BY TERRY BROOKS

SHANNARA

SHANNARA

First King of Shannara
The Sword of Shannara
The Elfstones of Shannara
The Wishsong of Shannara

THE HERITAGE OF SHANNARA

The Scions of Shannara
The Druid of Shannara
The Elf Queen of Shannara
The Talismans of Shannara

THE VOYAGE OF THE JERLE SHANNARA

Ilse Witch
Antrax
Morgawr

HIGH DRUID OF SHANNARA

Jarka Ruus
Tanequil
Straken

THE DARK LEGACY OF SHANNARA

Wards of Faerie
Bloodfire Quest
Witch Wraith

THE DEFENDERS OF SHANNARA

The High Druid's Blade
The Darkling Child
The Sorcerer's Daughter

THE FALL OF SHANNARA

The Black Elfstone
The Skaar Invasion

PRE-SHANNARA

GENESIS OF SHANNARA

Armageddon's Children
The Elves of Cintra
The Gypsy Morph

LEGENDS OF SHANNARA

Bearers of the Black Stuff
The Measure of the Magic

The World of Shannara

THE MAGIC KINGDOM OF LANDOVER

Magic Kingdom for Sale—Sold!
The Black Unicorn
Wizard at Large
The Tangle Box
Witches' Brew
A Princess of Landover

THE WORD AND THE VOID

Running with the Demon
A Knight of the Word
Angel Fire East

Sometimes the Magic Works: Lessons from a Writing Life

THE SKAAR INVASION

THE FALL OF SHANNARA

◆

THE SKAAR INVASION

TERRY BROOKS

DEL REY
NEW YORK

Copyright © 2018 by Terry Brooks
Map copyright © 2012 by Russ Charpentier

All rights reserved.

Published in the United States by Del Rey,
an imprint of Random House, a division of
Penguin Random House LLC, New York.

DEL REY and the HOUSE colophon are registered
trademarks of Penguin Random House LLC.

The map by Russ Charpentier was originally
published in *Wards of Faerie* by Terry Brooks,
published in the United States by Del Rey,
an imprint of Random House, a division of
Penguin Random House LLC, in 2012.

Library of Congress Cataloging-in-Publication Data
Names: Brooks, Terry, author.
Title: The Skaar invasion / Terry Brooks.
Description: New York : Del Rey, [2018] | Series: The fall of Shannara ; 2
Identifiers: LCCN 2018001392 | ISBN 9780553391510 (hardback) | ISBN 9780553391527 (ebook)
Subjects: LCSH: Shannara (Imaginary place)—Fiction. | Fantasy fiction. | Epic fiction. |
BISAC: FICTION / Fantasy / Epic. | FICTION / Action & Adventure. |
FICTION / Science Fiction / Adventure.
Classification: LCC PS3552.R6596 S57 2018 | DDC 813/.54—dc23
LC record available at https://lccn.loc.gov/2018001392

Printed in the United States of America on acid-free paper

randomhousebooks.com

2 4 6 8 9 7 5 3 1

First Edition

For Lisa,

Our Beloved Daughter,
Child of Nature,
Taken Too Soon

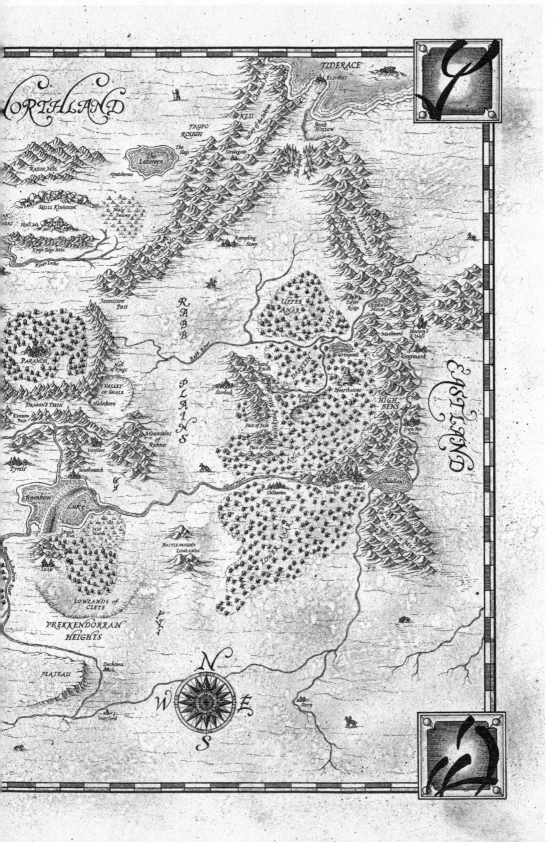

THE SKAAR INVASION

ONE

◆

"Darcon Leah," Ajin said, calm and composed, ignoring the sword at her throat.

A look of surprise flickered across Dar's lean features. Ajin sensed he was having trouble comprehending who she was. Or more likely, *what* she was. She was certain that whomever he had expected to find beneath her war helmet once it was removed, it wasn't a woman.

But she was used to such looks. When dressed in full armor with her dazzling white cloak draped across her shoulders, she presented an unlikely picture. Even now, ragged as she was from the night's battles, she was imposing. She was a woman who fought alongside men as an equal, a woman who led them in battle. In her Skaar homeland, she was regarded with awe and reverence.

Yet she was also a princess, the only daughter of her nation's ruling family, the firstborn of a king and a queen. A prime birthing, although her mother's replacement—*the pretender,* as Ajin insisted on calling her, though never to her face—had been quick enough to give him a pair of boy children once the former queen was banished. *The pretender* would have loved to banish the daughter, too—preferably to a burial plot—but Ajin was hard to kill. Just ask Dar Leah.

She waited patiently for him to say something, but he seemed unable to find the words. He simply stood there staring with the point of his blade at her throat and his expression unreadable.

"Not what you expected?" she asked. She gave him an encouraging smile, enjoying the moment.

"Who *are* you?" he managed finally.

Her smile broadened. She was tall and strong and beautiful, blond in the manner of most Skaar, her hair curled about her face in tight ringlets, framing startling blue eyes and fair skin. Seeing nothing more, you might still have thought her well bred and educated, but you would have missed much by looking no further. Only twenty-two years of age, she was a warrior skilled in combat arts and battlefield tactics. She had been born to it, her talents obvious even at an early age. Realizing the precariousness of her situation, with her mother gone and *the pretender* sitting on the throne with her father, Ajin had quickly decided to reinvent herself.

So she had joined the Skaar army. She had asked to be called only by her given name and not be accorded any special treatment. She was given none. She was harassed and abused, but she never complained. She was athletic to begin with, and she had refined her natural ability as she trained. Her willingness to place herself at risk and to suffer whatever hardships were required had endeared her to the soldiers who supervised her training or trained with her—all of whom were quick to tell others of her commitment. Her father, watching from afar, was one of those who paid attention. Ajin's perseverance—even in the face of her mother's banishment and the animosity of *the pretender*—only deepened his feelings for her. He was impressed by her determination and skill. She had excelled at everything asked of her and had evidenced an extraordinary understanding and appreciation of the lessons she was being taught. She advanced quickly through the army's ranks, becoming a battalion commander at eighteen. For her first assignment, she was tasked with leading a small number of Skaar soldiers into an outback country in Eurodia that had risen in revolt. She led from the front—she never asked anything of her soldiers that she would not do herself—and crushed the uprising in three days.

By then she had gained sufficient support from her father and the Skaar military that she was safe from *the pretender's* malevolent scheming. It was a bitter pill for *the pretender* to swallow, and that made Ajin all the happier.

One day, she might reveal all this to Dar Leah, should circumstances change. But lives were complicated and personal histories were not to be shared too hastily, so this day she would keep her story to herself. It was not the time or place for anything quite so intimate yet.

"My name is Ajin d'Amphere," she said. "I am a princess of the Skaar people."

Her words hung in the cool silence of the predawn darkness, joining shadows that rippled and shivered with changes of light as clouds passed across the moon. Even with the sword point at her throat, Ajin felt no fear or panic. Although Dar Leah did not yet fully understand it, she sensed there was a bond between them. He would not hurt her, nor would she hurt him. They had crossed paths three times now, and once she had held his life in her hands as he now held her life in his. To her way of thinking, they were warriors of equal stature, and she could not believe he would kill her while she was helpless and fully aware of how recently she had spared him.

"I heard your name inside the Keep," he said. "I heard them call out, '*Ajin, Ajin.*' A victory cry, I'm guessing. But it was really a massacre, wasn't it? A slaughter." He shook his head in disgust. "How do you know my name?"

"From my Penetrator, Kol'Dre. You know him as Kassen."

"I know him—and if I find him alive, I will remedy the situation immediately. All the Druids of Paranor are dead because of him!"

She shrugged. "And all my brave Skaar soldiers are dead, too."

"Is that supposed to balance out? I suppose you think so. Should I mention the Druids and the Troll guards and crew your airship destroyed?"

"Or I the two Skaar airships *you* destroyed first?"

For a minute neither spoke.

Then she gave him a questioning look. "The woman, the female Druid. She was special to you, wasn't she?"

He hesitated before nodding. "Once."

He looked as if he might say something more, but then he went still again.

"And are you responsible for what happened in the Keep?" she pressed. "Was that your doing? Was it you who freed that thing inside the walls—that monster and its poisonous mist—so it could feed on my soldiers?"

He shook his head, a dark look shading his expression. "That was another's choice. But what was the point of any of it? You killed all of us; we killed all of you. Now everyone's dead—and all for nothing."

"Not from where I'm standing. Paranor was our greatest threat, so we had to destroy it and the Druids. Now Paranor is gone, and I will not mourn it or its residents."

"No, I don't suppose you will." He gave her a none-too-gentle push. "Move back into the trees so we aren't standing out in the open, in case someone else from your little band of cutthroats survived. And don't even think about trying to run."

She walked into the forest, back where the darkness was so complete she could see almost nothing, the sword point prodding her along, removing her from any hope of finding help. The trees closed about her, Paranor's moonlit rise disappeared, and she was alone with the Blade.

"What do you intend to do with me?" she asked, once he had found a place he liked and brought them to a halt.

"I'm not sure, Princess. Maybe ransom you. Maybe use you as bait to draw out that traitor who gave up the Keep. Maybe I'll just let you wonder for a bit."

"Could you at least give me some space to breathe? Take your sword away from my throat. I promise not to run."

"Oh, please. You think I should trust you after what you've done? How foolish would that be?"

She could hear the disgust in his voice. It made her smile. "Would you at least stop calling me Princess? My given name is Ajin. Call me that."

"Fine. I'll call you Ajin. But I still don't trust you."

"You know the Skaar won't ransom me, don't you? Even my father, were he here, wouldn't ransom me. In spite of who I am, it isn't the way we do things."

"Then maybe I should just kill you, since you're so useless otherwise."

"Don't be ridiculous. You would never do that. Why don't you try telling me what I can do to put things right? Maybe we can reach an accord."

She heard his soft laugh. "An accord? Oh, well, that's different. I didn't realize you could bring the dead back to life. Or return the Keep from wherever it's been sent." The Blade shoved her up against a tree trunk. His sword shifted so that the edge was pressed against her throat. "Where are you from and why are you here?"

In the deep stillness of their forest concealment, she told him the details of the story behind the Skaar invasion—how their own land grew barren with an increase in severe cold and the coming of an endless winter, how their crops died and food and water grew scarce, how everything changed so quickly, how life became intolerable.

"The damage to our people is unimaginable. We are dying, our numbers reduced from millions to thousands. Our most vulnerable— our children, our old and sick, those weakened already from thirst or hunger—die every day. I have watched people I have known all my life perish. I watched my nurse and my favorite childhood playmates die. My dogs. My soldiers . . ."

Her words were bitter, her voice harsh. "It is the same everywhere— all throughout Eurodia, and in all of the other countries on the continent. Picture, if you will, whole populations who hunker down against the bitter winter and wait only to die. Without food and water, without warmth against the cold, what else is there to do? The weather changes are irreversible. The cold is deepening; even the southernmost lands of Eurodia are beginning to feel its bite."

She paused. "I had a younger sister. She's gone now, too. I tried to save her. I did everything I could think to do. When I wasn't in the field, I was sitting right beside her. I bathed and fed her and saw her through what I thought was the worst of it. But she had always been fragile. The sickness returned quickly enough. She developed a pox that covered her face and hands. She pleaded with me, begging for relief. When I saw there was no hope and she was gasping for each breath and straining against the pain, I placed a pillow over her face and let her slip away."

She paused, her eyes fixing on him. "When there is nowhere left to go and nowhere to stay, what do you do? I went to my father and begged him to send ships to search out distant lands in which we could make a new home. He did so, and our scouts found yours. We stole your airships and used their designs to build our own. Aquaswifts, we call them. Waters drawn from the oceans of our homeland and treated with chemicals power them. Aquaswifts are bigger and faster than your vessels. Our spies studied you for two entire years, here in your midst, and you never knew. Kol'Dre did most of the work. He is my Penetrator—my personal advance scout. He compiled information and sent it back for my father and his councilors. We knew everything about you before my father ordered me to come here with our advance force to prepare the way for the larger invasion. We knew you could be conquered. We know all your weaknesses."

"Or you think you do, anyway." Her captor's response was laced with scorn.

She shrugged. "We know enough to take advantage—as you have just seen. You are a nation of many different Races and peoples and governments, and you lack a central ruling power. You are fragmented, and thus you are vulnerable. All you really have is your magic, and most of that was concentrated in the Druids. Without them, you cannot vanish at will, as we can. You cannot create images to fool your enemies into attacking empty air."

"So you decided to eliminate them. You found a way into the Keep."

"With the aid of one of your own. A Druid betrayed you."

She saw recognition in his eyes. "Clizia Porse?" he asked quickly.

"Does it matter now?"

"It might, because she is still alive. I saw her afterward, when the Guardian was set loose. She was the one who sent Paranor into limbo. She's dangerous, Ajin. You might live to regret leaving her alive."

Ajin shrugged. "The end result is what matters. The demise of the Druids allows us to stop worrying about anyone using magic to oppose us. Now you must rely on your Federation's rudimentary sciences and inefficient weapons to resist us. And we will destroy you."

To her surprise, he smiled. "It sounds like you think this might be easy. Just walk right over us, cast us aside, settle in, and claim your new home. How long do you think it will take? A week or two?"

"I don't fool myself into believing it will be that easy. I am a seasoned commander, and I have fought and won many battles. I know what it takes to subdue a population. I know the time required and the costs that must be paid. I am prepared for all of it."

He gave a tired sigh. "You seem awfully young for someone so bloodthirsty."

Her chin came up, and her gaze found his and held it. "I have not been young since I was twelve years old and watched my father banish my mother, and her replacement begin to plot against me. Do not make the mistake of underestimating me."

"I would never do that," he replied. "Though I am sorry for your past."

"Do not be. I need no one's pity. I have made my own way in the world for this long, and I will continue to do so. You should worry for yourself. Why not talk to me about an agreement that will allow you to stay alive?"

"I'm not the one with a sword at my throat."

"But you were once, weren't you? And not so long ago?"

He stared at her, his face a mix of emotions. She had touched a nerve, reminding him of how she had held him pinned on a cliffside and then let him live. She might have been better off killing him, although she didn't think so. It had not felt right to kill one so brave and so loyal to his friends. It had not felt right to kill him when he was so helpless.

She saw that he remembered. Could she use it against him now?

"I think you must let me go, Dar Leah," she said abruptly. "You must do for me what I did for you. You must set me free."

He shook his head. "That would be a very bad idea, Princess."

"Ajin."

"Ajin," he corrected. "I would very quickly go from being your captor to being your captive, and I already told you how I feel about that."

Then be captive to my heart, she thought suddenly, impulsively—the thought exciting and forbidden. She could not deny how real and present her attraction to him was, how much it was a true measure of feelings she did not yet fully understand. But it had no place in what was happening now, so she shrugged it away.

"I don't want to be your captive," she said. "But I would have you be mine, once you realize there is no hope for you in the coming struggle. I have already saved your life once and would do so again. At some point, you will accept this and come to me. When you do, I will be waiting."

He stared at her in bemusement, and she reached up and gently pushed the sword blade away from her throat. "You don't intend to use this, so why threaten me with it? I am standing before you because I want to. Because I want you to understand my cause and to understand me. We are alike, you and I. I respect you and I think you respect me, too. We fight for what we believe in, but we do so with as much honor as we can manage. We share a code of conduct and a mutual admiration for loyalty and courage. We are not so different as it might seem."

"Different enough, when you keep advancing your plans for conquest. I would never do what you are doing!"

"Wouldn't you?" She cocked an eyebrow and took a step toward him. She was standing so close, they were almost touching again. She felt the urge to reach out for him. "If your land was dying and your people with it, would you not do whatever it took to save them? Even if it meant fighting to secure a place for them in another inhabitable land?"

She could see the uncertainty in his eyes. "You cannot know until you are faced with the situation. One day, you might be." She reached out and put her hands on his shoulders. It was a bold gesture, and she could see confusion mirrored in his expression. "You may continue to think us different, if you wish. But we are not, Dar Leah—and never will be. I don't know how this conflict will end. I don't know that either of us will survive it. But I do believe that, in ways neither of us yet understand, our fates are joined."

She reached up from his shoulders to his face and brought it down to hers. On impulse, she kissed him on the lips—a slow brushing followed by a hard press. She felt him resist, but only for a moment.

"You owe me my freedom," she said, releasing him and stepping back, "so I am taking it. I will not tell any of my people that I saw you. I will not reveal that you are here. Only you and I will know we shared this meeting."

She stepped past him, and he turned to watch as she walked away. A handful of steps farther on, she looked back. "I will miss you, Blade of Paranor, but we will meet again. Another time, another place. And very soon, I think. Look for me."

He shook his head, almost as if he couldn't quite believe what he was allowing to happen. "We are even now, Ajin d'Amphere. If I catch you again, I will not be so quick to let you go."

Her smile was dazzling. "Nor I you."

And then, as if to taunt him, she vanished.

TWO

◆

Kol'Dre lay in a crumpled heap just beyond the space where Paranor had stood not an hour earlier, oblivious to his surroundings. A heavy chunk of stone, broken free in the cataclysmic destruction of the Skaar advance force, had struck him on the head and left him in the path of the swiftly spreading green mist and the creature that it shrouded. He realized it was coming for him and knew he should bolt for safety. He could hear the screams intensifying behind him. He could see the wicked glow spreading through the hallways and into the rooms of the Keep, killing everyone it touched.

He remembered seeing some of his fellow Skaar turn back nevertheless, reacting instinctively to the shrieks and cries of their fellow soldiers, intending to help friends and comrades. But their efforts had been futile, and they had paid the price for their foolish bravery: Every last one of them was savaged by the horror that hunted them down. There was no standing against such monstrous magic, no device or weapon the Skaar possessed that could stop it. Courage for a reason was one thing, but blind, reckless bravery was another. Kol'Dre had his faults and occasional lack of good judgment, but throwing away his life had never been among them.

Yet his memories of what he had witnessed before the stone felled him remained hazy. He had no idea how he had gotten clear of the

Keep, or even why he was still alive. Nor did it matter. Not so long as he slept, careless and unknowing.

But then, suddenly, he was awake, shocked back to consciousness by the memory of lying next to a young girl in her bed beneath coverings turning red with her blood. The knife was in his hand, and he kept stabbing her, over and over again. And all the while she watched him, smiling with trust and love, attaching no blame to him even though it was his hand that killed her.

Kassen, she whispered.

He sat up with a gasp. The sudden movement made his head spin, and he lowered it between his legs and retched. The dream fragmented and the night closed about him. He was outside in the cool air, beyond the walls of Paranor, sitting in a patch of grass with trees to his left and empty space to his right. He turned his head to view the latter, sensing something wrong with it, and then he remembered that this was where the Keep had been. It was gone now. He blinked in disbelief, closed his eyes tightly, and looked again.

Still gone. Everything was gone.

Figures surrounded him, voices speaking urgently to him in the Skaar tongue, asking how he was, if he had suffered any injuries besides the one to his head, if he could see properly. He shook his head automatically, brushing them off, not even sure exactly what they were talking about.

Then he became aware of the hammering pain that ratcheted through his skull, spearing downward through his neck to his shoulders in steady waves. He reached up to touch the source of the injury and found a compress tied in place. Something had struck him hard enough to open a wound that had bled down the side of his face and onto his shoulder. He could feel the stickiness of freshly crusted blood and smell its coppery scent. He glanced down and found his Druid robes stained red. But the rest of his body seemed intact.

"Help me up," he ordered, and arms reached down to take hold of him and lift him to his feet.

A wave of dizziness and fresh pain nearly felled him a second time, but he managed to keep his feet, waiting for it to pass. He glanced again at the vast open space where Paranor had stood, just to be sure. "What happened to it?" he asked the men about him.

There were only five. Several of them shrugged. One said, "It just disappeared. Right after we got you through the gates of the outer wall and out here. Gone. Just like that."

Kol'Dre stared at him. "Is this all of us that's left? All that got out?"

The men nodded, stone-faced. Only one even bothered to look at him.

"Ajin?" he asked quickly, remembering he had left her there. "The princess?"

"Gone," one said.

"Gone? What do you mean, *gone*? She can't be gone! Did you look for her? Did you search?"

"Penetrator, it was all we could do to make it this far. Bringing you out took everything we had left. Most of us are injured—some badly. If she were here, she could find us easily enough." He shook his head. "She's dead."

Kol'Dre went numb and cold. He turned his head to hide his tears, looking over to where the fortress had been. He refused to believe it. Ajin was not gone! She couldn't be! He wiped at his face with his sleeve. Ajin d'Amphere was invincible. She could not be killed. Others among them, yes. They were Skaar and warriors. Death came frequently and never wandered far from where they stood, always hiding in the shadows, always waiting to leap out.

But never for Ajin. Ajin was different.

Yet he understood that these feelings were unique to him. To others she was flesh and blood like all Skaar, and she could be killed as easily. He saw her differently because he was in love with her. And he wanted her to be alive because he couldn't imagine a life without her.

Ajin.

His body shook involuntarily, and he stalked away to be alone with his grief. The others knew enough to let him be.

He stood apart in the darkness until the tears and the sobbing stopped and he was himself again. But the loss of Ajin d'Amphere was about more than just his personal suffering. She was the heart and soul of their invasion efforts, of everything they had given up to find a new land for their endangered people. She was the light that guided them and gave them their hope. To have come so far and accomplished so much, only to lose the one member of the advance force they could not afford to lose, was inconceivable.

He found himself thinking back over the weeks and months and years that had led to this moment. He had spent two long years living in this foreign land before standing on the shores of the Tiderace to greet the Skaar fleet as it landed at the far-northern edge of the Charnal Mountains. He had spent two long years preparing the way for this invasion. He had traveled widely and mapped the Four Lands thoroughly. He had recorded any relevant observations on the characteristics of its Races, the locations and designs of its cities and towns, the workings and proclivities of its governments. He had determined its strengths and weaknesses. He had cultivated various pliable government officials who would prove useful later. And all the while, he considered where the Skaar should strike first, where next, what sorts of obstacles presented the greatest dangers—which peoples would fight hardest and be most difficult to overcome and which would be most likely to see the futility of fighting and simply concede the battle before it was joined.

Kol'Dre had done this many times before in the countries of Eurodia, the continent that lay closest to the island home of the Skaar. His official designation was Penetrator—a scout, spy, assassin, and whatever else he needed to be, but mostly just a planner of ways to break down any form of resistance. Ajin d'Amphere relied on him as on no other to provide her with crucial information and advice on her potential conquests. She had always trusted in the validity and thoroughness of his assessments, and he had never disappointed her.

In return, she had paid him special attention—a reward for his services. She had given him access to her as she did to few others. He found her attentions and reliance on him flattering. And he found her, on a personal level, utterly irresistible.

Yet resist her he must if he valued his head. Everything was strictly business between Ajin and her Penetrator, in spite of his desire for something more.

Kol'Dre and those few he had chosen to serve him as guards and aides had come to the Four Lands in traditional sailing vessels shortly after the Skaar had determined it was necessary to find a new land to call home. They had crossed the vast blue expanse of the Tiderace in the old way, unaware of the existence of airships. Necessity was the mother of risk-taking, so you did what you had to, no matter the danger. What might lie on the far side of the ocean was unknown, but the Skaar believed that other countries must exist beyond those waters, and that other peoples must have survived the Great Wars that had destroyed the Old World.

It had been a revelation to find the extent of the opportunities this new land afforded. Kol'Dre was quick to recognize that this was where the Skaar were meant to be. Stealing the secrets of the airships was easy enough, and within a year the Skaar had built their fleet of aquaswifts and set about crossing the Tiderace not by navigating upon its waters as Kol and his crew had done, but by flying over them. As Penetrator, he had advised Ajin and the king to send only an advance force to begin with, to test the strength of those they sought to overcome. He had further concluded that the size of the country they were invading would prove a disadvantage to a larger force. A smaller, swifter, more mobile army would have better success and might just be strong enough to gain a foothold that would allow the larger army to cross and begin the greater task of carving out sufficient space for the bulk of their people to begin a new life.

His advice had been heeded, and the army Ajin had brought to the Four Lands had advanced to the fringes of the barren country belonging to the Corrax Trolls—a tribe that he found to be particularly barbaric and warlike, and not much liked by the other tribes. He knew the Corrax would attempt to drive them out, but the Skaar always chose a strong adversary at the start to set a persuasive example. So the Corrax would attack, thinking them weak and foolish to intrude—thinking victory over such a soft-skinned people would come easily and swiftly.

And the inevitable Skaar victory would be a valuable lesson to any who might think the same way.

As expected, the Corrax had massed in force within a week's time, coming directly for the Skaar. And the Skaar had formed their lines, pointed their weapons toward the Corrax, and waited.

The Corrax were eager to comply. But the battle they got was not the one they were expecting. Instead, it was a massacre.

The traditional Corrax attack relied on brute force and a reckless disregard for personal safety to overwhelm and crush its opponents. It was a strategy that had always worked for them before. Strike hard. Give no ground. Show no mercy. It should have worked here, had they been facing anyone other than the Skaar. The Corrax had hammered into the invaders' lines with all the fury and bloodlust that had destroyed so many other armies, fully expecting that this battle would end in the same way.

But the Skaar had simply waited for them to come, standing perfectly still in their precise but loosely formed ranks. Those in the front carried spears—eight-foot poles with hafts of pale ash, smooth iron-tipped heads affixed to one end and handgrips carved into the wood near the other. Those in the rear ranks bore short swords—blades of hammered steel with the surface dulled so that no light reflected, balanced and easily maneuverable in combat.

When the Corrax were within fifteen feet, previously designated ranks of Skaar soldiers utilized that part of their genetic makeup that allowed for it and, one by one, began to disappear. A curious shimmer rippled all along their lines, and it was suddenly unclear to the Corrax what was happening. And then, in another instant, whole ranks were not there at all. Only half of those who had been clearly visible moments before now remained, and their bodies were shimmering, too. There was a ghostliness about them, as if they were formed not of flesh and blood but of smoke and mirrors.

Although the Trolls could not see what was happening, those Skaar soldiers who had disappeared had shifted their lines left and right to come at their attackers from the flanks in a pincer movement. The Corrax experienced a few quick moments of confusion as they surged to the attack, closing on the Skaar who remained visible, and then they were being slaughtered. Real sword blades and spear points were skewering and slashing the Corrax from both sides in places where no one seemed to be, and there was nothing the Trolls could do to protect themselves. They tried to fight back, but they couldn't find their opponents. All they could see before them were empty images; the Skaar were gone, their bodies become no more than air.

The Corrax had fought on, anyway, almost to the last Troll, because this was all they knew how to do. But it had been hopeless, and they had died still not knowing what had happened. Even those who sought mercy, falling to their knees in abject surrender, had been slaughtered. Only those who had remained in their village were spared—the old, the infirm, and the young—allowed to live so they could carry word to other tribes, in other places, about what had happened. Once it was known what the Skaar could do, the other Troll tribes would be more willing to listen to reason. The Skaar army could then bypass these tribes and move down into the Borderlands and the more valuable prizes that lay to the south, east, and west.

The Skaar had left the bodies of the dead on the field of battle to rot, refusing them burial or even the flames of a pyre to send them to whatever afterlife they believed in. Their kin and friends were not allowed to claim them. They would be ghosts abroad in the land, their spirits left to wander endlessly, their history lost with their passing. This was the fate that awaited all those who chose to stand against the Skaar. This was power beyond anything those who inhabited the Four Lands had witnessed before, and they needed to respect how formidable the Skaar were.

Kol'Dre had known the impact this massacre would have. After all, he had helped develop this approach. His was a long and storied legacy. He was known throughout the countries of Eurodia, and coming to the Four Lands had given him the chance to further build his reputation, to test himself against men and women who were ignorant of his existence. He had relished the opportunity, coveted the challenge. In the conquering of the Four Lands, he would gain new respect and perhaps elevate himself further in Ajin's eyes.

Yet he understood the odds against fulfilling those ambitions. Any personal involvement with the princess had always been enormously complicated. A dozen years her senior and of common blood, he was not an ideal match by any measure. In fact, there was no reason for the king even to consider him as a son-in-law. None of this was helped by the fact that Ajin did not see him as he saw her. But he also understood you never got anything in this life by deciding you couldn't have it. So he had continued to dream, determined he would find a way.

Now the dreaming was over. Now she was dead, and there could never be a way.

It was exactly as this dark realization left him bereft that he heard gasps of surprise from a few of those who had hauled him from the Keep to safety. And when Kol'Dre turned around to look, Ajin d'Amphere was walking toward him.

That Ajin had had been able to escape from Dar Leah was something of a surprise. Certainly, she had done everything she could to persuade him it was the right thing to do, but it was still almost impossible for her to believe. It told her something about him that left her breathless with need. Here was a man, a warrior without peer, who was secure enough in his own skin to let a woman dictate his fate. One who placed respect and the settlement of personal debts above fears that it would cost him something down the line.

Few men she had known would have been able to do this. But for the Blade of Paranor, it had been no problem at all.

She thought again about how he had fought for the lives of the two Druids on the grasslands west of the Charnals when the Skaar had attacked them. Coming over the side of his warship so swiftly and charging to their rescue. Throwing himself into a battle that he must have known he could not win and still managing to save his female companion. Nearly escaping with her into the mountains with flying skills that matched her own, downing two of her airships and very nearly downing hers, as well.

It excited her all over again, just thinking about it, and she found herself smiling, in spite of the circumstances. Then her smile vanished, washed away by her realization of the darker realities. Yes, the Keep and its Druids were gone, but she had planned to make a present of the building and its treasures to her father, and now that was impossible. Most of her advance force—perhaps all, Kol'Dre included—was likely dead, destroyed by the creature that lived in the greenish mist. It was a hard, painful reward for all of their efforts, and she could only hope that it provided an example to the people of the Four Lands, showing them what the Skaar were prepared to do in order to make a home here.

She circled the perimeter of the grounds on which Paranor had rested, unwilling to step again onto that treacherous soil without a very good reason. She trudged through the darkness, searching for Skaar survivors, but found no one. In the surrounding forests, the birds and animals had begun to communicate again as they went about their lives with the coming of morning. Insects buzzed her heated face, and in the sky the diminished moon hung low against the horizon while the stars were beginning to fade again in the lightening sky. Morning was less than an hour away.

She had wandered along the perimeter of perhaps half of the Keep's barren grounds when she found the ragged little band of survivors and felt a small leap of joy. Even better, there was Kol, standing off by himself, staring at nothing. When the cries of the others alerted him to her presence and he turned and saw her, he raced for her, folding her in his arms with such happiness that she felt compelled to give him silent permission to touch her in familiar fashion this once.

"I thought you were dead!" he whispered, crushing her against him. "That was what they said. But I knew. I knew it wasn't so!"

"Yes, but it will be if you don't let me breathe soon," she complained.

He released her at once and stepped back. "Forgive me . . ."

"For what?" She gripped his arms to hold him in place. "For being glad to see me alive? For letting your usual cold and tightly wound emotions get the better of you?" She reached up to touch his cheek. "My brave Kol."

Without pausing to measure his reaction, she released him and walked over to the other men. She took each by the hand, praising him for his courage and determination, congratulating him on escaping a dangerous trap and living to celebrate the victory they had achieved over the Druids and their magic. The men nodded wordlessly or offered muted words of thanks, simultaneously embarrassed and proud, hauling their battered bodies upright long enough to face her and be recognized. She knew they loved her—worshipped her in some instances. She knew their loyalty was unquestionable. She spoke to each of them by name. Her soldiers had all been with her a long time, and before she was finished she found herself weeping for all the ones who were no longer there.

As she was finishing, she caught sight of Kol watching her from one side, his expression one of lingering disbelief and joy. As if he was making sure she was real and not a ghost. A complex man, Kol'Dre. In looks, he was unexceptional—of medium height, with a dark complexion and brown hair and eyes where most Skaar were tall and fair-skinned with blue eyes and blond hair. He was also not one to stand in the ranks and engage in hand-to-hand combat as she did. He was not a believer in the value of honor and glory, of proving courage through battles, of risking all for the sake of companions and country. He thought himself above all that—a shade more clever, a twist more intelligent. But this did not mean he was a timid man or a coward; he was a formidable opponent when he needed to be. He had killed other men without compunction—and some of them for her. But he was not fashioned in the traditional Skaar mold, and he was aware that it set him apart. To a very great extent, it was what defined him.

Which was what made him so valuable to her. A Penetrator must be a chameleon, able to think independently from those around him while remaining in the background, an unremarkable presence. He must have sharp eyes and quick wits and a good memory. He must be bold but not reckless.

She could go on, but all that mattered was how well Kol'Dre had served her in this capacity and how closely their fortunes were tied. Again and again, the two of them had led the way for the Skaar nation as they expanded their empire into Eurodia, claiming country after country for their king. Even if her upbringing had required more of her than his had of him, and even if he longed to bed and perhaps one day to wed her, he did not let this interfere with the job he had been given to do.

"Come," she called to him, beckoning him over to join the others. "We need two stretchers and four pairs of hands to carry Fer'Pas and Anan'Lor back to the airship. The rest of the advance force will need to be told what's happened before we set out again. Kol, set our brave soldiers to their tasks."

And Kol'Dre, his hopes renewed, jumped to obey.

THREE

Dar Leah stood in a dappled landscape of shadows and moonlight and watched Ajin d'Amphere walk away. On the one hand, he knew it was foolish for him to allow her to leave. She was the commander of a foreign incursion into the Four Lands—the leader of a force that had defeated two different Troll tribes and destroyed virtually the entire Fourth Druid Order. She was a large part of the reason Paranor had been sent from the Four Lands into a limbo existence, trapping Drisker Arc—the last honorable Druid—inside. Yet now he had set her free to return to what remained of her army and continue on with her plans for the Four Lands, whatever they happened to be.

On the other hand, what was he supposed to do with her if he didn't let her go?

His most urgent need was to find and retrieve Drisker Arc from within Paranor and get him back into the Four Lands to help deal with both the Skaar invasion and Clizia Porse, and there was little Ajin d'Amphere could do to help with this. She would be a distraction and a burden if he tried to keep her a prisoner. He would have to lock her up somewhere and find someone to keep an eye on her, since it was obvious he could hardly haul her along with him. Nor did he think she was a bargaining chip with the Skaar; she was probably right about how they would react if he tried to make her one. It didn't take much to realize he was a little short of choices, and his immediate efforts to help Drisker were what really mattered, even though he knew she was dangerous, an enemy of the Four Lands who would eventually come looking for him again.

Besides, he also knew she was right about his obligation to her. She was owed her freedom. She had done as much for him, giving him back his life when she could have snuffed it out. She talked about honor and courage as if they were a moral code she believed in, and from what he had seen of her actions, it appeared she did. He wasn't entirely comfortable admitting it, but he found that he admired her.

Maybe even more than admired her.

He watched her until she was out of sight, then continued watching for a few minutes more, trying to understand his behavior. When you felt closer to a young woman who had just killed virtually every last Druid you had sworn to protect than you did to the Druids themselves, it suggested you had your priorities mixed up. Or maybe your sense of loyalty. But he didn't think so. The truth was that, in retrospect, he really did admire her more than he had admired most of them.

He shook his head at himself, still lost in his thoughts, until he remembered what he was supposed to be doing. Ajin had said she would not alert any other Skaar survivors to his presence, but standing around to find out if she meant it did not seem wise. With a last glance at the empty ground where Paranor had stood not two hours ago, he sheathed his sword, turned around, and walked away.

His plans for helping Drisker were already forming in his head.

If things had been different, he would have sought out Clizia Porse. But having watched her dispatch the Keep to parts unknown, presumably knowing Drisker was still inside, he was pretty sure she was unlikely to help. Drisker had not trusted her, and in the end his doubts had proved well founded. It was clear enough that Clizia had betrayed him and had plans of her own regarding the Druid order, if there was ever to be another, along with any future return of Paranor. How she would manage all this he had no idea. Nor did it matter just now.

What he needed to know was this. How was he supposed to get Drisker Arc back into the Four Lands when, save for the Sword of Leah, he did not have any magic to call upon? He could only think of one person who might help, and that was Tarsha. She wasn't yet a Druid, but she was a Druid's student. She had studied under Drisker and she had powerful magic of her own, as heir to the iconic wishsong that had served so many Druid allies in the past—including members of his own family. If anyone could find a way to help Drisker, it would be her.

But first he had to find out where she was.

He knew where she was going; she had told him that much. But whether she was already there, still on her way, or finished and headed back to Emberen was unclear. At least as things stood just now.

So things would have to change.

He reached Drisker's little two-man and climbed aboard, powering up the diapson crystals and opening the parse tubes. He wasted no time giving further thought to his decision. Time was something he did not have to waste, and he had a long flight ahead.

As Dar Leah departed, dawn was beginning to brighten the edges of the eastern horizon from behind the jagged peaks of the Dragon's Teeth, and Ajin d'Amphere was standing watch over Kol'Dre and the five other surviving soldiers from the one hundred who had gone into the Keep. She had ordered them to move north from the battleground and deep into the woods where they would be hidden from view before she'd let them sleep. When they woke, she would dispatch the strongest of them to find the aquaswift they had flown in on and bring it back. It was much farther away than she would have liked, kept well away from Druid eyes on their arrival so there was no chance of it being seen.

For now, they all needed rest. But for her, sleep would not come, so she had risen and gone off to sit by herself.

Her thoughts should have been full of what to do next, with virtually the whole of the attack force she had brought to Paranor destroyed, but instead all she could think of was Dar Leah. She was well and truly smitten. She would not deny it—could not, in point of fact, do so honestly. She was attracted to him as she had not been attracted to another man. *Ever.* She had experienced her share of crushes and lovers, but they had come and gone, leaving virtually no impression. Yet in their three brief encounters, Dar had imprinted himself on her heart—despite the inescapable truth that they were more enemies than friends. It was stranger than strange, but it was exciting, too.

Dar Leah was everything she admired in a man, and she intended to have him, one way or another.

She was not so foolish as to think she could make this happen now. There were too many uncertainties and unexpected turns waiting ahead, and no amount of preparation would ever be sufficient. At the end of the day, she and Dar Leah were on opposite sides of a conflict that threatened to engulf the whole of the Four Lands. Time and circumstance would have to change that, but she was fully convinced it could happen. This was the nature of fate. She just had to be patient. She had to trust that she would be given her chances and that when she was, she would respond in the best way possible.

But whatever future there was for the Blade and herself, it waited somewhere down the road, and for now she had other concerns she must deal with. With the Druids dead and Paranor lost, she needed to redefine her goals for the Four Lands. The size of her original command of one thousand soldiers was reduced, but still sufficient for her to act.

Nevertheless, the first thing she had to do upon rejoining those she had left behind in the primary camp farther north was to convince them, down to the last soldier, that what had happened to the others not only had not been her fault but also had not been preventable. If they believed she had acted recklessly in attacking Paranor directly, she would lose control of her soldiers. She would lose their trust and their belief in her.

And that would be the end of everything.

She would return home in disgrace—a failure her quick-to-judge father might well use to determine she was both useless and expendable.

But her thoughts of such possibilities quickly faded as Kol'Dre joined her moments later, coming up silently and sitting beside her without speaking. Because she was used to having him close at hand and ready to offer advice in situations where she would never have suffered the presence of others, she let him stay.

Long minutes passed in silence, then she looked over at him and waited until he was looking back. "You needn't sit with me, Kol'Dre," she said. "I am well enough by myself."

His smile was wan. "I will leave if you wish, Princess."

She shook her head. "I don't wish it. You are welcome to stay. But you must call me by my given name. We are alone now."

"As you wish, Ajin."

His face was comforting in its familiarity. Calm and introspective, a reassurance. She had thought now and again about accepting him as more than her Penetrator and sometime confidant. She could hardly avoid it, given their proximity during their travels. But she could never quite make herself believe this was a good idea. She sensed that if she took that extra step, it would change their relationship, and she didn't want that. Besides, she valued him for his advice and his loyalty, not for his potential as a bedmate. However he saw things, she did not see a future between them that would allow for more.

"We've lost everything," she said after a few further moments of silence. "Paranor, its magic, the Druids, and our ability to use it all to bargain with. We've let it slip through our fingers by being inattentive and complacent. I should have done more to secure it. I should have been better prepared for a punitive response."

Kol'Dre shook his head. "What could you have done? How could you have foretold any of it? There was no way to prepare for what happened—no way to stop that thing from coming out and destroying us. We were helpless against it."

"That is a poor excuse. I am to blame. I overreached."

"It could be argued that way," he agreed. "But those who do not dare do not achieve. You took a chance, and you almost succeeded. Your father will be proud of you."

She snorted. "My father will skin me alive."

"You destroyed the entire Druid order, Ajin!" He was leaning close, his face intense. "You eliminated the single most dangerous threat to our success in claiming these lands. No one else has the strength or means to stand against us, and I should know. I've spent two years among these people. With the Druids gone, there is no other power that can prevent us from taking what we want—not even the Elves. And the Four Lands are too divided to unite as they should."

She felt herself go calm. He was right, of course. She had done what he claimed, and half a loaf was always better than none. She only needed to find a way to reimagine a Skaar victory in the aftermath of these events. She only needed to find a new path for achieving what her people expected.

"You have to let go of your guilt," Kol added a moment later.

She smiled. *It would surprise you, Kol'Dre, to know what else I probably have to let go of,* she thought. *But that information is for me alone.*

"I know," she said instead.

He heard something in the tone of her voice and lowered his gaze deferentially, as if he knew he had overstepped. She fought back a surge of satisfaction. "Come now. We have more pressing concerns to occupy our attention."

"Do you have a plan for addressing those concerns?" he asked.

She gave him a brief nod. "I'm working on it."

They said nothing to each other for a time afterward. Kol'Dre wanted to pursue the matter, but he knew it was better to just let her be. She was looking off into the morning, her thoughts clearly elsewhere. He had noticed it before when he came over to sit with her. She didn't look particularly troubled by whatever was drawing her attention. Rather, she looked almost pensive. An air of calm infused her countenance, defined her posture, and layered her gestures. She might be displeased with other things—the loss of Paranor, the deaths of almost one hundred of her best soldiers—but something besides these seemingly pressing concerns was preoccupying her.

"Where will we go once we leave here?" he said finally.

"What?"

"I'm sorry. I didn't mean to disturb you."

"You didn't. I was simply thinking about something else."

Indeed. "I asked where you think we would go after we leave Paranor."

She stared at him as if she didn't understand. "We return to the advance force and go on."

"Go on where?"

A flicker of irritation lit in her eyes. "Why don't you tell me, Penetrator? What would your advice be? Where would you have me go?"

"I think it would be unwise to turn back."

"Agreed. The Skaar do not retreat."

"So we go forward, as you said. Perhaps through one of the passes south and out onto the banks of the Mermidon, and see what sort of response we get?"

"That is what you would do? What you would have *us* do? Advance and wait to see what happens?"

"It has its merits."

"It is a lazy man's game. We need to do more. Why don't we fly to the Federation capital and confront them on their doorstep?"

He shook his head. "No need. Arishaig will come to us. Then we will seek an alliance with Vause."

Ketter Vause, Prime Minister of the Federation—a man Kol'Dre had studied and come to understand during his time in the Four Lands. Vause would recognize the value Ajin represented as an ally and come to meet her. He would offer her a partnership, an agreement—one that would give her access to the power her father desired over all the Four Lands.

She made a disparaging noise. "If he did as you suggest, I would not waste time on an alliance. I would face him down as we did the Druids and so many others who chose to underestimate us, and then I would destroy him."

Kol'Dre paused. Her answer was nonsense. What was going on? She was not thinking clearly, and that was very unlike her.

"The Federation has airships," he pointed out. "Many more than we do. They would outnumber us considerably on the ground, as well. We might do substantial damage to them, but in the end we would be the ones destroyed."

She made a dismissive gesture. "Do you think I don't know this? But we must do something to keep them at bay until the king arrives with the main body of our army and we are no longer so unevenly matched."

The king, she had said—not *my father*. He took note as he replied, "I would think a meeting of some sort might prove a better choice."

"We need to keep them off balance. We need to make them afraid of us. We need to keep them uncertain of what we might do. So we set a trap. We let them send their soldiers and their airships and destroy them before they realize how foolish they are being. Do we not know how to do this? Did we not do this at Rhemms?"

He nodded slowly, remembering. At Rhemms, they had discovered that an alliance of Bosch and Zekis was moving against them. This combined force badly outnumbered the Skaar, and even with their special abilities it would have been hard to defeat the foes head-on. So they had dug in along a riverbank with fortifications and blinds. Then they had taken almost all their soldiers to the enemy side of the river and hidden them well downstream of what would become their encampment. When the Bosch and the Zekis arrived, the Skaar attacked them from the sides and behind, pinning them against the river. Surprised and unable to maneuver quickly enough, trapped with their backs to the river, the alliance was cut to pieces.

"So, something of the same sort here, only using airships?" he asked.

Ajin nodded. "But I value your opinion, Kol. So tell me. Do you think such a plan will work?"

He felt her eyes on him, studying him as she thought it over. He did not look away. He knew better than to cede her any ground. If she thought him weak, she would never talk to him as an equal again, and he could not afford to lose that standing. So he sat staring at her while he took the space and time he needed to make up his mind.

"Maybe," he said finally.

"Then I will think on it further. But not today. I need to rest. You should sleep, too. I need my brilliant Penetrator to be sharp of mind in the days ahead."

She rose, touched him briefly on the cheek, and walked off. He stared after her, wondering if he was still in her good graces.

With Ajin, you could never be sure.

It took the last of the survivors the rest of that day and the next to return to the main body of the advance force, even with the help of their recovered transport. The injured were removed from the aquaswift and taken away for treatment while the others were given food and drink and told to use the remainder of the day to rest. The advance force had been making good progress coming south toward Paranor, and Ajin immediately announced it would continue south the next morning toward the Mermidon. But she made no clear verbal indication to Kol'Dre that she had decided what to do then.

He had no doubt what it meant should the Federation deem her a threat. He knew enough about Ketter Vause and the Ministers of the Coalition Council to be very sure they would not tolerate a Skaar presence in the Four Lands unless they could control it. So a Federation command would be sent to intercept them. Thus far, they had only engaged a few Troll tribes and eliminated the Druids. That should please Vause and his Ministers. But a rash act on Ajin's part could change everything.

His thoughts were interrupted by a familiar voice.

"You've cheated death again," Pre'Oltien observed wryly when he heard that the command had been given. "Lucky you."

His second was a stout, blocky fellow with laughing eyes and a ready smile. His life view was simple, and his needs small. He had found his way to Kol while both were in training to be Penetrators years ago. When Pre had seen he would not be among those chosen, he had come to Kol and asked to be his second. Kol had quickly agreed. Pre'Oltien was exactly the sort of man he was looking for—solid, loyal, dependable, and willing to do what he was told.

"Lucky enough," he agreed, realizing his second was talking about Paranor. "Things are back to normal here, it seems?"

Pre gave him a doubtful look. "Are they? Paranor gone, its treasures swept away? All those who went into the Keep save yourself and five others dead? There's talk, Kol. There's more than a little dissatisfaction and some real anger."

Kol'Dre made no verbal response, although he gave his second a nod of recognition. He had sensed the mood the moment he had returned and those left behind had learned what had happened to their fellows. It would be up to Ajin—Ajin, whom they adored—to find a way to make it right.

She did this later in the day, when she called her soldiers together in the twilight hours and explained why their companions had died and what those deaths had accomplished. She promised them that no further sacrifices of this magnitude would be needed, now that the Druids and Paranor were gone. They would fight again, but never be trapped as they were at Paranor. They would remember the sacrifice of those who had died and honor it with their courage and determination in the days ahead. Victory was almost within their grasp, as the Four Lands were rendered helpless without the magic of the Druids. One by one, the governments who stood against them would fall—just as the Troll tribes and the nations in Eurodia had.

Then she went down among them and took their hands in her own, one by one, reassuring and consoling, giving them renewed heart and belief in themselves and in her. It was typical Ajin d'Amphere—and because of who she was, the grumbles ceased and talk turned to the victory that waited just ahead.

Then in a heartbeat, everything changed.

Later that night, as Ajin and Kol'Dre were working on the details of their plan for a Federation entrapment on the Mermidon, one of her senior commanders, Sten'Or, appeared unexpectedly in front of them and stood waiting for an acknowledgment.

Ajin nodded a greeting. "Is there a problem, Commander?"

She was not fond of Sten'Or, although he was efficient and quick to assess an enemy's weakness when they were in the field. But of late he had become a rival for command of the Skaar army. She had repeatedly rejected his request to assume command, along with his advances as a suitable bedmate. Those alone provided him with sufficient incentive to seek to undermine her.

"There is a message from the king," he said without preamble. "It arrived yesterday, just prior to your return." He handed it to her. "I took the liberty of reading it, to be certain it was something worth bothering you about."

Ajin stared at him. He was too eager by half, so she took the letter without looking at it. "And is it worth bothering me at this hour, Commander? Since you admit you have already read it?"

Sten'Or shrugged. There was a delight reflected in his features that he did not try to hide. "That is something you will have to determine for yourself. I leave you to it."

And he turned away dismissively and walked off.

"That was rude," Kol'Dre declared angrily. "Who does he think he is to speak to you like that?"

Ajin did not reply, but her mind was racing. Something was very wrong for Sten'Or to treat her so. He was perpetually angry with her, but not usually so deliberately impertinent. For him to act this way, he must have reason to think he could do so with impunity.

She unfolded the message and read it through. A chill ran through her. Without looking at Kol, she read it through once more, as much to give her time to compose herself as to make certain of the contents.

Then she looked up. "My father is coming with the rest of the Skaar army. A full-fledged invasion force has been assembled. He will depart with his airships and arrive by the time of the next full moon."

"What?" Kol exclaimed in disbelief. "Why would he do that when you did not send for him?"

"Why, indeed?"

Kol hesitated. "He knows about Paranor."

"There hasn't been time."

"But why would he . . ."

A shake of her head. "Sten'Or is responsible for this. He was much too eager to give me the news. He might have sent my father a message earlier suggesting I had overstepped my bounds or trampled on his authority. Who knows? Such a message might have said anything, given who sent it. Sten'Or has always been ambitious, and his ambition might have gotten the better of his common sense."

"You must relieve him of command and have him flogged!"

Her lips tightened, and a look of determination washed over her perfect features. "Though it would give me great satisfaction to hang my scheming commander from the nearest tree by his private parts, it would not improve my situation. The damage is done. There is nothing that will help now. The king will come, whether I like it or not. When he confirms that I have lost Paranor and its treasures, he will have all the incentive he needs to take control of the army. He will claim my impending victory over the Four Lands as his own achievement and my efforts will be erased. My work will have been for nothing."

Her voice was calm and steady, but her heart was dark with anger and disappointment. "Still, he is not here yet, so perhaps I can outmaneuver him. You must help me."

"Of course," Kol agreed at once. Her Penetrator understood her well enough. Playing games with Cor d'Amphere carried more than a little risk for those involved—as Sten'Or would find out later. But refusing his daughter carried an even greater risk. "What do you want me to do?"

"We'll send the army to the Mermidon as planned. Once they arrive, I can put our plan into operation and await the coming of the Federation. In the meantime, you are going to take a small trip. You should be back before any engagement occurs."

"Where am I going?" he asked.

Her smile was cold. "Into the lion's den."

FOUR

It was silent and disturbingly spectral within the halls and chambers of Paranor. Everything exuded a transparency, vague and poorly defined, almost on the verge of disappearing. The absence of sound only seemed to enhance the feeling that Drisker Arc was living a ghost life. This world—this new world into which he had been banished—was a place in which color was diminished, clarity dimmed, and time suspended.

It must be like this in the netherworld where the shades were consigned, Drisker thought.

He had spent endless hours exploring a place so familiar to him he barely bothered to consider the paths his footsteps took as he struggled to come to terms with his situation. It was a confusing and disappointing effort that in the end yielded him little. Some things were apparent right away; others took forever to confirm. Others still offered no answers whatsoever and left him bereft of critical information. And none offered him even a small possibility of finding freedom.

First, no other living being was present. Even the dead had vanished, their bodies reduced to ash and bone fragments in the east courtyard. Any birds had long since flown elsewhere, and any mice had gone to ground. Tracing and retracing his footsteps was sufficient to reveal he was entirely alone.

Second, there was no way into or out of the Keep. He had tried over and over to find one and failed. He had attempted to open the gates and the smaller service doors set into the outer walls. He had tried to leave using the underground tunnel through which he had entered. He had attempted to use rope ladders and the foot- and handholds built into the walls, but there was an invisible force sealing away the entire Keep. It pressed up against the exterior of Paranor at every possible exit point and extended down into the earth. There was no way past it, and all his efforts to break through had been unsuccessful. Use of magic in every form he could think to conjure had failed. Even the talismans and magic housed in the vaults offered no answers. A few, like the Crimson Elfstones, were so powerful and unpredictable—as well as unlikely to be of help in his present situation—that he had left them alone. None of the talismans had provided him with an answer to his problem. He was trapped, and there was no way out while Paranor remained trapped in limbo.

Finally, no form of communication with the outside world existed. The scrye waters in the cold room could tell him when or where magic had been used in the Four Lands, but little else. Clizia had left him the scrye orb, but given the circumstances surrounding his imprisonment, it seemed unlikely she would respond to any summons he sent her.

Besides, no one who might want to help him even knew he was here save Dar Leah. And if anything happened to the Blade, Drisker might remain trapped in Paranor for the rest of his life—whatever sort of life he might have left in this limbo world. He couldn't even be sure of that. There was food and water within the Keep, probably enough for a few years if he used it sparingly. After that he would starve to death. In the meantime, he could not be sure what living in this half-life world was doing to him, anyway. Was he aging at the same rate? Was he being affected in ways he couldn't recognize? How much was he changing without even knowing it?

If all this weren't enough, there was the complicated question of why he was even still alive. It was hard to fathom. At Clizia's urging, Drisker had summoned the Keep's Guardian from the bowels of the earth, waking it for the express purpose of driving the Skaar from Paranor or killing them if they resisted. That it was capable of doing both was incontestable. But whether it could or would differentiate between those it had been woken to dispatch and anyone else it found in the process was unknown. It wouldn't have been so worrying if he were still a Druid, but he had resigned from the order, abdicated his position as Ard Rhys, and then been placed in permanent exile by his successor. There was no reason for the spirit creature to spare him. Even Clizia must have felt certain he would be killed, given how she had left him—helpless to defend himself and entirely at the wraith's mercy.

Yet for some reason it had passed him by. It had come down that corridor leaving only dead men in its wake and passed right over him—even *through* him, at one point—and left him unharmed. Why had it done that? What sort of distinction had it made between him and the Skaar? What had caused it to spare his life? He had never heard of this happening in the entire history of the Druids, all the way back to the time of Galaphile. What had been different this time? Because something must have been. He had mulled it over and still not found an answer that made any sense.

The Guardian was gone now, returned to the depths of the Druid's Well, subsumed into its slumber to await a new threat that would require it to come to the Keep's defense. It had cleansed its lair of Druid enemies—leaving it otherwise intact, if in limbo—and had disappeared.

His survival wasn't a riddle that required an immediate solution, but it was troublesome to ponder. Drisker knew he would not be alive without good reason, and he had no idea at this point what that reason was.

He sat against a passageway wall midway between the exit leading to the west gates and the assembly chamber used for convening the entire Druid order, his knees up and his arms wrapped about them, as he stared into space. If only he had the Black Elfstone. Then he could use it to bring Paranor back into the world of men and make his escape. He could go after Clizia Porse. He could help find a way to deal with the Skaar invasion.

"Isn't anyone else here?" he shouted into the empty silence, frustrated and angry.

He listened to the echo of his voice reverberate through the building and slowly die away. He looked up and down the hallway as if someone might unexpectedly appear, as if his words would bring them. Foolishness. There was no one here but him. There would never be anyone here but him. And eventually he wouldn't be here, either. Not alive and breathing, anyway.

"How am I supposed to figure out what to do?" he muttered into the shadowy void, his voice deliberately emphasizing each word, so that it echoed in the silence before fading.

"A little common sense might help," a thin, wispy voice replied almost immediately.

Drisker startled. The voice was right next to him. In the wall. He jumped up and faced its stone-and-mortar surface, hardly able to believe what he was hearing. The wall had spoken to him! There was no one there, so what else could it have been? Was the wall alive? Was the Keep speaking to him?

He dismissed this idea at once. There was no record of the Keep ever having spoken to anyone, not in its entire history—not since the day the first stones had been laid to form the foundation and the mortar between them layered with Druid magic.

He waited a moment. "Who's there?"

"Your conscience, Druid! Your inner Drisker Arc."

Drisker smiled in spite of himself. A wall with a sense of humor. "I find that hard to believe."

"You need to apply common sense; remember when you had some? It served you well over the years. I should know. I've been watching you make use of it. You and I are not so different, you know. I was like you once, rash and bold. Clinging to my precious principles. Led me to a rather lengthy period of rethinking my life. Which in turn led me to end up like you."

Drisker thought. *To end up like me. Trapped in Paranor?* For a second he couldn't think what the voice was talking about. Then he remembered. All those hours spent reading the Druid Histories. Just ancient legends and useless information from times dead and gone, the other Druids had scoffed. *Nothing there will help you with the present. Studying the world around you is all that matters. There is nothing to be learned by studying what's over and done with.*

Except that those who fail to pay attention to the past are doomed to repeat it.

"Cogline," he said softly. "Is it really you?"

"Not really. Because I haven't been me for a rather long time. Only a shadow of myself."

A transparent figure detached itself from the wall, oozing through the stone in lines and shadings until at last it was standing before him—an old man so worn and weathered, so wrinkled and gaunt, even in his present ghostly form, that he almost wasn't there at all. What there was of him was stooped and gnarled and skeletally thin, more an approximation than a representation of the man he had been when he was alive. Or so Drisker assumed, because Cogline had been dead for centuries, gone into the netherworld, another of its shades. No one had seen or heard from him since Walker Boh had used the Black Elfstone to bring Paranor back the last time it was banished from the Four Lands before facing the Four Horsemen in a battle that had claimed Cogline's life.

Drisker now remembered the story of how the old man had been trapped inside the Keep after he had sacrificed himself to Rimmer Dall and the Shadowen in order to save Walker, there to remain until the Keep's return.

And now, for reasons Drisker could only guess at, here he was again, returned in this half-life form.

"I suppose I must look a bit undernourished," the old man observed, glancing down at himself. "But all things are finite, and I probably don't have all that much time left."

"Do shades have finite lives once they reach the netherworld?" Drisker asked, intrigued. "I thought shades simply lived on in ghost form."

"Well, now you've learned something new, haven't you? Think about it. All those shades take up space. Where do you put them?

Eventually some have to give way to allow for new ones. When they do, they simply vanish. Poof. Gone in a moment's time."

"And what happens then?"

Cogline shrugged. "That's the question, isn't it? I will soon know the answer, but you will have to wait awhile. Which brings us to your present situation and the more pressing question of how long that wait might be."

"Can you help me get out of the Keep?" Drisker asked.

"Well, shades don't really help anyone, do they? You must know that much from the way living and dead Druids must meet at the Hadeshorn to converse. The living always desire answers from the dead, but the dead can't provide them. They can only hint or suggest or riddle. It is the way of things."

"So you can't help me?"

"I didn't say that. I can *try* to help you. But mostly you are going to have to help yourself."

Drisker sighed. "So far I haven't had much success. I've been trying for days and nothing works. Surely you can tell me something that would put me on the right track?"

Cogline shrugged, and when he did so his entire body shivered as if threatening to disappear. "You might try checking your pockets to see if there isn't something there that would prove useful."

"I already checked my pockets. I did that right away, just to see if I still had the Black Elfstone. I didn't. Clizia Porse took it from me when she left me here to die. All I have is the scrye orb."

Cogline looked decidedly disappointed. "You should check again. Maybe you missed something. In our tendency to be certain about what might or might not be true, we sometimes persuade ourselves things are different from reality. I wonder if it could have happened here?"

"I don't see how." Drisker was irritated now. All this back-and-forth talk was leading nowhere. He shook his head. "All right, I'll make another search. But I hope this isn't a game you're playing. Because I am not interested in games!"

The shade said nothing. It simply waited, head cocked. There was a curiously intense look on its face, readable within the shimmering of its features. Drisker stared at it, momentarily fascinated, and then began rifling through his empty pockets, reaching deep, fumbling around, finding the scrye orb and continuing to dig deeper.

"Nothing," he muttered, still searching. "Just the scrye orb."

"Hmmm. Well, then, at least we have eliminated one possibility." Cogline scratched his ghostly head. "Perhaps when you have finished rummaging about, you should check the chamber where the talismans curated by the Druid order are stored."

"So that I can discover it isn't there, either? I know what's in that chamber. I've cataloged it all myself, personally!"

"Have you anything better to do with your time?"

"Wasting it like this isn't helping!"

"But what if you're not wasting it?"

Drisker was about to offer a fresh retort when suddenly he froze, his hand still buried deep inside his pocket. His fingers explored carefully, and a shocked expression crossed his face. Then he slowly withdrew his hand.

In his palm lay the Black Elfstone.

Drisker stared. "I don't understand," he said quietly, looking up at Cogline. "How did this happen? How *could* it have happened? It wasn't there earlier. I would swear it wasn't." He glanced down, frowning. "This is your doing, isn't it?"

"There is so much to explain," the shade replied. "There are answers to be had to all your questions, Drisker Arc, although not all of them might be ones you will be happy to discover."

"I'll take my chances," Drisker replied. As maddening as Cogline was, he was clearly the only one who knew the story behind what had happened to the Elfstone. "Tell me what you know."

"I was about to do so. Let's begin with my recent past. I have been living in Paranor since before you became Ard Rhys. I was always fond of it there. Spent considerable time in it back when Walker Boh was struggling to accept his destiny. The netherworld was never for me. So when you left and Ober Balronen became Ard Rhys, I knew what lay ahead. The current Druid order was rotten clear through, made that way by the machinations of Balronen and his associates and their foolish indifference to the danger they were facing. But while a shade can observe, it can neither change the future nor interfere with the present."

He paused. "Mostly."

"Mostly?"

The shade made a dismissive gesture. "I was here when the Keep fell. I watched them die, all of them—all of the Druids trapped inside save Clizia Porse. But she had betrayed them, and she would betray you, as well. While you clearly distrusted her, I knew that alone would not be enough to save you. Your nature was to give the benefit of the doubt while hers was to take advantage. She would gain your help, then steal the Black Elfstone once you retrieved it and leave you to die. I could not stand by and watch it happen—it would put an end of the Druid order for good, destroying everything that had been established by Galaphile all those years ago."

Drisker nodded slowly. *All those years ago.* Thousands of years of Druid efforts expended to save the Four Lands. "So you did something, didn't you? Even though you weren't supposed to be able to do so?"

Cogline shrugged. "Shades cannot impact the lives of the living, but they can cause disturbances in other, smaller ways. Lengthy occupation of a place gives a shade a small amount of power over it. I discovered, quite by accident some years back, that my long tenure as a resident of Paranor had given me the ability to change things now and again without having to touch them. A sort of teleporting or rearranging, I suppose you would call it."

He looked off into the gloom of the Keep, as if remembering. "When I saw you go down, disabled by Clizia's magic, I knew what I had to do. I waited until she had removed the pouch with its Elfstone inside and then I—how shall I put this? I swapped what she had for something else. I waited until she had pocketed the Elfstone and was bending over you, and then I swapped the Stone for something else. Then I waited."

"For me to wake?"

The shade managed to look embarrassed. "Not exactly."

"What, then? Why did you wait to tell me about the Elfstone?"

"Rather unfortunately, I could not seem to find where I had put it. Or caused it to be put. I have trouble remembering things sometimes. The passing of the years does that to you—even if you are a shade. Then this morning, I remembered and transferred the Stone back into your pocket."

"And played games with me!"

"Drisker," Cogline said in an admonishing tone. "It's what shades *do*. You know this, so don't act so surprised. What matters now is you have the key to the door that bars your way back into the Four Lands. All is well. Except . . ."

Drisker felt a sinking feeling in the pit of his stomach. "Except what?"

"Except for one small complication that will surface sooner or later, so you might as well know about it now. We ought to visit the archives so you can see for yourself. Come along. Follow my lead."

He started off at a rapid glide, hovering just off the stone flooring. Reluctantly, Drisker followed, trudging after him as they passed down numerous hallways and descended several sets of stairs to the lower levels of the Keep. As he walked, Drisker kept one hand firmly fastened around the Black Elfstone and its pouch where they lay nestled inside his pocket. Shades were mercurial in their behavior, and there was nothing to say that Cogline might not choose to move the talisman about yet again—perhaps just for sport.

When they reached the archival chamber, Drisker triggered the locks and listened to them release, one by one. As he stepped inside, Cogline simply passed through the stone—as if to demonstrate how much easier everything was for a shade. The Druid ignored him, moving to the center of the room. "Well?"

Cogline shuffled his feet. "Clizia took something else that wasn't hers. From here, in the archives. She did so when you were otherwise occupied. It was a quick and furtive theft. She obviously knew what she was looking for and where to find it. I saw her commit her crime, of course. If I could have, I would have transferred that artifact out of her possession, as well, but there are limitations to what we can do as shades, and I did not yet know for sure that she would succeed in her efforts to take the Black Elfstone from you. So I knew it was better to concentrate on preventing that."

He pointed to a small cubicle set into the wall in a shadowed area where the light did not quite reach. Drisker peered at it and saw that the door was cracked slightly open. He tried to remember what it had contained. "What was in there—"

"Have a look," the shade said, interrupting him. "See if you can remember."

Drisker crossed the room, knelt to open the door all the way, and reached inside. "So she took whatever was in here, did she? I can't seem to recall . . . what was . . ."

He trailed off, a sinking feeling in the pit of his stomach. "No," he whispered.

Cogline nodded slowly, his entire body shimmering with the movement. "I'm afraid so."

FIVE

Before the last stones of Paranor's ancient walls had faded, Clizia Porse was well away from Paranor's graveyard and its few Skaar survivors and traveling south toward Varfleet. It wasn't where she wanted to end up, but she had contacts with people who could provide her with the supplies and transportation she needed. After all, she had been forced to abandon most of her possessions in Paranor, leaving with little more than the clothes on her back and a sizable number of credits in her pocket. At present, she was traveling with a goods caravan come down out of the villages and farmland west of the Mermidon—a collection banded together for safety against the raiders that had plagued foot and wagon traffic along the river for years. If she had been thinking more clearly, she would have arranged transport from somewhere closer to the Keep, but at the time she had been more focused on her plans for disposing of Drisker Arc.

Drisker, after all, was the sort of man you needed to pay close attention to if you planned to kill him.

That she had deceived the former Druid so utterly was something of a triumph—and a rigorous test of her acting abilities. She had to be entirely convincing in her insistence that they work together to protect the Druid legacy and the Keep. She had to pretend she knew nothing of Ober Balronen's increasingly erratic behavior or why Ruis

Quince had acted so recklessly when confronting the Skaar, when in fact she had been the cause of both. That she had not been instrumental in advocating for the young Skaar spy Kassen to be allowed into the Keep so he could set the stage for its fall. That her intentions for the future of Paranor were in keeping with Drisker's own. If he had suspected the truth about any of this, he would have dispatched her so quickly she might not have even seen it coming. Drisker was trusting but unforgiving of betrayal. If he hadn't been so passionately committed to saving Paranor and evicting the Skaar from her corridors, he might not have been caught off guard so completely.

But whatever had undone him—whatever the nature of his failure to recognize her intentions, whatever blindness he had developed to her larger, more personal goals—it had cost him his life. He might survive the deadly passing of the Guardian through Paranor's halls (although she seriously doubted it) or even linger on a few years afterward living off supplies that would normally provide for an entire Druid order and would be more than enough to sustain him. But in the end he would succumb. Drisker was gone, and he wasn't coming back.

Not while she had possession of the only magic that could allow him to escape his prison.

Which left her free to pursue her own goals without interference.

"Soup, Grandmother?"

A young boy held out a bowl of steaming liquid and a spoon. She took both with a nod and leaned back against the wagon wheel. The traders and their families had been more than kind to her, not even asking who she was or where she had come from. They had picked her up close to Paranor the day before, seeking transport to Varfleet and willing and able to pay for it. She could have gotten where she was going more quickly by air, but she was content to travel slowly and disappear into the populace of the Borderlands while she pondered the path she had set herself upon—one that had begun with the destruction of Paranor and would lead to a rebuilding of the Druid order in a way that would better suit her own purposes. Her journey was just beginning, and it would be a long one. But even though she was old and her years were numbered, she had the time to do what was needed and the patience to let it all play out properly. Rushing was never a good idea. Rushing caused mistakes, and mistakes could undo you.

She sipped her soup and thought briefly of the now demolished Druid order and how things might have gone differently if Drisker Arc had stayed on as Ard Rhys. As a leader, he was both capable and wise, but his inability to recognize fault in others was crippling. He wanted to believe the best of people, while she knew well enough that it was the worst that always surfaced sooner or later. She had seen the rise of Ober Balronen coming long before Drisker, and realized that if she was to change the direction of the order, she had to make an unappetizing alliance with him. She hated doing so—hated choosing Balronen over Drisker—but the latter simply wasn't strong enough to survive what was coming.

From then on, she had manipulated and deceived relentlessly, waiting for her chance to make the changes she had deemed necessary. In the beginning, she had only intended to rid the order of Balronen and one or two others. But when the Skaar had invaded, she seized upon the opportunity they presented and switched from ridding herself of a few Druids to ridding herself of the lot. A clean slate was always best, and this next time around she would hand-select the members of the new Druid order.

Her Druid order, with herself as Ard Rhys.

She finished the soup, and when the boy passed by again she handed him the empty bowl. In two more days, they would reach Varfleet, and she would find lodgings and begin planning for the future. Alliances must be formed, agreements must be reached, and the groundwork must be laid for what in five years would bring about the return of Paranor and the forming of the new Druid order. The whole process, she suspected, would take at least five years. So for now, she must bide her time.

Although there were a few tasks she must carry out fairly quickly.

She knew Drisker had taken books of magic from Paranor— books he had compiled on his own—and she wanted them. So first she must go to his cottage in the village of Emberen, which was north of Arborlon, up along the southern boundaries of the Streleheim. That way, his knowledge could live on through her.

There was also the girl. Tarsha. His student. She smiled, thinking of her. That girl was more than some callow acolyte. She possessed serious magic of her own; Clizia had sensed it the moment she had looked into her strange lavender eyes. You didn't get to be as old as she was if you couldn't recognize magic. Tarsha Kaynin could become a valuable ally if properly persuaded, and there were ways to make that happen.

Finally, there was the matter of what to do about the Skaar. She couldn't very well ignore them, or await the inevitable. She had to make contact with them and persuade them to support her when the time came. The rest of the Four Lands might believe the Skaar were nothing more than a temporary distraction, but Clizia saw things differently. In her judgment, the Skaar were here to stay.

So there was much to do, and she must start quickly. The larger plan could wait, but in the end it would only work if she successfully carried out the smaller parts first.

She picked herself up, still wrapped in her robes, and went off into the darkness to find a place to sleep. She would have been more comfortable by one of the many fires the traders were gathered around, but she preferred not to get too close to anyone. The less these people knew about her, the better. She would use them to reach Varfleet, then never see them again. They would remember her in a vague sort of way, but never with any real clarity. An old woman, quiet and aloof, her worn face immediately forgettable. She would leave them with no clear impression and disappear into the city to begin her new life.

Settling herself against the mossy trunk of an old-growth chestnut, she leaned back contentedly and patted the hard bulk of each of the treasures she hid inside her clothing. When she had taken the Black Elfstone from Drisker Arc, she had barely glanced at it before stuffing it into her robes. There had been no time for that, no time for anything but getting out of Paranor. Since then, she had left it where she'd put it that night, safely hidden away. After all, it would not be of use until the five years she had allotted for her plan and Drisker's lifetime were up.

Nor had she bothered with unwrapping the Stiehl once she had removed it from the archival vaults. It had taken her only moments; her knowledge of where it was and how its locks could be released was information she had persuaded a foolish Ober Balronen to entrust to her in a moment of weakness. She had coveted the blade since she had known it was there, but had been content to leave it where it was until she knew the Keep was going to fall.

Yet now, for the first time, she gave in to a sudden urge to look upon both, to revel for just a few moments in what she had accomplished.

She reached into her robes and drew out the Stiehl first, keeping her actions furtive and swift. A quick glance around and a scanning of the darkness with her Druid senses confirmed she was alone. She placed the blade in her lap where the moonlight could provide a sufficiently clear look once she had removed its wrappings. Her hands were shaking with excitement as she tore open the layers of leather and soft cloth and found the dagger nestled within. It was a wicked-looking weapon, its ebony handle carved with runes darker still and its blade matte black, deeply striated, and well over a foot long. She stared at it with keen anticipation for what it might be used for. It was the most dangerous weapon in the world, and now it was hers to do with as she chose.

After a few moments more, she slipped the Stiehl back into her clothing and brought out the Black Elfstone. She could feel the angles and planes of it through the fabric of the pouch in which it was kept. Such a pleasant feeling, she thought, as she caressed it lovingly.

Carefully, she loosened the drawstrings to the pouch and let the Elfstone tumble out into the palm of her hand . . .

And saw at once that it was something else entirely.

For a second, she was certain she must be mistaken. It was a stone. It had edges and planes. It was the right size. But it was not an Elfstone. It wasn't even black! It was just an unremarkable stone.

Her rage surfaced in a rush of white-hot heat that left her flushed.

She put the rock aside and rummaged through her clothing and pack. Nothing. But she had known that, hadn't she? She had taken what she believed to be the Black Elfstone and put it right where she could find it when she was ready to take it out. Except something had gone wrong. Had Drisker somehow scooped up the wrong talisman when he was rummaging through the archives? Had he mistaken this ordinary rock for the Black Elfstone, snatching it from its concealment and pocketing it without looking while she kept urging him to hurry?

Or had she somehow mistaken what she was stealing from him while he lay helpless on the floor of the Keep?

Everything was suddenly scrambled—all of her plans and schemes and thinking jumbled together in a confusing mix. Everything she had planned would fail if she could not get her hands on the Black Elfstone. Without Paranor, there could be no reformation of the Druid order. Without the magic and the talismans contained within, there could be no starting over. Did Drisker know she didn't have the Elfstone? Did he still have it himself? How could she find out without telling him the Stone was still inside Paranor? Only if she did so could the Stone's magic be used to bring Paranor back into the Four Lands!

Her ancient face, deep-etched by age and taut with renewed expectations, assumed an expression of cunning. She had to be careful about what she did next. She had to think of a way to get Drisker to reveal what he knew without his realizing it. Or find a way to turn him into her ally, willing or not. She needed leverage for this. But what sort of leverage could she apply that would rid her of Drisker and still allow her plans to go forward?

At the moment, she had no idea.

"She has the Stiehl!"

Drisker shouted it with such fury that it became not a question but a cry of despair. The extent of his anger was almost beyond measure. The Stiehl was a creation of dark magic with a history that went far back in time—so far back there was no clear record of how the weapon had been forged or who had fashioned it. What was known was that there was nothing it could not cut through and no one it could not kill. It had surfaced first in the days of Walker Boh and the assassin Pe Ell, while they were on their journey to the ancient stronghold of the Stone King, accompanied by the highlander Morgan Leah and Quickening, the daughter of the King of the Silver River. Pe Ell had killed the girl using the Stiehl, but had been killed himself later. Afterward, the Stiehl had been locked away in Paranor. Grianne Ohmsford and then Aphenglow Elessedil, both while serving as Ard Rhys, had determined it must never emerge again. Since then, it had remained locked away in the vaults of the Druid archives.

Until now. Until this.

Cogline, to his credit, said nothing, letting Drisker think it through. For a shade dead more than a thousand years, he possessed excellent instincts.

"I have to get out of here," Drisker said finally, staring down at the Black Elfstone, his gaze fixing on what he believed might still be the answer to his problems. "I have to use the Stone to free myself and go after her."

"Well, perhaps," the other replied.

"Perhaps? You don't think it might be dangerous to let Clizia Porse run around with the most dangerous weapon in the world while she implements her plans for . . . well, for whatever she's planning?"

"Yes, but what are her plans, exactly? I don't know. Do you, Drisker? How will she use the Stiehl to advance them? It might behoove you to think this through. And there is yet another matter to consider."

He went silent, his expression enigmatic as he waited for a response.

"Another matter," the Druid repeated. He shook his head. "Of course there would be another matter, and you wouldn't be happy if you didn't make me guess what it is, would you?"

"It should be obvious."

"Let's suppose that what is obvious to you—a shade with some insights that the living lack—isn't necessarily obvious to me. Please enlighten me."

Cogline shrugged. "You have to figure out how to use the Black Elfstone."

"What? You think it won't respond to me? That I am not a true member of the Druid order with the power to summon its magic?"

And suddenly it occurred to him that perhaps the Stone might *not* be his to use. He was no longer Ard Rhys. He was not even the last of the Druids. That alone might prevent him from employing its magic. What if he had disqualified himself by leaving the order and abandoning the post of Ard Rhys? Yet he could not imagine that Clizia Porse, complicit in the fall of the Keep, would be the only one who could wield it.

Cogline was watching him. "It isn't as simple as it seems," he said quietly, his body shimmering as if with a sudden chill. "It requires something to command such magic. It demands a price."

"What are you talking about? What sort of price?"

"It is not for me to say. It is for you to find out."

"Very profound. Well, then, I will do as you say. I will find out for myself. Care to come watch?"

He started off without waiting to see if the other would follow, stepping from the chamber and closing the doors behind him. *Let the shade pass through the walls if he wishes to follow.* Using magic, he reset the locks and resealed the chamber. The Black Elfstone was in his pocket once more as he strode back down Paranor's hallways, heading for the doors leading out to the Keep's west gates. His mind was spinning. Had Clizia discovered she did not have the Elfstone? And what were her plans for the Stiehl?

He stopped abruptly. He could find all that out easily enough. Both he and Clizia still had their scrye orbs. It would be a simple matter for him to contact her. They could speak to each other, and he could ask her what she knew.

But to what end? What would this accomplish? And what could he say to her that would matter? At best, she would be outraged both that she did not have what she needed and that he was still among the living. What sort of bargain could he hope to make with her that would help him but not her? It was likely to be a short conversation.

The complexity of the situation was daunting. Neither of them was about to give in to the other. Thinking on it further, he realized that the only advantage he had was that she couldn't be certain whether he still had the Elfstone. She might believe he was ignorant of the fact that it was still there somewhere in Paranor. She couldn't know that Cogline still lived on as a shade within the Keep and had purloined the Elfstone from her and given it back to him. She might even think he still believed the Elfstone was in her possession—that she really had stolen it from him.

He watched Cogline materialize beside him, bleeding through the passageway stone. He turned away from the shade. There must be a way he could take advantage of this knowledge that he had and she didn't. But he couldn't think just what it might be.

He continued down the hallway, reaching the west doors of the building and stepping out into the open courtyard beyond. The air was gray and misty, the skies a screen of impenetrable gloom through which neither moon nor sun was revealed. The outer walls of the Keep were blank screens ahead of him, barely visible through the haze. He already knew that from the top of those walls he could see nothing in any direction; the world of the Four Lands had disappeared, and what had replaced it was a vast emptiness.

He walked swiftly toward the gates, noting as he went that nothing seemed to have changed beyond the walls—no sign of life, no birdsong, no wind rattling the tree branches. Nothing. Only an immense void that threatened to crush his spirit.

But he would change all that. Standing before the west gates, he brought out the Black Elfstone and held it forth, summoning its magic to dispel the gloom and bring Paranor back into the world of the Four Lands.

Nothing happened.

He hesitated, not wanting to try again too quickly, afraid he was making a mistake. He walked through the steps he had taken to summon the magic—focusing on the Stone, binding to its power, speaking the words of summoning, the congealment of elements surrounding him that would ease the magic's passage. He had done them all, and if he was entitled to use the magic, as he had insisted to Cogline he was, it should have responded.

He tried again, taking his time, making sure he did everything correctly, and giving his words and gestures exactly the right amount of time and space.

Surface, he commanded the magic silently.

Once again, nothing happened.

"Surface!" he hissed aloud.

But the Black Elfstone remained dark. Drisker closed his fist on the talisman and stared helplessly at the closed gates and the gray haze that cloaked everything surrounding him.

"It might be that something more is needed," Cogline offered unhelpfully.

"Which I must discover for myself?"

"Well, you should at least think about what it might be."

"Suppose I simply don't qualify as a wielder of this particular magic? I've considered that possibility."

"As you should." Cogline gave him an appreciative nod. "However, I don't think that is your problem. You are a former Ard Rhys. You don't always shed that mantle simply because you cease to function in the job. I should know. I was once a Druid myself, if you recall my history. The Keep responds to truth and belief and commitment, not to a title. Are you Ard Rhys of the Fourth Druid Order or not, Drisker Arc?"

He spoke mildly and without hurry, but there was a hint of impatience to his words.

"I don't know," Drisker admitted.

"It always helps to know yourself before you try to know others. It helps to know yourself before you attempt to use certain kinds of magic, too."

"Well, maybe I don't know myself sufficiently well to use this particular magic."

Cogline nodded. "That could well be true. Why don't you let me know when that changes?"

And he turned away, walked into the wall, and disappeared.

SIX

---◆---

FAR TO THE SOUTHWEST of Arborlon, where the Rill Song wound toward the Rock Spur, Tarsha Kaynin was nearing Backing Fell and home. She had been traveling for three days, passing countless towns and villages, all of which she had avoided, spending her nights in wooded shelters along the river, limiting any chance encounters that might lead to delays.

As she journeyed, her night in Wending Way remained a vivid memory. It was there she had encountered the old woman Parlindru, the seer who had foretold her future with such gentle certainty while they sat together in the taproom of an inn. The old woman had read her future by taking hold of her hands, and had given her three promises of what was to be.

Three times would she love and all would be true, but only one would last.

Three times would she die, but each time she would come back to life.

Three chances would she have to make a change in the lives of others, and one of the three would change the world.

The rule of three, Parlindru had told her—a rule so embedded in the fabric of life that it was absolute. Three things could define all aspects of life. Three things could explain all events and all fates. It was true for everyone, and it would be true for Tarsha.

Yet did any of this really happen or had she imagined it all, her mind fogged by weariness and ale, her imagination run wild even as she sat wide awake at her table at that inn in Wending Way? Well, perhaps. She had drunk a couple of glasses of ale, but Parlindru, while seeming to drink with her, apparently had not taken a sip. The innkeeper who had served the ale and kept watch from behind the bar had not even seen the old woman. It was all mysterious and uncertain, and Tarsha had been left with a memory that was perhaps unreliable.

She had mulled it over as she flew on, trying to settle on at least one certainty, however small, that would tip the scales. In the end, she decided it was her instincts that mattered most, her always reliable sense of what was and wasn't real.

And her meeting with Parlindru felt decidedly real, so she resolved to stop doubting it and embrace the foretelling she had been given.

But as a result, she was saddled with expectations she could not stop thinking about—wondering when each of the three would occur, what they would look like, how she would be affected, and if she would recognize them for what they were. She did not feel fear—not even at the thought of dying three times. She believed that fate was to be taken figuratively rather than literally, and the prophecies felt like metaphors for something more complex than actual occurrences. After all, you couldn't die three times, could you? And change the world by changing someone's life? There were nuances to these fates, she believed—suggestions of things that would happen on a much smaller scale.

But whatever the case, the expectations were there, and the future she had been anticipating had suddenly expanded into something more fluid and at the same time settled.

So when Backing Fell approached, she put all of it aside and returned to thoughts of her brother. She wondered if her parents had ever brought him home. She wondered if he would be there when she arrived. She believed Tavo would be disappointed and hurt by her prolonged absence, but perhaps grateful, too, that she had returned. But whether he knew where she had been or not, she must find a way to reassure him that it had never been her intention to abandon him. She must explain what she was doing in a way that left him no room to doubt her intentions.

She must explain, too, about the path she had taken to find Drisker Arc and the work she was now doing as a Druid's apprentice.

The day of her arrival was sunny and warm, the skies clear and the world bright and shiny, as if newly made and still unspoiled. She crossed from the river into the forests, bypassing her village and flying on to her parents' cottage. When she was still a short distance away, she landed her small craft in a sheltered clearing where it was not likely to be disturbed and secured it. Leaving it behind, she began walking toward her destination. She was already rehearsing the words she would speak to her parents—and to Tavo, as well, if he was there—readying her explanations and her excuses and anticipating what lay ahead.

She passed out of the trees onto the pathway that led to her home, searching for what was familiar . . .

. . . and found instead the still-smoking ashes of what was gone forever.

Her home was in ruins, a pile of charred rubble and ash, burned to the ground, the earth beneath turned blackened and raw.

She slowed and then stopped altogether, staring in shock. There was nothing left. Everything was destroyed, everything she had expected to find, everything she remembered from her childhood. She started to call for her mother and father, then stopped. There was no one alive here; no one could have survived such devastation. What had happened? Where were her parents now?

Fearfully, she continued to approach the remains, trying to make sense of what she was seeing. It could be that her parents had chosen to find a new home, but why would their old one have burned to the ground? Was it an accident? Or was this perhaps why they had left? Deep in her heart, she knew the truth. This was Tavo's doing. Her brother had come home, found them, and punished them for abandoning him in the only way he knew how.

She stood where she was for a time, not ten feet away, memories flashing through her mind—insistent and vivid pictures of how she had grown up here with Tavo. She remembered playing together when they were younger—until he became too wild and uncontrollable. She remembered his behavior and how it had caused him to be banished to his uncle's farm. She remembered coming to her decision to leave home herself, knowing she must travel to the Druids if she wanted to help her brother by better understanding the magic both of them had inherited.

All that was wiped away.

She understood now exactly how Drisker Arc had felt when he had found his cottage burned.

She was crying without realizing it, and she angrily wiped at her tears and turned away. She had to find out what had become of her parents. She had to discover where they were.

She returned to the pathway and followed it until it joined the rutted dirt roadway that led to Backing Fell. In something of a daze, distracted and confused, she walked to the village. At first, she saw no one. Then, as she drew nearer to the village proper, figures began to appear and she hailed them, waving her arms and calling out.

But one by one, they either turned away or disappeared inside their homes—not gradually, but in haste. No one responded. No one made any attempt at all to talk to her. It was as if the very sight of her were distasteful, as if she were diseased and they feared catching what she had. Even when she started down the main street of the village, its residents fled from her. People she had known for years! Every man, woman, and child she came within sight of vanished. Worse still, some were calling ahead to others farther on, giving warning. She could not hear the words, but she could certainly detect the tone of voice used.

Frantic. Fearful.

She would have understood better if it were Tavo they were fleeing. But she had never given them any cause to be afraid of her. She had never experienced anything but friendship before now.

Something was very wrong.

She continued on. Finally, when she was midway through the village, the blacksmith appeared in front of her. Herkolan Kielson was a great, burly man, his size and strength well suited for his work, and he blocked her way with such determination that she slowed in spite of herself.

"That's close enough, Tarsha," he said.

Herkolan Kielson had always been a friend, someone with whom she had joked and told stories. With whom she had shared an occasional glass of ale. He had never spoken a harsh word to her, never been anything but a friend. But he was a friend no longer.

She stopped. "What's wrong, Herk?" she asked.

He shook his head, declining to answer. "You have to go. Leave Backing Fell and never come back. You're no longer welcome here."

She stared. "What have I done?"

"It is your brother who has committed the crime. But there is no place here for you, either. Your magic might be different, but the people of this village cannot afford to take that chance. Turn around now and walk back the way you came."

She was suddenly frantic, her lavender eyes flashing with unexpected anger. "Where is my brother? Where are my parents? Tell me!"

He shook his head. "Gone. And never coming back. Now go!"

She stood her ground, furious. "Not until you tell me more."

Suddenly she was aware of movement around her. Figures were gathering to either side—men with blades and axes and sharpened poles. Rudimentary weapons, but effective enough at close quarters. And they were drawing steadily nearer.

"Witch!" she heard someone say.

"Demon!" said another.

More epithets followed, vile names hissed and whispered. The faces of the men were dark and dangerous, their rage fueled by emotions she recognized all too well. She felt their fear and anger sweep over her.

"Go, Tarsha," Herkolan Kielson urged. "Don't let this go any further. There's been enough bloodshed. Your brother has seen to that."

Bloodshed? She felt a void open in the pit of her stomach.

"Leave now, Tarsha," Herk repeated, his voice more insistent.

The magic of the wishsong was rising within her, coming to her defense. She knew what it could do. She knew that these townsmen, once her friends and neighbors, could be swept aside like leaves in a strong wind if she used it. She was tempted; she was furious with them for their obstinate behavior, their foolish refusal to speak.

But she realized what it would mean to strike back at them. It meant hurting them, perhaps badly. It meant treating them as enemies when they weren't. It wasn't the homecoming she was seeking. It wasn't anything like what she had expected. She wanted answers, but she needed a better way to find them.

She nodded slowly. "All right. I'm going."

She backed away until she was in the clear. A wall of unpleasant but familiar faces watched her. She stared back at them defiantly, and then she turned around and went back down the road.

She walked from the village in a daze, aware of eyes watching her from behind parted curtains and half-closed doors. She knew there were people everywhere making sure she was really gone before coming out into the open again. All of them afraid of her, believing for whatever reason she might harm them or their loved ones. People who had never before worried about her, had never been anything but welcoming.

This was Tavo's doing. Herk had said as much, but she was afraid to consider what her brother might have done.

She was back out on the open roadway when she realized she had no idea where she was going. She had been told to leave, but she couldn't. Not without knowing more than she did. How else was she going to discover what had happened to her parents? If she was to solve this mystery, she had to locate them. Had they been driven out? She thought they must have been, if the reaction of the townspeople was any indication. But it seemed so unreasonable. She could understand driving Tavo out, if his offense was severe enough. But not her parents, too.

There's been enough bloodshed, Herkolan had said.

She slowed and looked back. Behind her, the streets of Backing Fell were empty. She turned around, determined to find out the truth.

But she had taken only a few steps when she heard a voice hiss in warning. "Don't do that, girl! Walk back the way you came in! I'll tell you what you want to know once you do."

The voice came from a cluster of bushes to her left, and she turned that way at once. "Who's there?"

"Just do as I say. Get clear of the village. I'll meet you down the road a way. Go!"

Tarsha did as she was told, walking until Backing Fell was out of sight. She continued to search for the owner of the voice but saw no one. She went a mile farther before an aged woman appeared—a scrawny, withered oldster with braided gray hair that hung to her waist and eyes that reflected a toughness that brought Tarsha up short.

"Over here!" the old woman snapped. "Get out of sight while we talk!"

Tarsha followed the woman into the trees, leaving the rutted dirt road behind. Neither spoke until the old woman turned, a hard, tight expression on her face.

"Tarsha Kaynin, you listen to me! You cannot go back there. You can *never* go back. These people won't tolerate you. They'll do whatever it takes to drive you out."

"Who are you?" Tarsha demanded.

"Name's Jes Weisen." The old woman frowned as she glanced back in the direction of Backing Fell. "I live in Yarrow, up the road. Do my business in gardens and plantings, but I know about some things I wish I didn't."

"Do you know about my parents? Do you know where they are?"

"Dead, girl. Dead and gone. Sorry to tell you this, but there's no way to spare you. Terrible thing."

Tarsha swallowed hard. Her eyes filled with tears. "What happened to them?"

"Torn to pieces in their cottage, they were. Like wild animals had got to them. Wasn't hardly anything recognizable left. Just . . . blood. A lot of blood. Wish to all that's good and merciful that I hadn't seen it for myself, but I was the one that found them."

Tarsha's legs gave way, and she sat down slowly. She didn't want to hear the rest, already fearing what it might be. But she knew she had no choice.

Jes Weisen sat down next to her. "I was bringing an order of plantings to them. I'd come up from Yarrow in my cart to make the delivery. Stumbled on this boy in the middle of a set-to with a larger boy. Didn't know who either one was until later. The smaller boy was your brother, Tavo. The larger was named Squit Malk. They were about to go at each other, but I broke it up. Sent the bigger boy packing when he threatened me, the fool."

She paused. "There was blood on your brother's clothing. I thought it was his at the time, but I was wrong. It was your parents' blood."

Tarsha closed her eyes in despair. "I knew it. I knew he had done something terrible." She began to cry. "Tavo killed our parents?" she whispered, still trying to make it seem real.

"He must have, because I continued to your cottage after meeting him and found two bodies. Couldn't hardly think it was anyone else under the circumstances. Given how fresh the blood on him was, it had to have been his doing. He was leaving Backing Fell when I met him, heading away east. He didn't tell me what he had done, but when I reported it to the townsfolk, I heard the stories about him."

The stories. About the things he sometimes did. About his use of his magic. About the wishsong.

She shook her head in despair. "Maybe he was seeking help."

"He wasn't running *toward* the town," the old woman said quietly. "He was running *away*."

Tarsha nodded, unable to speak. What more could she say? Jes Weisen's words only confirmed her darkest fears. She knew Tavo was capable of such madness. She had been witness to it. "Did they go hunting for him?"

"They did. They went after him as soon as they saw what he had done to your parents. Angry and frightened both, they were, but they went—until they found the other boy. He was in a field, miles away from where they had started the hunt. Or what was left of him was. They only knew him from a belt buckle some recognized. He was the same as your parents, torn all to pieces. This was half a day's journey farther on. But your brother was well away from Backing Fell by then, so the searchers gave up, realizing what they would be facing if they caught up to him."

Oh, Tavo! Tarsha's heart went out to him, in spite of the anger she felt for what he had done to their parents. Where was he now? She felt so many conflicting emotions, but she allowed herself to think only of her parents for now. Her mother and father were gone, victims of their son's madness—and of a magic wielded by a child who could no longer differentiate between right and wrong. They had tried to help him, to understand the forces that were driving him, but they had failed. Instead, they had made things worse by sending him to live with his uncle—a decision that had likely cost them their lives. A wash of regret and frustration surfaced, leaving her raw and torn.

"I'm sorry, girl," Jes Weisen said.

Tarsha nodded wordlessly. Her family was destroyed, her hopes for Tavo flattened, her plans for finding a way to help him scattered to the four winds.

"You must have seen what happened to your home," the old woman added. "The townspeople burned it right after they abandoned the hunt for your brother. I watched them do it. I told them not to, but they refused to listen. Perhaps they were just superstitious fools, not wanting any reminder of the terrible thing that had been done. Or maybe they just wanted to be sure there was no home for your brother to come back to. Or for you, either."

Tarsha was crying hard now, and Jes Weisen reached over and put a comforting hand on her shoulder. "There, now. You cry as much as you need, girl. It's a terrible burden you bear."

Tarsha shook her head wordlessly. Was her burden any worse than Tavo's? There was reason to think hers would ease. How would her brother ever find relief?

"I have to go after him," she said finally, wiping away the last of the tears. "What happened is my fault. I was the only one he would ever listen to. I can still help him."

Jes Weisen snorted. "You're taking an awful lot on yourself. You really think you could have changed things? You think none of this would have happened if you'd stayed in Backing Fell and tried to look after him?"

"He depended on . . ."

The old woman brought a finger up to Tarsha's nose and touched it reprovingly. "You listen to me, girl. Here's the rest of what you need to know. Your brother didn't tell me where he was going—didn't tell anyone, far as I know—but I know the direction he took and what towns and hamlets he would pass through on his way. A small village—if you could even call it that—was one of those on his route. Several days after leaving here, there was a report of something unspeakable happening there. Want to know what it was?"

Tarsha couldn't help herself. She nodded slowly.

"A boy went into a place he shouldn't have gone, a tavern with a rough crowd. Your brother, from the description we got. There was a fight—I don't know the details—that got out of hand. Fifteen to one, if the serving woman who survived could count properly. Your precious brother tore those fifteen men to pieces with that magic of his."

She paused, her gaze steady. "So you listen to me. Anyone who would do that is beyond help. He isn't thinking clearly, and one person can't alter the way another's mind works. So don't go thinking you should set off on some mission to save him. He's beyond that. He's beyond anything rational. Likely he'll be dead before you even reach him, if you're still foolish enough to try."

Tarsha nodded, appalled that Tavo had used his magic for such terrible destruction. But if he could kill his own parents, he could certainly kill anyone else who crossed him.

Including her.

Jes Weisen was right. Tavo had by now gone beyond her help—and probably anyone else's. The boy she had known was dead and gone, and in his place was this killing machine that might do anything if provoked.

Yet even as she admitted all this, she knew she was still going after him. She had to try. She would never be able to live with herself if she didn't.

Jes Weisen climbed to her feet. "I've told you everything I know, and now I have to be going. I only came back because I saw you walking into Backing Fell and knew what you would be up against. Those people are scared out of their wits. They don't understand someone like your brother, and they think you might turn out to be the same. So better to drive you away than to let you stay and take a chance."

"I only wanted answers," Tarsha told her. "I just wanted to find out what happened to my family. It was never my intention to stay."

"Best you get going, then. Like me. I'm not staying here any longer, either, and I might not come back at all. But take heed to what I said about your brother. Don't go doing something foolish. That boy is insane. A demon."

She reached down to touch Tarsha's cheek, then turned and walked away. She was through the trees and gone in moments, but Tarsha continued to stare after her, lost in thought. Everything she had hoped to accomplish by coming back was destroyed as completely as her home and parents. Everything about her former life was gone. Except for her brother.

She had to find him.

She stood up. It was nearing midday. There were still six or seven hours of light remaining in which she could safely fly.

She started for her airship.

SEVEN

ON THE THIRD DAY after departing the Skaar camp, Kol'Dre was in Arishaig, approaching the offices of the members of the Coalition Council for an unscheduled meeting with the Prime Minister of the Federation. It was well past noon, and he walked until he found the building he wanted and then entered, navigating his way along a tangle of hallways that wound through its interior. He was stopped repeatedly at checkpoints, but he had purloined the necessary passes from the admission offices at the building entrance. A meeting now, even on such short notice, would have been impossible. Besides, a surprise appearance would better achieve his purpose.

Ajin had been quite clear about what she wanted.

"Speak to Ketter Vause personally. Tell him we have taken Paranor and destroyed the Druids. Ask him to consider supporting our efforts to make a home for our people north of the Mermidon, in land we already hold. Advise him that he may choose to refuse us, but in that case we would have to consider approaching the Elves with the same offer and they might be more willing to accommodate us."

She paused meaningfully. "Do whatever you think necessary to persuade him, Kol. Make sure he understands that it would be in his best interests to accept our offer."

Kol had nodded his understanding. "But even if he agrees, he will seek to betray us. He is that sort of man."

"Of course he is. And I am well aware of what he will do. I am counting on it, in fact."

"Then what is the point . . . ?"

She put a finger to his lips. "It is not an alliance with the Federation I am seeking. It is an alliance with the Elves. Now go, and come back again safe."

Her hand came to rest on his shoulder, and her fingers squeezed to emphasize the bond between them. In that moment, he would have done anything for her.

Sending him into such danger demonstrated once again the degree of confidence she had in him. Others might have agreed to take the risk for her, but none had the experience or skill to achieve the desired results. When it came to assignments where death was only a heartbeat away, Kol'Dre was the best choice by far.

He smiled. He was an odd sort of man, and he recognized this about himself. The Skaar were a warlike people, and to survive as one of them you had to have a certain recklessness inside you. But for Kol'Dre, recklessness was a step away from carelessness. No, what he found invigorating and addictive was the excitement that came from taking highly calculated risks. He liked knowing he could do things no one else could ever hope to do—and not so much things of a physical nature as things that required a certain mental superiority and courage. He knew he was smart—smarter than most. And testing the limits of that belief provided reaffirmation. Giving himself challenges made life worthwhile. Kol'Dre had never valued staying alive more than he had valued accomplishment.

He thought again of Ajin, and he wondered if perhaps she shared these feelings. Certainly she was willing to put herself at the forefront of every incursion she led—never hanging back, never staying safe, always showing that whatever she asked of others she was willing to do herself. He admired her for this. Her father, Cor d'Amphere, was nothing like her. He was a king who ruled from his throne and not from the head of his armies. He was smart enough, and decisive when it was needed, but his courage was buttressed by his position of power and did not come from within. Stripped of his title, he would have been a very ordinary man.

Admittedly, it was dangerous even to think like this, but Kol'Dre was not afraid to give free rein to his thoughts. He was never one to fall into line with everyone else—never one to play things safe.

It would be the same this time. Here, in Arishaig, he would do what no one else could. He would do what Ajin had asked of him and walk into the lion's den, emerging unscathed. He would win the promise of an alliance, false though he knew it would be, and he would set the stage for whatever deeper plan Ajin was in the process of enacting. It didn't take a genius to see that she was calculating something that would either undermine or negate the power of the Federation. And his aid in bringing this about would open doors that were otherwise closed to him. It would elevate his stature in a way that nothing else could.

It would bring him one step closer to Ajin.

And perhaps even to the throne itself.

An ambition he would never dare voice aloud.

It was dim and institutional within the Federation office complex—a typical administrative warren housing functionaries and their directors. But he was patient and pleasant to everyone he met, doing nothing to suggest he was anything other than what he pretended to be, a visitor on state business. He took note of the fact that there were sentries everywhere. Apparently assassination attempts against Federation Ministers were not unfamiliar. Kol'Dre smiled inwardly. Had he wished any of these people dead, they would have breathed their last before their protectors knew what was happening.

When he finally reached the offices of the Prime Minister—a decided improvement in appearance over everything that had come before—he found himself in a sumptuous waiting room in the company of a dozen other visitors and four heavily armed guards. The guards stood to one side, watching closely but saying nothing. It was late in the day—the time reserved for personal requests and favors from members of the general public who had already passed through enough bureaucracy to gain admittance. Two hours was all that was allotted. You waited your turn, and if your turn didn't come within those two hours, you had to come back another day.

Kol'Dre sat with the others, used to waiting, indifferent to how long it might take. He used the time to look carefully at the weapons the guards were carrying—the diapson-crystal-charged flash rips the Federation army routinely issued. While the Skaar preferred blades to weapons such as these, it was always wise to know how your enemies fought and what sorts of tools they employed.

His wait to see Ketter Vause was shorter than he had anticipated. When the man seated next to him was called, Kol'Dre waited a beat and then rose with him, careful to stay a step behind and out of his view. He followed the man to an open door where a secretary waited and continued through as if he and the man were together, nodding and smiling reassuringly. *Just following my friend,* he seemed to be indicating, and the secretary smiled back.

As he passed through the open door and into the Prime Minister's office, he made himself vanish. The two guards standing watch on either side of the door never saw it happen. The man Kol had followed in was already moving forward to state his request when the Skaar Penetrator dropped one guard and then the other. Then he disabled the supplicant, as well. He was so quick that it was over in seconds.

Kol'Dre then reappeared and stood face-to-face with the Federation Prime Minister.

"Not a word, please," the Skaar Penetrator said quickly.

Ketter Vause, to his credit, did not panic. He gestured at the fallen men. "Did you kill them?"

"No. I only wanted them out of the way while we talked."

"Is that so? Well, maybe we'd better get started, then."

The Prime Minister was a man of average height and appearance; there was nothing about him physically that would suggest he was in any way suited to be leader of the most powerful government in the Four Lands. It was there, however, in the confident way he studied Kol, and in the unhurried inflection in his voice as he spoke. But mostly it was there in the calm he exuded as they faced each other. He had just watched the Skaar Penetrator disable two guards and a supplicant in the blink of an eye, all while invisible, and it didn't seem to bother him at all. It was immediately clear he was used to difficult situations involving difficult personalities, and he had learned how to manipulate and control both.

"I apologize for the intrusion, Prime Minister, but there was no time to arrange an appointment and I had an urgent need to speak to you quickly."

"Then perhaps we should sit while we discuss this." Vause was already moving to occupy the chair behind his desk. "I'm sure we can work something out . . ."

Kol made a hissing sound, bringing the other up short. "Stay where you are, Prime Minister! We will stand where we can see each other while we talk. Just in case you are tempted to use any weapons you might have hidden behind your desk. Turn and face me."

Ketter Vause stopped where he was, then shrugged and came back around his desk to stand not five feet from Kol. "It is not your intention to kill me, then?"

Kol shook his head. "If I wanted you dead, you would already be so. What I want from you is something else entirely. I am here seeking an accommodation."

"An accommodation? Of what sort?"

Kol took a moment to glance around the Prime Minister's office. The room was surprisingly spare and unadorned. The walls were mostly bare of decorations or art, the floor bereft of carpets and rugs, and the furniture old and unassuming. Vause's desk was cluttered with paperwork. There was a single chair behind it and two in front, but none indicating anything approaching comfort.

"You seem a no-nonsense man with a wish to get to the point. But give me a moment to explain a few things first. I assume you know of the attacks on the Troll tribes to the north? Two of them in the last few weeks?"

The other man nodded. "I do."

"And has a report reached you about what's transpired at Paranor?"

A long pause. "What is this about?"

"My name is unimportant, but you need to know I am an envoy for Her Majesty, Princess Ajin d'Amphere of the Skaar nation. We've come from across the Tiderace in search of a new country in which to settle our people, and we have chosen the Four Lands. Upon arrival, several Troll tribes attacked us, and we destroyed them as a warning to the others. Then we confronted the Druids at Paranor and they refused to hear us out. So we entered their Keep, killed them all, and caused Paranor to disappear. You will hear about it soon enough, if you have not already."

It wasn't entirely the truth, for the Skaar had nothing to do with making Paranor disappear. But it was better to let the Prime Minister think that all that had occurred was at their instigation.

Ketter Vause was staring at him, his features still expressionless. "How did you manage all this? You destroyed the entire Druid order? What sort of power do you possess?"

"The kind that allows me to enter a Prime Minister's offices without invitation. Shall I tell you the rest of what brought me here?"

"I hope you haven't come here to ask for our surrender, envoy."

"Hardly. To do so would be an insult. And think on this, for a moment. We have just done you a great service. We have rid you of the Druids, Paranor, and all its troublesome magic. Your greatest enemy is no more. You might doubt me at the moment, but it will be easy enough to determine if I am telling the truth. Assuming I am, you are in our debt. What I seek in payment is an alliance with the Federation—mostly, an agreement that each of us will stay out of the way of the other. You do not attack us; we do not attack you. We do not meddle in your affairs or encroach on your interests, and you do the same for us."

"I believe they call that mutual non-intervention." Ketter Vause stood with his hands folded in front of him. "You do not seek our support against other nations?"

Kol shrugged. "We don't require it. Perhaps there will be no need for us to act again, now that the Druids are gone and our presence is well established. We are trained fighters, Prime Minister—soldiers and warriors. We have conquered all the lands across Eurodia, far to the east. We are afraid of no one. But we would prefer to ally with our strongest neighbor. It is our intention to settle ourselves north of the Mermidon, in Troll country. It would be in the best interests of both of us if the accommodation I mentioned could be reached."

Vause smiled. "It would seem that way. But I am not convinced you have told me everything. What are you holding back from me, envoy?"

A long moment of silence passed as Kol'Dre let the other man think he was pondering how much he should reveal. Finally, he shrugged. "We may have to do battle with the Elves. They were more closely allied to the Druids than the Federation. If we have to go to war with them, we would prefer it if you kept your distance. Non-intervention, as you've so deftly pointed out. A battle on two fronts is not impossible, but it is impractical. Would you be willing to agree to this request?"

"It deserves consideration," Ketter Vause acknowledged. "I will need to think it over. I will send a delegation to Paranor to confirm what you've told me about the Druids."

Kol nodded. "I would expect no less. But you will find things as I have described them. In the meantime, think very carefully about what I've said. I can give you three days. I'll expect your response by then. Time and tide waits for no man."

He was out the door and through the waiting room and lost from sight in the tangle of hallways beyond before Ketter Vause could respond.

EIGHT

---◆---

AFTER LETTING AJIN GO, Dar Leah flew west through the remainder of that day and night, landing only to eat before continuing on. But he was still miles short of the Pass of Rhenn and the gateway to the Elven capital city of Arborlon and thoroughly exhausted when midnight on the second day approached. Choosing a spot situated on a wooded rise where he could view the sweep of the surrounding countryside for anyone approaching, he steered the two-man into the shelter of a cluster of conifers. The air was cool, so it was comfortable sleeping out in the open beneath a canopy of stars and a full moon hanging low in the eastern sky. White light flooded the open plains for miles and provided a welcome feeling of security.

He was tired, after all, of living every moment as if it might be his last, wondering from which direction the next threat to his life might come.

His sleep through what remained of the night was deep and untroubled in spite of the task he had set himself. And when he forced himself awake, the dawn was a thin golden ribbon bordering the horizon. He took just enough time to repack his sleeping gear and grab a quick bite before setting off once more. It was fortunate the little craft was already packed with blankets and food left over from the start of his journey with Drisker Arc on leaving Emberen; there had been no time to find either when he fled Paranor. At first, his thinking was vague and unfocused; he was still coming fully awake and still muddleheaded. But after a time, his thoughts coalesced and turned to the future and what waited ahead.

His decision to go to Arborlon was born of a desperate hope that what he found there would offer the best chance for Drisker. He had already decided that he had to find Tarsha Kaynin, and the person who could most likely help with this was his longtime friend Brecon Elessedil.

The two had met years earlier when they were both still boys. Dar and his father were on a delivery run to Arborlon carrying unformed diapson crystals from Dwarf miners in the Rock Spur. There was a time that the Elves would not have considered using the crystals for anything other than powering their airships, but over the past few decades they had been experimenting with capturing the sun's raw power for other purposes—ones central to their commitment to protect their Westland home and its resources.

Brecon had come down to the transport with his father—another in a long line of Elessedils to become the ruler of the Elven people—and asked Dar if he wanted to see inside the palace. Because the Leahs were staying the night, Dar's father had no objection, and the king seemed fine with it, too. So off the boys went, and that was the beginning of what quickly became a solid friendship that lasted even after Dar had migrated to the Druid order and became the High Druid's Blade under Drisker Arc and Brecon had gone on to serve his father.

It was an unlikely friendship; both boys knew it even then. But friendships are mercurial and often difficult to define. Relationships are based on all sorts of strange connections. And while it was odd to form such a close friendship out of little more than a chance meeting and a single day's visit, the two boys had liked each other instantly, finding they shared a handful of interests about which they were passionate. Both loved flying, and both were excellent pilots. Both were athletic and skilled in the use of weapons and could spend hours sparring or competing. Brecon was fascinated with growing plants and trees, and his talents were so impressive that his father would eventually appoint him caretaker of the Carolan and its Gardens of

Life. It was a suitable job for a fourth son who had no real expectations of ascending to the throne, and Brecon was content to accept it. Dar was skilled as a Tracker and a hunter, his education acquired in the outdoors and on journeys with his father. The two respected each other for their individual skills and knowledge and taught each other what they could.

But Brecon Elessedil had one thing more that Dar was hoping could help in the search for Tarsha Kaynin, and it was for that specific reason he had come to see him.

He landed the little two-man at the public airfield rather than the one dedicated to the king's private use so as not to draw attention to his presence. He was not there to see the king or appear before the Elven Council, but to see Brecon and Brecon only. He was not at all sure the Elves knew anything about what had happened to Paranor and the Druids, and he did not want to be the one to tell them. If he did, he would likely be detained while they endlessly questioned him on the details and debated over what they should do about this disturbing turn of events. The Elven High Council was like every other government in the Four Lands: It needed time and discussion to make decisions. It was more enlightened and generous than some, but it was a government still. Better that he should slip in and out of Arborlon unnoticed, speaking only with Brecon.

So leaving his two-man in the care of the airfield manager, he walked into the city, making his way along the winding pathways and through the crowds of Elves to the palace. No one gave him a second glance. Members of other Races came to Arborlon regularly, and it was not unusual to find Southlanders among them. A Troll might have drawn more attention, since Trolls seldom came down out of the Northland, but not Dar. And given his lengthy absence from the city, it was not surprising that no one recognized him. Nor did he do anything to give them the chance, keeping his head down and speaking with no one until he reached the palace grounds.

Dar might not have traveled to see Brecon for a long time, but he remembered which residence the prince had last occupied. So he started there, moving toward the Home Guards who warded the entryway to the family compound. A tall hedge closed off the yards and buildings, and the only entrance was through a flower-laden trellis. The prince had grown it himself when he had moved in five years ago. Gazing at it now, Dar couldn't help but be impressed. Flowers cascaded down in long streamers and stretched out from the trellis in all directions. He experienced a moment of pride. He had helped Brecon build that trellis, and seeing it now, in full bloom, made him smile.

Brecon was home, the guards informed him, and once advised of his visitor the Elven prince appeared almost instantly, grinning as he came down the walkway. He was taller and more slender than Dar, his gait gangly and loose, his blond hair worn long and tied back in the Highland style—an affectation he had borrowed from his friend. On spying Dar, his fine features lit up with pleasure.

"Took you long enough!" he exclaimed, as they embraced. "You were gone so long, I thought maybe you couldn't find your way back."

Dar shrugged. "Life intervened. Besides, it hasn't been *that* long."

"Long enough. Tell me, how is Zia? I'm still hoping to meet her before I get too old to appreciate the experience."

An awkward moment of silence followed, then Dar said, "Zia's dead, Brec. Killed more than a week ago. Can we take this somewhere a little more private? I'm here because I need your help."

The Elven prince flushed bright red and quickly nodded. "I'm so sorry. Come inside."

Brecon steered him through the gates and along the pathway that led to his cottage. For long moments, neither spoke.

"I wish I'd known about Zia earlier," Brecon said finally, giving Dar a wary look. "I feel stupid not knowing."

Dar shook his head. "Don't. It just happened, and I couldn't get word to you until now."

"Well, try not to let me make a fool of myself again. And I am truly sorry about Zia."

"Zia's death is part of what brought me here."

"Whatever it was that brought you here, it will have to wait. You need to eat a good meal, take a hot bath, and sleep for about twelve hours. You look all done in."

They passed through the front door of the cottage and into the main living space. It was neat and orderly and filled with baskets of flowers. Tapestries hung from the walls, and area rugs were scattered about the wooden floors. It was very much Brecon's dwelling, and it gave Dar an instant sense of peace.

"I don't know that it *can* wait," he began, but Brecon was already shaking his head.

And his friend was right. Dar was completely exhausted from the events of the past few days and not much ready to do anything further in his present condition. So he ate the meal Brecon served him, took a bath, and let himself be put to bed in a corner room with the drapes drawn and the silence deep and welcoming.

"Sleep as long as you can. We'll talk when you wake."

Brecon went out the door and closed it behind him. By then, Dar was already drifting away.

When he woke, Dar had no idea what time it was. The room was shadowy and still, but there were cracks of light through the drapes that told him it was daytime. He rose immediately and went to the windows to peer out. The sun was directly overhead. Midday. He had slept a whole day.

Way too long!

Hurriedly, he washed his face and hands, dressed, and went into the living area. Brecon was nowhere to be found, so he went out the door and walked toward the palace, thinking to find him there. But he was only halfway to his destination when Brecon appeared on the path ahead.

On seeing Dar, he glanced around as if looking for someone and rushed over. "You should have waited at the cottage. How are you feeling? Better?"

"After an entire day's rest? I would guess so."

Brecon grinned. "Almost two days. You never woke once."

Dar couldn't believe it. Now he really was worried. Too much time had passed to allow for any further delay. "Has word arrived about what's happened at Paranor?"

"So it's true?" Brecon asked. "The Skaar found a way into Paranor? The Druid order was wiped out? The Keep is gone?"

Dar stared at him. "I wasn't sure the Elves would have heard about it yet. Who brought word?"

Brecon did not answer, his blond head lowered, his blue eyes intense as he studied the path in front of him. "Hold that thought," he said finally. "Follow me."

They walked over to the palace, detouring to the far end where the reception rooms were located. Once there, Brecon led the way inside, his long stride lengthening as they drew closer to the building's south wing, nodding to the guards as they passed but saying nothing. At one point, Dar heard voices from down the hallway, and Brecon put a finger to his lips at once. Moving more quickly now, he took Dar into a room at the end of a hallway and from there into another room beyond, each time pausing to close and lock the doors behind them. Dar was looking around guardedly now, sensing that something was wrong.

"Not to worry," Brecon reassured him as he secured the second door and motioned to a grouping of chairs. Together they seated themselves, facing each other across a small, round table. Brecon glanced at a sideboard. "Let me get you something to drink. Is a glass of ale all right?"

Without waiting for a response, he filled glasses from a cask concealed in a cold box and carried them back to the table. There was a furtiveness about him, an uneasiness that told Dar something was definitely not right. But he held his tongue and waited for his friend to reveal it in his own time.

When Brecon was seated again, he raised his glass. "Health and good fortune." They drank deeply and returned their glasses to the table. "Are they all gone?" Brecon asked, then. "All of the Druids? Everyone who lived at Paranor but you?"

"Almost." Dar leaned forward. "I'll explain everything, but first tell me how you know so much about this."

The Elven prince made a face. "I was helping my father earlier this morning when he learned of it. Not an hour ago, while he was preparing for the morning Council meeting. My brothers were elsewhere. I was the only one present when word arrived."

"But who delivered it?"

Brecon hesitated. "Well, that part is a little strange. She says she is a princess of something called the Skaar."

Dar stared in disbelief. "You mean Ajin d'Amphere? She brought word *herself*?"

"Walked right in and told my father. Said she wanted us to hear it first from her."

Dar could not believe it—but then it was exactly the sort of impulsive, reckless chance she would take, confident that she could somehow walk into the lion's den and not be harmed.

"I couldn't believe it, either," Brecon agreed, seeing the look on his friend's face. "And she's with him now, addressing the High Council."

Not quite two hundred yards away, in a building that sat apart from the royal palace, the members of the Elven High Council were gathered in their assembly listening to Ajin d'Amphere explain what her people had done to the Druids and to Paranor. Gerrendren Elessedil, the Elven king, sat at the head of an oval table with five members of the Council seated to his right and five to his left.

And the looks of mingled shock and wariness mirrored on their faces were both priceless and gratifying.

Ajin was dressed in full Skaar regalia—white silk robes and scarlet accessories. Her weapons and armor had been abandoned, and she stood with her back straight and her head lifted as she spoke. She had appeared before foreign dignitaries and their councils many times before, and she knew that the secret to success lay in showing no concern for her safety and no hesitation in admitting her purpose. She knew she must convince them from the start that she was in command of the situation and its outcome, keeping her explanations spare and to the point, careful not to overemphasize or understate. She must never threaten or attempt to intimidate, but lay out her reasons with care.

When she had finished and stood waiting, there was a long silence. She resisted the urge to look over her shoulder to the grim-faced Home Guards, who stood behind her like expressionless statues. Unlike her, they bore swords and knives. But she didn't regret her choice to forgo weapons. She knew the nature and reputation of her audience. Coming armed would have sent the wrong message. Any sort of confrontation at this juncture would have been disastrous.

Finally, Gerrendren Elessedil shifted on his throne and shook his head. "You are bold to come to us with this tale, Princess," he said quietly. "Bold, and perhaps a bit foolish."

"Should I fear for my safety?" she demanded in reply. She was already calculating how many she would have to kill to reach the door leading out of the assembly. Quite a few, she thought.

"You've just admitted to wiping out the entire Druid order and you don't think we might be better off ridding ourselves of you before your soldiers come after us, as well?"

"You are not in any danger unless you intend to attack us, King Gerrendren. Our arrival in the Four Lands is not intended as a threat to you or your people. All we seek is a home for our endangered population waiting back in Eurodia. Make no mistake. We are facing extinction. We cannot remain where we are. If those Troll tribes and the Druids hadn't threatened us first, we would not have had to destroy them. But they did, so we protected ourselves—as I am sure you would do if the Federation, for instance, decided to attack *you*."

She used an example she was certain would resonate. Thanks to Kol'Dre's valuable information, she knew the history of these lands and their peoples. The Federation had, in fact, attacked the Elves on more than one occasion over the centuries, seeking to subdue or at least dominate them. This had been a part of their history with other nations, as well, for as far back as anyone could remember.

"So, you mean us no harm?" one of the Council members asked. "You expect us to believe we are safe from you?"

"As it happens," she said, "I've come to ask for your help."

It wasn't quite the truth, but it was not a big enough lie that she couldn't speak the words. She watched as the Council members exchanged uncertain glances.

"You've managed well enough without us so far," the king observed. "You seem a very capable young lady. And your soldiers seem a seasoned and well-trained unit. It's hard to believe you require help from anyone. What, exactly, are you looking for?"

"The Skaar are a strong and determined people, and we fully expect to succeed in our efforts to make a home here. But the bulk of our army, although it is on its way, has not yet arrived. My advance force has established a foothold and thereby demonstrated our determination to remain. We do not seek to dislodge those already living in these lands. We only seek a place for our own people. The Druids were a selfish, disorganized order that thought only of themselves. They were charged to be protectors of the land's magic, yet they squabbled and sniped at one another and did very little to aid those who were supposedly under their protection. I know this was not always true, but things had changed recently within their order. It became a sickness they could not survive. Am I not right?"

A handful of the Council members nodded, but the king shook his head. "An oversimplification, Princess. But let's get to the point. I am encouraged by your words, but not persuaded. It is easy enough to promise one thing while intending to deliver another. It has happened to the Elves on past occasions—and more times than I care to remember. So why should I believe it would be different with the Skaar? What proof do you offer that might persuade me?"

She nodded, acknowledging his reasoning in a small act of deference. She knew how she appeared to him, and she was using that. She was young and beautiful and seemingly vulnerable, standing there in her silken robes, unarmed and presenting no discernible threat. She could have been his granddaughter and seemed little more than a supplicant. Her candor and apparent lack of guile were disarming and encouraging. Gerrendren Elessedil and this Council believed themselves in command of the situation, and she made no attempt to persuade them otherwise. She was there at their sufferance and stood before them at their mercy.

But these were the Elves, after all, and of all the Races that occupied a place in the Four Lands, none was more honorable or fair-minded than they. Their entire history had proved it. They were an ancient people who had come out of centuries of hiding at the conclusion of the Great Wars in order to lead civilization back from the brink of extinction, and they had demonstrated their worth as leaders and healers. They were wedded to the care and maintenance of the land and its peoples. And as much as they were capable of fighting for what they believed necessary, they were children of the earth first and foremost. Their moral code was strong and their adherence to it deeply ingrained.

"I have only my words to persuade you, High King. I have only myself. So I will lay my situation and my intent before you for your examination. Then you will decide for yourself. May I continue?"

Ask his permission. Always demonstrate deference first before seeking a favor.

He nodded. "Please do, Princess."

"I am here with a thousand members of the Skaar army—minus those who perished in battle since our arrival. With the passing of the Druids, I have performed a service to the Federation and its hierarchy—one which they sought and approved. I asked them myself before I set my soldiers and myself on our path to Paranor if they would agree to let me face the Druids alone and promise not to interfere. They agreed readily enough because they hated the Druids and wanted them gone. I acted with their approval and tacit support. But now that is changing."

For the first time, she had deliberately lied. But she looked squarely at the faces of her audience, taking her time, her expression revealing no trace of her deception. "There are those within the Federation who would like the Elves gone, as well. I expect this does not come as a surprise to you. But before that happens, they intend to eliminate us. Though we do not threaten them—though we have no intention of intruding into the Southland regions—they fear us. Already, they are preparing to dispatch a large force to intercept us where we are encamped just north of the Mermidon. Once again, we will be forced to defend ourselves. Once again, there will be no attempt at a meaningful negotiation."

None of this was necessarily true yet, but it would be soon enough if her plans unfolded as she intended.

"Surely, you cannot know this," one of the Ministers interjected quickly.

"I can, and I do." Ajin did not hesitate in her reply. "As I indicated, we have been scouting the Four Lands and its people for several years. We have learned of the Federation's desire to dominate the other Races. It will be no different with the Skaar. The Federation will try to wipe us out. They see us as dangerous—especially now that we have eliminated the Druids. So they will eliminate us, as well."

She paused. "But here is something you don't know. With the Druids now gone from the Four Lands, the Federation intends to abolish all magic. They will demand that you give over your talismans and your Elfstones and all the rest for safekeeping and cease all practice of magic in any form. If you refuse, they will declare war on you, as well."

Immediately there was a terrible uproar—a cacophony of dismay and anger. Everyone began shouting, saying it would never happen, decrying the duplicity and arrogance of the Southland government. Ajin left them to it, delighted by their response. She did not try to interrupt them; she simply waited for order to return.

What she had told them was true enough, although not quite the imminent threat she had suggested. The Federation did want magic stamped out, but they did not necessarily anticipate forcing the Elves to comply. But it was a reasonable assumption that with the Druids gone, they would look very hard at some form of action that would achieve this result.

The king quieted the Council members, standing to emphasize his displeasure with their outburst, lifting his arms to gesture for compliance as he shouted them down, motioning for those who had risen to sit once more.

"Ministers, please remember yourselves! We have a duty to act responsibly. We are not animals that strike out in response to every slight or threat. We are men and women of reason, and we think things through and then act. Let it be so here." He turned to Ajin. "Princess."

She gave him a low bow. "High King," she acknowledged.

"You are certain of this?"

"I would not be here otherwise."

"Nonetheless, I will seek confirmation from other sources. Your accusations are very serious. Meanwhile, tell the High Council and myself exactly what it is you are asking from us."

Ajin straightened. "What I once asked from the faithless Federation government, my lord: an agreement not to interfere in whatever takes place in the forthcoming confrontation between the Skaar and the Southland. Let it happen as it will, but do not intercede. Give no aid to the Federation. Give no aid to us, either—unless, of course, you determine that our cause merits it. In return, we will promise not to intrude into Elven territory in our quest for a new land for our people and to be a good friend to our Elven neighbors."

There was a guarded murmuring among the Ministers. Gerrendren Elessedil rose quickly. "Please step out into the hallway, Princess. We will discuss this among ourselves and then advise you of our decision. Our full consideration will be given to your request."

Ajin bowed and turned away. She had done what she could. With the Elven Home Guards as her escort, she departed the room.

NINE

Dar Leah's face was flushed with outrage. "Are you telling me Ajin d'Amphere has been allowed to speak to the Elven High Council?"

Brecon shrugged. "It wasn't my decision. It was my father's, and I couldn't very well tell him not to hear her out when both he and the High Council wanted details about Paranor and the Druids."

Dar slowly sat down again. "Surely the Elves knew about the Skaar invasion beforehand? They must have known about the Troll tribes the Skaar wiped out."

"We knew, but not because of the Druids, Dar."

"You mean there hasn't been *any* communication about this between the Druids and the Elves? The Ard Rhys didn't send you a message or ask what you knew or anything?"

Brecon held up both hands to signal a stop to the discussion, then rose and walked over to the storage cabinet that held the ale. He filled a pitcher, then returned and poured generous amounts into both their glasses, which had somehow gone empty.

"Things aren't as simple as you might like." The prince was seated again, and he took a long pull of his ale. "In fact, they are much more complicated."

"I don't care how complicated they are!" Dar snapped. "There should have been some sort of communication between the Druids and the Elves!"

"You make it sound like this is something new. There hasn't been any real communication between the two for a long time. Didn't you know?"

The Blade shook his head. "I was gone too often to notice, I suppose, and Ober Balronen wasn't one to share his business with anyone. But no one else tried communicating? And Arborlon let things stay that way? Why?"

"My father made a few attempts in the beginning, but they were never reciprocated. And yes, we knew right away about the Skaar when they landed on the northern shores of the Tiderace, but it was Wing Riders who brought us word. We learned later about the Corrax and the others. We tried to communicate what we knew with the Druids, but we heard nothing back. When they failed to respond, we tried sending word to the Federation. They ignored us, too."

"So you gave up?"

"Essentially. My father and the Council decided that if there were any real danger, we would have heard something. Besides, this wasn't Elven business, and for a long time now the Elves have been withdrawing further from the other Races, having less and less to do with them. Save for the Dwarves, with whom we still interact regularly, we share almost nothing with the rest of the Four Lands."

Dar shook his head. "This is madness! Do you have any idea what the Skaar can do? How dangerous they are? Especially that princess!"

"I did what I could, Dar. I don't believe in isolation as either a political or economic policy. But these days, I am definitely in the minority. And the Druids had no use for us other than to keep pressuring us to let them take control of our magic. Recently, they asked to send members of their order to aid in managing it—and not in a polite way. More as an unstated threat, an obvious insult. We Elves have managed our own magic for centuries, long before humans even existed. We have trained endlessly to understand how it functions and have made better use of it than the Druids ever thought of doing. The Federation is no better. They want the same things from us as the

Druids, except their plan is to see magic eradicated from the Four Lands completely. They would see us eradicated, as well, if they could find a way to make it happen. To take our magic is to steal our heritage. It is unthinkable."

"Well, you can stop worrying about the Druids."

Brecon nodded. "I know that now. I'm sorry. And I wish I could change it. I wish the Elves had chosen a different course of action. But my father is a stubborn man. I'm a good son, and he appreciates how talented I am at growing things, but he doesn't think me of much use beyond that. He seldom listens to me."

Dar leaned back in his seat and shook his head. "Well, he *should* listen to you. He has some very big problems. Ajin d'Amphere devised and executed the plan that led to the destruction of Paranor and the Druids. Whatever she wants from the Elves, it will only be to serve her own purposes. Your father needs to be warned."

Brecon shrugged. "I can warn him, but I can't make him listen. Growing older hasn't made him any less stubborn."

"You are his son! You have to make him understand."

"Dar, you and I are friends, but you haven't been here in well over a year. You don't understand how things are. So let me explain it to you. I told you my father doesn't consult with me on matters of court. He didn't invite me to this morning's Council—or invite my brothers, for that matter. He wanted to handle this by himself." He paused. "I met Ajin d'Amphere. She is very beautiful, and I know my father thinks so, too. It's never too late to have a brief fling, you know, and he's been looking; I can tell. I keep it from my mother, but she's probably noticed, anyway."

"He'd better keep a blade under his pillow if he plans to sleep with her," Dar muttered.

"So what do you want to do?"

Dar was uncertain. Charge over to the Elven assembly and question whatever it was Ajin was telling the High Council, demand that she be sent away at once? Somehow he didn't think that was a good idea. He was not an Elf and had no standing in Arborlon. Besides, Ajin was too clever to be brushed aside so easily. She would find a way to turn the tables on him, and he would have lost any chance he had of putting a stop to her plans.

Besides, it was more important just now that he find Tarsha Kaynin.

"What did you come here for, anyway?" Brecon asked suddenly.

Dar leaned back in his seat with a sigh. "Well, not for Ajin d'Amphere. I need to find someone, a young girl Drisker has been mentoring over the past few weeks. She is exceptionally skilled in the use of magic. Drisker has been training her."

Brecon stared. "But he never trains anyone."

"He's made an exception for Tarsha Kaynin. She's an Ohmsford descendant. She's inherited the wishsong."

His friend drew a sharp intake of breath. "Well, no wonder you want to find her. I didn't think there was an Ohmsford descendant left in the entire Four Lands. She must be the last of that line."

Dar shook his head. "Not quite. She has a brother who can use the magic, too. But he is deeply troubled, and she is worried about him. She went to find him about a week ago."

"Do you know where she went?"

"A village called Backing Fell, in the deep Westland. I don't know where it is or even where she is at this point. But there's a reason we have to find her and find her quickly. I haven't told you this, but the Keep was betrayed by one of the Druids—an elder of the inner circle, a woman who has been with the order for years. Her name is Clizia Porse. She helped the Skaar get inside the Keep, making it possible for the Druids to be destroyed. She was one of only two Druids who survived."

"One of *two*?" Brecon looked confused.

"Drisker Arc was the other."

"But he left Paranor months ago. He was exiled. What was he doing there?"

"He found out what was going to happen and tried to stop it. I went with him. But he trusted Clizia, and she betrayed him. She was the one who used her magic to send Paranor from the Four Lands and into limbo. When she did so, Drisker was inside. So now he's trapped there."

Brecon shook his head. "But you escaped, and now you want to find a way to get him back."

Dar nodded. "I'm hoping Tarsha Kaynin is the answer. The wish-song is a powerful magic. If anyone can help Drisker escape his imprisonment, it would be her. I don't know whom else to turn to. I have to find her."

"I know of Backing Fell," Brecon said. "I can get us that far. But if she's left and gone elsewhere . . ."

"We have to assume she has. I can't track her at this point. I need another way of finding her."

Brecon stared at him for a long moment. Then realization set in. "No," he said emphatically.

"There isn't any other way." Dar held his gaze.

"Then find one."

Dar brushed back strands of his long red hair where they fell across his face. "You have to remove them from wherever your father has them stored and come with me to find her."

"My father would have me thrown out of the city and banished for life!"

"Only if he finds out what you've done. You can return them before he even knows they're missing."

Brecon made a rude noise. "You make it sound so simple. But it isn't. He's got them locked away. In his chambers. In a steel box sealed inside the flooring! Even I can't get at them."

"What do mean?" Dar interrupted. "Since when did you ever let a lock stop you? If you know where they are, you can figure out a way to open it! You probably already have, if I know you."

The Elven prince gave him a long-suffering look. "The Blue Elf-stones. The Seeking Stones. Magic that can find anything hidden or lost. You want me to steal them from my father, and then use them to find this Tarsha person. But you don't seem to realize what you're asking of me. You don't seem to appreciate the risk you are asking me to take."

"I understand perfectly." Dar sighed. "And I am not suggesting you should steal them. I'm only asking you to *borrow* them. I wouldn't ask it if there were any other way, but there isn't."

"Borrow, not steal. There's a distinction without a difference." Brecon was drinking the rest of his ale, one large swallow at a time. "The Stones have been locked away for decades." He looked back at Dar. "I knew you were here for a reason." He set his glass on the table with a thump. "I hoped it might have something to do with wanting to see me."

"It does. You know that." Dar leaned forward, his face intense, his mouth tight. "But it's more than wanting to see an old friend. My entire life has been destroyed. The Druids are all dead. Paranor is gone. I have nowhere else to turn. I cannot abandon Drisker; I will not. He is the best hope for the Four Lands. The best hope for all of us. He can find a way to stop what's happening."

"You need to find someone else to help you."

"Brecon, listen to yourself! Let someone else handle this? Who else is there? I am here because I think that, together, we can find a way to make all this right—the loss of the Druids and Paranor, the imprisonment of Drisker, your father's possible infatuation with an enemy who will likely cut his throat if he pursues her, and a foreign Race that clearly has ambitions that go far beyond finding a new homeland."

He paused and shook his head. "Please, don't refuse me this. Help me. I need you!"

Brecon Elessedil studied him some more, then sighed. "Even if I wanted to get you the Elfstones, I couldn't."

"Maybe we can find a way," Dar said. "They're in a lockbox in the floor of your father's bedroom? Can we get in there without being seen?"

Brecon stared at him. "What are you up to?"

Dar kept his face expressionless. "You're pretty good at opening locks, remember? And you've opened this one before. Let's find out if you can open it again."

Ajin d'Amphere had waited impatiently for the Elven king and his High Council to make their decision, believing that it would go in her favor but at the same time worrying it wouldn't. She prowled the hallways restlessly, her Skaar escort of two soldiers trailing after her like loyal dogs. Not that she thought of them that way. Such an assessment was too limiting. They were there to ward her against harm. They were there to do her bidding whenever summoned. But they were more to her than that. *All* of the soldiers in her small command were more than just names and faces. She was close to them, the result of years of shared experiences. They were friends.

She knew it was wrong to think of men under your command that way, to allow yourself to feel anything for them. A leader should not be personally affected when individual soldiers were lost while in her service. But that was not who she was, and she had known it since she had begun her training with members of her command almost a dozen years ago. During her formative years, they had struggled together to endure both emotional and physical hardships, comrades frequently closer to one another than to their families.

Her thoughts shifted momentarily to her relationship with Kol'Dre. He had served her for years in her campaigns across Eurodia, repeatedly making it possible for her to turn adverse situations to her advantage. Over and over, he had given her invaluable information and advice. That spoke volumes about his devotion to her. But he was too ambitious for his own good. And while she trusted him, that trust was not as complete as she would have liked—especially when it came to his feelings for her. He wanted more from her than she was willing to give. She would have to keep an eye on him. She could not allow her emotions to undermine her authority or to paint her as a vulnerable woman.

She stopped at the end of the hallway on what might have been her twentieth circuit and stood looking at the Home Guards and the closed assembly doors. If the Elven king refused her, she would have to reevaluate her whole plan. But there was no help for it. She had done her best to convince him; she had made certain he knew she favored him. Brief furtive looks, small acknowledgments, and words that carried possible meanings beyond what they conveyed openly. Tricks of seduction, and she had used them all. Overt actions would not work with Gerrendren Elessedil. He was too proper and restrained for that. He would expect her to exercise discretion and show consideration for his place in the Elven hierarchy. He would not be immune to her charms—a princess of another people, a young woman who was barely more than a girl—but he would not risk mistaking the nature of her interest and looking foolish. For now, just piquing his interest was enough. She was planting seeds for the future, for a time when something more would be required.

"Princess," one of her escorts whispered.

At the end of the hallway, the doors to the assembly were opening, and the king and his Ministers were filing out. She stood where she was, waiting. But when she saw the king come toward her, she went to meet him halfway, not bothering to hold back.

"Princess Ajin," he said with a small bow.

He had used her first name—a small gesture that gave her hope. When he reached for her hand, she gave it to him. His fingers squeezed hers lightly. Her bow in response to his was much deeper and more profound. "King Gerrendren."

His smile was genuine. "The Ministers of the Elven High Council and I are in agreement. You shall have what you have asked for. Whatever you choose to do about any aggressive acts on the part of the Federation will not concern us, so long as the Skaar stay clear of the Westland and Elven interests in the other lands. You've indicated what you will do to keep your end of the bargain, and we will hold you to it."

"As you should, High King. And the Skaar will not disappoint you."

"The Federation are no friends to the Elves, Ajin. They never have been." He bent a tad closer. "I think I may speak for the High Council when I assure you that if their aggression threatens you, we will take steps to back them away. I think we will make good neighbors, the Skaar and the Elven people."

She managed not to roll her eyes. Instead, she gripped his hands tightly. "This means so much. You have my eternal gratitude. I shall not forget your kindness."

He stepped closer. "I hope you mean that, Princess. I hope our alliance will bring you back to Arborlon soon—as my personal guest. I would like to know you better."

Ajin smiled, her eyes never leaving the king's face. "As I would you. Until then, *Ac're dorst juin bei.*"

"Which means?"

"In the Skaar tongue? It has no literal translation."

"An approximation, then?"

Her smile was dazzling, and she managed to blush. "I think it best I keep it to myself until my return. I leave it to your imagination until then."

She backed away, signaling to her Skaar soldiers.

"I shall have my Home Guards guide you back to the palace where you can retrieve your belongings," the Elven king said.

He turned from her with a final smile and went back up the hallway. When he had disappeared out the door of the assembly building, she looked at her soldiers. The older, Jen'Na, gave her a conspiratorial wink.

"'Aren't I much too young for you'?" he translated. "Tender words, Princess."

"He will never learn their real translation." She smiled. "Unless you tell him."

She indicated their readiness to depart to the Home Guards assigned to escort them and did not bother to note the look she was certain her soldiers were exchanging. In a group, the five of them walked back through the palace grounds, following the pathways leading to the royal quarters.

When they reached their destination, they entered through the east doors and walked to the rooms where the Skaar had left their weapons and cloaks. The Home Guards left them there, advising them to continue down the hallway until they were out of the palace. It was midday by now, and Ajin and her companions had flown here directly from their encampment. They were tired and hungry, but Ajin had made it plain beforehand that they would not be staying in the city any longer than they had to. Instead, they would fly east until they were beyond the borders of the Westland and make camp for the night on the Streleheim Plains. They would eat and rest then and resume their journey back to the rest of the advance force on the following day.

She thanked the Elven Home Guards for their assistance; gathering up their weapons and cloaks, they went out the door and down the hallway as directed. Behind them, the Home Guards watched them go.

Ajin walked slightly apart from her companions, lost in thought. There was a great deal to consider and not a lot of time in which to do so. The variables of her plan worried her, especially when it came to her father. He was growing steadily less dependent on her. She still had his ear, but she did not feel he was as strongly inclined to defer to her judgment. She worried that he no longer trusted her as he once had. On every one of her other campaigns, he had awaited her summons before acting. But this time, his precipitous departure for the Four Lands was a clear indication of his loss of faith. Whether this was due to the rumors of men like Sten'Or or his own misguided lack of faith, it was hard to know. But overall, his trust in her had eroded.

She did not like to think what that meant. But she knew she would have to do something about it.

Still in the lead, she rounded a corner in the hallway and watched a door open ahead of them. A familiar voice was speaking, a voice she could not mistake. She slowed, then stopped short in surprise.

She was face-to-face with Dar Leah.

TEN

◆
———————————————————————

FOR A TIME THAT neither could have measured, Dar Leah and Ajin d'Amphere just stared at each other. Then, unexpectedly, she smiled. "We just can't seem to stay away from each other, can we?"

She stepped closer to him. Their eyes locked, then she looked past him to Brecon. "And look who you have with you! The king's youngest. What sort of mischief are you two up to, I wonder?"

"You should look to your own conscience, Princess," Dar snapped.

Ajin's exquisite features showed an exaggerated dismay. "Should I? Whatever for?"

"What did you tell my father?" Brecon demanded, stepping forward to confront her. "What did you say to the Elven High Council?"

Ajin spared him no more than a momentary glance. "Perhaps you should ask him. If he wants you to know, I expect he will tell you. It isn't for me to say."

"It's a bold move, coming here like this," Dar said. "You risk much in revealing yourself this way."

She shrugged. "No more than I am willing to risk. Confrontation is better than hesitation, and I've always believed caution is overrated."

"So what are you doing here?"

She seemed to give the matter a few moments of thought. "I don't suppose there is any reason not to answer. I came to offer an alliance. I want the Elves and the Skaar to become friends."

Dar shook his head. "A nice sentiment, but I suspect your friendship comes at a price."

"My enmity comes at a price, Dar Leah, not my friendship. Only those who stand in my way need fear anything from me."

"The Druids, for example? They paid a rather high price—even the ones who were unaware of what was happening right up until the moment of their deaths. So how did they stand in your way?"

"You were there on the Plains of Rabb. You saw it all yourself. Those Druids who accompanied you acted impulsively and foolishly. They threatened us, and it cost them. Those at Paranor turned a blind eye to what their leadership was doing to them. They did nothing to hold those leaders accountable and thereby invited their own fate. The Druid order was sickened from head to foot. It would have come down eventually, like any dying tree, even if I had not acted."

Dar raised an eyebrow. "Not a conclusion I would have reached. The Druid order was a living, breathing, working collection of men and women who were doing something they strongly believed in and they did much good over the years. The head might have been muddled, granted, but the body was functioning. But then, I think we see things a bit differently, you and I."

She stepped back, as if giving herself space. "It's a difference mostly of degree." She paused, giving him a look, her blue eyes taking his measure. "Why are you here? Have you come for a visit with the Elessedil family? Or for something more pressing?"

He smiled blandly. "The Elessedils are friends from a long time back, Princess. I haven't visited for a while."

"And you decide to pay a visit at a time when the Keep has disappeared and the Druids are mostly gone? An odd choice."

"I have nothing better to do. Besides, I thought they should know what you did at Paranor. But I suppose you already told them, didn't you?"

"I thought it should come from me. But if you worry for their safety, you needn't. I am no threat to them, and Gerrendren knows this. I intend the Skaar and the Elves to be allies, just as I said. A simple enough arrangement that will benefit us both."

Dar didn't miss the way she used the Elven king's first name. As if they were already close friends. He remembered Brecon saying that beautiful women easily charmed his father, and he experienced a moment of intense frustration.

"You wish to ally with us?" Brecon was openly appalled. "An invader who covets our land and would kill our people?"

Ajin turned on him at once. "Caution, Prince Brecon. You speak harsh words without cause. The Skaar do not covet your land and have no intention of killing your people. We have come to find a new home, yes—but not at your expense. Our interest in the Four Lands lies elsewhere."

"Yet what happened to Paranor and to those Troll tribes would suggest your interest lies *everywhere*," Dar countered.

Ajin shrugged. "Things are not always as simple as we would like them to be. You will come to realize this in time. Now I have to go. This unexpected encounter has been pleasant, but I have work to do."

Brecon stepped forward to block her way. "Maybe you should be made to come to terms with what you've done first. Perhaps letting you leave would be a mistake."

Despite his anger with Ajin, Dar Leah stepped between them, sensing that matters might be getting out of hand. There wasn't much to be gained by picking a fight at this point. And trying to stop Ajin from leaving was pointless. Any guest of the Elven king was under his protection, and any attempt to interfere would win a harsh reprimand and perhaps cost both of them the king's good graces.

"Peace, Brecon," he said quietly, drawing his friend back. "Let her go for now." He glanced at Ajin. "Another time."

She smiled in response and put her hand on his chest. "I told you we would meet again. I suspect we are not yet done with each other, Dar Leah. I believe we will have further encounters down the road. I hope so. I look forward to them."

"You should be careful what you wish for, Princess," he said.

She removed her hand and stepped back. "And you should be more astute at recognizing who your friends are."

She brushed past him and did not look back. Her Skaar companions trailed after her, giving the Elf and the highlander sharp looks as they passed by.

Dar watched her go, reflecting. She was dismissing him for now. She would learn nothing more of his intentions today, and that was enough. She realized he was not there because of her; he could not have suspected she was coming. Their encounter was simply by chance. But she knew, as well, that he was in Arborlon for more than a simple visit to Brecon Elessedil and his family. She knew his reason for coming would have something to do with the loss of Paranor and the Druid order. She might wonder what that something was and how much trouble it might cause her later, but she knew better than to pursue the matter now.

Just as he knew better than to underestimate the purpose of her visit and its impact on the king.

"She's planning something," Brecon said quietly, a troubled look on his face.

"She's always planning something," Dar replied, looking back at him. "It's unfortunate we had to run into her like that. I would have preferred she not know I was here at all. She'll want to discover what I've come for, and she'll keep nosing around until she does."

His friend made a dismissive gesture. "Let her try. No one knows the reason you've come but the two of us." He paused. "Still, she does seem inordinately interested in you, like there is something between you that only you and she know."

Dar sighed. "In a way, perhaps there is. She saved my life once. And then I returned the favor—though something tells me I might live to regret it. I'll tell you about it later."

"I think it's more than that. I saw how she looked at you. Sort of like a hungry cat eyeing an appetizing mouse."

Dar ignored the comment. "She's right about one thing. You should ask your father what was said in the assembly. Find out exactly what she came here for. But for now we need to get to the Elfstones before either she or your father finds out what we're up to. So lead the way."

They went deeper into the palace, following a series of hallways to Gerrendren Elessedil's private quarters. No one was about, so there was no one to question where the two of them were going. When they reached the king's bedroom, they slipped inside, closing the door behind them and locking it, then went into the small room off the sleeping chamber that served as his private office. Dar looked around with appreciation. Gerrendren's quarters were sumptuous— beautifully decorated with tapestries, paintings, precious glass, and thick rugs. Flowers in vases had been placed throughout. Sunlight flooded through windows from high up on a south-facing wall, streaming across a desk and chair and cabinets situated against the wall opposite.

Brecon pulled back a rough woven rug laid out in the center of the room, then ran his hands across the smooth flooring in a series of sweeping motions that seemed to brush away an invisible veneer to reveal the outline of a panel set into the floor.

"My father told me about it once when I was much younger," he said. He had a mischievous look on his face. "I had asked him about the Elfstones, and I think he didn't see the harm in showing them to me. After all, I was a boy, and the door was concealed and secured by magic. What harm could it do to tell me? Except that I was one of those precocious children who couldn't let well enough alone. Having seen the Elfstones once, I wanted to see them again. I had the concealment unlocked within the week. I knew a few things about magic, even then."

"You took the Elfstones out?" Dar grinned. "He would have skinned you alive if he'd found that out!"

"At the very least. But I was careful. I put everything back the way it had been. You know how it is when you're young. You have to test your boundaries, find out what's being kept hidden from you. I didn't tell him what I'd done, but I told my mother."

"And she didn't tell on you?"

"No, not her. She thought I could do no wrong. She still feels that way. I'm her youngest. She loves it that I won't be king. Prefers it that I am the designated chief gardener of the Carolan. After I shared my secret about accessing the vault to get to the Elfstones, I think she thought that giving me up to my father would stop me from ever sharing anything with her again. She would have been right, too."

Dar pictured a younger Brecon Elessedil with his mother. Arialena Elessedil was a small, lively woman with exquisite features and a wonderful laugh, but also a quick temper. She had always been kind to Dar when he had come to visit, and she liked it that he and Brecon were close. She hadn't changed much over the years, and Dar regretted that he probably wouldn't have time to see her on this visit.

Brecon knelt and lifted away the floor panel by placing his hands carefully on its surface so the wood adhered to his fingertips. The panel was thick and sturdy, yet it seemed to weigh nothing as he pulled it free and set it aside. Another small Elven magic, Dar presumed. Over the past twenty years or so, the Elves had returned to mastering arts they had let slide for many centuries, their slow retreat from the other Races apparently giving them the impetus to seek out knowledge they had once possessed and lost. Theirs was a culture of magic established before the coming of humans and the Great Wars, and it felt right that they should seek it out anew. Dar only wished he had such a heritage to reclaim, but when it came to magic he had only the sword he wore strapped across his back. A fighting weapon. A bringer of death, not life.

He brushed these thoughts aside and watched as Brecon reached into a shadowy interior not brightened even marginally by the sunlight that fell across its opening. Slowly, he extracted an odd container. It appeared to be a square box constructed of silvery metal, but it revealed no joints, openings, or locks and instead was perfectly smooth on all six surfaces.

"The Elfstones have been in this box ever since I last saw them," the prince observed, his voice gone distant and soft. "I always thought we should have been doing something with their magic, employing them for some useful purpose. My brothers openly urged our father to do so, but he just brushed us off. One time, some years back, he said something about their history being darker than we realized, but he never explained what he meant. But I know it had to do with the past, when the Druids and the Ohmsfords used the Stones on all those dangerous quests."

He held the box carefully in front of him. "The Druids wanted these Elfstones, you know. They tried very hard to persuade us to give them up. Aphenglow Elessedil gave them back to us years ago after she became Ard Rhys. She was an Elf, and she thought they should be with her people because only Elves could use them, anyway. She wouldn't return the Crimson Elfstones, though—the ones that were brought out of the Forbidding when the Ellcrys failed during her early years in the Druid order. She thought them too dangerous to be anywhere but locked away in Paranor. But these, the Seeking Stones . . ."

He trailed off. Dar nodded. "She was probably right, even though the Druids didn't prove to be any better at keeping their magic safe. They couldn't even keep themselves safe in the end." He gestured. "Let's have a look."

Brecon glanced down at the box, his narrow features tightening as he worked his fingers around its surface, searching. His concentration was visible on his face and in his eyes, and eventually he found the places on the smooth sides he was looking for and pressed hard. The box shimmered and the top slowly lifted away.

Inside was a leather pouch, closed tightly by drawstrings.

"How did you discover the secret of opening this puzzle box?" Dar asked his friend. "You were what? Midteens?"

Brecon nodded. "The secret is in the nature of the material that makes up the container—an organic substance with which I am familiar. It serves to ward sections of the Carolan, and the exploration of its properties taught me how it functioned. It took me awhile, but I knew what to look for. I just kept experimenting until the secret revealed itself. It wasn't words or gestures or anything so mundane. It was a bonding of flesh to metal."

"Another kind of magic," Dar observed.

"Another kind. An Elven kind."

"Earlier, you hinted you couldn't even get inside the lockbox." Dar gave him a look. "Testing me, were you?"

Brecon pulled a face. "Just wanted to see how determined you were to do this—how serious you were about using them. It doesn't mean I don't think it's any less risky or dangerous to take them out."

He reached into the container and removed the pouch. Setting aside the container, he loosened the drawstrings and dumped their contents into his palm. The three brilliant blue gems glimmered as if alive, their hue reminiscent of a twilight summer sky. Dar stepped close and peered at them in awed silence.

"So when do we leave?" he asked.

They quickly decided that sooner was better than later, but Dar thought Brecon should first inform his mother of their plans. She would be more understanding and more willing to help cover for them, should their absence be discovered too quickly.

Not to mention that she would be more cautious about revealing what she knew to Ajin d'Amphere, should the princess or her Skaar come sniffing around.

So Brecon closed the box and resealed it—the Elfstones removed and tucked away in his pocket—and then lowered it back into its hiding place and returned the floor to its previous condition. Dar pulled the rug back in place, and they retraced their steps down the hallway to the reception room Brecon had taken Dar into earlier. Leaving the highlander to himself, the Elven prince went off to speak with his mother. Dar was prepared for a long wait, but it took Brecon less time than he had expected; he was back within the half hour, his mission completed.

"Mother sends her love, and says you are responsible for me."

Dar smiled. "She would say that."

"She also said you can justify her faith in you by bringing me back safe and sound."

By now Ajin and her Skaar companions would have made their departure from Arborlon. Assured there would not be another unexpected encounter, Dar and Brecon set out for the Elessedil private airfield to prepare for their own impending journey. As an Elven

prince, Brecon had an airship designated for his personal use, which was kept housed and serviced year-round. Since the vessel was always fully provisioned, there were no further preparations necessary once they reached it, and the friends boarded and were quickly away.

They flew out of Arborlon heading southwest in the general direction of Backing Fell. Their craft was an expanded single-mast sloop that could easily hold six but still be flown by a single pilot. Even though his help wasn't needed, Dar worked the radian draws and light sheaths while Brecon manned the helm. Once they had crossed the Rill Song and come in sight of the eastern borders of the Sarandanon, Dar tapped Brecon on the shoulder. "Find a place to land so you can use the Elfstones. We need to be sure of our direction."

Brecon immediately took the airship down to a clearing at the edge of the forests bordering the Sarandanon. Dar secured the radian draws and then lowered the mooring lines that would hold the airship in place. Once they were hovering just a few feet off the ground, he threw out a rope ladder, went over the railing, and anchored the lines to tree trunks and exposed roots so the vessel was stable.

Brecon followed him down and together they moved to a rise overlooking miles of farms and cultivated fields that made up the bulk of the soil-rich valley.

Dar shielded his eyes. "Pretty country. I could live here."

His friend nodded, a crooked smile spreading across his lean face. "I've actually considered it. I'd leave Arborlon and move here in a second flat, if I could. I'd even leave the Carolan. There are others who could do my work."

"But?"

"I don't want to leave my mother alone. She's not close to my father these days—hasn't been for a while. My brothers don't seem to see it, but they have their own lives and families. So she turns to me. I don't want to abandon her."

Dar nodded. "We all make such choices. I had thought to go back to my family when I saw what had been done to Paranor. But I don't think I can abandon the Druid's Keep, either. Or Drisker."

"Neither one is your responsibility."

"You could argue that. But it's more in how you see it than how it is." He gave Brecon a nudge. "Might as well use the Stones, Brec. See if you can find Tarsha."

The Elven prince pulled a face. "This isn't going to be as easy as you seem to think. First of all, I have no idea what this Tarsha person looks like, and I have to picture her to find her. Or at least provide the Elfstones with some identifying characteristics. Second, I've never used this magic, so I'm not entirely sure what I'm doing."

Dar stared in disbelief. "What do you mean you've never used the magic? Not even once? Just to see what it can do? How could you resist? You had access to it anytime you chose."

"You haven't been paying attention. I told you I hadn't taken them out of their hiding place again since I found them. There's a reason for that. Using magic triggers a response. It . . . calls attention to itself. I didn't want to risk Father finding out what I'd done. So I looked at them that one time and then left them alone."

"You are a true disappointment," Dar declared in frustration. "I'd assumed you must have used them at least once! How could you stand not knowing what it felt like?"

Brecon laughed. "Not everyone thinks sticking their head in a moor cat's mouth is a good idea."

Dar stared, surprised at the rebuke. "If you say so . . ."

Brecon was grinning broadly. "Glad we have an understanding. Now describe Tarsha."

Dar did, focusing on her more memorable characteristics—the white-blond hair, the lavender eyes, and the sculpted features. Then he described her dress—although it was hard to be sure what she would be wearing now. He described how she had moved and responded during their conversations, how she used her gestures and facial expressions.

When he was finished, Brecon shrugged. "I'll do my best. Maybe the hair and eyes will be enough."

He fished the pouch from his pocket and spilled the Elfstones into his open palm. In the bright daylight, they seemed to absorb the sun's

rays, their deep-blue color enhanced until they appeared twice their normal size. Dar stood back as Brecon gathered his thoughts, the Elfstones clutched in his fist. Then the Elven prince closed his eyes and went perfectly still.

Finally, after long moments, he lifted the hand with the Elfstones until it pointed southwest in the general direction of Backing Fell. Brecon stood like a statue, arm raised and outstretched, eyes closed, face mirroring an intense concentration. Dar watched silently, wondering if anything was going to happen.

It wasn't. The Elfstones failed to respond.

Brecon lowered his arm and looked over, giving a reluctant shrug. "Nothing."

"Try again," Dar urged.

Brecon resumed his stance, his arm lifting once more. This time he kept his eyes open, looking off into the distance as if willing Tarsha Kaynin to appear. The concentration on his face was total. Dar waited, but the Elfstones remained dark.

"Picture her in motion," Dar said quietly, firmly. "As if she's struggling with something or perhaps trying to defend herself."

The Elven prince did not respond, but he remained in place, his arm still stretched out. He inhaled deeply and then exhaled, and his body tensed as his free hand closed about the one that held the Elfstones, both arms now extended out from his body.

A glimmer of blue broke through the cracks between his fingers.

"Yes!" Dar hissed excitedly.

Then shards of indigo exploded from Brecon Elessedil's clenched fists and shot away into the distance in a ribbon of brightness that carried both watchers with it—down from the rise and across the Sarandanon sharply south and over the Rill Song once again, past forests and hills, gullies and streams, and farther still. The Rock Spur Mountains rose in the distant west, and the light swept past them and angled east toward where the Tirfing bordered the edges of the Matted Brakes, and then curled in on itself until it found a solitary traveler standing next to a small aircraft. It was Tarsha Kaynin, looking north toward Elven country in the direction of Dar and Brecon.

But it wasn't at Dar and his companion Tarsha Kaynin was look-ing; it was at three ragged figures approaching from the north.

Dar caught his breath. Beneath the shifting shadows of the cloaks the three wore draped over their gnarled forms, he spied the glimmer of unsheathed blades.

ELEVEN

◆

Immediately after speaking with Jes Weisen about Tavo, Tarsha Kaynin departed Backing Fell to renew her search. Hearing the old woman tell the tale of what had happened to her parents and brother had left her shaken and unsure of what she was doing, but Tarsha had made up her mind to continue on. No matter what her brother had done, no matter how sick or angry or disturbed he was, she had to try to help him. If she abandoned him now, he was lost. There was no one else who would bother looking for him or to whom he could turn. He would continue on his rampage through the Westland villages and beyond until someone imprisoned or killed him.

No matter the danger to herself, she could not allow this. She could not live with herself if she let it happen.

So she flew her small airship east in the direction Tavo had taken, stopping frequently at small villages and outlying camps in an effort to find his trail. There was no other way for her to track him—no other way that made any sense. He was traveling alone and with a purpose that only he could know, so she had little to go on.

She found the village Jes Weisen had described to her—a tiny hamlet with a scattering of shacks and ramshackle homes and a tavern and smithy's forge—much later that same day. A rumor of its misfortune had spread to other, larger villages not far away and led her to it. She left her airship concealed in nearby woods and entered near dusk, a solitary presence entering a ghost town. No one was about; only a few lights shone in the windows of the shacks. But a solitary light was visible through a boarded-up window of the tavern, so she entered.

The barroom was empty, the serving counter deserted. The light emanated from a candle-lit lantern hanging from the back wall. In its feeble glow she could see the remains of smashed tables and chairs and holes in the walls of the building. There were dark stains all across the wooden floor, and in places pieces of the ceiling had been torn away. At first, she thought the building deserted, but then a haggard, empty-eyed serving woman walked out of the kitchen area from behind the bar and stared at her. "We're closed," she said.

Tarsha walked over to her. "I'm looking for the person who did . . ." She hesitated, then gestured at the room. "All this."

The woman frowned. "What's he to you?"

Tarsha hesitated. Best not to reveal too much. "We grew up in the same village. I heard what happened here. I thought maybe I could talk to him."

The serving woman shook her head. "Last one to try *that* ended up that stain over there." She pointed at a particularly large spattering of dried blood. "I carted his body out back with the others. Burned them all to keep any sickness from spreading to those of us who are left." She gave Tarsha a sharp look. "What makes you think he would listen to you? He isn't in his right mind, you know. Wouldn't listen to me or to any of those men he killed. So why would he listen to you?"

"We were friends when he was younger. Before . . . any of this. Are you saying talking won't work anymore?"

"I'm saying exactly that." The woman brushed back her lank hair and frowned some more, remembering. "I could tell something was wrong with him the moment he walked in. I tried to help him—even told him he maybe ought to go somewhere else. It's a rough crowd comes into this place, men who don't treat strangers well. He wouldn't listen. Didn't even seem to want to. Then he got into it with a few of the regulars—bad men, all of them."

She paused, locking gazes with Tarsha. "He just exploded, girl. Went all the way crazy. He had some sort of terrible magic in his voice. He sang, he did—an awful sound—and he tore those men and everyone else in the room apart. Made them explode! It was terrible to watch. I was hiding in the kitchen, one eye watching through the door when I could stand it. Tables and chairs flying, bodies tossed about, blood everywhere. I couldn't do nothing. I didn't even want to try. Not with him."

Images of what had happened flashed through Tarsha's mind, raw and ugly. Everything she was hearing about her brother suggested that he had passed beyond her reach.

"Do you know where he went afterward?" she asked.

The woman nodded. "Funny about that. There's an old woman who lives up the road a ways, just at the east edge of this village. She found him and took him in. Crazy thing to do, you know. He's all covered in blood when he comes up to her door, and she takes him in, anyway. He stays the night with her, leaves in the morning, and the woman's none the wiser about what he's done. Calla Lily, she calls herself. For the flower, you know. Lucky she's still alive, but she is."

So perhaps Tavo isn't beyond helping after all, Tarsha thought, allowing herself a small shred of momentary hope. "Did you speak to her?"

"Of course I spoke to her. How else would I know all this?"

"Did she say where the boy went after he left her?"

"Didn't say 'cause she didn't know. He just left. Hardly spoke to her at all. He went east, I think she said. Just walked away." A pause. "You got to be going now, girl. Like I said—we're closed. But take some good advice. Turn around and go back to wherever it is you come from. Don't waste your time on that young man. He's just marking time until someone does for him."

Tarsha went back to her airship and flew on. She thought about visiting Calla Lily, but decided there was little else she would learn from her. She needed to keep moving, to keep trying to find him before he did any further damage. And there was every reason to believe he would. His mental state had deteriorated beyond anything she had ever imagined possible. The danger of him harming anyone who crossed him in even the smallest way was now undeniable.

Even if it happens to be me.

But she had made up her mind. She would take her chances.

She slept that night in fields beyond the forest regions that surrounded Backing Fell and the unfortunate hamlet where Tavo had done so much damage, unwilling to stay anywhere that reminded her of what she had come home to. She curled up in the cockpit of her aircraft and wrapped herself in blankets against the cold of the night air. But there was nothing she could do about the chill that had settled into her bones with this day's discoveries. She wondered if she would ever rid herself of the horror that was consuming her every time she thought of her brother.

As a result, she slept hardly at all and woke worn and dismayed.

From there, she continued eastward, conducting a leapfrogging search of the countryside, following the shores of the Rill Song toward the Tirfing, stopping frequently to ask the same questions, over and over again. There were a few who had seen a young man such as she described, a solitary bedraggled figure passing close by homes and towns but never entering. There were one or two who had talked to him. They remembered him as hollow-eyed and withdrawn, barely able to voice the two questions he asked each of them.

Do you know a girl named Tarsha?

Do you know where she might have gone?

Until finally, toward the end of the day, she found someone who remembered the questions differently.

Do you know a Druid named Drisker Arc?

Do you know where he lives?

She felt a sinking feeling in her stomach when she heard this. Somehow, Tavo had found out where she had gone and was tracking her. Somehow, he must have stumbled on one of the people she had talked to on her way to Emberen while searching for Drisker, and she had been remembered. It wouldn't have been difficult for them to recall; her physical appearance was distinctive enough. And there would have been no reason for them not to reveal what they knew.

So now he had a specific destination.

But what did he intend to do once he reached it?

She thought of her parents, torn to pieces, bloodied beyond recognition, victims of his fury and his vengeance. Did he plan to do the same to her? Or did he seek her because she was all he had left, and he was desperate to find her so that she could help him?

"Oh, Tavo, why?" she whispered to herself, saddened by both possibilities.

She turned northeast to fly back to Emberen. She might as well return there and face him.

She was reminded of Drisker Arc's journey to Paranor with the highlander Dar Leah, and she wondered what had happened to them and if they had returned yet. Drisker's mission to reach the Druids had been so urgent, and there was reason to be afraid for him. She hoped he had settled things by now. But even so, she did not care for the prospect of his returning only to find her brother waiting for him. Even with the Blade to help protect him, he could be facing a serious threat.

And the thought of Drisker being forced to hurt or kill Tavo because she wasn't there to intercede was even more troubling.

So she pressed ahead, flying deep into the night, sleeping poorly once more to rise early and continue on the second day in the same fashion. It was arduous and debilitating, her time spent turning over and over the possibilities of what she might find when she reached Emberen, of what sort of disaster awaited her there. None, she kept telling herself, but she didn't believe it. She understood how unlikely it was. There was no point in pretending otherwise, and she knew it, even if she couldn't help herself.

Then, well into the afternoon of that second day, her airship broke down. She felt it begin to lose power, and she was quick to land on a barren stretch of plains not far from the juncture of the Matted Brakes and Drey Wood. Once on the ground, she began an examination of the vessel's workings, her knowledge minimal enough to cause her to wonder if she would even recognize the problem once she found it.

She was in the midst of her investigation when she caught sight of three ragged figures approaching from the north. She stopped what she was doing and moved away from her craft to watch them. They were ragged, soiled creatures—hard men with hungry looks and little kindness in their faces. She was in trouble, although not the sort she couldn't handle.

And then—suddenly, unexpectedly—she sensed someone else watching her. No one she could see—just eyes watching from a place far away by a means she could sense but not identify. *Magic,* she thought at once. *But whose?*

A few moments later, the sensation faded. Whoever had been watching her had ceased to do so. She wondered at once if it was Drisker. He would be the one most likely to use magic. He could have returned, found her gone, and decided to come after her.

"Troubles, little lady?" one of the men approaching asked in a harsh whisper.

It sounded to her as if his vocal cords had been damaged in some way, as if speaking was difficult for him. His companions said nothing, but she caught a glimpse of a knife beneath one's tattered clothing, the blade held close to his body.

She faced them squarely. "Do you know anything of airships?" she asked them pointedly. "You don't look like you do."

"Looks can be deceiving," another said—the one who was hiding the knife. "Let's have a peek, see if we can help you out."

She didn't think he was talking about her vessel. She raised her hand. "Stop right there."

Her tone of voice brought them up short. There was iron in it, a clear indication that she believed she was able to back up her warning. The men exchanged glances. "Now, that's no way to be," said the first.

"Maybe not, but that's the way it is. So turn around and walk away."

The men had sullen, dangerous looks on their faces. "We're not leaving until we're ready," said the one with the knife. "And we ain't any sort of ready just yet."

"Don't be foolish," the first said to her. "We can do this the easy way or the hard way. Makes no difference to us. But you can be sure of this. It's going to happen."

Tarsha shook her head. "No, it isn't. I'll say it one more time. Walk away. Don't make me hurt you. Because if you take one more step, I will."

"Aw, missy, that ain't how you should be talking to us." The knife man was whining. "You should be careful what you say . . ."

His body uncoiled in a snake-like motion, and the hidden knife flashed through the air. Before she could act, the blade buried itself in her shoulder, knocking her backward and leaving her sprawled on the ground, grimacing with pain.

The men charged her in a flurry of arms and legs and shouts, trying to overwhelm her. They might have done so easily enough if it had been anyone else. But even injured, Tarsha Kaynin was more than a match for them. She howled in fury, and the wishsong instantly halted their charge as suddenly as if they had run into a stone wall. They crumpled to the ground, gasping in anger and pain. One tried to rise, and she used her magic to pick him up and toss him twenty feet away. The other two watched it happen and then scrambled to their feet. Picking up their companion, they staggered away without uttering another word, looks of disbelief etched on their faces.

An odd pang of guilt struck Tarsha in that moment. What she had just done had not been so different from what Tavo had done in that tavern. She had used the wishsong as a weapon. Admittedly, to defend herself—but hadn't that been true of her brother, as well? The wishsong was a heavy burden; it imbued the user with both great power and great responsibility. But there was one difference in the ways she and her brother had used it. Her victims had been allowed to walk away alive. Tavo's had not.

Tarsha watched her attackers until they were out of sight and then pulled the blade from her shoulder. She was bleeding freely, and she felt flushed and shaky. She rose and stumbled over to the airship. In the storage bin were bandages and healing ointments, and she quickly tended her wound. The knife was not clean, and she worried about infection. But there was nothing more she could do about it now. What mattered was that she repair the airship so she could fly for help.

She opened the parse tubes and began to test the diapson crystals for effectiveness. The crystals were charged, so she moved to the radian draws. Halfway through her investigation she found the problem. The left parse tube connector had worked its way loose from its seating. She tightened it anew, and within minutes she was setting out once more.

By then it was late in the day. She knew she should stop and rest, but she also knew she should hurry. So she flew on until nightfall before setting down only a few miles below the Rhenn. There she changed her dressing, ate a little food, drank a little water, and went to sleep.

When she woke the next morning, her wound was throbbing painfully, and she knew she was in trouble.

In the city of Arishaig, far to the east of where Tarsha found herself, Ketter Vause sat behind his desk in the Prime Minister's office and stared silently at the man standing before him. The man was a junior officer of a Federation garrison stationed in Varfleet who had been dispatched to investigate rumors of a disturbance in the vicinity of Paranor several days earlier. Vause's own first commander of the main body of the Federation army, who had been summoned to hear the junior officer's report, stood off to one side, listening to his scout.

All bore stunned looks on their faces.

"The Druid's Keep is gone?" Vause said after long moments, repeating the newcomer's words in a tone of clear disbelief. "You are certain of this?"

"I was there. I saw for myself." The other man shifted his feet uncomfortably. He was clearly unhappy with having been delegated by his commanding officer to deliver the news personally. "There's nothing left of it. The ground on which it stood is empty. It's as if nothing was ever there."

The Prime Minister steepled his fingers before him in contemplation. *How is this possible?* The question frightened him. Did the Skaar invaders possess such terrible power? That envoy seemed to hint they did, although Vause had not for a moment believed it possible. But there it was. This messenger from Varfleet had just said the Skaar had disposed of the Druids, and it appeared they had.

"The Druids are gone, too? All of them?"

"There were no Druids at the site, although it is possible some fled. In any case, there were no witnesses to what happened. None that I could find, at any rate. Paranor and its Druids have disappeared, Prime Minister. Every last vestige of the order is vanished."

"You searched?"

"There wasn't much searching required. The truth of it was mostly in what I could see for myself. Or not see."

Vause's narrow features tightened. That the Druids were gone, their order wiped out and their members dead or scattered, was the best news he had received in a very long time. Paranor had been a thorn in the Federation's side for countless generations, but no one had thought it possible to eliminate them altogether. Yet the Skaar had accomplished this practically overnight and the Federation war against magic and its uses appeared to be over. Without the Druids to collect and manage magic in all its various forms, the Elves were left isolated—the only Race solely dependent on such power. Without the Druids, the employment of magic might well be stamped out entirely.

"We can't be certain exactly when it happened," Arraxin Dresch, his first commander, observed. "No one seems to know. Word's gotten back to us quickly enough, but even so—"

"Even so," Vause interrupted, "not quickly enough for us to find witnesses or survivors, so we are left to imagine the particulars." He paused. "What's become of these invaders? Where are they now?"

The messenger glanced at Dresch for support and found none. "I don't know, Prime Minister." He spoke quickly, nervously. "I was told to come at once to Arishaig to report what I had seen. But there was no one at the site of the Druid's Keep. There might be a report by tomorrow."

Ketter Vause nodded. If he wasn't so bothered by the implications of all this, he would have been more willing to celebrate what on the face of things was a stunning accomplishment.

But his moment of jubilation had already turned to one of concern. What did the Skaar intend next, and what was he going to do about it? Could he rely on the envoy's promise that the Skaar were seeking an alliance? Could he believe the Skaar would leave the Southland alone if Vause agreed to their terms?

The answers to his questions were swift in coming. By the following day, a second messenger had arrived. First Commander Dresch brought him before Vause immediately. From the look on the commander's face, the news was not good.

"Tell me what you found," Ketter Vause ordered brusquely.

"Prime Minister, we discovered the main body of the invader's army encamped on the north shore of the Mermidon River. They number somewhat less than a thousand soldiers. There is no clear indication of what they are preparing to do next. My commander positioned men on this side of the river to monitor their movements and report back when they know anything further."

Ketter Vause nodded, expressed his thanks, and dismissed the man, gesturing for Dresch to remain behind. He was not happy to discover the Skaar were right up against Federation territory. The messenger from the Skaar princess had promised they would not attempt to occupy any part of the Federation. But the Borderlands were a Federation protectorate, and the Mermidon was their northern perimeter. If they weren't intending an invasion of the Borderlands, then why were they setting up their camp at the edge of its borders?

He remained where he was for a moment, looking out the window across the vast expanse of the city of Arishaig. Arraxin Dresch stood perfectly still, waiting patiently. Vause expected as much. He had rid himself of the last man to hold the commander's position, irritated by his constant insistence on questioning his decisions. This one had a reputation for complying with orders—a quaint but otherwise praiseworthy approach to the concept of chain of command.

He sighed. What did the Skaar intend? Advancing as they had to the banks of the Mermidon revealed they were up to something, but a force of less than a thousand was too small to risk exposing itself to the much larger Federation army—a force that could crush it like an eggshell if its full strength were brought to bear. Surely the princess and her commanders must know that. So what were they doing?

"Commander?" he said, without turning. "What do you make of this?"

"I don't think we should sit around waiting to see how it turns out" was his immediate response.

Dresch was a big, bearded man with his best years still ahead of him, his loyalty long since established, and his bravery unquestioned. He had experience on the battlefield. He had put down a Dwarf uprising in the Declan mining region five years earlier. His sole weakness was his tendency toward caution. But caution wasn't always a bad idea.

"Would this Skaar princess really dare to turn on us?" Vause shook his head. "It would be foolhardy to risk doing so. We have been offered an agreement, an alliance of non-aggression. Would she choose to go back on her promise to let the Federation be? What would persuade her to change her mind?"

"Greed. Hunger for more than she already has. Who knows?" Dresch paused. "Have you received any communication since the offer was made? Perhaps it has been withdrawn."

Vause wasn't sure, but for him to assume it was no longer on the table didn't seem wise. "We must take steps to see that she behaves herself. Take two companies of Federation army regulars and a warship escort to the Mermidon today, and have them camp directly across the river from the Skaar. I want you with them to observe. Get word back to us if any attempt is made to cross the Mermidon into the Borderlands. Do it now."

His first commander nodded and left without a word.

Vause went back to staring out the window. He would give this a few days, just to see if the princess or her envoy made any further attempt to contact him. If they did not, he would send someone to confront her. Whatever was going on, he wanted to know the details.

This whole business with the Skaar was making him increasingly uncomfortable. He was beginning to think they could prove to be more trouble than the Druids they had somehow dispatched.

If that feeling persisted, he would have to do something about it. And do it soon.

TWELVE

CLIZIA PORSE HAD CONTINUED on with the trading caravan to Varfleet following her discovery that she had somehow failed to gain possession of the Black Elfstone. That she did not have the talisman she needed to bring Paranor back into the world of the Four Lands was galling enough. The fact that in all probability it was still inside the Keep—where Drisker, if he was still alive, could lay hands on it—put her at a decided disadvantage.

So for the day following her unpleasant discovery, as she walked beside and sometimes rode within the caravan wagons, she puzzled over what to do. By the following morning, on arriving at their destination, she still did not have an answer.

Her choices were admittedly unattractive.

Because she had left Drisker's scrye orb behind, she had some connection with Paranor, however tenuous. Her decision on the matter had been deliberate and purposeful. Should Drisker somehow survive the Keep's Guardian—unlikely as that seemed—she would want to know. The orb would provide her with a way. But now matters had moved beyond simply satisfying her curiosity. Now it appeared that her only chance for recovering Paranor lay in Drisker having succeeded in doing what she had intended he not do—avoid the death she had so cleverly arranged for him. And if he was still alive, she needed to not only confirm it, but also learn whether or not he actually had possession of the Black Elfstone.

Just at the moment she could not think of a way to proceed without tossing everything up in the air. She needed to be certain if he was alive—but without giving anything away about the Elfstone. If she found he was unaware of the truth and she left him that way, he would eventually die—which would be the simplest outcome. But then Paranor and all its vast and treasured magic would be lost to her and her plans to rebuild a new Druid order severely compromised. If, on the other hand, she told him the truth, how could she do so in a way that would further her own interests yet not put her in danger?

So which way should she jump?

The answer to this conundrum eluded her, so instead she quit thinking about it and went off to find an airship. That she would stay only a short time in Varfleet was a given. What she needed to do was travel west to the village of Emberen and Drisker Arc's home to find those books of magic he had purloined on leaving. Yes, they were technically his, but the work had been done while he was a Druid at Paranor and so should belong to the Druids. And since she was the sole survivor of the old order and in the process of forming a new one, they should be hers.

That Drisker would never return to make use of them personally only strengthened the case for making them hers and finding a way to put them to use.

She had no regrets about what she had done to him—just as she had no regrets about how she had manipulated Ober Balronen, Ruis Quince, and all the other Druids to arrange for their demise. Nor did she have regrets about how she had betrayed Paranor to the Skaar so that she could form a new Druid order and begin a new era in the history of the Druids. To her way of thinking, it was a necessary sacrifice. To make a new start, you had to first put the past behind you. The members of the Druid order were irrelevant and divisive. They had lost their bearing and diminished their ability to impact the future. Increasingly, they were becoming dangerous in their blindness. She might have saved them, had they chosen her as High Druid rather than Balronen, but you lived with your mistakes in this world, and she had done nothing more than give a nudge to what was certain to happen eventually.

For Clizia Porse, everything was expendable in the quest to achieve her desires.

So once she had secured and provisioned an airship, she departed the city and set out for the Westland. A three-day journey lay ahead—though at her age, she required little sleep and could probably be in Emberen in two more days if she drove herself hard. It was a small concession to discomfort given what she hoped to achieve. She could have secured the services of a pilot and avoided expending the energy to navigate and fly the airship on her own. But then she would have had to decide what to do with him afterward, and there was only one acceptable choice given her determination to keep her movements secret.

Besides, she was a passable flier with years of experience—even if most of those years were in the past—so she opted to keep herself to herself for now. And she believed the time spent flying alone would provide her with a chance to think through her plans and divine the means for carrying them out. There was much to consider, and it would be best accomplished if she was left undisturbed.

One of the more intriguing prospects she found herself considering for the second time since leaving lost Paranor centered on what use she might make of the mysterious girl Tarsha, who had accompanied Drisker that first visit when he had sought to gain an audience with Ober Balronen. A student he was mentoring, the Druid claimed. Seemingly a young girl with no visible talent and no skills worth mentioning, his tone had suggested. But Drisker did not waste time on those lacking ability to employ magic, and she sensed there was something more to this Tarsha than what the Druid had suggested. There was an air of secrecy about her, revealed not by any obvious deception but by her presence alone.

And from the way she had looked at Clizia—from the caution and wariness she had displayed—she was clearly more than she appeared.

Clizia Porse was very good at reading people. She prided herself on being able to see right through anyone. Tarsha was a book waiting to be read, and if she was still in residence at Drisker's cottage in Emberen there would be a chance to do so. For now, Clizia could enjoy anticipating what truths might then be revealed and how she might somehow prove useful for what lay ahead.

She arrived in Emberen close to sunset on the third day of travel, weary and hungry to get on with things. She brought the airship down in a landing field occupied by less than half a dozen other vessels, all worn and ragged and looking decidedly unsafe. Her ship was not new, either, but it was well maintained and fully provisioned. She left it under the care of the field manager—a man who seemed willing enough to look after it, especially after she promised him a sizable bonus if she found her craft to be in the same condition when she departed as it was now. A more extensive inquiry into the location of Drisker's home than she had anticipated proved necessary; it appeared that it had been burned to the ground some weeks earlier and a number of brigands had paid the ultimate price for doing so. Informed that he had found temporary lodgings, she set out to find them, carrying a sack filled with food and clothing—a black-cloaked wraith, bent and gnarled and unapproachable.

She found the new home dark and silent amid other similarly shadow-bound residences, its bulk hunkered down within a heavy screen of trees and noticeably set apart. A brief scan with her magic revealed no one waited within. She climbed the porch steps, opened the locked door with ease, and entered. She had hoped to find the girl still in residence—assuming she hadn't been scared off—but it appeared no one had been there for at least several days. There were clothes in a back bedroom that might have been Tarsha's, but no other trace of her presence. She undertook a cursory search, but she did not waste her time trying to discover where the books of magic might be hidden, saving that for when she was better rested.

Then she ate her dinner by candlelight and went to bed.

When morning came, she rose, washed and dressed, ate her breakfast, and began her search for the books in earnest. Whatever else he had lost in the fire that had destroyed his earlier home, he would have made certain to protect those books. She went from room to room, a determined huntress, beginning with Drisker's sleeping quarters and using her magic to aid her in her search. She took her time, considering every possibility as she went, her sharp old eyes missing nothing. She rummaged through all the drawers and closets, hunting under and behind furniture, moving quite deliberately from one room to the next. Afterward, she went on to consider what might be under the home or in the attic above. She searched every place she could think of, no matter how far-fetched, but turned up nothing.

The day was nearly done when she finished, and she had nothing to show for her efforts. It was disappointing, but she was not discouraged. She had never once believed that finding something of such importance would be easy. Drisker was nothing if not clever, and he would have been more so concealing those books.

Toward evening, an oddity surfaced, one she could not explain. Glancing haphazardly into the trees surrounding the cottage, she caught sight of movement. It was gone as fast as it came, but she thought from the glimpse she caught that it might be human. She saw it again a little later, no clearer than before. Who or what was out there or what its purpose might be in prowling about remained a mystery. She thought to lie in wait for it or track it or even set a trap. But that seemed a foolish waste of her time, given what little she was apt to discover.

Lingering at the periphery of her expectations was the faint hope that Tarsha might appear, but still there was no sign of her. Clizia Porse was determined and strong-minded, but she was also very old and tired more easily than she once had. As a result, she began to wonder if she should abandon this effort and go in search of something more productive. The books would be useful, but forming alliances with those who might support her in establishing her new Druid order was important, too. Quite possibly, she began to think, it might be the better choice.

And then abruptly, on that same evening, everything changed.

Tarsha Kaynin was hot and feverish by the time she arrived back in Emberen, only barely able to land her airship, coming in too fast and hard, and skewing the vessel sideways as she set it down. Her knife wound was badly infected, and her efforts to cure the infection had failed miserably. Her arm and shoulder had been swollen and painful for the last two days, the wound festering and leaking fluids, her head pounding with her sickness. She managed a quick hello for the field manager as she stumbled past, leaving the two-man for him to put away, wanting only to reach Drisker's cottage and go to bed. She had no idea if he would be there, but at this point it didn't matter. She would have a decent, warm bed to sleep in, food and drink to consume, and a guarantee of safety for at least one night. There were some medicines waiting, some of which would help her, and if she weren't better by morning, she would go to the village healer.

She trudged into Emberen and up the roadway toward her destination, paying almost no attention to anyone around her, head down and body hunched in an effort to lessen her agony. It seemed apparent that the grime-encrusted knife blade had done its job. It all seemed a very long time ago, and she didn't care to think on it. Even Tavo seemed far in the past, and just then she found she didn't care if he was still coming to Emberen or not. Simply recovering from her wound would take all the strength she had left.

She had just come in sight of the cottage when she saw the cloaked figure sitting on the porch and felt a surge of relief and joy. Drisker had returned from Paranor, and now everything would be all right!

Except it wasn't Drisker. She knew it almost at once, and as she drew nearer, it became clear the occupant of the chair was Clizia Porse. Tarsha felt a sinking in her stomach, but there was no help for it now. She was too close to turn aside, even had she wished to, and given her present condition it made no sense to go anywhere else.

She watched the old woman rise and pull back the hood of her cloak, revealing her sharp old features—a pinched and wrinkled image still all too familiar from their last encounter.

"Tarsha, isn't it?" she said. "Do I have it right?"

Tarsha nodded, irritated. "Where is Drisker?"

Clizia Porse pursed her lips. "I'm not sure. I left him at Paranor, assuming he was on his way out. I came here to find him. I thought he might be waiting, but he isn't." She paused. "I thought I might find you, too."

Tarsha shook her head. "I went back home to see my family." She dropped her backpack, suddenly unable to hold it any longer. "I need to sleep."

"Your bed is waiting; your room is ready. I have not disturbed either. Would you eat first?"

"No, I just need to sleep."

She took two steps and dropped to one knee, the strength gone out of her. Instantly, Clizia Porse was beside her, arms about her waist, helping to hold her up as she guided her inside. "You've been hurt, girl. I can smell the infection. We have to get you treated at once."

Tarsha shook her head stubbornly. "The village healer . . ."

"Knows not a tenth of what I do. I can help you far more than anyone else. Now, come inside."

The old woman was far stronger than expected, and Tarsha let herself be led to the bedroom and put into the bed. Without asking permission, Clizia began to remove her clothing so she could get a look at the wound. When she had Tarsha stripped to the waist and the infected wound was revealed, she made a disparaging sound. "You've let this go far too long. It needs cleaning, medication, and binding anew. A knife wound, it appears. Wait here."

Tarsha closed her eyes, and it seemed only seconds later that she felt hands on her shoulders. Clizia was holding a cup of steaming liquid in front of her face. "Drink this. All the way down. It will help with the pain. It will also help you to sleep when I am finished."

The girl drank the bitter, pungent brew without objection, no longer wanting anything but to be cared for. The Druid took the empty cup, set it aside, and began to clean out the wound. The pain was excruciating, but Tarsha said nothing, determined to keep her feelings to herself. She remembered how Clizia Porse had made her feel during their meeting at Paranor—exposed, uncomfortable, at risk. Even Drisker had been wary of her, warning Tarsha to reveal nothing, to keep her own counsel.

She would do so here.

When the wound was washed clean of infection and blood, the old woman applied a poultice and then wrapped it with a bandage that felt snug without applying too much pressure. It should be left open to drain at present, she advised. Tomorrow, she would stitch it up and reapply the bandage. By now, Tarsha was almost asleep. She stayed awake only by telling herself she must know everything that was happening while Clizia Porse was in her bedroom. So she fought sleep just long enough for the old woman to complete the treatment and rise from beside her.

"You rest now," the other said. "We will talk in the morning. I will keep watch and wake you if there is need. Sleep."

And Tarsha did.

She dreamed of nothing at all.

When she woke it was light out again, the midday sun high overhead, the birdsong bright and clear, and the forest air filled with the smell of leaves and grasses. She felt markedly improved from the previous night, but she tested herself anyway by moving her arms and legs. To her surprise, there was almost no pain at all, and what remained of her injury seemed to be all but healed. She sat up slowly, looked around, swung her legs out of the bed, and stood. A little bit of dizziness, but otherwise she was fine, save that she was very hungry.

She shed her nightclothes and put on forest garb, taking her time, listening for Clizia Porse and hearing nothing. Once dressed again, she slipped from her bedroom and walked out into the main part of the house.

The old woman sat at the small kitchen table sipping liquid from a cup. Without comment, she rose, poured a second cup, and handed it to Tarsha. "Drink it," she ordered.

Tarsha drank, frowning. "This is ale."

"Ale with herbal medicines to help you heal. You're clearly better, but not yet completely back to yourself."

"I feel well enough. The medicine you gave me and a good night's sleep did wonders."

The other's long face took on a look of amusement. "You've been asleep for almost two days."

The girl stared at her. Two days? No wonder she was so hungry. And no wonder she felt so rested. But two days? Without once waking? How could that be?

The Druid seemed to read her mind. "The medication I gave you was very strong. The infection needed healing without interruption. That meant you had to sleep for more than a single day. Can you feel how it helped you?"

Tarsha nodded. "I am grateful."

Clizia made a dismissive gesture. "You must be hungry. Let's get you something to eat. Then I will sew up your wound." She paused. "Proper young ladies don't fight with knives."

Tarsha grimaced. "It wasn't much of a fight."

The old lady nodded. "I imagine it wasn't."

As she prepared a meal for them, Tarsha was surprised to find herself liking Clizia Porse better than when they had first met. In spite of Drisker's warning, Clizia appeared to have good intentions toward her. If the old woman had not cleaned and bandaged her infection and given her the healing medicines to drink, it was hard to say how things would have turned out.

On the other hand, she was still not convinced that she knew where Clizia's loyalties lay. After all, she had lied to Drisker about knowing Kassen. And Tarsha felt that, in spite of her kindnesses, Clizia was keeping something back from her. So it might be best if she kept a secret or two of her own for now.

While they were eating, Tarsha asked again about Drisker, and this time Clizia told her what had happened. While the two of them were inside Paranor attempting to summon the Guardian of the Keep, Drisker had decided at the last minute to go in search of Kassen. On his orders, Clizia had gone ahead, relying on Drisker's promise that he would quickly follow. But once she was safely outside, she had witnessed the conjuring of a Druid spell that must have been cast by Drisker and Paranor had disappeared, sent into a limbo existence.

"He has the means to bring himself and the Keep back," she finished, giving a perfunctory shrug. "I am certain of that much, if nothing else. But it will not be easy. In the meantime, he is trapped there."

"Is there nothing we can do?" Tarsha pressed.

Clizia shook her head. "Nothing of which I am aware. Although . . ." She hesitated, as if she had remembered something. "Drisker brought several books of old magic with him when he left the Keep and went into exile. I searched for them everywhere, but could not find them. There might be something in there that could help him, if we just knew where they were hidden."

A whisper of warning surfaced in the back of Tarsha's mind. *Be careful.* "I know of the books," she said, "but I think they were still here when I left for Backing Fell. Are you sure they're gone?"

The old woman nodded. "I've run out of places to look. Maybe someone else has them. But let that go for now. You said you went to Backing Fell? In the deep Westland? Whatever for?"

Tarsha had been open and aboveboard with Clizia until now, and it was tempting to be so again. But she was bothered about the woman's rather too keen interest in Drisker's books of magic. Besides, she had kept the secret of her brother's use of the wishsong for so long she found it easy to do so now.

"My family lives there. I went home to see how they were."

"An odd time for a visit all the way back there when Drisker was risking himself at Paranor. Are you not his student and is he not your mentor?"

Tarsha hesitated. "I am and he is. For about a month now. I would have gone with him, but he insisted I remain behind. He also insisted I go back to see how my brother was doing. Tavo has been very ill, and Drisker knows I am worried about him."

The sharp old eyes studied her. "There's more to this story, I suspect, but it can keep until you are stronger. I want to know why Drisker took you on as his student. This is very out of character for him, you understand. There must be something rather special about you for him to make an exception."

Tarsha smiled. "I guess he must have thought so. We never discussed it." She pushed back her plate. "Can we go outside now? I think it might be good for me."

So they cleaned up their dishes and put them away, and then left the cottage for a walk. They traveled a couple of miles down the roadway, ambling along companionably. They were a good match this day, the old woman and the still-recovering girl—the former asking questions at every turn while the latter answered those she didn't object to and slid past the ones she did. It was an odd cat-and-mouse game that Tarsha quickly found required cautious navigation. Clizia Porse was no fool, and she knew how to find things out. But the questions she pursued—of family and of magic—were ones Tarsha was used to avoiding, and she was able to do so here, too.

They walked until the sun had moved well past midday before returning, and then Tarsha went off to have a nap. She remained in her bedroom for the rest of the afternoon, trying to decide how much more she wanted to reveal and what she was going to do with herself now that Drisker was gone. At one point, she wondered what had become of the highlander, Dar Leah. Had he gone into the Keep with Drisker? Was he trapped in lost Paranor, too?

By bedtime that night, she still had more questions than answers.

When Tarsha had retired for the night and Clizia Porse was certain she slept, she went out onto the porch and sat in a high-back wicker chair to think things through. While the girl was skillful and practiced at avoiding questions when she did not wish to provide answers, she had nonetheless revealed herself in other ways. Clizia was now in possession of answers she had not known she was looking for.

That the girl was hiding something was undeniable. Why she was dissembling was a matter of debate, but the evidence was there. Something was wrong with her family, and she had been hiding it long enough that doing so was second nature. She was also hiding the reason that Drisker Arc had taken her on as a student when he had refused to do this for anyone else since leaving Paranor. Clizia was certain it had something to do with a magic she either possessed or could access. But the exact nature of that magic remained unclear.

Even without knowing the answers to any of these riddles, the old woman had found out something more important—what she should do about Drisker Arc and the Black Elfstone. When the girl spoke of him, she did so with special fervor and respect, with compassion and tenderness. It wasn't overt, but it was there. She cared for the Druid, and Clizia was willing to bet he cared for her, as well.

So if Drisker still lived, Tarsha Kaynin could provide Clizia with the leverage she needed to persuade the Druid to do something he clearly would not do otherwise—to use the Black Elfstone to bring Paranor back into the Four Lands. The trick was in determining how best to present an offer he could not refuse—one that would seem to be the key to his freedom while at the same time hiding the fact that it would lead him to his doom.

After all, she still needed to find a way to rid herself of him. Once she had possession of the Black Elfstone, she could do this.

She was aware suddenly of another presence. A shadowy figure that lacked substance or identity was passing through the trees just beyond the fringe of the clearing and her range of vision. She recognized it as the shadowy movement she had sensed earlier. She sought it out anew with her magic, trying to reveal its identity. But it blocked her efforts, a conscious act that shut her out, almost as if it sensed what she was doing—which meant it had the use of magic.

She waited on it, but eventually it disappeared and the night was empty of everything but what was usually there. She found herself wondering how long she could stay in Drisker's house and remain safe from the creatures she now realized were watching her.

She shook her head as she rose and went inside. Sleep now, worry later. Tomorrow would be a big day. For her. For Tarsha.

When she woke, she would know better what the future held.

THIRTEEN

IN THE SHADOW-LAYERED PASSAGEWAYS of Paranor, in the gloom of a halfway world, Drisker Arc walked alone, wrapped in dark thoughts. All around him the silence was an intense, suffocating presence. Only the scrape of his boots on the stone flooring and his own measured breathing broke its spell. Time had passed, but it was difficult to know how much. There was nothing by which to measure it. There was no day or night, no full dark or light, no sun or moon. The shadows did not alter, frozen in perpetual twilight and so fixed they might have been painted on the walls and floors of the Keep. While Drisker moved about the buildings, the courtyards, the towers, and the walls, he could feel growing within him the certainty that he was losing ground. Chances were slipping away. Opportunities remained hidden and secretive, and still no solution for escaping his prison had presented itself.

Shades knew he had tried to find one. He had tried to use the Black Elfstone over and over again. He had done everything he could think to do to bring its magic to life. He had willed it to surface; he had threatened and cajoled. He had pictured what it would do if it were triggered and when that failed had given himself over to a blind faith and desperate plea that it would do anything at all.

And still nothing had happened, and he remained imprisoned.

He began to imagine that like the Keep he was fading away. He could tell he was becoming less substantial, more ephemeral, the longer he remained trapped in this endless limbo. He wondered if eventually he would lose everything that made him who he was and become a shade that would wander endlessly in search of meaning. It did not feel unlikely. He had kept despair at bay until now, but he was beginning to feel it press against him with inexorable determination. And once it took hold, he knew he was finished.

Helplessness was already an insistent presence in his life. He found himself struggling with visions of what might be happening back in the Four Lands. Clizia Porse was free to carry on with her machinations, the Skaar were relentlessly foraging deeper into the lands south of Paranor—perhaps preparing to challenge the might of the Federation itself—and Tarsha Kaynin was searching for her brother with no one to protect her against her own bad judgment.

All of it was maddening.

That Dar Leah might have located Tarsha and be looking after her as she searched for her brother—since by now it was clear that Drisker and Paranor were gone—provided some small consolation. But nothing changed the fact that there was nothing he could do about any of it while he remained trapped within the Keep.

He slowed for a moment, thinking once more of the archives, wondering for what must have been the thousandth time if there might be something in there that could help him. But he could think of no artifact or talisman or magic that would free him from his prison and return him to the Four Lands other than the Black Elfstone. His frustration surfaced anew. When he could call upon so many forms of magic to serve him, why couldn't he find a way to call upon this one? What was he missing?

He revisited his efforts—every one of them. He took his time, cataloging and examining each carefully. Was there something he hadn't tried? Was there another summoning spell, another method of conjuring he had failed to remember? Was there something he could do differently? Cogline had seemed to suggest there was, that he was not doing something that was needed to make the magic respond.

What was it the old Druid had said to him? *It requires something of you to command such magic. It demands a price.*

But what sort of price?

He looked around, almost expecting to find Cogline watching him in his struggles, thinking perhaps to ask him for more information. But shades rarely helped the living, and when they did it was always in an enigmatic way. They gave hints at solutions, but it was up to the one who needed the answers to unravel them. In any case, there was no sign of his ghostly companion. For the moment, at least, Cogline had chosen to let him reason things through on his own.

As if that were possible.

His emotions overcame him—frustration, rage, and despair—and tears filled his eyes. His dark face grew darker, and he hunched over as if in pain. For an instant, he was overwhelmed. He was never getting out of Paranor. He was never going to find a way to return it or himself to the land of the living. He would never see Tarsha or Dar Leah or Fade or even Flinc again. He was going to remain trapped within the Keep's walls until he simply faded away.

He was going to die here.

It was this last conclusion that proved intolerable and brought him back to himself. Calm once more, he cast off the negative feelings and began tightening his resolve. There would be no giving up, no quitting, no acceptance of a fate he could not envision for himself. He would simply keep searching for a way out of this prison until he found it. He stared around at the shadowed walls, searching for what he knew was hiding there.

An answer to his problems, a way out of the Keep.

Cogline.

There had to be something more the old man could tell him, even if only speaking in riddles.

But that isn't the only way he can communicate with me, Drisker realized suddenly.

He raced for the stairs leading to the higher floors, heart pounding. *The Druid Histories.* Why hadn't he thought of them earlier? All of the long and storied writings of the Druids were chronicled there.

Surely something about Cogline must be included, and perhaps something about how the Black Elfstone was employed to open the Keep while he was imprisoned all those centuries ago.

So anxious was he to get there, he slipped twice on his way to the third level, where the Histories were stored, barking his shins. All of the despair and depression had dropped away, and while he knew he could not be certain what he would find or how much help it would provide, at least he had a place to begin.

The pounding of his boots on the stone energized him, the rhythm urging him to go faster, but he slowed as he reached the third floor, winded and not wanting to get ahead of himself. Before him, lounging in the hallway, he could see the ghost of Cogline waiting for him, an expectant look on his withered face.

"I was curious to see how long it would take you to figure it out."

Drisker gave him a look. "Not all that long. But you could have told me to come here in the first place."

"Life is an education, Drisker. It is learned mostly through what you discover on your own and not through what others tell you."

"So you don't have anything new to reveal, I gather?"

"Not really."

The shade looked rather more pleased with himself than Drisker thought reasonable. "Why don't you wait out here, then?" the Druid suggested. "Stay out from underfoot."

Cogline shrugged and melted into the walls. It was growing annoying to watch him do this. But then, it was worse than annoying to have him hanging about when he was of so little help.

Drisker opened the doors to the office that served the Ard Rhys and walked over to the curtained wall that hid the books. When he pulled back the covering, there was nothing to be found, only the stone and mortar of the bare wall. Drisker stepped back, summoned his magic, placed his hands on the wall, palms flat, and began to murmur softly. Light rose from where his hands moved across the wall's surface, growing steadily in intensity until it was nearly blinding.

Then the light pulsed as if expanding, enveloping the Druid completely before sharply dying away. In the aftermath of its disappearance, the gloom and shadows closed about once more, and the silence returned. Drisker stood quietly staring at the space the wall had occupied, the wall itself gone.

Beyond, a bare room waited, its walls fashioned of materials that few had ever seen. A huge table with twelve chairs dominated the center of the room. Both table and chairs were constructed of finished pieces of timber with metal enhancements and fastenings and had an ancient, immutable look to them. But the Druid ignored both and walked to the walls. Starting on the right and working his way left, he ran his hands across the smooth surface, palms brushing lightly and moving in circles—as if to scrub clean something the eye couldn't see. It took him a long time to circle the room entirely, and when he was finished he stepped away and waited.

Slowly, the walls began to dissolve. Their surfaces ran like melting ice and faded away, leaving rows of books bound in leather and iron cord, so clean and well preserved they looked newly made. Everything about the books and the shelves shone and gleamed, the pale light of the half-world to which Drisker had been sent catching new brightness. The Druid walked around slowly, studying the tomes, pulling out one or two to judge their place in time, and then finally settling on one that recounted the events of the era surrounding Cogline's previous life.

He laid the book on the heavy old table, opened it, and began to read. The jolt of expectation he felt at that moment was immeasurable. Hope was at hand.

Several hours later it had all but vanished. He had scanned the book from end to end and found no mention of Cogline. In disbelief, he pulled the volumes on either side of the one he'd finished and scanned them, as well. Still no mention of Cogline.

A fresh wave of frustration swept through him. How could the old man not have been mentioned *somewhere*? He was a seminal figure in Druid lore and in the history of the Four Lands. A failed Druid who had survived death to come back when the Druids were gone and Paranor had been consigned to limbo by Allanon just before his own demise, he had helped persuade Walker Boh to become the next

High Druid and was responsible for urging him to use the Black Elf-stone in order . . .

He caught himself.

. . . in order to bring Paranor back into the Four Lands.

Wait. Maybe he had this wrong. It was *Walker Boh* who had used the Black Elfstone and returned Paranor, not Cogline. Cogline had helped to persuade him, but he was a failed Druid. Not even a Druid at all, really. So would he even be mentioned in the Histories?

Maybe not. But Walker Boh would. Drisker saw it clearly now. That was where he should be looking for an explanation.

He was turning back to the Histories to begin his search anew when he felt the scrye orb, ever present in his pocket, begin to tingle.

He knew without looking it was Clizia Porse.

Clizia had waited for what she believed to be a suitably long time be-fore using her scrye orb to attempt to contact Drisker. She had spent most of the day until then considering what approach she should take to get the Druid to do what she wanted. She had woken that morn-ing knowing exactly how she would use Tarsha Kaynin, but she had waited through most of the day to act. Best not to rush things. Best to think them through. It was midafternoon, and the girl was nap-ping in her bedroom. Clizia had given her tea with a little something added to keep her out of the way while she carried out her plan. The drug she had added to the tea would keep her sleeping for several hours, so there was little reason to worry while she was using the scrye orb. The time she required was assured.

All this assuming, of course, that Drisker Arc was still alive. But she couldn't help thinking that he was. It was an irrational conclu-sion, given her certainty just days ago that there was no possibility that he could have survived. But she had learned over the years to pay attention to those kinds of premonitions.

She gave herself a chance to think through again what she in-tended to say and how she would say it. She would only get one chance, and it was important that she not make a mistake. It would be easy enough to do so, after all. Drisker was no fool.

So she waited patiently until she could be certain Tarsha was asleep, sitting on the porch and looking out into the sun-streaked trees that allowed her brief glimpses of the surrounding homes, which housed the neighbors she never seemed to see. Her secretive watcher was absent today, off doing whatever it did when it wasn't spying on her. The whole of the forest was filled with birdsong and flashes of brightness as reflective surfaces caught the sunlight and spun it away again in tiny bursts. Except for the watchers, she liked it here and could have stayed and been comfortable. But once she had Drisker and Paranor back, she needed to move ahead with her plans to deal with the Skaar. How she would do so remained a moving target, but one step led to another, and until you took each step you could not be entirely certain where the next would lead.

So when she was certain Tarsha slept, she brought out the scrye orb and called upon its magic, turning its all-seeing eye on Drisker. She wondered belatedly if it could penetrate the veil that enfolded both the Druid and Paranor, but she needn't have worried. Within moments of her summoning, he appeared before her, very much alive. She allowed herself a quick, pleased smile.

"How nice of you to visit," he said. His voice was calm enough, but his expression was dark and menacing and there was weariness visible in his eyes. "Surprised to see me?"

"I want to make a bargain with you," she replied, ignoring the question. "How would you like to get out of there?"

He gave her a doubtful look. "What mischief are you up to now, Clizia?"

"It appears I was a bit hasty in sending you off in such a rude manner. I should have thought it through better. Perhaps you would like to come back and join me in creating my new Druid order? I find I am not quite equal to the task I have set myself."

Now there was merriment in his eyes. "I would rather crawl across broken glass than help you. But thank you for asking."

"Don't be so hasty. I can't believe you are so anxious to stay locked away in an empty fortress. You could be there for a long time."

"Wasn't that your intention?"

"It was my intention to see you dead. But as I've said, I've reconsidered."

"You shouldn't have bothered. Just because you failed once doesn't mean I'm going to give you a second chance. Find another way to amuse yourself. This conversation is over."

The scrye orb went dark. Clizia waited patiently for several minutes before summoning him again. She knew this wouldn't be easy, and she was determined not to let him distract her from her purpose.

His face reappeared, bladed and hard. "I'm busy, Clizia. Trying to get out of here on my own. What is it now?"

"Do you know where I am?" she asked. Without waiting for his response, she flashed the orb about the entry to his cottage and then settled on herself sitting in the wicker chair. "I'm comfortable here."

He took a deep breath. "I'm happy for you. I liked my previous home better, but as you probably know someone burned it down. Still, that one's adequate. If you stick around awhile, I will find a way to repay you for looking after it."

"I haven't showed you the new addition. It was added after your departure. It brightens up the place a bit. Your decorating tastes are a bit ordinary. But this helps change that."

She rose and walked into the house, pointing the scrye orb's eye ahead of her so that Drisker could follow where she was going. She took her time, letting it settle in for him, giving him a chance to figure out what she had done. When she reached Tarsha's bedroom, she was sure he knew what she intended to show him. But she entered, anyway, so he could see the sleeping girl for himself. She let him have a good look at her young face, white-blond hair sprawled on her pillows, her features relaxed and beautiful as she breathed softly.

Then she backed out of the room, closed the door behind him, and turned the orb back on herself. "She's my guest now. We are becoming great friends. I am keeping her safe and sound for you." She paused. "For the moment."

"She is a child!" Drisker spit at her, not bothering to hide his disdain. "You walk dangerous ground, Clizia. More dangerous than you know."

The old woman nodded her agreement. "I expect so, Drisker. But great risk sometimes brings great rewards. And I think it might be so in this case. I think maybe she has talent with magic."

Drisker stared at her wordlessly.

"About my bargain," she said. "Are you ready to listen?"

"It seems I must. What is it?"

Clizia let him wait a few unnecessary moments. "Just this. I need you to bring Paranor back into the Four Lands. I need the Black Elfstone to accomplish this. I don't care if you want to help me or not. I don't care if you don't choose to be a part of a new Druid order. But I do need Paranor. You can help me with that."

There was a long pause. "You might remember that you stole the Elfstone from me when you left me to be devoured by the Keep's Guardian. Without it, I can't do a whole lot."

"This is what we both thought, but we were wrong. I took the Elfstone from you but discovered later that what I really had was a cheap imitation. I don't know how it happened, and I don't care. What matters is that the real Black Elfstone is still somewhere inside Paranor."

He gave her a look. "I'm surprised you are telling me this."

"Why shouldn't I tell you? What do I gain if I don't? You remain trapped, but I've lost Paranor. If I ever want access to the Keep again, I need the Black Elfstone. So there you are, still in the Keep, ready and able to find it and use it. It's worth risking your anger to get you to do so."

She did not want him to gain an advantage over her, even though she was asking for his help. The advantage, she believed, was all hers. She had Tarsha to bargain with, and she was betting that would change things considerably. Whatever the case, he would not be able to resist the prospect of freeing himself, so he would use the Elfstone to do so and bring back Paranor.

She waited, but he didn't say anything.

"Did you hear me, Drisker? You have the means to free yourself."

There was a funny look on his face. "Or something bad might happen to my student. You forgot that part."

She shrugged. "I've made no threats. You can assume what you want."

"Where you are concerned, I am inclined to assume the worst." His face was expressionless. "Tell you what, I'll think about it."

"I wouldn't take too long to do so," she warned. "Things have a way of changing."

"Now you are threatening."

She smiled. "If you say so."

Drisker nodded. "Goodbye, Clizia."

Then he was gone and she was left to ponder what he might do next.

Drisker gripped the scrye orb tightly in his fist and stared off into space. That was unexpected, Clizia asking him to find and use the Black Elfstone, confessing she didn't have it, insisting she needed him back in the Four Lands. But only to be sure that she got possession of the Black Elfstone before she killed him. Only to be sure he was really dead this time. She would use Tarsha to make this happen—use her as a bargaining chip and as a means to weaken him sufficiently to leave him vulnerable to her magic.

So what was he going to do?

Return himself and Paranor to the Four Lands. It was the obvious choice. But first he had to find a way to make that happen. He had to wake the Elfstone's magic so it would do what it was supposed to do. And so far, he hadn't discovered how to do that. But he had to figure it out soon because Tarsha was in real danger as long as Clizia Porse had her.

In all likelihood, the girl didn't even realize how bad her situation was. Clizia was trying to win her over, and this was something she knew how to do when she set her mind to it.

He turned back to the Druid Histories and began searching anew. Somewhere in their pages was the solution to his problem.

He pulled the volumes in which the details of Walker Boh's life and times were chronicled and began to read. He skipped past the parts devoted to his early life—before the years leading up to his time as a Druid—not believing he would find anything useful there. When he reached the sections involving Walker's interactions with Morgan

Leah and the elemental Quickening, he slowed and studied what was written down.

Here, for the first time, Cogline was mentioned. Drisker bore down, reading everything there was to read about the old man and Walker that led up to the search for the Black Elfstone, his return from the city of the Stone King to the former site of Paranor, and his attempts to bring back the Druid's Keep from its limbo existence. It was a slow, tedious process, and after dozens of pages he still didn't know why the Black Elfstone would not respond to him.

But he stopped reading when he found something else, something of equal importance.

He had found a way to save Tarsha.

FOURTEEN

TAVO KAYNIN HAD BEEN walking for days. How many, he didn't know. Time had lost meaning for him. Everything had lost meaning except his search for Tarsha. Since the tavern massacre in that small Westland village, he had made it a point to stay away from everyone when not engaged in asking about his sister. Every so often he would find someone who had seen her. Tarsha was memorable, the color of her eyes and hair unusual, and those who had encountered her remembered. Most knew nothing more than from which direction she had come and in which direction she had gone. So he followed along as best he could, picking up just enough scraps of information to be able to continue his search.

Until, finally, he found someone who knew something more useful.

His source was a man he encountered on a lonely road outside another unfamiliar village he was avoiding while following the steadily disappearing trail Tarsha had left in her passing. It had been several days since there had been any new information, and he was still traveling eastward, still tracking along the southern borders of the Mermidon, when he caught sight of the man approaching. He almost stepped off the roadway, intimidated by the other's clean, well-tended dress and air of confidence. He had endured enough raw looks and rough comments about his own dirty, disheveled appearance to want to avoid inviting any more. He was afraid of his own temper by now. He knew what he was capable of doing if he became angry or frightened, and he was intent on avoiding any further incidents.

But on a whim he decided not to give way and continued toward the other traveler until they were face-to-face. Then he asked the same two questions he had been asking everyone he spoke to. *Have you seen a girl with white-blond hair and lavender eyes?* And when he saw the hesitation in the other's eyes, he felt a surge of excitement and pressed on. *Did she say where she was going?*

"Who are you?" the man asked. Not unfriendly, but clearly wary. "You don't mean her harm, do you?"

Tavo could barely contain himself. "She is my sister!" he exclaimed. "I am searching for her because I think she needs my help. Please, tell me if you know anything."

His words were persuasive and his voice filled with desperation. He was clever, and he knew how to pretend. His skill at deception was improving, and he was paying close attention by now to the advice offered by his friend and companion, Fluken, who was standing just off to one side.

Make him believe, Fluken urged him wordlessly. *Do not anger or frighten him like you did those others. Give him a reason to want to help.*

So Tavo did as he said, and avoided calling on the magic that roiled within him, eager to be unleashed so that it might crush this stranger and force the words from his dying tongue. Instead, he remained outwardly calm, but concerned in what he believed to be a brotherly way.

The stranger looked at him doubtfully. "You look all done in."

"I have traveled a long way to find her," Tavo continued when he sensed the hesitation. "I have no credits or means of transportation. But I continue on, anyway. I won't let anything stop me. I must find her."

The young man hesitated a moment more, then nodded. "You look like her. I can see the resemblance. So, yes. I did meet and speak with her maybe a month ago. I gave her food and water, too. She was all alone and looked very tired."

"That was kind of you." Tavo made a show of gratitude, forcing a smile. "Do you know where she was going? Did she say?"

"She did. To a small village, but the name escapes me. North, somewhere, in the Westland. I think she was looking for someone." He shook his head. "I just can't seem to remember."

"Please take a moment to think about it. Maybe it will come to you. Anything at all will help . . ."

They stood together in silence for long minutes, the man with his head lowered and his eyes fixed on the ground while Tavo stared at him impatiently.

Finally, the man sighed and lifted his head, smiling. "No use. I just can't seem to remember it."

Tavo was enraged. His face reddened and his neck muscles corded. "Then I'll help you!"

Ten minutes later he had the answers he wanted. Tarsha was headed for the village of Emberen to find a man named Drisker Arc. She had not said why she was looking for him. She did not say what she intended to do when she found him. She did not say anything about who he was. Not that it mattered; he would find all that out eventually. What he'd learned was enough to give him a fresh start.

He would have thanked the man if he had told him all this willingly, but then maybe he really couldn't remember. In any case, it was too late. The magic of the wishsong had destroyed his mind and left him a babbling idiot standing in the road mumbling and jerking like a puppet hitched to invisible strings. Tavo did not laugh. It wasn't funny. The magic was serious business, and he took it that way. He could use it for anything if he was prepared to accept the consequences, and by now he was. He saw it as necessary, and that was sufficient to give him license to do what he had just done. The man would never be the same, but he had served his purpose.

Tavo considered leaving him as he was, but then thought it would be a kindness simply to put an end to him.

So he did.

A single note, high and haunting, and it was done.

He went on alone, completely unaware that his sister was now tracking him as he was tracking her. He would have found it ironic, had he known. He could have stopped where he was and waited for her to catch up to him, but he thought her arrived and settled in Emberen by now and had no reason to believe anything else. Least of all that she had returned to Backing Fell, had discovered what he had done to their parents and uncle, and had gone off to look for him as a result.

He had no reason to know that she was simply trying to help him and had never intended to abandon him. But maybe it didn't matter. By now he was well past complex rational thinking, and he could only manage situations as they happened. Being in the moment was simple, uncomplicated, real. He could handle what that required of him, but not much more. Thinking beyond the moment was no longer possible.

The trek went on for several more days, taking him along the shores of the Mermidon and onto the grasslands that spread east toward the distant mountains of the Dragon's Teeth. He wasn't entirely sure where Emberen was, but he took time to ask people now and again so he could continue. Most were happy to provide him with the help he needed. Only one or two turned away, but he let them go.

He stole a horse to help him with his search. He didn't have to hurt anyone to take the horse, and so he didn't.

He was trying to be good now.

Or at least to go unnoticed.

Fluken walked with him, singing and reciting poetry and offering words of advice. His voice was comforting, his presence reassuring. It was good to have a loyal friend. Fluken was always there for him.

And he always would be.

When the Elfstones went dark, Brecon Elessedil and Dar Leah hurried back to their airship, powered up the diapson crystals, and flew south in the direction of the vision the magic had shown them. Neither talked about it; neither questioned the decision to begin searching. They were simply doing what needed to be done in order to find Tarsha Kaynin. Dar was piloting the airship now, while Brecon used the Elfstones to help set their direction. But the Elfstones, after projecting a few final faint images of Tarsha, went dark.

Brecon shook his head as he lowered the Stones and turned to his companion. "I remember my father saying something once about movement disrupting the search power of the Stones. If either the searcher or the object of the search is moving too quickly—in an airship, for example—the Stones have difficulty tracking. Maybe that's so with Tarsha. We need to go to where we saw her with those men, in any case. Just to see what happened. We can try to find out more when we get there."

But it took them the rest of that day and the following two before they located the place they were looking for on the morning of the third day, and when they got there Tarsha was nowhere to be found. They walked the entirety of the area where the airship had landed, searching. After several minutes, Dar knelt in what seemed to be a patch of scorched earth. His hands moved across the damaged ground. "Look at this."

Brecon walked over. "Magic has been used here," Dar announced. "I can smell its residue."

He rose. "Tarsha defended herself against someone or something, then got back in her airship and set out again." He thought a moment. "I'm guessing, but maybe she's gone back to Emberen."

"But Drisker isn't there," Brecon pointed out. "You said so yourself. He *can't* be there. He's trapped in Paranor."

"She doesn't know that. She doesn't know anything about Paranor. Whatever happened with the search for her brother, it doesn't involve Backing Fell anymore or she wouldn't be flying the other way. Maybe she found him and maybe she didn't. Maybe she decided to go back to Drisker to see if he's returned. Maybe to ask his help, if she didn't find Tavo."

Brecon looked doubtful. "Awful lot of maybes. Let's try using the Elfstones again. Maybe this time we'll have better luck."

He retrieved the pouch from his pocket and dumped the Stones into the palm of his hand. Tightening his grip on them, he lifted his arm and pointed north, eyes closing. Moments passed, but there was no response.

Then, abruptly, an image of Tarsha sleeping in a bed surfaced once and was gone. Dar and Brecon exchanged glances. "Did you recognize anything?" the latter asked.

Dar nodded slowly. "The room was too dark to be sure, but it might have been the cottage Drisker moved to when his own was burned down."

"Burned down?"

"Long story. His house was attacked and burned not too long ago. He told me the story while we were flying back to Paranor. I didn't see much of the inside, but that might have been a bedroom."

Brecon clapped him on the shoulder. "So let's you and I go there and find out."

He nodded, but the expression on his face indicated he remained dissatisfied. His friend put the Elfstones away and walked back to the airship.

Moments later, they reboarded their airship and set out once more.

Tarsha was deep in slumber when the dream came. She felt its approach—a kind of tingling in the air, a drop in the temperature. A presence nudged up against her, and she was aware of someone standing next to her bed. She lacked any interest in knowing who it was and did not allow the dream to wake her. It was unobtrusive and only vaguely interesting and the simple fact of it was not enough to trouble her.

Then a voice spoke.

Wake up, Tarsha.

She ignored the command—and it was a command because there was considerable force behind it. But dreams are insubstantial, and she felt no urgency to respond.

Tarsha, you must wake!

Forceful now, more insistent and sharp-edged with concern. She felt a shift in the nature of its intent, and she wondered in a vague sort of way if this was a dream, after all.

Tarsha! Now! Look at me!

Definitely not a dream. She rose from the depths of her slumber, finding her way to consciousness even as the sleeping potion sought to hold her down.

Her eyes opened, and she was looking at Drisker Arc. Which, of course, was impossible. According to Clizia, he was imprisoned in banished Paranor. He didn't even look like himself, but rather appeared as a sort of insubstantial, ghostly version of the man he had been, his features shifting as if formed of mist, threatening to evaporate at any second. There was no weight to him. There was nothing to suggest he was anything but a wraith.

"Drisker?" she said, disbelieving.

Her voice was sluggish, weary. She was awake, but struggling to stay there. She took note of her darkened room; night had clearly fallen in Emberen. The sole light was provided by Drisker's ghost, its body radiating a strange whiteness that suggested glimmerings of movement seen most often from the corners of one's eyes.

With great effort, she raised herself on one elbow. "Drisker? What happened to you?"

The wraith knelt by her bedside but made no move to touch her. It seemed likely that he couldn't, that his form would not permit it. There was a shimmer to his body, and its smallest movements cast shadows across the walls and floor of the darkened bedroom.

I am trapped inside Paranor. Even his voice sounded otherworldly, a faint echo skidding off each word before trailing away. *I cannot stay long. The spell won't let me. But I have information you need to know.*

She stared at him. "How can you be here if you are trapped inside Paranor?"

Magic. This happened to a Druid once before, hundreds of years ago. His name was Cogline. He was a failed Druid, and his story is too long to tell. What matters is that magic placed him inside Paranor after the Druid Allanon had consigned it to limbo. While he was there, he could not escape on his own. But he discovered he could send an image of himself anywhere he wanted to—just as I am doing.

She nodded slowly. "So you're not really here. But this isn't your shade, either. You aren't dead."

I'm not dead. Clizia Porse wishes I were. It was she who did this to me. She tricked me while we were inside the Keep summoning its Guardian, and left me for dead while she fled. Once clear of Paranor's walls, she used her magic to send the Keep out of the Four Lands in order to keep it safe for her personal use later. She betrayed Paranor to the invaders, and the Druids are no more. She plans to rebuild the Druid order with herself as Ard Rhys. Listen to me now. Clizia is play-ing a game, and you are her pawn. She is not your friend.

"I don't understand. It was Clizia who helped me recover when I returned from searching for—"

She is not your friend! She is pretending. While you have been sleep-ing, she has been busy trying to use you against me. You will remember she has a scrye orb, just as I do. Well, she used it to contact me and offer me my freedom if I would bring her a powerful magic called a Black Elfstone. She showed me an image of you sleeping and hinted that you would be safe only so long as she got what she wanted. She keeps you with her to use as a bargaining tool. As long as she thinks I will bring her the magic she wants, she won't hurt you. But she won't wait long. I need you to get out of there as soon as you can, any way that you can.

Tarsha was fully awake now, sitting up and facing Drisker. "What about you?"

Do not worry for me. I will find a way out on my own. Go to Dar Leah, if you can find him. If not, go to the Elves and ask for sanctuary. Do it right away! But be very careful. If she finds out what you are try-ing to do, she will bind you so securely you will never get free! You will likely only have one chance, so wait until you find it. Then run and don't look back. She will come after you, but you must hide yourself.

"Not very comforting." Tarsha was struggling to accept that she had been wrong about Clizia, even given Drisker's earlier warnings and her own suspicions when the old woman had asked about the books of magic. She was angry for allowing herself to be deceived. "I don't know where Dar Leah is. Can you help me find him? Can you go to him as you've come to me and ask him to help?"

Coming to you wasn't as easy as it might seem. It don't know how many more times I can do so. I wouldn't have known I could do it at all if not for the Druid Histories. In their recordings, it told of how Cogline

was trapped within Paranor. But he found he could leave by project-
ing his spirit self, his almost-shade, out into the world. He only needed
direction and knowledge of his destination. He used it to search out
Walker Boh, the Druid of his time. But there was a price for doing so.
Each time he projected himself as a spirit, it took something from his
corporeal form. He became further weakened and diminished. If he
were to continue, he would disappear altogether. That is the risk I run,
as well.

"Then you must go now. Don't stay any longer. I can manage well
enough now that I know the truth about Clizia."

He rose and stood looking down at her, his face a mask of worry.
Be wary, Tarsha. Clizia Porse is extremely dangerous, and she would
snuff out your life without a second's hesitation if she thought it neces-
sary. You must not reveal I was here. You must not reveal what you
have learned from me. You must not let her discover what you intend.
This is asking a lot, but your life depends on how well you are able to
manage the charade I am asking of you.

She nodded. "I understand. Just try to find a way out quickly. I
need you. Tavo has killed all my family, and it may be that he intends
to kill me, as well. He was coming to Emberen, so I came back here to
find him. But now I don't know what to do."

Do only what I told you for now. That is enough. I will find a way to
reach you. Look for me.

And he was gone, vanished from her sleeping chamber as if he
had never been there, the room gone dark again, the air gone still
and empty. Tarsha stayed propped up on one elbow for a moment,
struggling with what she had been told, still not entirely sure it was
real. If she hadn't been a wielder of magic herself and aware of the
strangeness that magic could perform, she would have doubted her
senses. But she knew Drisker had been there, even if in diminished
form, and had spoken to her. She knew everything he had said was
true, and now she must do what she could to save herself.

She lay back slowly, eyes peering upward into the darkness. So
much had happened in so short a time. She had made the journey to
find Drisker and ask him to train her, and the Druid had taken her in.

The Skaar had invaded the Four Lands and taken Paranor, killing all the Druids. Drisker's home had been burned. Someone was trying to kill him, and now it appeared it was as he suspected—a fellow member of the fallen Druid order. Yet he had gone to Paranor, anyway, to try to save those he had once led. And she had gone in search of Tavo and found only the horrific death of her parents, the destruction of her home, and the enmity of her friends and neighbors.

What had she accomplished in all this?

Not much, she decided. Mostly, she had been struggling to find her way in the world, and her way remained a mystery. She remembered the old woman Parlindru, and her prophecies. The rule of three would be her fate, she had told her. Three times she would love, but only one would endure. Three times she would die, but each death would see her rise anew. And three times she would have a chance to make a difference in the lives of others and three times would do so, but once only would her actions change the world. So the old woman had told her—an old woman no one else saw, even though they had shared glasses of ale openly in a public house.

Tarsha's thoughts shifted away from the prophecies and returned to her present predicament. There was no time for worrying about something so abstract and distant. She had to deal with the problem at hand. She had to get herself beyond Clizia Porse's reach, but she had to plan carefully how to do so. She had to fool the old woman into believing nothing had changed while she prepared to slip away. She had to be smart. She had to be wary.

She could not afford to be afraid.

But it was too late for that. She was terrified.

Her eyes were suddenly heavy. The medication, she thought at once. A drug. Perhaps intended to keep her in line. But she needed to rest in any event, her recovery not yet complete. She would think about things once more when she woke.

Nevertheless, it took her a long time to fall back asleep.

FIFTEEN

Arraxin Dresch, first commander of the Federation army, assembled two companies of front-line soldiers in response to the orders from Ketter Vause, provisioned a transport, readied three warships, and set out for the Mermidon on the same day, as ordered. Even before departing, he sent a flit ahead to provide him with a more up-to-date report on the movements of the Skaar. Whatever lay ahead for his men, he intended to be ready for it.

He was a lifer, a career soldier with more than thirty years of service. He had begun as a lowly lieutenant but rose swiftly through the ranks to his present position, which he had assumed five years ago when his predecessor retired. He had fought in the Dwarf wars at the edge of the southern Anar and subdued an uprising of miners that threatened the Southland's monopoly on the metals needed for making weapons and airships. He had hunted Gnome raiders in the far Northland when they began interfering in the shipping of goods to and from the major Southland cities, smashing a ring of pirates that had virtually shut down the air lanes north and east. His record as a commander was impressive and distinguished, and he did not intend to let it be sullied by some barbaric foreign invader. Another few years and it would be time for him to take retirement, and he wanted his career to end well.

As a result, he was determined not to be overconfident or reckless in his present undertaking. He understood better than most the risks you ran as a Federation army commander. He understood the value of being able to ascertain when to hold back and when to strike hard. He relied on tactics and experience to see him through the tougher assignments. He chose his subordinates wisely, and he listened to what they had to say, even when they disagreed with him.

So it was now, as his command vessel led his fleet north out of the Southland and into the Borderlands, flying just west of the Duln Forests in a direct approach to Callahorn and the Mermidon. He stood with his subcommanders, Croix and Pressalin. Both had been with him for more than ten years, and each of them pretty much knew what to expect from the other. Ahead, the day was sunny and clear, and the sweep of the Duln's green canopy was bright with promise. They had flown most of the day yesterday and through the night, and now they were only a few hours from their destination. The three were discussing what lay ahead and what sort of difficulties or threats might be facing them.

"These Skaar can—how did you put it?" Edeus Pressalin was saying. He was a short, powerfully built man, blunt-spoken and aggressive. In battle, he had no equal, a warrior through and through. "Did you say they could appear and disappear at will?"

Dresch nodded. "So it is reported. But we have no firsthand experience with this because we haven't faced them ourselves."

"But they annihilated the armies sent against them by several Troll tribes," Croix observed. "They must possess some considerable advantage to achieve victories of that sort."

Tall, slender, and diffident, he was the more cautious and far thinking of the two subcommanders. To Dresch's way of thinking, he was the perfect complement to the more fiery Pressalin.

"Because they succeeded in defeating a couple of bands of disorganized, undisciplined savages?" Pressalin dismissed Croix's words with a wave of his hand. "A Federation command would have done the same."

"They managed to get inside Paranor and destroy the Druids,"

Croix added. "I don't recall that Federation forces have been able to do that."

"They are dangerous, and we need to think of them that way," Dresch interrupted before they could start arguing again. He valued their differences of opinion because they approached problems from polar-opposite mindsets, but it was also sometimes annoying. "We don't want to assume anything else until we've taken their measure."

Pressalin made another dismissive sound. "Doesn't matter to me if they can disappear or not. Give me a Federation phalanx with airship support, and I'll blanket the whole killing field with fire and iron, then see how many are left standing!"

"Well, we have to determine if they are a threat to the Federation, first." Dresch was looking out toward the first silvery glimmerings of the Mermidon. "Our orders are very clear. We are to defend the south shore of the river and not cross over. If the Skaar attempt to cross from their side, we can retaliate. But we need to be certain they have aggressive intentions."

"Because maybe they intend to enjoy a nice holiday after coming all the way from another continent? Any fool could ascertain their intentions, Commander. All we are doing is marking time until they make their move against us. And they will. There's no other reason for them to come this far south, no reason for them to have fought those Troll tribes. And I don't care what their precious princess says about their plans."

Dresch gave him a disapproving look. The way his subcommander was dismissing Ajin d'Amphere worried him. Pressalin clearly assumed a young woman could never be a match for him in battle, but Dresch was not so sure. He was a firm believer in never underestimating an opponent. If her skills in future battles were anything close to what they had proved to be thus far since coming into the Four Lands, she could be very dangerous, indeed. But he let his subcommander's comments pass for the moment. There would be time enough later—in private—to address his misguided sense of superiority.

"How will we set our defensive lines?" Murian Croix asked.

"Line the south banks with one company directly across from wherever the Skaar have set their camp. Divide the other company in two and place half on each wing, far enough back so that they cannot be seen from the other side of the river—a precaution against any attempt to outflank us. We will hold the airships safely behind the lines, ready to come to our aid should the need arise."

"But shouldn't we be worried about who might come to their aid?" Croix asked softly.

Dresch turned to him. "What do you mean?"

"How did they get all the way here from their homeland? Sailing ships? Perhaps. But what if they have airships, too? What if they have warships equal or superior to ours? How do we defend against that?"

The other two men stared at him. "There have been no reports of airships, Commander Croix," Pressalin snapped.

Dresch held up his hand to silence him and faced Croix. "Explain your thinking, Commander."

"The fact that no one has seen any Skaar airships doesn't mean they don't exist. This advance force, commanded by a warrior princess whom you admit you think is intelligent, has penetrated deep into the Four Lands. By marching all the way to the banks of the Mermidon, she has effectively cut herself off from any retreat or escape by foot. How much sense does it make for her to do that unless she has a method of escape beyond retreating on foot?"

"Go on." Dresch was experiencing a sudden misgiving.

"It makes sense for the Skaar to have airships waiting to carry them out, should the tide go against them. Also, they must know that we have such vessels. So even if they brought none with them, they will have commandeered some of ours by now."

Pressalin nodded slowly, grudgingly. "I agree. It would be insane to advance against the Federation if they didn't." He paused. "Unless they have no intention of advancing farther and are only doing what they told the Prime Minister they would."

"Even if that were so," Dresch replied, "they could not be certain a third party wouldn't attack them at some point. No, I feel certain that Murian has it right. The Skaar must have airships waiting in reserve."

"Which means," Croix interjected, "we need to be prepared to neutralize them if they attack us. Because besides having transports, they are likely to have warships, as well."

"Which also means," Dresch added pointedly, "that we must find and monitor them in case the need to neutralize them arises." He gave his subcommander a nod of approval. "Well reasoned, Murian. I am giving you the task of finding those ships and preventing them from acting against us. They are to be found and watched. Any antagonistic movement on their part is to be halted by an incisive and dominant retaliatory strike. Those are your orders, Subcommander."

The other man nodded. "I will make certain they are carried out. Give me command of two squads equipped with diapson-powered explosives and you will have no reason to worry."

They talked further, but the greater part of their plan was now in place. Dresch was grateful to Croix for thinking of the possibility of Skaar airships, but chagrined at his own failure to think of it first. He was reminded that Murian Croix was the logical choice to succeed him when he retired. Edeus Pressalin was too unimaginative and hotheaded to ever be first commander of the Federation army. Croix had always been better suited for the position.

At the same time, he didn't want to retire until he was ready. But what if he was incapable of realizing when it was his time? What if his age was already catching up with him and he couldn't see it? If Ketter Vause took notice of his failure to consider certain obvious possibilities, he might be forced to step down more quickly than he had planned. And he didn't like thinking that the choice might be made for him.

After his subcommanders had departed, he retired to his quarters to stand at his desk where maps of the Mermidon and its north and south banks were spread before him and studied them intently. Given that the Skaar had annihilated two Troll tribes and the entire Druid order, anticipating what they might do once their army faced his was important. Their small numbers—somewhere around a thousand, the reports said—did not suggest they would risk a full-blown assault against even a single Federation company, let alone two. They would be woefully outnumbered in unfamiliar territory. Moreover, the reports received so far indicated they found antiquated weapons—blades, spears, bows and arrows, and the like—adequate for modern battles. Which made no sense. Flash rips and rail slings, combined with cannons, would cut them to pieces. There was no reason to believe they would chance so much by launching an attack on a superior and better-equipped force.

On the other hand, they had somehow gotten through Paranor's considerable defenses—past walls and gates and wards of magic—to destroy virtually all the Druids within the Keep. They had essentially wiped the Druids and their order off the face of the Four Lands. Even Druid magic had not been enough to stop them.

It was troubling beyond words.

Dresch stepped away from the maps. He was going to have to be very careful in the days ahead.

The Federation command had arrived to establish camp across the Mermidon from the Skaar at midday of the previous day—a day after Ajin herself had returned from Arborlon. Now, as twilight was approaching and the Federation soldiers were once again preparing to settle in for the night, the Skaar princess stood with Kol'Dre on a rise to the north, less than a mile across from the other encampment, studying its impressive sprawl. The smells of cooking drifted in on the back of a warm south wind, and the shadowy figures of the soldiers were visible as they passed between tents and patches of firelight, busy at their tasks, seemingly heedless of the Skaar advance force.

Ajin was satisfied to leave it that way. She wanted them to think little or nothing of what the Skaar might be up to—less still of any potential danger. They should lose interest as routine and familiarity blunted the edges of their caution. She wanted them overconfident. They would begin to decide that nothing was going to happen, that this was a preventive action and the Skaar were doing exactly what Ajin had told Ketter Vause they intended to do. The Skaar had arrived and taken a defensive position, and any difficulties with the Federation would be settled by negotiation—by words rather than weapons.

After all, theirs was the strongest army in all the Four Lands, and what sense did it make to offer a challenge with so few aggressors? The Skaar numbered less than a thousand, and the contingent of Federation soldiers dispatched to keep an eye on them numbered more than twice that. Plus the Federation had warships and advanced diapson-crystal-powered weapons. Alone in the middle of enemy territory and facing a seasoned command, why would the Skaar even think of tempting fate by provoking an armed response? Only a fool poked a sleeping bear with a sharp stick.

An old bromide. But Ajin had never been one for bromides.

Yes, she wanted them confident and complacent for a few short hours. And then she wanted them angry and confused. Because frightened, confused men made mistakes.

"Are you ready, Kol'Dre?" she asked him. He had arrived back in camp the same day she had, albeit a bit later.

"Of course," he answered impatiently, a hint of reproof in his voice.

"Patience in all things. It was you who taught me that. Now, then, I want it done while they still think nothing is going to happen."

He nodded. "Are you sure about this, Ajin? Once we do this, there is no going back. They'll respond with everything they've got—and we don't have the full army behind us yet."

Ajin considered for a moment. It *was* a risk, striking at them like this. A big risk. But if they succeeded—which she was certain in her Ajin fashion they would—it would leave the Federation hierarchy deeply unsure about what it could expect its army to achieve in an all-out battle against the Skaar, and open up new possibilities for negotiations.

"If you do what you are supposed to, we won't need my father's intervention. By the time my father arrives, I will be in complete control of the situation. He would never consider dismissing me then, even with Paranor lost. Sten'Or will look like a fool."

"Sten'Or has his ear, Ajin," he said quietly. "Your father's man, his spy in your camp. I wouldn't be so sure of this."

She gave him a look. "My father's man? I don't think so. *The pre-*

tender's? Most definitely. Besides, things might not be entirely as Sten'Or believes them."

She skipped right past any attempt at an explanation. "I am entrusting you with our future, Kol'Dre. Am I right to do so?"

His look was dark and angry. "How can you even ask me that?"

She shrugged. "Because I worry. Too often you have to play the chameleon, Penetrator, and even I am not always sure of your true feelings. That girl, the one at Paranor. Allis. She caught your eye, didn't she? You thought I didn't know, but I did. I know everything about you, Kol'Dre. I had once thought you loved me. Now I wonder."

She watched him squirm—just as she had intended. "I do love you!" he insisted. "You know I always have. But it is hard to feel as I do and know it will never come to anything. So, yes, I was tempted. But it was only momentary. I killed her in the end, didn't I? I know where I belong. I know who my people are."

Cleverly said, Ajin thought. But how truthful was he being? Did even he know? Time to offer him an inducement. "There are other ways you can be with me," she said quietly, offering him a glimmer of hope.

He stared, surprised. "You have never said so before."

"Some things take longer than others. I have cared for you all along, Kol. You must have sensed that in the way I treated you. I did not take you to my bed because I did not want our relationship to change. And perhaps I was cruel in not doing so, especially when inviting so many others. But you are my favorite. You always have been."

He shook his head. "I wish I could believe that."

"Oh, so now I need to prove myself?" she snapped. When he started to protest, she gave him a hard shove. Let him squirm a little more. "No, don't deny it. You want to see proof of how I feel about you, but you'll just have to wait. I do care for you, and I don't want to feel any doubt about that reliance. And I need to be sure you can stay loyal to me, no matter what. I need to know, too, that in this one instance particularly—in this place and time—you will stay strong and do what you have said you will."

He studied her a moment. "This is about your father, isn't it? When he arrives, you want to know if I will still stand with you or side with him. Am I correct?"

She kept her expression neutral with considerable effort. "No. This is about you and me, Kol. This is about how the rest of this campaign is going to turn out. I have already suffered betrayal from Sten'Or, who goes behind my back to involve my father and bring me to heel. I am merely a woman, of course—young and weak and callow. Don't I need minding? Many still think so—from either misguided concern or jealousy at my success. I know this is true. And so do you.

"So, if I cannot depend on you to treat me differently—as an equal at the very least—I need to know. This is my life we are talking about. And your eyes have wandered once already on this expedition. I want to know it won't happen again. I want to know you will stand by me every time I am threatened, even if it means your own life might be at risk. I am alone, Kol. My soldiers are loyal, but not at the expense of defying my father. You are the only close friend I have and the only one I trust. So tell me. Am I mistaken to think so?"

Kol'Dre stared at her for a long moment, and then he dropped to one knee, keeping his gaze on her face. "You are not mistaken. Not now, or before. I will never betray or abandon you, Ajin—not even if it means defying your father. Not even if it costs me my life."

A surge of satisfaction rippled through her, and she reached down to take him by his shoulders and raise him back to his feet. "I am pleased to hear you say so," she whispered, not bothering to hide the strong emotions she was feeling. "I accept your word and will not question it again."

Alone, in the darkness, they embraced and held each other. Kol'Dre had responded to her prodding exactly the way she wanted him to. He was still hers in all the ways she needed him to be. Ajin found the moment incredibly satisfying.

Two hours later, Kol'Dre flew out of their encampment with five other Skaar soldiers, following the north bank of the Mermidon River west for several miles before crossing over to the south and turning back toward the campfires of the Federation army.

Ajin went with them, of course. Kol'Dre objected vehemently, reminding her of how dangerous this excursion was and what the cost would be if she were killed or captured. She smiled at his concern and told him not to worry. All would be well.

Because Ajin d'Amphere never asked her soldiers to do anything she wouldn't do herself—and after the disaster at Paranor, she felt she had something to prove.

Midnight along the Mermidon, and the sky was clear and filled with stars. A moon descending to the southeast gave that quadrant of the heavens an even brighter glow. The air was fresh and sweet with the smells of the forest and a river far enough removed from the city of Varfleet that none of its industrial stench was in evidence. A rustling in the grasses signaled the approach of some small nocturnal animal, its passage audible only because of the deep night quiet. Even the hunting owls and the smaller night birds made no sounds as they swooped from tree to tree, their winged flights nothing more than the passage of shadows.

The Federation guards on the western flank took disinterested note of everything, spread out in a precisely staggered pair of sentry lines stretched across the very perimeter of their encampment, keeping their eyes directed toward the space from which any danger might approach. They were seasoned veterans, and there was little they had not witnessed personally during their various tours of duty.

All were wakeful and doing precisely what they had been taught to do, the ones in the forward line keeping a lookout for what might move in the dark in front of them and the ones in the back keeping an eye on the ones just ahead of them.

A good system in most cases.

But not this night. Not when these men needed to be looking behind them.

The Skaar raiders—seven in all, including Ajin—swept in from the south, well behind the entire Federation encampment, cutting through a corridor that separated the watch on the western perimeter from the main body of the army. They had scouted the watch the night before to determine numbers and positions, so the Skaar knew

whom to look for and where. They were swift and sure—seven le-
thal ghosts invisible to those they passed, man and animal alike. They
started with the back six guards, coming up on them without a sound
and silencing them with knives driven straight through the base of
the skull or across the throat, lowering each dead body silently to the
earth before moving on.

Not one sound was given to alert the front line of seven. And all
seven went down in the same fashion as their brothers-in-arms, their
lives ended in seconds.

The Skaar assassins revealed themselves long enough to be sure
that all their victims were dispatched, then converged on Ajin and
Kol'Dre. No words were spoken. None were necessary. The plan had
been carefully detailed earlier, and all of them knew what to do. Retreating the way they had come, they melted into the darkness, disappearing as if they had never been there, making sure they were well
away before allowing themselves to become visible again.

They found their aircraft, boarded, and flew westward, their return following the exact same path as their arrival, crossing the Mermidon to the north bank when well upstream and winging their way
back to the Skaar encampment.

"Now we will see," Kol'Dre whispered in Ajin's ear as they drew
near to their own fires.

She nodded wordlessly. It was a big gamble, but a necessary one.
She needed it to work in order to set in motion the events that would
gain her the edge she needed over the Federation. And to manipulate
things once her father arrived with the rest of the army and learned
of her failure to prevent the loss of Paranor.

Because she knew what would happen otherwise. He would strip
her of her command and send her home in disgrace.

It was what she would do if she were him.

SIXTEEN

---◆---

BY THE TIME HE finally reached Emberen, Tavo Kaynin had been on the road for ten days. It would have taken longer, but in the end he had stolen a horse and ridden for the last three days of his journey. He was worn down both mentally and physically. He had killed twenty-three people—his parents and his uncle, Squit Malk, the men in the tavern, and the man on the road whom he had broken in order to find his sister—but it meant nothing to him. He no longer felt anything was wrong with killing when he could justify it by pointing to the ways he had been mistreated. Fluken was quick to reassure him that he should not allow others to abuse or mislead him—and that anyone who did should expect to pay a price. If the cost of their transgressions was their lives, it was unfortunate for them but no blame should attach to Tavo.

That was Fluken's thinking—and now Tavo's as well. That was who he was. He was, in short, a creature he would not have recognized a few months earlier. His mind no longer worked as it once had. Yes, he still sought his sister with the same relentless determination that had driven him from the beginning of his flight from Backing Fell, and nothing had changed to his way of thinking where Tarsha was concerned. She had betrayed him. She had left him in his uncle's care just as their parents had and then abandoned him. Like everyone else, she deserved the retribution he planned to deliver.

He entered Emberen, a ragged and soiled creature—his demons raging inside him and his desperate need to exact revenge on his sister beyond understanding—sitting astride the stolen horse he had ridden half to death. Fluken sat behind him, invisible to all who glanced his way, whispering steadily in his ear, urging him onward, prodding him relentlessly. Fluken was his friend, and he listened. But in truth, he felt the hold that Fluken once had on him beginning to weaken. He no longer needed Fluken as he had before. He better understood how powerful he was, how much in control of a magic that for so long had been in control of him. He understood that letting the magic guide him, that letting it *think* it was in control when actually it wasn't, allowed him to be its master.

He saw no problem with this reasoning. He saw nothing wrong with his newfound conviction that he had mastered something so powerful simply by deciding to go along with its urges.

It was early morning in the village and there were few people about. Most who saw him turned their heads. Most sensed in him something they did not want to get close to. But these people did not matter. They were no different from trees or storefronts or animals; he would suffer them but not allow them to deter him.

Twice he stopped people to ask after Drisker Arc—one a man, one a woman. Each time they were quick enough to respond, pointing him down the road and beyond the town. The woman gave more explicit guidance, however, telling him exactly where to go and what to look for. The Druid had moved recently, she revealed. Someone had burned down his cottage. There was in her eagerness to reveal what she knew both fear and loathing. Which of these emotions was for Tavo and which generated by mention of the man he asked after, it was difficult to say, but it didn't matter. A path to his destination had been provided, and Tarsha would be waiting not too far ahead.

He abandoned his horse just outside of town, climbing down gingerly and setting the animal loose to wander where it wanted. A man passing gave him a questioning look, but Tavo ignored him. The horse was a burden he no longer needed. The man hesitated as if to reprimand him for his lack of care, then appeared to decide against it and passed on. Others he encountered gave him looks, as well. He knew he was a sight, unwashed and bloodied, his clothes ragged, his face drawn and scarred. He had eaten nothing in three days save an apple and a half loaf of bread another traveler had offered him. He had found water easily enough, but nothing else. Not that either food or water much mattered. He wasn't thinking of sustenance and didn't miss it. All of his attention was focused on reaching Tarsha and putting an end to this part of his journey.

Fluken walked beside him, jaunty and fresh-faced. He never seemed to change, not even in the smallest way. No dirt ever appeared on his face or hands or clothes. He never ate anything—at least not that Tavo saw—preferring to sit back and watch his friend eat. Perhaps it was his unselfish nature that caused him to forgo food for the benefit of his companion. Perhaps he just didn't care all that much about food. It was hard to say. Everything about Fluken was confusing and vague save his insistence on tracking down Tarsha.

They passed out of Emberen, leaving its shops and businesses behind, and moved into a residential district where stretches of forest separated the houses and outbuildings. A pair of children came running out of a patch of woods off to one side, caught sight of him and hesitated, then raced back into the trees. A dog barked at him from the end of a heavy chain. The dog was big and dangerous-looking, but Tavo just stared it down. In moments the dog had turned back, slinking away with a low growl.

When he reached Drisker Arc's cottage, he recognized it right away from the description the woman in the village had supplied. It was set well back from the road, a small building of white-painted boards and a brick chimney. A broad covered porch ran the length of the front side, enclosed by an ornate metal railing and a broad wooden capstone. A pair of ancient straight-back chairs and two small tables occupied the available space and seemed entirely insufficient for the job.

Tavo stood looking at the cottage for long minutes, trying to decide what to do. He needed to find his sister, but he didn't want her to see him and flee. He thought to call out, then stopped himself. Better just to walk up to the door and knock.

He was on his way up the gravel pathway when the front door opened and an old woman clothed in black appeared on the porch. She didn't see him at first; her clear intent was to sit in one of the chairs. But even without looking at him, she seemed to sense him and turned. And the expression on her face stopped him in his tracks.

"Who are you?" she demanded in a tone of voice that suggested he ought to answer.

"I'm looking for my sister," he said.

"Why look here?"

"This is Drisker Arc's home, isn't it? I was told she was coming here."

The old woman studied him a moment. "What is your sister's name?"

Tavo was growing irritated. He didn't like being questioned, and it felt like this delay might be purposeful. What if Tarsha was already slipping out the back?

"Tarsha," he said.

The old woman shrugged. "She's not here. She was, but now she's gone."

Suddenly Tavo was infuriated. The old woman was lying; he could feel it. She was trying to help his sister.

"I know she's inside. You better tell her to get out here!"

"You better watch your tongue."

Tavo smiled. "You don't know what will happen if you don't do what I say! You don't have any idea what I can do."

The old woman smiled back. She took a few steps along the porch and came down to the bottom of the steps. "No, I don't. But I know what I can do, and it would be a whole lot worse than anything you could possibly imagine. I know about you. Your name is Tavo, isn't it? Are you like your sister, Tavo? Do you have magic, too?"

Tavo's face went dark with fear and anger. There was something about this old woman that made him pause. Even Fluken, standing off to one side, seemed hesitant. He did nothing to urge Tavo on, neither moving nor speaking as he stood there, eyes on the old woman.

"Now do as I say," she said quietly, "and don't press your luck. I have magic, too, Tavo. And I have spent many more years than you have discovering what it can do."

Then, abruptly, the door behind her opened, and Tarsha stepped out onto the porch.

Tarsha was still bleary from her meeting with Drisker—real or imagined—the night before, but she had heard the voices, and even in the warm cocooning wrap of her slumber she recognized Tavo's. She had not believed it at first, but as she became more certain she knew she had to go to him. She forced herself all the way awake, climbed from the covers, and walked through the cottage to the front door, still in her nightdress, listening as Clizia and Tavo conversed, and growing increasingly concerned over the tone of their voices.

When she opened the door and stepped onto the porch, both stopped talking instantly.

She gave Clizia a look. "I want to talk to him," she said. "I have to."

The Druid gave her a doubtful look, then stepped back to clear a path. Tarsha came down the steps and walked past her. "Hello, Tavo," she said when she was a dozen paces away.

She stopped, waiting on him. His face was hard to read. There was anger, but confusion, as well. As if now that he had found her, he didn't know what to say. Or didn't know if this meeting was even what he wanted. He stood there for long moments without speaking or moving, his eyes fixed on her.

"You left," he said finally.

She nodded. "To find help for you. To find the Druid who lived here so he could teach me how to help you with your magic."

He shook his head, an angry look in his dark eyes. "No, you ran. You ran as fast and as far as you could to get away from me! You abandoned me to those creatures that called themselves my parents! And you left me to that monster, that . . ."

She could see him spiraling out of control, and she held up her hands quickly to placate him. "I know. I returned to Backing Fell after you left, Tavo. I know what you did to them, and why. I know you are hurting. You have to let me help you."

"You don't want to help me!" he screamed at her. "You wish I was dead! You *hoped* I was dead!"

She shook her head. "No, I don't wish that. I never wished that. I just didn't know what to do to help you. You told me to go away when I came to see you, even though I didn't want to. I knew you were in trouble, but Mama and Papa couldn't see it. But now I know better what the magic is and how it works. I know how to manage it—and how to help you manage it. Just let me . . ."

Tavo's fists were balled up at his sides, and his entire body was rigid. "You filthy liar! Fluken knows! He knows you're lying! He can see you're trying to hide the truth, and he tells me!"

She looked to where he had glanced, but there was no one there. Who was Fluken? She tried again. "What can it hurt to let me try to make things better, Tavo? What if I really can make the pain go away and the magic behave? What if I really can help you? Tavo, I love you. You're my brother. I would never leave you and not come back. Can't you see that?"

And for a moment, it seemed he could. The tenseness left his body, and his face softened. He was back to being the boy he had been all those years ago when they were still close—before their parents had sent him to their uncle's farm to live. He blinked rapidly, tears welling in his eyes, and he shook his head as if waking from a dream. "Tarsha?" he asked softly.

She nodded, sensing she still had a chance. "It's me, Tavo. I'm glad you've found me. I will do everything I can to help you. I will try hard to make you feel better. We can work together . . ."

He seemed to be listening, responding, then suddenly he wasn't doing either. His expression became distracted and then turned vacant. With a swiftness that was terrifying, he transformed from the boy of ten years ago to the enraged young man who had come to find her. All the softness disappeared, and the hard look that replaced it was so frightening it caused her to take a step back.

"Tavo . . ." she whispered but got no further.

"You witch!" he screamed at her. "You were going to trick me again, weren't you? Do you think I am so stupid I cannot see it?" His

fists opened and his fingers crooked like claws. His arms came up threateningly and thrust toward her.

"Tarsha!" Clizia Porse called in warning.

"Leave us!" Tarsha shouted back. "Tavo and I must settle this ourselves!"

She was conscious of Clizia's sharp hiss of disapproval; then the other woman stepped away. Tavo was screaming something at her— sound and fury that defied any comprehension—and abruptly the madness that had recaptured him released in the howl of his wishsong. His wild magic slammed into her with such force that she was thrown backward onto the gravel walkway. She did not lose consciousness, but she was dazed and weakened by the force of his attack. Even so, her own magic quickly sprang to her defense—a wall of sound that blocked Tavo's attack and shattered his efforts.

Her brother staggered back but recovered quickly, staying upright as his eyes cleared, and he came at her again. His power was stronger than she remembered, more fully developed and less raw. It slammed her down once more, even before she could regain her footing, pinning her in place as he advanced. Wrapping herself in a new defense, she rolled away from his strike and managed to get to her knees before he changed tactics. But this time she was ready for him, and she lashed out in retaliation. Their magic collided in midair before bursting apart in an explosion of light and energy so powerful it shook Drisker's cottage to its foundation and knocked Clizia backward out of view.

Tarsha rose once more, her body aching. Her brother glared at her, breathing hard, trying to recover himself. "Tavo, stop this!" she cried to him. "We need to talk! There's no point in fighting."

But her brother wasn't having any part of it. He attacked again, his magic coalescing into a barbed whirlwind that would have torn her apart had it been able to reach her. Yet it still came close enough to leave the exposed skin of her hands and face torn and bloodied and her body bruised. She broke his attack once more, but now she was nearly played out. She still hadn't recovered from her journey; she was still in need of rest. He was too strong for her. If the attack continued, he would destroy her.

Which, she realized for the first time, was precisely what he wanted. He was far beyond reason. Like her parents and her uncle, she was going to die.

So she had to find a way to bring him under control physically, to stop the attacks and make him listen to her. Looking into his eyes as he prepared to come at her one more time, she found no hint of the brother she had known as a child, no indication of affection or trust. He was a soulless monster consumed by rage and hate and driven by a mindless need for revenge.

She felt herself lose hope.

Tavo's voice rose to a crescendo and hammered into her. It struck her with such force that it effortlessly broke apart her defenses, throwing her a dozen feet into the air, holding her in place three feet off the ground, and then slamming her down. The air went out of her, her vision wavered in a wash of pain and sadness, and everything went black.

From where she crouched at the corner of the porch, Clizia Porse watched Tavo Kaynin walk forward to stare down at his fallen sister. She was probably already dead—and if she weren't, she soon would be. Tavo wasn't looking at his sister with anything that even approached compassion. He was clearly trying to determine whether she really was dead or if more was needed to make her so.

So Clizia acted, knowing that if she let him end Tarsha's life, it would ruin everything she needed to accomplish with Drisker Arc. And she wasn't about to let that happen just to satisfy some half-mad sibling's insane compulsion.

At the same time, she was wondering if perhaps there might be a use for him. After all, he did possess the most powerful magic she had seen in many a moon. If it wasn't the wishsong itself, it was a close approximation. And if it was the wishsong, that meant both brother and sister were descendants of the Ohmsford bloodline—perhaps the only ones left in all the Four Lands. Which would explain Drisker Arc's decision to accept Tarsha as his student.

But whatever she was going to do about Tavo Kaynin, she had to do it fast and she had to handle it in the right way. No ordinary approach would work with someone this irrational.

She rose, watching for any threatening movements from him, but he just stood staring down at his sister, seemingly oblivious.

"Tavo!" she called.

"Go away!"

"Step away from Tarsha. Let your sister be."

"I'll let her be when she's dead! And she's not quite dead yet."

Clizia exhaled. Good news, if so. "Why don't you hear me out first? I have a use for Tarsha. An important use, which might be good for you, as well. So perhaps you would consider waiting a bit longer to kill her? I know she deserves to die, but why not let her live awhile in expectation of what might happen? If you kill her while she is unconscious, it will mean nothing. She won't have a chance to regret the way she hurt you. Tavo! Look at me."

Tavo looked, his gaze blank, his face expressionless once more. The anger was gone, and he no longer seemed to be interested in talking to whatever ghosts accompanied him. Whoever Fluken was, he seemed to have faded from his consciousness for the moment.

"You and I are not so different." She spoke quietly, her voice modulated to be persuasive and calming. She knew how to do this, and during the long years of her life it had served her well. "We have both suffered grave hurt at the hands of others, our lives tortured and twisted by those who wanted us gone. We have both endured injustice and misunderstanding through no fault of our own. You have great magic. So do I. You have suffered because of how you have struggled with it. So have I. We are so much more alike than we are different. Give me a chance to tell you more."

She was pleading with him as an equal, a fellow sufferer at the hands of an amorphous, faceless array of enemies. Ingratiating herself by identifying with him and letting him identify with her.

Tavo stared at her a minute and then nodded.

"Your sister said she would try to help you master your magic, to find a way to bring it under control. I will do much more than that. I will teach you *how* to use it, so that it will serve your purposes. I will give you a way to vent your hatred and gain revenge over those who would make your life miserable. I will give you access to a power you have not even begun to dream of! You have power in your voice, granted—but you don't yet understand all the ways that power can be used. Even more to the point, you don't have all the tools you need to accomplish the great things you were born to do."

His brow knit and his face darkened. "Why would you do this?"

"Why not, if you can help me in return? If it allows us to help each other? Do we not need to band together, we who are the victims of uncaring parents and neighbors and friends? We do not deserve to be victims; we should be victors!"

He was nodding with her now, agreeing with her assessment, even though she was doubtful he really understood what she was saying. She resisted the urge to step closer to him, standing hunched over in her dark robes to make herself appear less threatening, more innocuous.

"Here is what I promise you," she continued, now that she had his undivided attention. "Stand with me, Tavo, and I will give you power that will allow you to punish all those who might hurt you! I will give you a chance to discover how you might change the very world you live in! No one will ever lock you away again. No one will ever threaten you again. Others will stand back from you in awe, and they will fear you. They will treat you with respect! This is what I will give you if you will let me make use of your sister for a short time."

She had no intention of doing any of this, but her plans were not fully formed as yet, so mostly she was buying time for herself and Tarsha. This brother of hers was clearly insane and incredibly dangerous. That she could bend him to her will, persuade him to her cause, was a risk she must take for now. She must lead him to believe she would do all the things she had promised. But in the end, he was expendable and must be eliminated if for no other reason than to assure her personal safety.

"You could be lying," he said, as if reading her mind.

"There would be no point in lying." She came forward a few steps now, hands held out as if in supplication. "You are too powerful to be lied to, and I would be a fool to trifle with such power. Your magic is familiar to me, and there is no limit to what it can do. If I help you to master it, you must agree to help me. This is the way things should be, Tavo. Now step back from your sister and let me see to her."

He did so, arms hanging limply at his sides, head lowered as his eyes fixed on her. There was still something there between them, Clizia judged—still a hint of caring that transcended the madness that otherwise ruled his existence. "Fluken" would attempt to change this, and she must be careful to see that this other self, this imaginary friend, did not interfere with her plans.

But there were ways to do this, and no one knew them better. "Pick her up and carry her inside," she told him. She had walked over, bent down, and found a pulse. Weak, but there. "Gently, Tavo. She is the key to everything. I will explain it all to you once we are inside. There will be a bed for you in which to rest and sleep. There will be food to eat and ale to drink. And medicine, Tavo. Medicine to help calm you and keep your thoughts directed as they should be. Come now, pick her up."

Tavo did so, cradling her in his arms and lifting her effortlessly from where she lay on the ground. "Tarsha," he whispered. "I'm sorry for what I did."

He started for the porch, walked up the steps, and disappeared through the open door. Clizia Porse followed, allowing herself a surreptitious smile. He was hers now, and she would make certain he remained so.

SEVENTEEN

LATER THAT EVENING, IN the city of Varfleet, a boy of capable skills but limited means was watching a game of Pickroll. The game was taking place in the gambling room of the Sticky Wicked Hall of Chance, a popular gaming palace down near the docks, where men of hard lives and questionable morals gathered nightly to find new ways to part with their money and their patience. Because the loss of the first frequently led to the loss of the second, big men with scars and frowns stood against the walls of the room at regular intervals in spaces specifically designated for them, each providing a clear view of and a short path to the gaming tables should trouble arise.

All of which provided Shea Ohmsford with a small financial opportunity he was quick to recognize.

It worked like this. Servers employed by the Sticky Wicked were there to provide food and drink to the patrons, and it did not do to get underfoot when they were on the floor. On the other hand, they were not required to perform other types of fetch and carry, so they made it a hard-and-fast rule not to—and signs above the serving counter and on each of the walls of the room said as much. They also described in graphic terms what could happen to you if you made the mistake of trying to sidestep the rule.

But sometimes other forms of fetch and carry were necessary, and young Shea Ohmsford was quick to recognize an opportunity. Messages needed to be conveyed to friends and family, offering reassurance that long hours of absence did not signal permanent abandonment. Or pleas for help needed to be speedily dispatched for players who found themselves suddenly short of credits. Or excuses needed to be proffered for failure to appear for work. Then there were the items to be fetched: medicines to sharpen the mind and quicken the hand—none of which were on the gaming hall menu of food and drink—or fresh clothing to replace that damaged in a brawl.

And so on and so forth.

Shea Ohmsford—small and slender and wiry and easily able to navigate the sea of larger bodies—was there to provide any of those services, circling the room with catlike ease to respond to a beckoning hand raised by an eager customer. And all for a coin or two—though sometimes more since the market was fluid and the law of supply and demand reigned supreme.

The boy worked at the sufferance of the establishment, but the owner liked him and knew him to be dependable. She understood the need for the services he offered, yet preferred that it be Shea who carried them out, since the boy represented no threat and was well known about the quarter to be honest and circumspect about what he saw or heard—all good qualities for anyone who worked in a place like the Sticky Wicked.

Shea Ohmsford was not particularly fond of the work. It was mostly boring, payment was spotty, and the gaming room's players were frequently unpleasant. Nor did he need the credits. The black-cloaked grandfather he had encountered a few weeks back had paid him handsomely, and he had squirreled that money away against a future that was always uncertain. But he did not want to use those credits to live off because they were his stakes in a larger future that waited a few years farther down the road. So he worked both to make enough to survive from day to day and because he knew that if you expected to find opportunities you had to make space for them in your life. Better to keep your hand in even when things were going well, at a place where keeping your eyes and ears open might present you with such opportunities. He had grander plans for his life than spending the rest of it in Varfleet, and whether those plans came to fruition or not it was better to avail himself of the chance that they might.

Tonight was an ordinary sort of night—the number of players about average and the number of tables in use about the same. Shea was watching with half an eye for a raised hand, but for now they were few and far between. He could have spent the night in bored disinterest, but instead he had found something to help him pass the time.

At a table not ten feet away, a game of which he knew almost nothing was under way. Pickroll, it was called. Only men and women with credits to burn played it. The stakes were high and the odds against winning long. The game involved the use of both cards and dice, along with expenditures of large numbers of credits during the course of play. Three of the four men sitting at the table were Sticky Wicked regulars—men of questionable practices in their ordinary lives (some of those practices legal and some not). All three were well known for their skill at games of chance, and each possessed the experience to know and anticipate how other players might react in any given situation. None were men Shea Ohmsford much cared for, although all of them, at one time or another, had enriched the boy with credits in return for services rendered.

The fourth man was the wild card, a newcomer to the gaming hall and perhaps to Varfleet, as well. Shea knew he had never seen the man before, nor seen the fetching creature that clung to him as if to imprint herself upon his body. She slid over and around him as if she were oiled, and draped herself about him like a second skin. She was stunningly beautiful—long and lithe, with the most flawless white skin and catlike golden eyes Shea Ohmsford had ever seen. She laughed and whispered and winked at her companion in a teasing fashion, but never with anything that suggested an attempt to distract him.

Still, the dock marshal sitting directly to the newcomer's right had apparently begun to grow weary of her. Leaning back, he coughed loudly and looked the newcomer directly in the eye. "Your pretty cloak appears to need its drawstrings tightened," he growled. "Better straighten her up before she falls on the table."

The dock marshal was a lean, rawboned man of considerable size—fully six and a half feet and 270 pounds at a minimum. When he spoke, his voice rumbled out of his belly like the low growl of a furnace burning hot. His glower was deep and threatening, and his big hands were knotted before him in fists.

The newcomer nodded but did not otherwise respond. He was not a big man, but he was a commanding presence nevertheless. He wore his dark hair long and tied back and sported a closely shaved beard and mustache. He was a cool one, the boy thought. He had been winning steadily, never taking his eyes off the dice or the cards, humming softly now and again, giving the astonishingly fetching woman who hung on him little more than the occasional glance and wink. He did so now from beneath his heavy brow, his eyes the color of storm-clouded skies. The silken creature that clung to him went instantly still, fixing herself in place and staring directly at the dock marshal.

The dock marshal returned her look with a baleful stare and went back to his cards. "Shouldn't allow her at the table, in any case. She's not a player. She's nothing but a bit of pretty fluff. You want to play the game, you should play it alone."

The newcomer shrugged. "I can quit now, if you wish. All right with everyone if I cash out and leave you to it?"

He glanced casually about the table. Heads remained lowered, but the disgruntled murmuring was unmistakable. None of them would be happy if he left now, carrying away almost all of their credits. And the other two men were no better to cross than the dock marshal— one thought to be a successful assassin attached to one of the guilds, and the other a high-placed member of the city's governing body of Ministers and a member of the Federation military.

The dock marshal glanced at his companions and made a dismissive gesture. "Never mind. Leave it for now. But as for you . . ." He looked again at the newcomer's sinuous companion momentarily and then at the newcomer. "Don't bring her back tomorrow. You hear?"

The newcomer glanced at the woman draped across his shoulders. "Hear that, Seelah? My friend the dock marshal doesn't much like you, I'm afraid."

Seelah's features tightened, and her strange slanted eyes found the dock marshal's. For the first time, the boy noticed them change color, from golden to a smoky crimson. He watched in fascination as her lips parted with a soft hiss, revealing wickedly long and razor-sharp teeth—better suited to a Parkasian wolf than a sensuous girl.

The dock marshal hesitated, then looked away quickly.

What is she? the boy wondered.

The newcomer cleared his throat. "Regardless of who does or doesn't return tomorrow, it's one more round tonight for me, and then I'm through. Make your best play, friends."

The other three glared even harder, their expressions bitter and their eyes filled with malice. No one spoke. The dock marshal had the deal and the roll, and so he commenced the round. All of them turned their attention back to the game. The dock marshal won the first hand and began to smile, sensing that things were turning his way at last, while the other two men continued to fume. The newcomer seemed almost disinterested.

"Boy!" he called suddenly, turning to Shea, his hand beckoning.

Shea hesitated, not sure for a moment if he had heard right. Then, seeing the other continue to make impatient gestures, he hurried over. When he was beside the newcomer, the woman with the cat eyes slid close to him and placed a slender white hand on his shoulder.

"Your name?" the newcomer asked softly.

"Shea Ohmsford."

A long stare. "You wouldn't be having me on, would you?"

The boy shook his head. "That's my name."

"Well, well. Small world, it seems." He laughed softly. "So, Shea Ohmsford, are you for hire this evening?"

"Of course," the boy answered, growing marginally bolder. "What's your wish?"

The cards were being dealt, the dice placed in front of the military man. The newcomer bent close, and his voice dropped to a whisper. "How would you like to engage in a bit of excitement? Something you've not been asked to do before?"

"You'd have to pay well," Shea said at once. "More than you've probably been asked to pay before."

The newcomer smiled. "An excellent riposte. Well done, young Shea. Are you ready or not?"

"Stop all that whispering and play the game!" the dock marshal snapped. "Chat with the boy later, if you admire his company so much."

The woman slid off the newcomer like a sheet of silk and onto Shea, wrapping herself protectively about him. Her deep-auburn hair tumbled over his shoulders and brushed his face. The boy went rigid all over at the touch of her body enfolding his, and his eyes fixed on the newcomer. "She's awfully close," he whispered. "Can you ask her to move?"

The man smiled once more. "Cross the room to the doors leading to the street," he replied. "When things start to get rough, as I think they will, I will signal you with a raised arm. When I do, scream *Fire!* as loud as you can. *Fire!* Scream it. Then throw open the doors and step away from them at once."

"If I do that," the boy replied, eyeing the newcomer, "I'll lose my job."

The other smiled. "I don't think so. But if you do, I'll give you a new one. With better pay."

He reached into his pocket and produced a leather pouch. The boy could tell by the bulge of its contents that it was chock-full of credits. A second windfall in one month, he thought—and this one perhaps larger than the one resulting from his encounter with the black-cloaked grandfather. Still, he hesitated.

"Just shout *Fire* and nothing more?"

"And step clear of the doors."

"Are you playing or not?" the purported assassin demanded, sharp eyes fixed on them.

"I've been watching you," the newcomer said to Shea, a hint of urgency in his voice. "You're a sharp young lad. A better future than this awaits you. A richer future. Take a chance, and don't disappoint me."

Seelah slid off the boy's back and onto the shoulders of the newcomer once more. Her eyes had turned a curious fragmented gold and green, and they glittered like gemstones as they watched him.

Shea accepted the bag and tucked it away. "I won't," he managed.

The entire conversation had taken no more than a minute, and no one had heard a word save the newcomer and the boy. Shea backed away into the crowd and then moved off as if to fulfill whatever errand had been entrusted to him. Behind him the game resumed. Everything returned to the way it had been before—as if time had stopped for a few moments and then started up again. Yet Shea Ohmsford knew something important had happened, even if he had no idea yet what it was.

At the very least, he was about to make a change in his life, and he had to hope it was a change for the better.

He edged his way through the crowd of men and women, sidling past the gaming tables until he had reached the entry. Once there, he positioned himself by the closed doors and waited, a rush of expectation surging through him, wondering what would happen next.

For long moments, nothing did. He waited patiently, on edge for the disruption the newcomer had promised, with one eye on the table and the other on the closed doors. The minutes passed. He found himself wondering just what it was he thought he was doing. What did he know about this man and his . . . his creature? Neither one might be anything like what he thought them to be. This was dangerous ground he was treading, allowing himself to become involved in a scheme that could very easily get him killed. He was violating his own rule about avoiding such situations, even if he was a child of the streets and used to such risks. The credits mattered, but not at the cost of his life. He resisted the urge to look around the room and see if anyone noticed what he was doing, just standing there. Someone must, he reasoned. He began to feel self-conscious about his presence and his inactivity, and then he began to worry that some other patron would summon him and he would have to find a way to ignore them without calling attention to himself.

Then all of a sudden he noticed that Seelah was no longer clinging to the newcomer. She had disappeared.

He glanced hurriedly about the room, searching for her, but she was nowhere in sight. He had not seen her go. Nor, apparently, had anyone else. Or if they had, they were not remarking on it or responding in any way. Everyone's attention seemed to be somewhere else.

A moment later the round ended, and the newcomer gathered up his credits, shoving them into his pockets as he rose. Instantly the other men began shouting at him, their accompanying gestures expressing their displeasure. Even from across the room, Shea Ohmsford could tell they were not going to permit the newcomer to take his winnings and leave without giving them a further chance to win them back.

From their positions against the wall, a few of the big men who served the establishment as peacekeepers stirred to life. The dock marshal was on his feet now, too, blocking the newcomer's way. The other two men were starting to rise with him. A knife blade glimmered in the assassin's hand.

The newcomer's arm shot upward, his closed fist opening to release dozens of tiny fireflies that scattered everywhere, their tiny bodies glowing a brilliant white against the gaming room's backdrop of shadows and smoke and gloom.

An instant later the fireflies burst into explosions of flame.

"Fire!" Shea Ohmsford cried out.

Men and women were already overturning tables and chairs and surging for the exits. Shouts and screams filled the Sticky Wicked, bodies slamming up against one another and the furniture and walls as patrons and servers alike sought to escape. Bits of fire tumbled from the ceiling, and the room was in chaos.

As the gambler had instructed, Shea threw open the doors to allow for easy flight, thinking as he did so that the other had been right—none of this was his fault or was likely to get him fired. He just barely managed to get out of the way as the first members of the surging crowd reached the entry and disappeared into the night. Outside the building, passersby were gathering, trying to see what was happening, heads turning and people slowing to gawk, hampering the escape of those inside and adding to the general confusion.

Across the room, the four Pickroll players were all moving. The boy caught a glimpse of the assassin's blade as it was thrown, but it was the dock marshal the knife struck. He grunted at the impact and charged the assassin in response. The military man was calling for help in restoring order, his voice booming out. But no one was paying attention and no one was stopping, military or otherwise.

The newcomer had backed away from the table and was moving across the room toward Shea. But the dock marshal and the assassin both saw what he intended, and instantly broke apart to come after him with long knives in hand.

What they might have done if they had caught up to him would forever remain a subject of speculation, because before either pursuer could manage to lay hands on the newcomer a massive form sprang up from out of nowhere—seemingly from the floor itself—to intercept them. A moor cat of enormous size filled the space separating the pursuers from the pursued, all bristling fur and wide-spread jaws, teeth gnashing as it roared, great claws tearing at the wooden floorboards. Another man might have tried to face it down, but neither of these two cared to try. With cries of mingled fear and anger, the dock marshal and the assassin began scrambling for the protective barrier of the serving counter.

Within seconds they had disappeared into the kitchen, and the moor cat had vanished. And just as suddenly the newcomer was beside Shea, taking his arm and steering him out the door and into the night.

"Now, that was exciting, wasn't it?" He shouted to be heard above the din of the crowd surging now through the streets. He glanced at the boy. "You handled your part perfectly. I was right, wasn't I? You won't lose your job over anything that happened tonight. You're a quick and willing lad. I'd like to hire you for something more."

They stumbled ahead, the man turning him toward the docks.

Shea broke free of the grip on his arm and began walking on his own, keeping slightly apart. "I'll at least listen to your offer, but let's settle up on tonight's work first. Is your promise of a better job and a richer future still good?"

The newcomer laughed. "Of course! I always keep my promises."

"You'd be the first," the boy muttered under his breath as they disappeared into the shadows of the buildings and hurried on toward the docks.

Their passage through the lower end of Varfleet was swift and silent. They kept to the seclusion of back alleys and side streets, and when they were almost to the water Shea's companion turned to him.

"Do you have somewhere to go tonight?"

Shea hesitated, uncertain where this was leading. "I have a place to sleep, if that's what you mean."

Though what he had was the back room of an inn that was mostly used for storage but contained a bed he was allowed to sleep in as payment for sweeping out the front rooms and cleaning up the trash each morning. But that was for him to know and not this stranger.

"Come with me. I have a bed for you and we can talk a bit about your new job."

The boy shook his head. "I don't need it. I have my own place."

"A place known to the gaming house owner and soon to be known by those men who will start to put two and two together."

"They're not that smart. I wasn't doing anything odd. They won't even remember me."

"They'll remember you were the last one who talked to me and want to find out if you know anything. No, you shouldn't go back tonight. Come with me."

Shea frowned. The offer troubled him. This gambler was too quick to want him close. "I don't even know your name."

The man laughed. "Well, you ought to know a man's name before you agree to work for him. I'm Rocan Arneas."

Shea had never heard the name, but he nodded in response without making any further effort to follow the man. "I don't know."

He was thinking of the bag of credits in his pocket and the long knife strapped to his ankle. It didn't pay to be careless in the Dock District. Rocan Arneas seemed sincere, but you could never be sure. Shea hadn't survived on his own for this long by being foolish, and he wasn't about to abandon the habit now for the promise of a few more credits.

Then again, the lure of additional credits kept him from disappearing into the night. Like anyone in need, he could be tempted.

Rocan had moved over to stand close to him, and Shea realized he was not as big as he had appeared earlier. He was sturdy but not tall, and solid rather than large.

"I live right here," he said, gesturing to the building behind him. "Doesn't look like much on the outside, but that's to prevent those who might wish me harm from finding me."

"Like those men tonight."

"They're not too happy with me just about now, even though they have no reason for it. I took their credits in a game of chance—one I just happen to be better at playing than they are. But that doesn't change things. There are others, too—men of even worse dispositions and intentions. So I try not to let them know where I sleep."

"But you're telling me. And you barely know me."

Rocan nodded. "Listen to me, Shea Ohmsford. I was serious before. I have work for you, if you want it. I will pay you well. I saw the way you worked the room—a boy with sharp eyes who takes everything in and makes up his own mind. I have uses for those skills. Don't misjudge my intentions and don't disappoint me in my evaluation of you."

Shea pulled a face. "When you've got no one, you've got to be good at looking after yourself. If I trip up, no one's going to pick me up and put me back on my feet."

"I understand that well enough. We're not so different, you and I."

Shea thought it unlikely, but gave him a nod, anyway. "So what sort of use do you have for me?"

"I need someone to scout out the gaming halls I might want to play in. It's not always wise for me to go in ahead of time, so I need someone else for that. Someone to get the lay of the land, so to speak.

Someone to make a judgment on the character and appearance of a place and then report on what they've seen. A boy like you can do this and not be noticed. You're sharp enough, and I judge you to be honest. What do you think?"

"I think you might have trouble with appearing in any gaming hall in all of Varfleet after tonight. Word gets around."

"Which is why we are leaving Varfleet and going elsewhere. Another city might prove safer for the time being. And my skill at gaming tends to work better in places where I am not known."

Shea froze. Leave Varfleet? Leave his home—the only home he had ever known?

"But don't they know you everywhere by now? How long have you been doing this?"

Rocan Arneas gave him a look. "If you come inside, I will be happy to tell you. I have an aversion to speaking of private matters in public places."

The boy looked around. They were deep down a side street with no lights and no sign of another living soul. He felt uncomfortably vulnerable. Still, he understood the reason for cautious practices in a city like Varfleet.

He shrugged. "All right. If you think you can behave yourself."

Rocan gave him a wry look. "I think I can manage that."

He took Shea farther along the building to a heavy metal door inset into a stone-block wall and flush to its rough surface. There were no windows and no signs of a lock or handle. Shea studied it a moment, then looked at his companion. "How do you get in?"

Rocan grinned. "That's the point."

He walked along the wall for perhaps a dozen yards, Shea following, to where a series of metal spikes protruded along the length of an attached drainpipe. He pulled on several of them in turn. When he finished, the door opened.

"Built it myself," he said, walking back to the boy. "I have talents other than gaming. Some of them are rather useful."

Shea was impressed. In spite of his misgivings, he wanted to know more about this man. He started through the open door and then stopped, remembering.

"Where's Seelah?" he asked, looking around. "What happened to her?"

Rocan Arneas clapped a hand on his shoulder. "Another mystery. Where did she go? She was behind us for a while, watching our backs. Didn't you notice?"

Laughing softly, he guided Shea Ohmsford through the doorway and into what the boy hoped was not a mistake.

EIGHTEEN

WHEN TARSHA WOKE AGAIN, the day was dark and threatening, clouds washing across the sky and mounding up on the horizon to form huge banks. The air smelled of rain, and she could tell a storm was on the way. She lay in her bed for long moments, trying to remember what had happened to put her there. She knew she had risen at some point and gone outside, but what . . .

She caught herself, the memories flooding back.

Tavo.

She had gone outside when she'd heard his voice. She had tried to reason with him. She had tried and failed. He was beyond reason, and he had attacked her. Using the magic of his wishsong, he had struck out at her. He had tried to hurt her, overpowering her with the strength of his violence. She had fought back against him because he had given her no choice, but she was no match for him.

In the end, her defenses had been smashed and she had fallen, battered and broken.

And after that, nothing.

But she knew one thing for certain now. He had tried to kill her.

Yet she was still alive. It did not seem possible. She looked about with bleary, unfocused eyes. She was back in her bedroom. Clizia must have brought her here and put her to bed. The old Druid woman must have fought off Tavo or intervened to save her life. She had been quick to tell Clizia to stay out of it, that this was her battle to fight, her life and Tavo's to reconcile.

It was a bad decision. She had clearly not been up to the task.

She wondered if it was the same day or another.

She tried to rise and couldn't. Her limbs were leaden and her willpower sapped so completely she could not make herself move. At first, she was certain she was mistaken and this was just an aftereffect of her struggle with her brother. But several tries later she found that nothing had changed. She wanted to rise, but her body would not obey her. She was completely limp and helpless.

Her capacity for reasoning was likewise impaired, but she knew something had been done to her beyond what might have resulted from her battle with Tavo. She did not feel any pain and she could sense her body parts. She was not crippled or broken. She simply couldn't make herself move.

Instinct nudged her into concluding that, since this wasn't the result of something Tavo had done, Clizia must have caused it. Again, she heard Drisker speaking to her in his spirit form, warning her against the old woman, telling her she was dangerous and would use Tarsha if she could.

"Clizia," she hissed softly, the sound barely recognizable in her ears.

Within seconds, Clizia Porse was there, entering the bedroom swiftly and taking a seat next to her on the bed. "Awake at last," she observed with a thin smile.

"What . . . have you . . . done to me?"

The old woman shrugged one shoulder. "What I had to, to save your life. Your brother wanted to kill you, so I convinced him to spare you long enough to serve other purposes. A lie, of course. He thinks I can help him improve his magic, and I let him believe this as a way to keep him under control. I had to agree to give you a potion that would keep you immobile in order to convince him I was not trying to find a way to help you escape him—which I am, naturally. Then he agreed that he needed to rest. I used a spell to put him to sleep, and there he remains for the present."

A lie, Tarsha thought at once, but nodded agreeably. "What . . . day?"

"A day since your battle with Tavo." She paused. "You inherited the wishsong, didn't you, Tarsha? That was why Drisker took you on as his student, because you have the use of such powerful magic. You should have told me earlier."

"I . . . know that . . . now."

"Do you? I wonder. You're a headstrong, independent-minded young lady. I imagine even Drisker had to worm it out of you. But enough of that for now. You need to rest further. You took a terrible beating, and you're lucky to be alive. Your brother wanted you dead, you know—until I stopped him. By almost any measure, you should be dead, anyway. I was sure he had killed you."

In that moment, a strange certainty struck Tarsha. She had died—just as Parlindru said she would—for the first of three times. But instead of dying, she had risen anew. The seer's prophecy had begun to take form.

"Your brother is insane, girl," Clizia was saying. "He blames you for whatever it was that happened to him. He speaks with someone named Fluken, who is invisible to us, but who tells him what to do. A twisted projection of his own identity—a conjuring from his demented mind—or I'm a Troll's plaything. I asked about Fluken, but he wouldn't talk about it. He is very cautious, even now that he says he trusts me. He *half trusts* me, so he will watch whatever I do carefully. We must be circumspect about how we handle him, you and I. We must find a way to try to rehabilitate his mind, to clear it of its madness and make him whole."

"Can it . . . be done?"

Tarsha realized she was growing weaker just from the effort of speaking, of trying to be understood when the words were flitting about her like wild things. She was drifting away, and she could not help herself.

Clizia Porse shrugged once more. "Perhaps. Perhaps not. His madness is far advanced and has been part of him for a long time."

"You have . . . to help me . . . wake up . . ."

"Shhh, time enough for that later. For now, sleep." Cool fingers brushed strands of hair from her forehead. "Sleep, Tarsha. Much awaits you when you wake. You will need all your strength. Sleep, girl."

There was something in the words that was more a warning than a comfort. And Tarsha felt it deep in the back of her mind, down where a few things still seemed to make sense to her. Clizia Porse was her enemy, not her friend, and it was a mistake to fall asleep while in the old woman's care or to listen to what she was saying. It was intended to lull her, but it would lead to something very wrong and very frightening.

Yet her body betrayed her. Her eyes closed, and she drifted away.

"That's his cottage," Dar Leah whispered to Brecon Elessedil.

They crouched together at the forest's edge, off to one side of Drisker's temporary home, watching for signs of life. In the distance, thunder rumbled in a long, slow peal. Dar's gaze drifted west to the darkening sky. Another storm was moving in and would reach Emberen by nightfall. It would be the third storm in four days.

His friend nudged him. "Do you think anybody is in there? It looks deserted."

"Maybe." Dar shook his head doubtfully. He didn't want to make a mistake about this. The home looked deserted, but you never knew. "Let's watch for a bit. We don't want to walk into a trap."

He said this without any real idea of what sort of trap they might stumble into or who might have set it, but his instincts warned him to be careful. Drisker would not be there, unless he had managed somehow to find a way out of Paranor. Tarsha might have returned and be sleeping. But if so, Dar wanted to make sure she was alone. There were too many enemies out there looking for him since the Keep had fallen.

It had taken them four days to reach Emberen—impossible on the face of things, given that under normal circumstances it would have taken them one day—but life has a way of dashing expectations.

They had departed the site of Tarsha's encounter with the three men as planned, flying north toward Emberen. Things should have gone smoothly after that, but they did not. The day was already cloudy and gray, and within a short time the winds picked up. Within an hour, a fierce storm roared in out of the west, packed with lightning and thunder, dragging in its wake a deluge of such proportions that the friends were forced to seek immediate shelter. The refuge they found was inadequate for their needs; the rain pretty much soaked them through, helped by gusts of wind that blew water at them from all directions.

The pair had no choice but to hunker down to wait it out.

But the wait turned out to be much longer than they'd anticipated. It rained all that day and into the night. When it finally wore itself out as dawn approached, the Blade and the Elven prince began their journey anew. They barely got off the ground before the airship lost power. Landing, they began a search to discover what was wrong. Both were experienced fliers and aircraft mechanics, and as such had learned how to fix all sorts of problems. But in this case, the solution was simple enough. Rainwater had soaked through the cracks in the parse tube casings and left them flooded and mud-stained. Both crystals and tubes needed to be dried out before they would function.

But they had persevered, and eventually gotten the crystals cleaned up sufficiently to supply power. Between the storm and the malfunctioning crystals, they had already lost two days. Then a second storm blew in, every bit as fierce as the first, forcing them to abandon their attempts to set out and to take shelter once more.

"Is this really happening?" Dar demanded in frustration.

"It seems Mother Nature has it in for us," Brecon agreed. He grinned. "What did you do to make her so angry?"

This second storm lasted through the night and until sunset of the third day, and by then they were soaked through all over again and their airship was once more without power. Working together, they discovered that three of the diapson crystals had gone bad and had to be replaced. By then, night had fallen and clouds masked the sky so thoroughly that they had no way of navigating. Both were cold, hungry, and disgruntled, and too exhausted to do much more than try to get some sleep. They ate first, drying out their clothing by a fire as they sat close to the flames and told stories of what had happened to them since they had last seen each other. Eventually, they slept. But by the time they rolled into their blankets for the remainder of the night, it was close to midnight.

The morning of the fourth day of travel had dawned bright and clear. Neither had any idea of where they were, but it wasn't where they had expected to find themselves. The first storm appeared to have blown them far out onto the grasslands of the Tirfing. Undaunted, they boarded their airship once more and began flying north toward Elven country, arriving in Emberen the next morning, tired and hungry.

Now here they were, crouching in the woods, watching the seemingly empty house in the clearing ahead, frustrated once more. They had not been able to learn anything else about Tarsha's fate during their travels, and Dar was worried that something very bad had happened to her in spite of Brecon's encouragements.

"If she has use of the wishsong, she can take care of herself," the Elven prince had said. "That sort of magic can stand up to anything, and apparently Drisker thought she had promise. So stop worrying. She'll be there waiting for us."

Dar wasn't so sure. She was young—still a girl—and magic alone couldn't always save you. Besides, now that they were at the cottage, she didn't *seem* to be there. He felt fidgety and irritable, anxious to do what Brecon wanted and just knock on the door and see who answered. Likely no one—unless Tarsha really was there. It was logical enough that she could be there—that this was where she would go to find either her brother or Drisker or both—but logic didn't always determine direction or destination.

Impatience tugged at him, but he held himself in check, and they remained where they were, sitting together in the woods, tucked back in among the huge dark trunks, tall stands of wild grasses, and brush, and watched. Time slipped by at a glacial pace, marked by the passage of the sun west. Sunset was slowly approaching and the darkness beginning to close in. The sounds of the forest, lively before, quieted in expectation, and a hush settled across the land.

"So how much longer are we going to sit here?" Brecon whispered, failing to hide his irritation.

Dar didn't know. All he knew is that something about the cottage didn't feel right. Its deserted appearance felt misleading, and he was determined not to rush into anything.

"When it gets dark," he whispered back, "we'll have a look through the windows. If a light comes on, we'll know someone is in residence. Then we'll just have to find out who."

Brecon was looking off to his right across the clearing where the shadows were deepest. "I thought I saw something move," he said.

Dar glanced over to where he was looking, but he didn't see anything. "Maybe a badger or a fox?"

"Bigger. Much bigger."

Their attention was still focused on the darkness where Brecon had seen the movement when the front door of the cottage opened momentarily and then closed again. Dar put a hand on Brecon's arm and nodded in that direction.

A few minutes passed in which nothing happened, and then a black-cloaked figure stepped onto the porch and shuffled over to one of the straight-back chairs. An unlit lamp dangled from one hand and, once seated, the shadowy figure lifted its glass door and reached inside.

Instantly the lamp flared to life, emitting a soft golden glow that revealed its bearer's dark features clearly.

"That's Clizia Porse!" Dar hissed. "What's she doing here?"

Brecon nodded wordlessly, and together they watched for a few minutes as the old woman sat back and stared toward the descending sun, watching as it set.

Dar Leah realized Clizia must have come here after leaving Paranor. But what was here that would make her choose to occupy Drisker's residence? He wondered if his suspicions had been right—that Tarsha had returned and was inside. At some point, they would have to find out. But asking Clizia was out of the question. Even if Dar pretended to know nothing of the events at Paranor, she might see through his lie.

They continued to wait patiently, and after the sun had set, its last brilliant streaks of red and purple disappearing into the gaps below the storm clouds, Clizia rose. Picking up her lamp, she reentered the cottage and closed the door behind her, the latch clicking audibly as the lock was set. No interior lights were lit. The entire cottage remained dark.

With the latest storm approaching more swiftly now, the winds picking up and the air turning damper and tasting of copper and the peals of thunder coming closer together, Dar and Brecon were left in almost total blackness.

"Do you have a plan yet?" the Elf asked Dar.

"No. I've still got a few problems to solve first."

"Do any of them include the fact that we still don't know if Tarsha is even inside the cottage? Or that we don't know who else might be in there? Have you considered that neither your sword nor my Elfstones will work against anyone or anything that doesn't use magic first? And there are only two of us against a woman who tricked Drisker Arc and left him trapped in Paranor. No easy thing to do, I suspect. Have I missed anything?"

Dar shook his head. "Not that I care to know about." He glanced at the darkened house, then off toward the approaching storm. "I'm going down for a look. Wait here for me. Watch my back."

Brecon grabbed his arm. "I don't know about this, Dar . . ."

"I don't know about it, either." Dar gripped his friend's hand momentarily. "But I'm going, anyway."

He was rising to leave when a voice from behind him said, "That would be a very bad idea."

Dar and Brecon whirled about as one and peered into the darkness.

There was no one there.

Inside the cottage, Tavo Kaynin was waking up. He had fallen asleep right after eating and taking the medication the old woman had suggested. It was still light then, and now it was nighttime. He lay where he was for a moment, supine on a sleeping pad she had arranged for him in the living area, wrapped in a blanket. He did not know how long he had slept, but he knew why he had come awake.

He'd been dreaming of Tarsha.

In the dream, she was standing over him with a huge blade gripped in both hands as he lay in his blankets, smiling at him like a predator finding prey. She waited until his eyes were open wide, then she slowly began to lift the blade over her head. It was a broadsword of considerable size, yet she barely seemed to feel its weight. He knew what she intended—how could he not? But when he tried to rise, intending to stop her from killing him, he found he could not move. He was tangled so tightly in his blankets that try as he might, he could not break free of them. He writhed and kicked, but the blankets would not release their grip.

And the sword kept lifting, the blade gleaming wickedly.

The smile on his sister's face grew enormous. "You shouldn't have come after me, Tavo," she hissed at him. "You should have stayed where you were!"

Down came the blade, a whirling, glittering sharpness that would cut him in half, the whistle of its descent through the stillness plainly audible, with nothing to slow it, nothing to stop it from striking . . .

And then he woke, in the here and now, and there was no sign of Tarsha in the darkness.

He breathed heavily for a moment in relief. But fear and rage roiled within him, and he flung aside the blankets and rose from his sleeping pad in a frenzy of need. He should never have listened to the old woman. He should never have let Tarsha live. He had been a fool not to kill her right away and put an end to the reason for his journey to find her.

Why hadn't he?

He paused, his mind a jumble of confusion. Everything was so hard to understand. The only time things were clear was when Fluken was there. But Fluken never came inside strange houses, so he couldn't help now. Tavo tried hard to think, to remember. He had been persuaded to let Tarsha live, hadn't he? That old woman—Clizia something—had persuaded him. She had backed him away from his sister and then ordered him to carry her inside so she could be put to bed. He had gone along with this for reasons he couldn't explain, because it had seemed a good idea. Just as it had seemed a good idea to take the medicine she had insisted he needed. All this without knowing why he was doing it. There was something about her, something both scary and at the same time comforting. He trusted her. He could not have explained the reason for it, but he did. She spoke in a way that convinced him of everything she said. The sound of her voice soothed him. He wanted to believe what she was telling him. He wanted her to be right about what was best for him.

But now this dream was tearing at him, and he no longer felt so certain.

He no longer felt like he wanted to listen to her.

He no longer wanted Tarsha to live another day.

And he knew how to kill quickly and quietly. He had done so at that tavern when he had used his magic to punish the man who had lied to him. It took almost no effort at all to cause the man to choke to death. He remembered the satisfaction he felt when it was done.

Tarsha's life could be snuffed out just as easily. It would all be over in minutes.

His eyesight had adjusted to the darkness, and a quick glance around the room revealed no sign of the old woman. He stood for a few minutes more, making sure. Then he turned and started down the hallway to Tarsha's bedroom. He went silently, cautiously, aware that Clizia was somewhere in the cottage. He didn't want her to find out what he was doing until it was too late. He had made up his mind that he would not allow her to stop him, but he didn't want to have to confront her if she tried, either.

He paused at the bedroom door and listened. His thoughts were suddenly clear. *Just do it. Just go inside and do it. A few quick moments is all it will take. Then go back to bed and sleep again.*

He released the latch on the door and opened it a crack. He could see Tarsha lying on the bed asleep, curled on her side, facing away from him. He hesitated once more, gathering his resolve.

Then he entered the room.

Leaving the door open behind him, he walked over to the bed and looked down at his sister. She was deep in sleep, so much so she would be dead before she even realized what had happened. He glanced at her curtained window as the branches of bushes slapped against the glass. A storm was coming on, and the night was black and deep. There was no light from either moon or stars. No night sounds from birds or animals. Nothing but the howl of the wind ripping through the trees.

It was time.

He was just about to summon his magic, to bring its power to bear, when he sensed another presence. He turned slowly toward the darkness behind him and saw the glimmer of eyes in the darkness at the back of the room. The old woman was sitting in a chair, watching him.

The magic died in his throat.

She never moved, she never spoke, but he could feel the force of those eyes bearing down on him. Without stopping to question it, he turned from his sister and left the room.

Dar Leah and Brecon Elessedil exchanged hurried glances in the pitch-black of the forest before turning back to the invisible voice. It was impossible to see anything, and there was no movement of any kind, either visible or audible.

"Who are you?" Dar asked softly, trying to beat down the surge of adrenaline the voice had caused him and keep calm.

"No one," came the answer. "A creature of the forest. An ancient. You don't know me, but I know you. I saw you before with the *russ'hai*, Drisker Arc. Where is he?"

Dar edged a step closer. "He's at Paranor."

"But you went with him. Why didn't he come back with you?"

Dar took another step. "He couldn't. He had business there."

A pause. "If you take one more step, *chil'haen*, I'll leave. You can't see me if I don't want you to. And right now, I don't want you to."

Dar backed off. "What is it you want? Why are you even talking to us if you don't want us to see you?"

"It seemed only right, since I can help you. Drisker Arc would want me to—even though I was bad awhile back, and he might still be mad at me. We share a mutual friend, he and I. Is it possible you share the same friendship?"

"It is," Brecon said at once. "She's called Tarsha Kaynin. We think she is inside the cottage."

"She is. I saw her carried in after the battle with her brother. At least, that's what I think he is. The witch keeps her prisoner, but she doesn't realize it. She thinks the witch is a friend, but she isn't. I can tell such things, and the pretty girl can't."

Dar and Brecon exchanged another glance. *Pretty girl?* It sounded as if there was a connection between Tarsha and whoever was speaking—something that predated Clizia's arrival.

"She fought with her brother?" Dar pressed, realizing what that meant. "Is she all right?"

"If she weren't, what would be the point of rescuing her? Now, do you want to help or not?"

"We do," Dar said, taking a chance. "And Tarsha needs to help Drisker, in turn. Drisker is in trouble, and maybe she is the only one who can get him out of it."

"Then you will need *my* help," said the voice. "The witch is very powerful. *Ten'aren col haist!* I don't think she plans to let Tarsha go."

Probably not, Dar thought. "Anyone else in there?" he asked.

"One other. A boy, I think."

"A boy? What boy?"

"Enough questions! Stop wasting my time. Do you want me to help you or not? I can tell you how to rescue her, if you want me to."

"Tell us," Dar urged. "How would you get her out of there?"

"Ask nicely."

Dar gritted his teeth. "Please tell us how to get Tarsha out of there."

"Much better. But first I will tell you my name and you will tell me yours. I am called Flinc. I am a forest imp."

Which meant nothing to either of the other two. "I am Dar Leah," the highlander said. "My companion is Brecon Elessedil."

"There! Now we all know one another. So back to your question.

How will I get the pretty girl out of Drisker's cottage? Quite simple. A diversion."

With that, he appeared suddenly before them. He was a small stooped figure with a weathered face, a bald head, and a great drooping mustache. He was very old; only his bright eyes suggested even a hint of youth.

Dar stared. There was nothing about the forest imp that seemed the least bit imposing, so how could he possibly help?

"You're to be the diversion?" he asked.

The little man shook his head. "No, you are." He paused. "With a little assistance."

And the biggest moor cat either Dar or Brecon had ever seen appeared beside him.

NINETEEN

---◆---

THE NIGHT WAS STILL in its deepest sleep, the hour gone far past midnight but not yet halfway to dawn. The storm had blown through in a final rush of downed limbs and scattered leaves, and the resultant silence was so hushed it might have been a mother's soft endearment to a sleeping child. Slowly and with caution, the sounds of the forest returned, and life crept out of its shelters until all was as it had been.

Clizia Porse was still dozing in the armchair she had dragged into Tarsha's room, setting her watch early in case the girl's brother forgot his manners. As she knew he likely would. She had slept little and not well, but when he came for Tarsha, she was ready and waiting. He had been sleeping soundly, but something had woken him and brought him to his sister's room. There was no mistaking his intent; his stealth and his body language gave him away. The potion she had given him had tamped down his darker self for a time, but it was not enough to hold him for long.

Still, her potion had done its work better than she could have hoped for, even if it hadn't made him sleep as long as she had wished. For it had stolen his will so completely that he was now her creature. She merely had to look at him, and he hadn't argued or pressed ahead with his intended attack on his sister, but had turned about obediently and departed. Even without her speaking a word.

She rested better after that, and even slept now and then—although with one eye open and her senses pricked to detect any further intrusions.

But in that deepest hour of the night, she came awake again—fully this time, and knowing as she did so that something was wrong. She looked around the room carefully, searching for whatever had intruded, but there was nothing to see. Tarsha was still asleep in her bed, and no one else was present. She rose slowly, reaching out with her senses. What had disturbed her was not in this room, or apparently even in the cottage, but outside, in the dark.

She shuffled from the bedroom and out into the living quarters. Tavo was asleep again on his pad, his breathing deep and even. So nothing of what had roused her had to do with him. She went on, moving toward the front windows, lifting away the curtains and peering out.

The moon had come out again with the passing of the storm and its attendant clouds. Patches of open sky revealed a scattering of bright stars, and their combined light canted through breaks in the branches of the trees but failed to disperse the misty gloom that shrouded Drisker's home. The temperature had dropped, and the change had generated a ground fog that crawled across the forest earth like a living creature, tendrils reaching between the trees as the body shifted and roiled atop the scattered woods that surrounded the cottage. Bits of the mistiness rose as high as the lower limbs of some of the ancient trees, twisting and stretching.

But Clizia's eyes were on the clearing that fronted the cottage—the open space before the trees where the fog was thickest and its movements most seductive. Not much scared the Druid—especially not things made of mist and fog and shadows. But what moved through the cloaking was something decidedly menacing, something that didn't belong and might present a threat. It was huge and long, a beast of some sort. She couldn't tell what, even watching as closely as she was. It came and went as if it were a part of the brume itself.

"What manner of creature are you?" she whispered to herself.

She had warded the house with magic to conceal Tarsha from

anyone searching for her, but not the surrounding grounds. Had she been careless in not doing so?

Casting aside her uncertainty, she moved to the door, flung it open, and walked out onto the porch.

Fifteen feet away, hip-deep in the roiling fog, stood Dar Leah.

"It's the dead of night, Blade," she growled irritably. "What are you doing here?"

"Looking for Drisker Arc," he answered. He was wrapped in his Blade's cloak, and as he stood amid all the white brume in the moonlight, it gave him a wraith's appearance. She did not miss the fact that he was holding the black blade of his office at his side, as if he intended this to be a confrontation.

She made a dismissive gesture. "Drisker isn't back yet. Why are you searching for him at this hour, Blade? Surely this could have waited until morning."

Dar shrugged. "I was at Paranor with him when he went into the Keep that night. He told me he was going to meet you to try to save it—something about releasing the Keep's Guardian. But when you came out, he wasn't with you. Now it turns out he's not here, either." He paused. "You were the last one to see him."

She stared in him with undisguised malice, trying to decide what this was about. Was he really daring to challenge her? Drisker had clearly been very careful to keep the Blade's presence at Paranor a secret from her or she wouldn't have found herself blindsided like this, but what could she say to him now that would send him away? She couldn't have him hanging around—not with Tarsha and her brother inside.

"This is not the time for this conversation!" she snapped. "I can't say what happened to Drisker. We parted ways inside the Keep, and I lost track of him. It was his choice to stay, not mine. I did what I could to get him to leave with me."

"Oh, I don't think you did anything of the sort." Up came that black blade, the moonlight glinting brightly off its polished surface. "Otherwise, you wouldn't have been so quick to use your magic to send Paranor into limbo while he was still inside. I saw you, Clizia. I was watching."

She felt a cold rage building inside. She should have left him to Ober Balronen rather than trying to make use of him. Or simply killed him herself.

"Who do you think you are to question me?" Her warning was unmistakable.

"Someone looking for the truth. Why don't you try admitting it?"

"I think you'd better go. You've worn out your welcome."

He shook his head slowly. "I don't think I want to."

At the rear of the cottage, Brecon was crouched in front of the back door, trying to release the lock. It was a simple enough mechanism, but he was working in shadow without any sort of light to aid him. Flinc stood close behind, urging him on.

"Quickly now, young Elf! We haven't a second to lose. Get us inside, for cat's sake! Your friend won't last out there alone for very long. As a distraction, he's a bit lacking in imagination."

"I thought the moor cat was there to help!"

"Fade will do what she can, but moor cats are notoriously fickle and inclined to wander off. Hurry, will you?"

Brecon *was* hurrying, and Flinc wasn't doing anything to help. He wanted to mention this, but let it go. Flinc had supplied the plan, even if it didn't require much from him.

The moor cat, on the other hand, might prove a much-needed ally. Fade was her name, Flinc had informed him. Besides being huge, Fade seemed able to disappear and reappear at will with barely a noticeable transition between the one and the other. Granted, all moor cats possessed this ability, but not with the dexterity and thoroughness of Fade. Also, Brecon did not think the cat was Flinc's creature. She might be responding to commands he was giving, but somehow the Elven prince doubted it. Once or twice, the forest imp had instructed her to do something while they were creeping through the trees to reach the cottage from separate directions, but the cat had pretty much ignored him.

Now Dar was tasked with confronting Clizia, and Brecon and Flinc were responsible for getting Tarsha out of the cottage. Where Fade was and what she was planning to do was a mystery to all of them—including Flinc. For when Dar asked the little man to explain what the moor cat would be doing while the rest of them carried out their parts, he had shrugged.

"Oh, Fade will do what moor cats do, you can be sure. Whatever it is, it will be helpful to us. No need to give it another thought."

All well and good for him to say, but Brecon wasn't so sure. He fumed and fumbled and somehow the lock released. With Flinc breathing down his neck, he opened the door a crack and peered inside. No one visible, no sounds of anyone moving about, no lights.

He looked back at the forest imp and nodded, and they slipped through the doorway and into the cottage.

Right away Brecon sensed the presence of another person. Then he remembered Flinc mentioning there was someone besides Tasha and Clizia inside the house. He crouched down and listened for a moment. His Elven senses were much better than those of most other Races, and he could tell from the sounds that there were two people sleeping somewhere ahead of them.

"Two sleepers," Flinc whispered needlessly in his ear, his breath hot and musky. "One on the floor directly ahead, one in the room on the left."

Brecon nodded without comment and moved ahead toward the door on the left. If Tarsha was still here, she was most likely the one in the bedroom. They moved soundlessly through the darkness, feeling their way along the wall, conscious now of a barely audible conversation that was taking place ahead of them, just outside the cottage.

Ignoring the urgency of their situation, the Elf and the forest imp eased through the doorway toward the sleeper in the bed. Moving swiftly to make sure who it was, they were rewarded with a clear view of Tarsha Kaynin, revealed in a filter of moonlight shining through the bedroom window. Even Brecon, who had never met her, knew who it was.

He started to lift the girl off the bed, but Flinc stayed his arm and pulled him down so he could whisper in his ear.

"She knows me, but not you. If she wakes and sees you, she might scream or struggle. Best if I be the one to carry her."

Brecon frowned. "No offense, but are you strong enough?"

Flinc gave him a look. "I carried her almost a mile from where I found her after the fire burned Drisker's home. I think I can manage here!"

He was insistent to the point of snappishness, and the Elven prince hesitated. Then he shook his head. "No, I'll do it."

He rose quickly before the imp could voice any further objections, sliding his arms under the sleeping girl, drawing her close to him and gathering her into the cradle of his arms. For just an instant, her eyes seemed to open and then close again. Brecon took a closer look. Had he seen correctly? But she was sleeping so soundly it appeared it would have taken a great deal to wake her, so he dismissed the matter.

"Time to go," he whispered.

They turned for the doorway and found themselves face-to-face with Tavo Kaynin.

For a few endless moments, Dar Leah and Clizia Porse stared at each other in a confrontation that both knew neither was about to back down from. Dar tensed as he watched tendrils of steam leak from Clizia's fingertips. In a moment, she would strike at him. He held his sword before him like a shield, wondering if he had the strength to withstand what was about to happen.

"You were warned," Clizia said softly.

There are moments in life so charged with terrible possibility and so rife with hushed warnings that everything seems to slow to a near stop in anticipation. Those who experience such moments always remember later how clear everything seemed—how much they distinctly recalled—or they remember nothing at all. For Dar Leah, it would be the former. His gaze fixed on Clizia Porse with an intensity that, if visceral, would have burned a hole completely through her. When he saw her hands move—a barely noticeable shifting of fingers that a less experienced man would have missed completely—he threw himself to one side. Even so, the fire whips she uncoiled from her fingers to lash out at him whistled close enough that he could feel their heat.

As he struck the ground, he rolled. He was buried now in a deep layer of fog, momentarily invisible within its blanket. She would come after him, he knew; she would search him out and finish him. As if to prove his point, he watched the burning ropes slice through the insubstantial brume of his concealment at the place where he had landed moments earlier, flames bursting brightly as they struck the hard earth, leaving scorch marks in their wake.

Dar got to his knees, his sword still in his hands, as he waited for whatever was to happen next. The fire whips crackled with dark magic, and he knew Clizia was hunting for him. He flattened himself against the ground within the mist, scooting swiftly to one side as the magic-born fire burned all around him in bright lines. He told himself to be patient, not to panic. All he was doing was buying time for Brecon and Flinc.

But how much more was required before his companions had Tarsha free?

Then he heard someone scream from inside the house, the sound sharp and piercing, but he could not tell whose scream it was. A roar of anger surfaced at the end of the scream, high-pitched and terrifying, dying almost immediately into an oddly strange growling that then went silent.

The flame whips Clizia was holding disappeared. She would be wondering what was happening, too. Dar sprang to his feet in response, certain the old woman suspected the truth—that Dar had come for Tarsha and likely had not come alone. She would be quick enough now to abandon the attack on him and rush back into the cottage.

Emerging from the layer of fog, he saw her already turning toward the front door of the cottage, her dark form slouching for the opening. He yelled her name, and his blade blazed to life with the glow of its magic. She turned back momentarily, then gave him a dismissive look and took another step toward the door before shrinking from what she found blocking her way.

Fade filled the entry with her considerable bulk—snarling jaws, muzzle pulled back to reveal her huge, curved fangs.

Even from where he was standing almost twenty feet away, Dar heard the gasp that escaped Clizia's lips. She was momentarily paralyzed by the suddenness of the big cat's appearance, but in the next instant it had disappeared. By then, Dar was moving toward the cottage, yelling Clizia's name to make her turn back. But almost without looking, she cast a spell on the fog surrounding him, and it began to swell, growing taller than he was and wrapping about him.

In seconds, there was no air, and he was suffocating.

Inside the cottage, another stare-down was under way. Tavo, having entered the room soundlessly, was confronting Brecon Elessedil and Flinc, who had just turned to leave, the former carrying Tarsha in his arms. Brecon had the Elfstones, but they were tucked in his pocket, and unless he set down the girl he couldn't reach them. Even then, he wasn't sure if they would be of any help.

He might have been undecided about what to do, but Flinc was not. The forest imp launched himself at Tavo, wrapped his scrawny arms about one leg, and bit down. The resulting howl was blood-curdling. Tavo gritted his teeth against the pain, emitting a dangerous growl, then shook his leg to rid himself of Flinc. The forest imp bit him again, but this time Tavo's response was more a roar than a scream. When shaking his attacker off failed to work, he finally reached down with both hands, fastened his fingers on Flinc's clothing, then yanked him loose and threw him across the rom.

What else he might have done after that was more than Brecon cared to imagine, but Tavo never got a chance to demonstrate. Releasing his grip on Tarsha while keeping one arm locked around her waist as he swung her into an upright position, the Elven prince took two quick steps forward and slammed his fist into the side of Tavo's head. Tavo's face turned white from the force of the blow, and he dropped to the floor unconscious.

Flinc was back at his side. "Give her to me!" he snapped. "You need to use the Elfstones against the witch! We may have to fight our way out of here."

Brecon obeyed, knowing the other was right. Clizia was still out there, possibly blocking their path. Gently, he lowered the still-unconscious Tarsha into the forest imp's arms. To his surprise, Flinc took the girl from him and held her up with no apparent effort. Brecon hesitated a moment—just long enough for Flinc to give him a look—and then they were out the door, Elfstones in hand, running . . .

Right into Clizia, who was just entering.

Brecon ran into her with such force that he knocked her backward onto the floor. Clizia's head slammed against the wooden planks as she fell, but it seemed to have no effect. Her eyes fixed on him, filled with malice, and her hands began to summon her dark magic.

Then Fade was there, huge and forbidding, towering over the fallen Druid, one great paw holding her down, pushing on her chest. Clizia gasped, the breath rushing from her lungs from the weight of that paw. In seconds, she was unconscious.

Again, the moor cat disappeared.

Had there been more time to think about it, Brecon might have considered binding and gagging both Clizia and Tavo Kaynin, but at this point he was only thinking about getting out of there as quickly as possible—of taking Tarsha somewhere safe. And just about then he was distracted by Dar shouting the Leah battle cry, flashes from his dark blade visible through the front windows of the cottage. Yelling for Flinc to follow, he charged down the hallway, through the living quarters, and out onto the porch. The fog had risen considerably; it was now almost to the cottage roof. Deep in its midst, the magic of the Sword of Leah was scattering arcs of brightness as it cut at the vapor.

"Dar!" Brecon yelled for him.

"Brecon!" his friend managed to yell, and then his breath was cut off.

The Elven prince realized what was happening and responded at once, pointing the Elfstones toward the sound of his friend's voice. Brilliant blue light blazed to life and flashed into the thickest of the mist. As it burrowed in, the tentacles drew back with a shudder, shrinking away from the Elven magic as if burned.

Seconds later it was back to its former depth of about three feet, and Dar could be seen standing within it. The Blade was choking and gasping as he breathed the night air, but he signaled to Brecon that he was all right. Together, they made for the concealment of the woods, anxious to get clear before either Clizia or Tarsha's brother woke up again.

"Where's Tarsha?" Dar asked as they reached the fringe and plunged into the trees.

"Flinc has her." Brecon stopped and looked back uncertainly. "At least, he did when I came to help you. He was right behind me."

Dar wheeled around, seeing no one following. "We have to go back!"

Brecon grabbed his arm. "We can't do that. Look, that forest Gnome—or whatever he calls himself—has her safely in hand. He might have gone out the way we came in, through the rear door. We have to return to where he found us and wait for him to come back. Both Clizia and Tavo were unconscious; they couldn't have recovered fast enough to do anything to stop him. He just went another way."

Dar looked uncertain, but finally nodded. "Let's hurry, then."

They passed deeper into the trees and began working their way to where Flinc had found them watching the cottage and its occupants. They went swiftly, not bothering with stopping to see what was happening in the clearing, leaving that for when they reached their destination. As they crept through the trees, both were searching the dark for some sign of Tarsha and the forest imp, half expecting to see them emerge from the shadows. But neither appeared.

They were not at the agreed-upon meeting point, either. By now, Dar was almost certain they had fallen into Clizia's hands and were prisoners. He mentioned it again to Brecon, but the Elven prince shook his head.

"The imp was halfway out the door behind me. He was safely away from both Clizia and Tavo. If he had fallen or been grabbed or otherwise attacked, he would have gotten off a warning and I would have heard. I still think he went the other way—out the rear door of the cottage. Maybe that moor cat found him. Maybe the three of them went somewhere and are waiting for morning. The imp might have decided that was safer than coming back here."

As if to emphasize this, Clizia appeared on the cabin porch, her black robes wrapped about her, with Tavo a step behind. The two stared out into the dark for a few moments and then huddled together. Dar could hear nothing of what they said, but he could guess the gist of it. He waited to see what they would do, but to his surprise they did not set out to search for their attackers or Tarsha but turned around and went back inside.

Although Dar and Brecon waited a long time afterward for one or the other to reemerge, neither did, and the cottage remained dark and silent. Finally, Dar nudged Brecon and they slipped back through the trees, far enough away from the cottage that they could speak without risk of being overheard.

"Something isn't right," the Blade said, when they were safely away. He sat down on a log, his chin in his hand, thinking. "There's an explanation here that we're not seeing."

Brecon nodded. "A different explanation than we've been considering."

They were silent a moment. "Remember when Flinc said Drisker would want him to help us, even though he was bad awhile back?" Dar asked suddenly. "Bad about what, though? What do you think he was talking about?"

"No idea."

"He made their relationship sound rather tenuous. So what if it had something to do with Tarsha?"

"That's a bit of a stretch, isn't it? But then, the imp was pretty insistent that I let him carry Tarsha. I didn't agree at first, but then it seemed I might need to use the Elfstones, so I gave her to him."

Dar stared at his friend. "You know what? I don't want to wait until morning. I want to find Tarsha and Flinc right now. Can you use the Elfstones to find out where they are?"

Brecon didn't bother with a response. He simply brought out the Stones, clasped them in his fist, and held them up to the night.

TWENTY

———————————◆———————————

CLIZIA PORSE WOKE TO discover that Tarsha was gone and Tavo was lying unconscious on the floor. She was incensed beyond words, but anger quickly turned to cold and calculating determination. Dar Leah and his friends might think they had gotten the best of her, but they would find out differently soon enough. She had not outlived and outsmarted all her enemies over the years to be tricked by the Blade and his foolhardy accomplices.

For just an instant, as she bent to revive Tavo, she wondered if it was possible that Drisker Arc had somehow escaped his imprisonment in Paranor and come back to set things right, but she dismissed the idea almost at once. If Drisker were behind this, he would have been the one confronting her and not Dar Leah.

She roused Tavo, brought him to his feet, and determined his head was clear enough when he began to rant about Tarsha. She leaned close, a bony finger to his lips. "Say nothing more until I tell you to," she hissed. "We'll get your sister back. Be quiet and come with me."

They walked through the house and onto the porch and stood looking out at the night. For long minutes neither spoke, and then the young man whispered, "Why aren't we doing something?"

She leaned close once more. "We *are* doing something. We're letting those fools who have Tarsha see us. They will be out there watching. They will want to discover what we intend to do. So we're going to make them believe what we want them to believe. This is a game we're playing, and I want to be very sure we end up the winners."

She turned away, took him by the arm, and led him inside again. "They split into two groups," she whispered as she walked him through the house. "Dar Leah—formerly Blade to the High Druid and Drisker's friend—was alone. He was the one distracting me when the others came in the back way to retrieve Tarsha. Who were they? You must have seen."

Tavo frowned and shook his head. "I don't know. A small furry creature of some sort; I've never seen one like it before. Like a rodent that could walk. And an Elf. They took Tarsha!"

"As I've already pointed out. So let's just go find them."

She took him all the way through the cottage to the rear door. Once there, she made a series of gestures and spoke a few strange words. Then she led him outside, hurrying him away from the building and into the woods. She was aware of the way Tavo was looking at her—as if wondering what sort of trick she might be playing—so she stopped just inside the trees and turned to him.

"I provided us with a momentary cloaking so we would be hidden from watching eyes. That way they will believe we have settled down to sleep for the rest of the night, intending to search for Tarsha when it is light. They likely think we will have to track them, having no idea of where they might have gone. But they are mistaken."

"You know where Tarsha is?" He sounded excited. His lips curled into a snarl. His hands curled into fists. "Once we find her, I'll finish what I started and punish her for her betrayal! I'll make sure she doesn't get away from me again."

Clizia took hold of the front of his tunic and yanked him close. "You listen to me. You want to find your sister? You want to see her dead? Fine by me. But you won't achieve either one if you don't do exactly what I say. We'll find her because she carries my mark and will be easy to track down. But she is not to be harmed—not until she has fulfilled her purpose. Not under any circumstance. Do you understand me, Tavo Kaynin?"

He shook his head slowly, a sullen and defiant look crossing his face. "You don't want to make me angry," he spat at her.

She laughed. "I know what sort of power you have—and I know what you can do when it's working properly. But for the moment, it isn't—not against me. I shut that part of it down with a little magic of my own when I took you in. Do you wish to test this? Or will you do what I say?"

The dark look faded a shade. "All right," he muttered.

"Then let's go find your sister. Remember what I said about Tarsha. No harm must be done to her." She paused. "Though you can do what you want with her kidnappers once we find her; they don't matter. They are bad people. They don't deserve to live."

He nodded. "I know what to do."

She did a conjuring, and images formed on the night air, revealing Tarsha and the furry creature that had taken her. Clizia wondered where the other two were, but would be satisfied just to find the girl.

Beckoning to Tavo, she set out.

Together, the pair walked through the forest for a long distance, navigating by moonlight shining down from a sky cleared of clouds by the passing storm. Tarsha and her captor were easy to track, thanks to the mark she had placed on the girl. She walked without speaking, but her odd companion mumbled and growled with regularity, speaking to himself or to the one he called Fluken. The young man was unbalanced but he was also functional, and the combination made him dangerous. After this was done, she would have to decide what to do with him. It would be better to kill him and be done with it, but she kept thinking there might be a use for him—a use she hadn't yet recognized.

And for that, of course, she needed the girl.

Flinc had watched Brecon Leah hurry toward the front of Drisker Arc's cottage; he heard the Elven prince calling for him to follow. Still cradling the pretty Tarsha Kaynin in his arms, holding her close enough that he could feel the beating of her heart, he waited until the other was out of sight, then promptly turned the other way.

There was no reason to expose this beautiful creature to further danger by going the Elf's way. She was deep in sleep, still lost in her dreams, and he had to do what was best for her while there was yet time. She might have died if she had remained the old woman's prisoner. She might have been tortured or been subjected to further indignities by her brother. The Elf and his companion had good hearts, and they clearly wanted what was best for her, but did they even know what that was? Did they understand how precious she was? He didn't think so. Not like he did.

He hurried to reach the back door, the sleeping girl no burden to him at all, in spite of his size. For a small fellow, he was surprisingly strong. He would not have stayed alive for all these centuries otherwise. Even the passage of time had done little to weaken him. He remained very much the same as he had always been—and that was true in ways that only Drisker Arc understood. Even if the Druid didn't always approve of those ways or the choices Flinc made . . .

Forest imps were unusual creatures. Some would say odd. Drisker Arc might agree, although he would never admit it to Flinc. But he understood how Flinc was susceptible to rash and selfish behavior, given the right impetus.

Such as a reason to indulge his desperate craving for someone to love him.

Like this pretty girl, Tarsha.

Flinc understood this weakness, but now and then it proved too strong for him to resist. He glanced down at the girl and smiled. White-blond hair and lavender eyes, skin smooth and white as chalk. Possessed of beauty and magic and charm. Exotic in a way only great treasures were. Tarsha was a rare creature; she deserved to be cared for. No one saw this quite as clearly as Flinc did, so they were less cautious about the dangers she faced. He had looked after her when the assassins had come to Drisker's home and set it on fire. If not for Flinc (and, to a less important degree, Fade), she might have been killed or badly injured. But he had saved her and taken her away to his home to make sure she remained safe.

He thought about how good it had felt to have her there in his underground home—his special guest, his private treasure. She had been sleeping, of course, because it was necessary. First, because she was exhausted and damaged and needed to rest and heal. Second, because if she were to agree to stay with him permanently, she needed time to get used to the idea that living with him was something to be desired.

Drisker hadn't seen it that way, but the Druid didn't understand everything about how the world worked—not even as wise as he was. Flinc, on the other hand, had more experience, having lived so much longer and thereby gained a more extensive worldview and a deeper understanding of life. Tarsha would have come to see that if she had spent more time with him. She might have come to love him. Not in a physical way because he was well beyond that, but with a deep and abiding friendship. Time was a healer and a teacher—and people just needed enough space to allow for understanding and acceptance.

He had thought he might find this the last time he took Tarsha, but Drisker had prevented her from staying with him then. Now Drisker was no longer here, and if the Druid was truly trapped in the limbo existence of Paranor, he might never return.

Flinc had to make plans accordingly. He had to accept that now it would be up to him to care for this lovely child.

So he carried Tarsha Kaynin from the cottage and into the forest, moving steadily but carefully so as to leave no trail, picking his way over ground that would reveal no sign of his passing, then angling back toward his own stretch of the woods and his home. He was sorry he had to do this to the Elven prince and the Blade, but they would never have let him take Tarsha otherwise. They would have kept her with them as they tried to find a way to bring back Drisker—even when the odds were so steeply stacked against them. They would try and fail, and in the process they might get the pretty girl killed. He could not allow that to happen. Not when he was being given a second chance. Not when he was so certain this was the right thing to do.

It was still dark when he neared his underground home, but the first tinges of morning light were appearing through gaps in the trees, and in an hour it would be full daylight. He approached his home with caution. There were no indications yet of a pursuit, and he detected no sounds or movements. He stood before his hidden entry and prepared to trigger its release.

Off to one side, right at the edge of the trees, something moved. He froze momentarily, his gaze shifting toward the movement. Fade slid from the shadows, her huge gray-and-black body sinuous and sleek in the near darkness. She came out of the trees and stopped, looking at him. Then she sat back on her haunches, her lantern eyes fixing on him and holding him in place. She was making a judgment, he realized. She could not communicate, but she was letting him know she was taking his measure for some reason. Likely as a warning she felt he needed.

About the girl, perhaps? He frowned. Well, if Fade was giving him a warning about that, she was wasting her time. It was not her place to pass judgment on him—a creature so many times older, an ancient being whose ways she was not in the least familiar with.

Yet she continued to watch him.

Dismissing her with a mental shrug, the forest imp knelt, lowering Tarsha Kaynin to the ground. He felt for the release to his trapdoor and turned it a half twist counterclockwise, then a full twist clockwise. Then he found the handle and opened the grass-and-weed-covered hatch and laid it back. Picking the girl back up again, he carried her down the waiting stairs and into his home.

After laying her on his bed and covering her with a blanket, he went back to close the trapdoor. A quick glance around when he poked his head up revealed Fade still sitting off to one side, watching. Flinc stared back at her a moment, a twinge of doubt tugging at him. Something wasn't right. The big cat wasn't sitting there because she enjoyed looking at Flinc or had decided to take up a watch on his abode.

She was telling Flinc to be careful.

The forest imp regarded the moor cat for a few moments longer, then pulled the trapdoor closed behind him and locked it.

• • •

Tarsha Kaynin was sleeping deeply until she felt something nudge her consciousness, bringing her out of her comforting rest and back toward wakefulness. It was a familiar voice, a rough rumble she had heard and listened to before. There was no face, no presence, just the voice as she stirred beneath the covers of the bed on which she lay, pulling herself back into the present and whatever was waiting for her.

It would be . . . best if you . . . find another shelter . . . quickly and . . . look for Dar Leah to protect . . . and stay away . . . but go at once to . . .

Drisker Arc!

All the rest of what he was saying was lost to her. It was as if a filter was separating and breaking apart his sentences, but she sensed fear and urgency in the words nevertheless.

Her eyes opened in response, and to her surprise she knew right away where she was. No longer in her bedroom in Drisker's cottage, but once again in the underground home of Flinc, sleeping in his bed. She forced herself to gather her wits and sit up. A quick look around confirmed that everything was just as she remembered it from before, although there was no sign of the forest imp.

Then suddenly he popped up from behind a stack of crates off to one side, his wizened face scrunched up in a mix of excitement and uncertainty.

"Tarsha of the beautiful eyes, welcome back to my home. You are my guest once more. I brought you here from Drisker's cottage. It wasn't easy, you know. I had to steal you away from the witch, who was keeping close watch over you. Did she hurt you?"

The girl shook her head. "You stole me? How did you manage that?"

"I am a clever fellow, that's how. I waited until the witch was sleeping, caused a distraction to bring her out front, and while she was still muddleheaded packed you up and whisked you out the back door. Now you are safe!"

She fixed him with her sharpest gaze. How much of this was true? With Flinc, it was difficult to say. "And what about my brother? Did you see him?"

"I saw him. He was sleeping. I was so quiet he never even stirred while I was carrying you out. Is he really your brother? He was attacking you. He wanted to hurt you."

"He is my brother nevertheless. Tavo doesn't understand things as well as he needs to. And he does things he shouldn't."

"He is dangerous. He has powerful magic, and he used to it to hurt you. You mustn't let him near you again."

She nodded, not wanting to talk about it further. "Thank you for bringing me here, but I have to leave right away. Clizia will come looking for me. She is a Druid, not a witch. If she finds me here, she might try to hurt you for helping me. I have to go before she finds out where I am."

Flinc shook his head vehemently. His gestures were frantic. "No, no, Tarsha, no! You must stay here where I can keep you safe. If you leave, they will find your trail and hunt you down. But they cannot find me. They cannot find my home. I was careful to leave no sign. They will find you gone, but they will not know it was me who took you. The witch will not find you here."

Tarsha swung her legs over the side of his bed. Her head was cotton-filled and her eyes still heavy with whatever had put her to sleep. The tea Clizia had given her, perhaps, with a drug slipped into the brew to make sure she could not function. But she felt the same way she had after Drisker had found her in Flinc's underground abode and carried her out several weeks ago. She was reminded of it right away, and she found herself wondering if the forest imp had drugged her, as well.

She stood up slowly, allowing herself a few moments to make sure her sense of balance was functioning. "Clizia Porse can find anyone anywhere, I think. I can't stay, Flinc. And not just because of Clizia but because Drisker is in trouble and needs my help. He sent an apparition of himself to me while I was in his cottage. He managed to contact me and told me he was trapped in Paranor and trying to get

out. But mostly he warned me about Clizia and what she might do to me."

"There you are, then! You have to stay here—and stay safe! You can't just leave! Where would you go?"

"I have to find the Blade, Dar Leah, and go with him to Paranor—or at least to where Paranor was—to help Drisker. I have to help him, Flinc. You should want this, too. He is your friend, isn't he?"

"Yes, yes." The forest imp made an impatient gesture.

"Would you want to come with me?"

"No, I can't leave here. This is my home. This forest is where I belong. My kind doesn't wander." He sounded miserable. "I thought maybe you belonged here, too. With me. You would be happy here, Tarsha. You would, really."

She smiled, running her hands through her hair as she considered how to respond. She saw now what he wanted. He was desperately lonely and had decided she could be the cure. But it was wishful thinking, entirely misguided.

"My kind does wander," she said finally. "And I have responsibilities that I cannot shirk. I must leave. I am sure you would make me happy if I could stay, but we have to be what we are. We can be friends, Flinc. I hope we can settle for that."

"It is too dangerous," he tried again.

"Yes, it *is* too dangerous, but so is staying here. Not just for me, but for you, as well. If something happened to you because of me, I would never forgive myself. Do you see?"

Flinc gave her a reproving look. "Forest imps are quite capable of looking after themselves. We have not lived long lives by being incautious and unprepared. You are making a mistake by leaving, pretty Tarsha. If you will just stay another day or so, I think you will see . . ."

She held up her hands to stop him there. "No, I am determined in this, Flinc. Drisker needs help, and if I can provide it, I must. Will you take me outside again and guide me to the edge of the forest so I can find my way?"

He was about to reply when the trapdoor to his home exploded.

• • •

When the trapdoor to Flinc's home tore open, revealing Clizia and Tavo, it heaved upward momentarily before slamming back down again at a crooked angle that blocked entry once more. Tarsha instinctively backed away, trying to summon the wishsong to her defense, but she realized at once she couldn't. The magic was beyond her. Whether because of her injuries or something in the tea Clizia had given her, she had no command of the wishsong whatsoever.

But Flinc was already moving, grabbing her hand and pulling her after him. "This way! This way! Now!"

She went with him, borne along by the urgency of his words and her own substantial fears. Deeper into his home they rushed, through a curtain and into another tunnel. Once within the darkness, Flinc yanked her to a stop.

"Tarsha Kaynin, you must go alone now. Down this tunnel to its end and then out into the trees. Go find Dar Leah. He is somewhere nearby. I will stop those who are following. Go!"

Numbly, she did as she was told, moving off into the darkness, her eyes adjusting to an almost total absence of light. All that saved her from having to find her way blindly were glowing bits of stone embedded in the tunnel walls that gave off just enough illumination to reveal the curve of the passageway. She did not look back, knowing what was about to happen. Flinc intended to face Clizia and Tavo alone. How he would stop them was impossible to imagine. She did not think the forest imp was a match for the Druid or her brother separately, let alone together.

Without the wishsong's magic, she could do nothing to help. Rationally, she knew this.

But to just leave him . . .

She was crying, but she brushed away the tears and hurried on.

The tunnel was narrow and winding, and it took her a long time to reach its end. There she found stairs leading upward to another trapdoor and an exit out. The trapdoor opened easily—perhaps because she was opening it from within rather than without—so that she emerged into the forest once more. From there she began to run, heading toward the glimmer of the rising sun, away from what she believed to be the direction of Flinc's underground home. She ran as fast as she could, not bothering to try to hide her passage, not worrying that any pursuers might try to track her, all of her concentration on simply escaping.

She soon lost her way. Tree limbs crisscrossed overhead to create a thick canopy, and even though the sun had risen high enough that its brightness flooded the sky, it was no longer clear which way was east. She was still moving as fast as she could, but already she was beginning to tire. Her strength was not yet fully restored, and her stamina was quickly sapped. She felt she might not even be traveling in a straight line. She thought she heard a voice calling her name, but was frightened of who it might be and veered sharply toward the heavier shadows amid the larger of the forest's ancient trees.

She had begun to pick up her pace again—propelled onward mostly by fear—when abruptly she ran right into someone. Strong hands seized her arms, and she found herself looking up into the blue eyes of an Elf.

"Tarsha." He spoke her name softly and smiled. "It's all right. You're safe now."

A weary, resigned Flinc watched Tarsha Kaynin disappear into the dark, then turned back toward his underground home. Already he could hear the intruders smashing apart the trapdoor that blocked their way in. The locking mechanism within the frame was designed specifically to keep an enemy from just smashing through directly. If he had not long ago taken such a precaution, it would have been impossible for pretty Tarsha to escape at all. He regretted that she was lost to him, but he understood that it was the only choice left if he wanted to keep her unharmed. And he wanted that more than anything.

Still, it was hard to accept what that meant. It was an acknowledgment of the reckoning he had been putting off for centuries, the conclusion of a life that, at times, had seemed to him as if it might never end. But he had not lived this long to pretend he did not understand that it was inevitable, that it was the necessary consequence of his decision to save the girl. It would have been wonderful if he had been able to persuade this rare and lovely creature to live with him, to be there to keep him company and share his lonely existence. But she had made it clear that this would not happen no matter what he did, and so now he had to choose whether to save her or give her over to her enemies.

Which was really no choice at all.

Now he must do what he could to slow them down before his inevitable demise. He found himself wishing that he could see Drisker Arc one last time. He had never shared such a close friendship with another human in all the years gone by.

He arrived back inside his home just in time to see the witch and her young companion push their way through the debris that had barred their entry. The witch looked furious, the young man sullen and dangerous. Bad people who would try to do him harm if he gave them cause and opportunity.

"Welcome," he said, executing a small, precise bow.

They looked at him as if he were insane. "Where is she?" the witch snapped.

"Gone." No need to pretend he didn't know who she was talking about.

"Gone? Gone where?" Her ancient face was wrinkled deep by lines of displeasure. "Speak up, creature!"

Flinc drew himself up to his full height of four feet six inches. "I am a forest imp, and I was born to a species that found its beginnings in the time of Faerie. I am a rare and special creature, so treat me with respect!"

The young man sneered. "What are you again? You look like a large rodent of some sort. Are you a mole or a badger?"

"I am more than you will ever be," Flinc answered. Shifting his gaze to the witch, he added, "As for the girl, *shrig-hai obscenen,* she is beyond your reach."

The old woman actually smiled. "No one is beyond my reach—

especially not that girl. I have placed my mark on her and can find her again whenever I wish, no matter where you might have sent her. You may be very old, but you aren't very wise."

Flinc shrugged. "Perhaps not, but I am very determined. Tarsha Kaynin has been sent to safety, and even though you may try to track her, you will not be able to. Your search ends here."

"If so," the witch hissed, "then so does your life."

"Perhaps that is a trade worth making. My life is my own, to do with as I choose."

The witch took a step forward. "Not while you stand in my presence. Right now, your life belongs to me, and what becomes of it is not for you to decide. You overestimate your abilities, little imp."

"Or you do. Why not simply leave and go find sweet Tarsha if you think yourself so clever? Why even bother with me? Are you so afraid of me? Am I such a danger to your plans?"

"Let me have him," the young man said suddenly. "I will make him tell us what he knows! I will flay the skin off him if he refuses! I will strip him of his sanity!"

"Not just yet," the witch replied. "I want to spend some time with him myself. I want to know why he feels so confident when his instincts must surely tell him he has met his end. What say you to that, imp?"

She was a creature of darkness, both without and within, and clearly capable of terrible things. Flinc could see it in her appearance, hear it in her words, and feel it in her very presence. He curled up inside himself, a protective response. He had thought that taunting her about finding Tarsha on her own might send her away, but the witch was not that sort. She was the kind that hunted and killed and felt no remorse in doing so. She believed in tying up loose ends and disposing of all potential problems that might otherwise return to haunt her later. She would not be leaving Flinc alive, no matter what else she might decide.

He squared himself away, blocking her path. It was time. It was the moment he had expected, and he was ready for it.

"You will do what you must, and I will do the same. But you will never have the part of me you want, witch." He lifted his wizened face slightly, a cunning look on his face. "Come show me what you intend to do."

Enraged, she took a step toward him, hands formed into claws lifting to shred his face. But then she saw something in his eyes, the truth of what he intended, and threw herself backward into Tavo.

"Get down!" she screamed at him.

Then Flinc went rigid, his body stiffening, and with shocking suddenness thousands of barbs exploded from his flesh, rocketing in all directions at once. Most struck the stone of the walls and ceiling and floor of his home, but enough to matter embedded themselves deep inside the flesh of his enemies.

When the air cleared of deadly missiles, Flinc was no more.

Right away, Clizia could tell the barbs were poisoned. She could feel the poison's fire burning through her. She struggled to her feet and summoned a negation spell to counter the effects, swaddling herself in a smoky haze that shrouded her entirely as it began an extraction of the poisoned barbs. Nearly frantic with pain and a numbing sensation that was working its way through her damaged body, she then conjured an antidote that coated her like a second skin from head to foot. She worked on herself first, then on Tavo.

Although she thought more than once as she struggled to save him that it would be far easier if she just let him die.

In the end, she was so exhausted that she collapsed in a heap, waiting to see if her efforts had been successful. Either she had acted quickly enough to save them both or they would die writhing in pain. She had been careless and foolish in allowing herself to get so close to that vile creature. She had been overconfident, and that was inexcusable. No matter the rage and frustration his persistence in resisting her engendered, she should have known better.

She called Tavo's name several times, but there was no answer.

After long minutes—how many, she couldn't have said—she felt a hint of strength returning to her body. She felt a marginal lessening of the pain; sensation was returning. She breathed long and deeply, promising herself that if she recovered she would not make a mistake like this again, swearing it on everything she held dear.

She glanced over to where the forest imp had been standing when he exploded. Nothing recognizable left. A dark residue formed a wide stain on the floor. Particles of ash floated on the acrid air.

She heard Tavo's whisper of disbelief. "Why did he do that?"

"He is a Faerie creature," she answered. "They are not and never were like us. They can do things that are beyond us. He willed himself to die, and tried to take us with him."

His whisper twisted into a snarl of rage. "Now what do we do? You let this happen, old woman! What about Tarsha? How do we find her without him?"

"Try listening to what I say. Your sister bears my mark and she is mine whenever I wish it. We will find her easily enough. This imp thought to send her to safety, but he has merely postponed the inevitable. Stop your whining!"

Tavo moaned. "Something's wrong with me. My head hurts. There's something in my eye . . ."

And then he screamed, a long dreadful wail of despair.

She crawled over to him and dragged him around to where she could see his face. His left eye was gone. The poison had dissolved it.

His good eye fixed on her. "Don't look at me like that!"

"Like what? Like you're missing an eye? It's nothing. You have another."

"What do you mean, nothing? It's my eye!"

She seized the front of his tunic. "I'm tired of you, little man. I offered my help in finding your sister, and all you can do is whine about how things aren't going your way. Did you think this would be easy? Did you think she would just lie down and let you finish her like some helpless animal? How stupid are you?"

His face had gone white. For the first time since she had encountered him, she saw fear in his eye—a reflection of doubt that he was capable of doing what he had set out to do.

She patted his face. "Relax, Tavo. I will help you still."

"I don't need you to help me," he blurted out, his voice shaking.

There were tears in his remaining eye—the tears of a little boy. "I don't need anyone! You said you would keep her a prisoner, but you lied! You let those men and that creature take her from me. Why should I trust you with anything?"

Clizia fixed him with a gaze that would have turned a sane man to stone. One aged finger reached out and tapped him on his nose.

"I have great things planned for you," she whispered. "I would make you the most powerful man in the world—greater even than the Druids when they walked the Four Lands. But for that to happen, you must do as I say and not question me. You must give me the chance to prove I can do what I say. So decide now. Are you going to listen to what I tell you or go off on your own? If it is the latter, you will certainly cause problems for a while wherever you go, but in the end you will die. You will be killed and quickly forgotten. You will never know what you can be."

She held his gaze. "Which path will you take? Choose quickly; I have no more time to waste on you."

His eyes were bright with fear and loathing, and there was a glimmer of madness in his gaze that was unmistakable. His nod was barely perceptible. "I will go with you. Can we leave now?"

"Soon enough," she answered. She dragged herself to her feet and waited for him to do the same. "Come with me."

Together, they climbed from the forest imp's underground lair and back out into the morning light. Clizia was already thinking ahead to what she would do next. Suddenly, her plans for Tavo Kaynin were taking shape, formulated in a moment's inspiration while they lay exhausted and half dead underground, the poison of the barbs only just defeated. It was all so simple. That Tavo had to be killed was indisputable. He was much too dangerous to be allowed to live—too unpredictable, too wrapped up in a struggle to control his own demons. But perhaps before she disposed of him he could be made useful enough to advance her plans for the future.

Even the most insane could sometimes serve a greater good.

Clizia did not notice the lantern eyes watching her as she began the journey back to Drisker's cabin. Nor did the young man. Their thoughts and their cautions were directed elsewhere. The eyes watched as they disappeared into the trees, then blinked once, and Fade materialized within the shadow of the huge old trunks of the forest, her massive body stretched out in the undergrowth. She remained where she was long after the intruders departed, her senses directed toward the lair of the forest imp.

She was waiting for him to emerge. She had waited for him before, sometimes for hours, sometimes longer. It was a ritual they shared.

But on this day, he did not appear.

TWENTY-ONE

IT SEEMED ROCAN ARNEAS was not one to sit around mulling things over. So once he decided he was leaving Varfleet behind, he wasted no more time. The very day after the incident at the Sticky Wicked Hall of Chance, he packed up his clothing and personal effects, strapped on his weapons, closed and shuttered his warehouse lodgings, and—hauling a somewhat skeptical and reluctant Shea Ohmsford with him—set out.

He had brought the boy into his private quarters the previous night to explain why he wanted to bring him along, which had left Shea more confused than he had been before. The boy was nothing if not quick-witted—you didn't survive long on the streets of a city like Varfleet otherwise. He was swift of foot, and instinctually sharp enough to recognize the truth of things long before others did, making him more than able to smell out a scam. But Rocan Arneas was every bit as smart as Shea was, and his ability to explain something without actually saying much at all was unparalleled.

What he told Shea was that he needed someone who could provide several valuable services, including a willingness to fetch and carry, provide a second set of eyes and ears, get into and out of tight places, and be willing to work long hours without complaint. The pay would be good initially, but if he continued to excel at his job, it would eventually be great.

Shea, he advised—in his matter-of-fact way of tacking something important on at the end of things—could end up wealthy.

The boy took all this in without getting too excited. He liked Rocan's enthusiasm and found him fascinating to be around. But he had learned a long time ago that lack of substance frequently meant a lack of moral commitment, and he was worried that this might be the case here. Deep involvement with games of chance like Pickroll did nothing to lessen his concerns. Rocan could persuade the bark to peel off a tree and join the logs in the fireplace, and this was not reassuring.

"It's this way, young Shea," he said at one point, as they feasted on cold quail and hot bread late that first night. "What I do is collect things. I am a scavenger of a sort, but I am very particular about what I scavenge and why. I relieve other people of what they least need or understand how to use wisely. I select these people out of the wider population, and I sit them down and usually persuade them to donate what they have without realizing they are doing so."

Shea, no fool he, understood at once. "You're talking about taking their money at games of chance. Like earlier this evening, playing Pickroll."

Rocan laughed merrily. "I knew you were the right lad! So quick to see the truth. That skill will serve you well in the years to come, young Shea. Don't you ever lose it."

"So you take money from those who have plenty to spare by playing games with them. Then you pocket the money and keep it for yourself. But even if they don't need it, why is it right for you to take it from them and call it a donation? Seems to me this makes you just like them."

It was bold talk directed to a man like Rocan, about whom he really knew nothing. But Shea knew that you had to stand up to such men and challenge them if you wanted their respect.

Rocan leaned forward across the small dining room table and fixed his eyes on the boy. "I am nothing like those men. They have no other thought of what to do with their money than gamble it away. Their goal is to enrich themselves further by foolishly believing they can win, thereby ensuring a softer, more decadent life. They seek greater prosperity without purpose. I, on the other hand, game not to enrich myself, but to change the world for the better."

Shea stared. "How do you do that? How are you changing the world?"

With a slow smile and a shrug of his shoulders, Rocan leaned back again. "Why don't you come with me to Arishaig and let me show you?"

So Shea allowed himself to be persuaded even though he hadn't the faintest idea what this was about. He had always told himself not to get into anything he didn't fully understand upfront, and mostly he had done so. But this time, he didn't. He was persuaded to make the deviation from his hard-and-fast rule for several very different reasons.

First of all, he thought it was time to move on from Varfleet. Things had been stagnant of late and now—since his last two jobs— increasingly dangerous. Besides, he had lived here his entire life and seen almost nothing of any other part of the country. Rocan was providing him with transportation out. It was a free ride to a new home.

Second, he had a considerable amount of money in hand after combining the payments from the black-cloaked grandfather and Rocan. It was reasonable to assume there might be more to be earned from the latter, and once he had accumulated enough he could settle permanently, be it here in Varfleet or another city in another part of the Four Lands. He was working toward a better life—one in which he no longer had to scurry about like a rat gathering bits of food. He wanted a real home. He wanted sufficient credits to merit recognition. He wanted to be valued; he wanted his advice sought after.

But as an orphan who had lived most of his life by his wits and luck, he had learned one indisputable truth—you never got anywhere without taking a few risks. He had reminded himself of that earlier with both the grandfather and Rocan. Now and then, you had to step across forbidden boundaries and jump into the fire. He felt strongly that this was one of those times. Something about Rocan suggested this was an opportunity not to be missed—even if he was still not sure he trusted the man.

So after a quick stop to gather up his meager possessions, off he went with his benefactor, boarding a public transport that traveled once every other day from Varfleet to Arishaig. Rocan purchased passage that provided them with a private cabin and special services including food and drink and an attendant ready to see to their needs at any time during their journey. Seelah did not accompany them to the loading dock, and once inside their cabin Shea was about to ask why she wasn't going with them when suddenly she appeared out of nowhere. She was as silky and irresistible as he remembered, and he smiled in spite of himself. Recognizing his response, she leaned into him to kiss his cheek.

"She likes you, lad," Rocan observed. "Should be interesting to see how that plays out down the road."

Shea wasn't sure he was the least bit ready to find out something as wild and mysterious as that promised to be, so he was quick to take his seat and turn his attention to watching the countryside as their vessel lifted away. Off to one side, he could hear Rocan cooing to Seelah in an unfamiliar language, his words low and calming—as if she needed reassuring for some reason. He had to force himself not to look over at them. Some things were best left to the imagination.

Nevertheless, when temptation got the better of him and he risked a quick peek, he found Seelah making soft noises as she rubbed against Rocan, and he looked away again quickly.

They rode most of the way without talking, the three of them remaining in their cabin for the duration of the two-day journey. When the attendant appeared to bring them breakfast and later lunch—and much later dinner—the boy waited to see what his response would be to Seelah. But the instant the door opened, the strange creature simply disappeared, gone beyond sight and sound. Only when the door closed behind the attendant did she materialize once more.

More than once Shea thought to ask Rocan more about where they were going and why. But in the end he decided against it, remembering that Rocan had spoken of letting Shea see for himself. So he decided it was better not to appear too eager for answers. Besides, if he needed to extract himself from this situation later, it might be easier to do so if he kept a safe distance between himself and Rocan now.

They spent the night in their cabin sleeping on benches that were adequate, though far from comfortable. Neither Shea nor Rocan slept particularly well, but curling up on a padded bench seemed to be no problem for Seelah, who was asleep in minutes and did not stir the remainder of the night. Shea sat across from her for a long time, puzzling through what sort of creature she might be, wondering how she and Rocan came to be . . . *To be what? A couple? Friends?* The boy didn't know. They were clearly close, but the nature of their relationship was still unknown—along with any definition of what Seelah actually was.

At one point during the night, when he saw Rocan was awake, too, the boy leaned over and whispered, "How did you and Seelah meet?"

Rocan blinked and smiled. "We met in a bar one hard rainy night. The shadows wrapped around us like a cloak to hide from anyone watching what we saw in each other's eyes. We touched, we kissed, we shared a molten red ale that brought tears to our eyes. Later, much later, after we had spent ourselves in a room . . ."

Shea held up his hands, making warding motions. "Seriously, even I can tell you're making that up. Tell me the truth or don't tell me anything."

Rocan shrugged. "I have no reason not to tell you. She was trapped and caged by some very misguided people. I saved her at some risk to myself. We became friends and partners. Companions. Fellow travelers on the road of life." He paused. "To spare you time and effort, I'll answer the question you cannot bring yourself to ask. No, we are not lovers."

"I wasn't going to ask that . . ."

"Maybe not, but you want to know. What do you think she is?"

Shea turned crimson. "I wasn't going to ask that, either."

"Doesn't matter. What do you think?"

The boy shook his head, not trusting his answer to words. "I don't know. She's beautiful, I can see that much."

"And very, very dangerous."

"I imagine."

"But not quite human, right?"

Shea nodded again, thinking. "Kind of magical."

"Ah, bright lad! Right again. She's one of the Faerie—a creature out of time, ancient."

"Which means she's . . . what?"

Rocan shrugged. "Hard to say. She won't talk about it. She's one of the Fae. Maybe the last of her species; I don't know. She has magic; she can shape-shift when she chooses. But she's not like the other shifters you've heard about, the ones that were born into the Four Lands. Not like the kind that are wicked and deceitful and sometimes go mad. She is as sane as you or I. An original."

"She looks a little like a cat."

"A form she prefers to take now and then, but cannot sustain for long. Mostly, she is what her body wants her to be. So even though she has shape-shifting abilities, she is for the most part the creature she shows us."

Shea looked back through the darkness at the sleeping Seelah. "I've never seen anyone so beautiful," he repeated, unable to put the thought aside. "The prettiest girl I've ever known doesn't begin to approach her."

"Beautiful and dangerous—a useful combination. She and I, we are a pair to draw to, as they say."

"Will you tell me more about how you found her?" he asked Rocan.

The other shrugged. "One day, maybe."

He drifted off again after that, leaving Shea to ponder his revelations about Seelah. A strange, wild creature, the boy thought. Not one to trifle with; not one to challenge. But he was drawn to her, anyway. He wanted to know more about her. He wanted her to tell him about herself.

He fell asleep imagining how that might happen.

It was nearing noon the following day when Rocan shook Shea awake from a doze he had fallen into an hour or so earlier, thanks to his inadequate sleep the previous night. His eyes blinked open and he found Seelah staring at him from across the cabin, curled up on the other bench like a cat, her golden eyes glittering.

"Take a look outside, young Shea," Rocan told him. "There's our destination approaching."

Shea shifted to a sitting position and peered through the open viewport at a sight that left him breathless. For as far as the eye could see, buildings of all sizes and shapes sprawled across the landscape. Those closest were fewer and more widely spread apart, many of them attached to fields and pasturelands. Farther on, dirt roads rutted and narrow gave way to ones that were smoother and wider, some covered with paving stones and some graveled, and the homes became residences clustered more closely together.

It wasn't until well beyond the outlying buildings that the city walls appeared—sizable to begin with, but growing steadily larger as they approached. These formidable barriers encircled the city proper— huge and sheer and bracketed by weapons towers and landing pads on which various types of airships were settled. Some were huge battle cruisers, some flits and Sprints, but all were at the ready. Soldiers of the Federation were visible atop the walls, as well—hundreds patrolling the seemingly endless string of battlements as they stretched away into the distance. Within their protective grasp, at the very center of the city, great towers rose against the bright-blue skies south, closely gathered like sentinels. Other, smaller towers were gathered in clusters elsewhere within the walls, looming over the smaller warehouses and shops that filled the city from end to end.

"They always build the strongest walls for themselves, the rich and powerful," Rocan muttered, his bitter words so soft the boy almost didn't catch them. "They always protect themselves, even if it's at the expense of others."

Their transport continued on, and soon they were close enough to the perimeter walls that Shea could see how the city had been constructed like a wheel, with the largest buildings and highest walls at the very center and other walls radiating out toward perimeter walls like wheel spokes. It was the most astonishing achievement the boy had ever witnessed, and he could barely bring himself to grasp the whole of what he was seeing.

"How can you even find your way around?" he asked.

Rocan shrugged. "Practice, practice. Or asking directions, of course. It takes time to get acclimated."

Shea could just imagine. For the first time, he was intimidated by the idea of trying to survive here. Varfleet seemed tiny in comparison with this behemoth. It had taken him all his life to learn everything there was to know about his home city. How long would it take him to learn just a tenth of that in Arishaig? He immediately began making plans for departure, overwhelmed beyond reason by the magnitude of what he would be facing if he stayed—a cold chill running up his spine at the thought of it. And then abruptly his stubborn side surfaced and reminded him that he was not a quitter. If he had to leave at some point, fine. But he would not commit to leaving before he had even set foot on the ground. He would wait until Rocan had revealed what it was he had brought him here to see and then decide.

His attention was diverted to the city again as they passed over the perimeter walls and angled toward the landing pad designated for their craft. Below, the roofs of the city passed beneath like a parade of soldiers, all looking much the same—salmon-colored tiles with black chimneys stacked on top of whitewashed walls. The streets below were crowded with people on foot or riding in passenger coaches, carts filled with dry goods and foodstuffs, and a smattering of the newly developed ground speeders that only the rich could afford.

Shea had never seen these machines before, and he hadn't really been all that sure they were not simply another wild rumor. Each carried only one or two passengers and was built for speed. They were fueled by the converted energy of diapson crystals connected to thin light sheaths mounted on hoods or roofs contoured to match the shape of the vehicle so that the fit was seamless. They were slow moving and out of their element on the heavily trafficked city streets, but the boy had heard that once outside on the flats and grasslands they could fly as swiftly as airborne Sprints.

He had a sudden urge to drive one, just to see what it would feel like. But his chances for doing that seemed slim, at best.

When they landed, Rocan got to his feet at once, snatched up his backpack and travel case, and went out the door without looking back. Seelah had already disappeared. Shea hesitated, then heard Rocan calling for him to get moving and quickly followed, his own backpack slung over his narrow shoulders. He went down the airship's central corridor into the cheaper public seating section, already crowded with departing passengers unloading through the main doors. Ahead of him, he caught sight of Rocan's long dark hair as he bobbed and weaved his way forward. The boy was quick to imitate him, although careful not to bump anyone on the way even while he was being jostled himself.

Outside, he caught up to his companion and they walked across the elevated landing pad to a stairwell and started down.

"Our luggage and a coach should be waiting," Rocan advised. "Otherwise, it's a rather long walk."

Shea could imagine. Nothing could be very close to anything else in a city of this size.

The promised coach was waiting—an arrangement Shea did not pretend to understand, given the distance they had traveled already with no evident mode of communication. Their luggage was already gathered and stowed in the coach, and they climbed aboard and settled into the plush, comfortable seats.

Seelah appeared beside Rocan just before they started to move.

"All right, I give up!" the boy exclaimed in disgust. "How does she do that?"

Rocan looked puzzled. Then he gave a quick nod in recognition. "You want to know how she appears and disappears like she does? Well, it must seem very strange; it did to me the first few times. And the explanation is even stranger. I've told you she is one of the Fae. Her exact species is not clear to me. It appears she has something of sylphs or sprites in her—river, air, land, one of those breeds. Supposedly, they could shift out of themselves and become a part of the element that was at the core of their identity. So, since she just disappears into thin air when she vanishes, I have to assume that's the element that defines her. Or some part of it, anyway."

Shea stared. "So she's an air sprite?"

Rocan shrugged. "In part, at least."

The boy crossed his arms, a perplexed frown on his face. "Then what am I doing here when you already have Seelah? Can't she do whatever you need done? She's ten times more capable than I could ever be."

Seelah gave him a dazzling smile, perhaps acknowledging the truth of this claim. Slithering down off the bench on Rocan's side of the coach, she nestled against Shea—or more accurately, *into* him, stroking his hair and cheeks. Shea squirmed with discomfort, but at the same time found the touching undeniably pleasant.

Rocan chuckled. "Seems she's taken with you, lad—more so than with anyone else I've encountered. Maybe she'll answer your questions sooner or later. She's never answered them for me, though I've asked often enough. For now, though, I think it might be better to accept her company and let the rest of it be."

Which is where things remained for the rest of the ride to their destination, Rocan burying himself in logbooks and sheets of paper filled with numbers and figures as Seelah continued to rub up against Shea until he found himself wondering which would be worse—if she continued or if she stopped. She seemed intent on sticking with the former, and all he could do in response was sit there and endure it. Any resistance on his part might send the wrong message—or maybe the right one—and he was wary enough of her not to want to make a mistake.

Trying his best to forget the beautiful creature nuzzling him, the boy looked out the window at the city they were passing through, trying his best to get a sense of things. One discovery took almost no effort at all. Whatever else Arishaig was, it was militarized on every level. There were soldiers everywhere he looked—some at designated stations along the roadways they traveled, some patrolling in squads along the walkways and streets, some marching in formation, some standing at attention, some on horseback, and some in flits passing overhead. The boy could not tell what any of them were doing besides keeping watch for trouble. All of them carried weapons and looked ready enough to act if the need should arise. Now and then, they would stop someone on the streets and ask for what appeared to be some form of identification. Once in a while, they would seize someone, lock their wrists in iron bracelets, and lead them away.

Although they were passing through distinctly different parts of the city, some grander and cleaner, some less so, he saw almost no evidence of begging or homelessness. When he asked Rocan about this, the other told him such unfortunates were consigned to those portions of the city that lay outside the walls and were not allowed inside for any reason. He did not look up when he said this, and Shea did not ask about it further.

They traveled in the coach for almost an hour, their pace dictated by other traffic and the driver's unwillingness to try to force his way through. Rocan barely spoke to him, his mind on his books and papers, but Shea imagined the driver had his orders. The boy shifted his position over and over, but Seelah simply shifted with him and stayed close, nuzzling contentedly.

A couple of times, in spite of his reticence, Shea found himself nuzzling her back.

When the coach finally began to slow further and the traffic grew sparse and the way forward clear, Shea sat up in anticipation.

Rocan put away his logbooks and papers and said quietly, "Did you know there is a tendency for people to ignore anything that makes them uncomfortable? They will look briefly, perhaps—a glance, no more—but then look away. For instance, when they see a young couple pressed up against each other in a coach, involved in matters of the heart. They appear to all those who see them to be in love. And love is, for the most part, a private matter. That being so and not wishing to intrude, they look away without thinking further about what they have seen. What further reason is there to stare when the evidence is clear?"

Shea flushed, realizing what the other was telling him. He had been used as a decoy and hadn't realized it. He hadn't given a thought about how anyone outside the coach might respond to what was happening inside. But he had been schooled before, and he was pretty sure this wouldn't be the last time.

The coach rolled to a stop. "Come, Shea," Rocan said. "We're here. The lesson's over."

Forcing a smile, the boy gave a slow shrug in response and was the first to climb out of the coach.

When the baggage was unloaded, the driver accepted payment and drove off, leaving Rocan and Shea standing at the door of an unobtrusive storefront with what appeared to be lodgings above. Seelah had vanished before they even left the coach. Shea glanced around on the chance he might notice something that would give her away, but the Fae was not to be so easily found.

"Is this where you live?" the boy asked.

"Sometimes." Rocan started for the front door that adjoined the entry to the storefront. "Come inside. This is where you will be living, too, for a while."

Maybe yes, maybe no, Shea thought, but followed him through the doorway without comment. A set of stairs leading up to the second floor greeted them, and with baggage in hand, they began the climb.

"We won't be here long," Rocan said. "Just long enough to let you have a look around. Then we'll need to gather up Tindall and discuss what lies ahead. I'll tell you what it is he and I are about and let him explain why it's so important."

At the top of the stairs, there were doors to the left and right. Rocan chose the first, released the locks that secured it, and stepped inside, with Shea on his heels. He had barely finished closing the door when armed soldiers stepped out of hiding from a closet and behind curtains, flash rips pointed at the pair.

"We've been waiting for you, Rocan," one said. "Welcome home."

TWENTY-TWO

To his credit, Rocan Arneas did not appear in the least bit surprised or flustered. He turned to face the speaker, who was standing off to one side—a short, stocky man with a series of small white stars sewn onto the breast of his black tunic. "Nice of you to come greet me, Commander Zakonis," he said, smiling.

Shea, standing just behind Rocan, did not have the faintest idea what was going on save for the obvious fact that the Federation had apparently been hunting and had now found his companion. The why of it was impossible to guess, but he found himself wishing once again that he had paid better attention to his instincts.

"You have misbehaved, Rocan, and this time you are going straight to the prisons where you will remain until we can sort out what it is you and Tindall are up to."

"So you have made him your prisoner, as well?"

"It wasn't all that difficult. He doesn't move around as quickly as you do. We found him, scooped him up, and took him to Assidian Deep. Once he was down in the dark and the quiet where he could scream as much as he wanted, we asked him a few questions about you. He didn't want to say anything, of course, but it turns out his tolerance for pain is rather low. So here we are, the two of us, come together to reach an accord on the nature of your immediate future."

"I think maybe you assume a bit too much about any accord between us."

"Oh, I think we will reach one quickly enough once you hear what might happen to your friend if we don't."

"You've hurt him already, haven't you? Is he dead?"

"He's a bit banged up, nothing more." Zakonis glanced over at Shea. "Who is this piece of street trash? Are you recruiting boys for your little rebellion these days or is he here for something less palatable?"

Rocan did not spare even a glance for Shea. "I picked him up on my way here to carry my luggage and perform a few other minor duties I don't care to bother myself with. He doesn't know the first thing about any of this."

"So you say. But is it the truth? With you, Rocan, it's always so hard to tell. Where's your pretty friend? Lose interest in you, did she? I expect you like to try out new women like new clothes. I'm sorry to have missed her. I would like to have questioned her a bit, too, maybe seen how well she stood up to the sort of pain I intend . . ."

His voice caught in his throat as Seelah materialized right in front of him. Zakonis made a choking sound and tried to say something more, but the Fae was already lifting him off the floor by his neck and throwing him across the room into two of his soldiers. She went through the rest like a whirlwind—so quickly Shea had trouble following her movements. A dazzle of golden eyes turned crimson here; a flash of long hair whipping about her face there. One soldier got off a single shot before he went down; another took a swing with his weapon in a blocking effort that failed. Seelah swept them aside as if they were made of paper, leaving them slumped on the floor of the apartment, their weapons broken and the pieces scattered.

Rocan grabbed Shea by the arm and propelled him out the door. "Seelah hates Federation weapons," he offered, practically dragging the boy down the stairs. "Knives and swords, bows and arrow, are all fine. But diapson-powered stun guns and flash rips and all the rest? That bunch back there is lucky she didn't tear them apart along with their weapons."

"Are they dead?" Shea blurted out.

"Probably not. Although you never know. She has a temper."

They were down the stairs and out the door in seconds, heading back the way they had come, toward the city. Or at least two of them were; Seelah was gone again. Rocan began to run, and Shea had no choice but to run with him. His arm had been freed, but he didn't think much of his chances alone in this monster city with no knowledge of where anything was. No, he had thrown in his lot with Rocan Arneas by coming here in the first place, and now he was going to have to see things through.

When they had run the equivalent of perhaps a mile, Rocan slowed and turned off the larger road they had been following into a narrow passage that was little more than an alleyway. They followed this route for a while as it twisted and turned through one cluster of buildings after another, crossing broader streets in the process without ever turning onto them. Shea glanced around trying to get a fix on where the sun was, but he couldn't manage it. Not that it mattered. It made no difference where the sun was since he didn't know where anything else was, either. What he really wanted to find were the gates that would take him out of Arishaig to the open grasslands beyond.

"What about all your personal stuff?" the boy asked, for Rocan had left his luggage behind in the apartment.

Rocan had slowed almost to an amble, although he kept them moving steadily onward. "Stuff, like you say. Nothing I can't afford to lose. What matters most is either on me or in storage where no one will ever find it."

"You've probably lost your apartment, too. You can't go back there now, can you?"

"Probably not."

"That Federation commander? You seem to have some history between you."

Rocan shrugged. "He hunts me; I avoid him. He thinks I am a danger to the Federation, a rebel intent on bringing down the entire government through nefarious means. He has no idea."

They broke through the scramble of taller, more densely situated buildings into a forested park that ran on as far as Shea could see. There were people sitting on benches and eating lunch on blankets and enjoying a day filled with sunshine and warmth. Here, unlike the rest of the city, there were no soldiers and weapons. The buildings closest to the park were residences of varying sizes and shapes, and the sound of birds was audible through the muted din of the distant, larger center of the city.

"So you are not a rebel?"

"There are no rebels. They've all been stamped out. I wish it weren't so, but it is."

"Is Tindall a rebel?"

"No, he's a scientist. Quiet, now. Save your strength for walking. We've got a way to go. We can talk more later."

So the boy lapsed into silence, still as confused now as he was before about what was happening and why. But he recognized a distinct hardening in Rocan's voice, and he knew it wasn't smart to ask anything more just now. The other would tell him when he was ready. Or not tell him at all, perhaps. It didn't matter to Shea in the larger scheme of things, because he was already looking for a way to get out of this mess.

They walked for a very long way—long enough that, by the time they reached their destination, the skies were darkening. They were well beyond the park and the houses and into an industrial part of the city that was decidedly less pleasant, old and run-down, the streets littered with trash. Huge warehouses hunkered in deepening shadows, a handful with lights shining bravely through barred windows and everything beyond cloaked in darkness. Only a few people were out and about, shadowy forms that were ragged and tattered and slipped through the twilight like ghosts.

Shea felt a shiver creep up his spine at the haunted look of the area and its denizens. Everything felt dangerous.

He forced the feeling down, although he couldn't quite banish it entirely. Oddly, he was reminded of Varfleet, and an unexpected nostalgia crept over him. He couldn't find a reason for it beyond a sense of familiarity, but he understood districts like this one—places of fire and iron, of forges and giant presses where the melting and re-forming, fabrication and finishing of goods were carried out in cavernous spaces. Where workers suffered burns and slashes and sometimes loss of limbs, and their hands and faces were always black with ash. But these were places, too, where vagrants and homeless found shelter and desperate men and women took advantage of those weaker than themselves. They were there, in the shadows, waiting; Shea could sense their presence. The smell of iron and coolant, of forge fires and their ash residue, wafted thick and pungent on the air. Odd clangs and bangs from hammers and presses echoed down the streets, punctuated by sudden yells and sharp-edged warnings.

Shea walked with his eyes lowered but watchful, aware that dark figures were moving off to either side, not yet threatening, but near enough nevertheless that it might be only moments before they were.

"This doesn't feel very safe," he said quietly.

Rocan grunted. "Because it isn't. Stay close."

They moved deeper into the warehouse district, a threatening silence closing about; all the buildings ahead were unlighted hulks, and the inhabitants of this part of the district prowled in the shadows soundlessly. One or two approached, hands outstretched for credits, low voices pleading. Rocan shook his head and gestured them away. One was so bold as to clutch at Shea's arm, but the boy quickly pulled free. Laughter, low and mean, trailed after him as they passed on. The sky was growing thick with clouds and mist, and the vague light from the moon and stars was disappearing.

"How much farther?" Shea whispered.

"A way yet. Just keep moving."

No problem there, Shea thought. He was walking practically on top of Rocan, his eyes shifting constantly to keep watch, his senses alert for signs of danger.

When they reached a place between buildings where there seemed to be no one about, Rocan brought them to a halt, swung his backpack off his shoulders, and opened it.

"Here," he said, hauling out a small, bulky object that he unfolded carefully and locked in place with a series of sharp metal clicks before handing it to Shea. "Take it."

It was a mini-crossbow, much smaller than those of regulation size—almost a toy. Shea examined it. It was not much more than two feet across, with a looped ring on the business end for drawing back the bowstring, a slot for the bolts, and a notch for the trigger.

Rocan then handed him a pair of ten-inch bolts. "Just in case," he said. "You probably won't have time to use more than one, so be sure you don't miss. Load it now, and keep it close to your chest while we walk."

Shea did so, finding its workings supple and smooth. He drew back the string to the trigger, laid the bolt in the firing slot, and, with the point directed to one side, tucked the crossbow against his chest.

"What about Seelah?" he asked hopefully, remembering how she had rescued them at the apartment.

Rocan shook his head. "She's no longer with us. We're on our own."

Shea wanted to ask why she wasn't there, but really he didn't need to know. All that mattered was that if she wasn't there, she couldn't help them.

Shea caught a glint of steel in the fading light as Rocan drew a pair of long knives from his backpack and tucked them beneath his cloak.

Then they set out once more.

Now any remaining light was almost entirely gone. The warehouses were reduced to vague hulks in the background, and the beggars prowling the streets had faded away. Now and again a shadowy movement revealed a lingering presence, but for the most part these faceless wraiths remained concealed by the dark. Rocan kept the boy to the middle of the roadways, avoiding the walls, doorways, and overflowing trash bins on either side, stepping carefully around the vague bundles they encountered lying in their path. Shea had a death grip on the mini-crossbow by now, realizing he was probably going to have to use it. How could he think anything else? Rocan wouldn't have given it to him if he hadn't believed there might be a need for it before they reached their destination.

The wind had picked up, steady gusts ripping down the empty streets, further scattering the loose garbage that was already strewn about, whipping around corners and across roofs with howling shrieks that foretold the coming of a sizable storm. Shea glanced skyward. Heavy, dark clouds were rolling in, and a haze of rain was clearly visible above the lighted buildings of the city to the west. If they didn't reach their destination soon and take shelter, they were going to end up soaked.

"Is it much farther?" Shea asked once more—this time a little louder to be heard over the wind.

Rocan started to answer and stopped abruptly, his eyes shifting to something ahead. Three ragged figures were approaching, spread out in a line, slouched down against the force of the wind, cloaks billowing out behind them, hoods drawn up. They held weapons in their hands—blades that glinted in momentary flashes as lightning streaked across the sky.

Rocan slowed, apparently deciding that flight was not going to save them. "There will be more behind us," he said quietly.

Shea glanced over his shoulder. Indeed, two more were already coming up behind them to cut off any chance of escape. Caught between the men ahead and behind, and the buildings to the left and right, Shea and Rocan were penned in.

We've escaped one trap only to fall into a second, Shea thought in despair. He wondered momentarily if the two were connected, and decided they weren't. There wasn't any sensible way they could be, given the participants. The Federation soldiers had their orders regarding Rocan; they believed him a seditionist. These men were thieves and cutthroats with no interest in anything but stealing credits and valuables.

Shea took a deep breath. They were going to have to fight their way out of this, and they might have to kill someone in the process. He had never killed anyone before, and he wasn't much interested in doing so now. But he also wasn't much interested in dying.

"The two behind are yours," Rocan said under his breath, drawing to a halt and standing his ground. He had blades in hand, and his

cloak lay on the ground, temporarily discarded. "Do the best you can. Try to hold them off. I'll help if I'm able."

Shea wanted to say that he had never been in a situation like this and wasn't sure he could do anything even to save himself. He had come to Arishaig to make his fortune, but it was beginning to look like he had really come here to die.

Time slowed and then stopped. A deep silence broken only by the whistling of the wind settled in, enfolding the combatants.

Then the five rushed the two, and there was no longer silence or time left. Shea brought up the crossbow and held it with both hands. The gloom was sufficiently deep that there was every chance neither of his attackers realized what he was holding. They were coming at him side by side, so he quickly stepped left to disrupt their formation. As he had hoped, the one closer increased speed and moved in front of the other, anxious to get there first.

He was within six yards of Shea when the boy released the cross-bow trigger. The iron-tipped bolt slammed into his attacker's chest, throwing him backward into the man trailing, sending both sprawl-ing. The boy was already reloading his weapon as they went down, the toe of one boot tucked in the holding strap to brace the crossbow as he drew back its drawstring. For a moment he thought he would not be able to do it; his hands were shaking and all the strength seemed to have gone out of him. But then the drawstring yielded to his efforts, rising to the fastening notch and hooking itself in place. Into the slot went the second bolt, and he dropped to one knee, sensing the sec-ond attacker back on his feet and closing fast. When he lifted his gaze and the bow, the man was right on top of him. Instantly, Shea re-leased the trigger, not bothering to look, firing blindly because there wasn't enough time for anything else.

The man screamed, but the sound died into a terrible gurgle of blood and air. The man fell on him—a huge weight that knocked him backward. His knife dropped and skittered away. When Shea rolled away from him, just trying to get clear, he saw that the bolt had taken him through the throat. The man was lying with his hands clawing at the shaft, which had entered his neck and was sticking out the other

side. His eyes were glazed and his movements feeble, and in seconds he was dead.

Shea scrambled back to his knees in time to see Rocan standing over the bodies of two of his attackers while locked in combat with the third. This man was long and lean and wiry, and there was a frantic determination etched on his hard features. Blades glittered as the two grappled, each holding a weapon high in one hand while trying to keep his opponent at bay. There was barely any movement at all as they struggled, just a terrible straining of muscles and limbs and a series of grunts as each sought to break the other's grip and drive his knife home.

Shea hesitated only a moment; then he was rushing to Rocan's aid. With no other weapon at hand and no bolts left, he jammed the empty crossbow into the attacker's spine as hard as he could. The man did not go down, but the blow momentarily distracted him. It was enough. Rocan's knife hand twisted free and the blade disappeared into the man's chest.

And that quickly, it was over. All five attackers lay dead in the empty street. Shea stood looking about, breathing hard as he stared at the bodies, scarcely able to believe what had just happened. He kept searching for something to help him make sense of it, but his efforts failed.

Then Rocan gripped him by his shoulders and knelt before him. "That was as brave an act as I have ever witnessed, Shea Ohmsford. I believed you would measure up, and you did—even to something as terrible as this. Deep breaths, lad. Take a moment to recover yourself. Look at me. In my eyes, now. Look deep."

The boy did so and found his companion studying him intently. "Tell me, now," he whispered, "are you all right? Are you all of a piece?"

Shea nodded. "I don't want to have to do that again. Ever."

"Can't promise that. No one can. But for tonight, I think we are done. Are you ready to go? Come, then, we haven't much farther to travel."

Shea felt a surge of relief push aside the fear and horror that still

clung to him like a second skin. He exhaled sharply, thinking he had already traveled just about as far as he cared to this night.

They walked away swiftly from the bodies, anxious to get clear of the stench of death and the chance of any similar encounters. Shea could feel eyes watching them from the shadows as they moved farther along the roadway, but he couldn't see or hear anything in the deep gloom. Then he realized he might be imagining the eyes, and that no one was really there—especially given the growing storm. After what had just happened, it was no wonder he was on edge.

He could still see the faces of the men lying dead on the stones of the street, their eyes staring at nothing. He believed he would see those eyes for a long time before the memory began to fade.

They went on for perhaps another half hour without incident. No one appeared to bar the way, and no one called out in challenge. In the shadows, scattered figures were now visible, prowling the refuse bins and doorways, looking for food and shelter. Rocan glanced their way but said nothing, locked within himself as he scanned the otherwise deserted streets. Shea let him be, busy wrestling with his own emotions.

Finally, they arrived at a building that looked for all intents and purposes the same as every other building they had passed on their way—a blocky, darkened structure with vast roll-up doors on one wall and barred windows high up on another with a pair of heavy iron doors midway along, which the boy assumed were the main entry.

Rocan proved him right when he led Shea over and released a series of locks embedded in the steel casing. The doors immediately swung open on a black void. Rocan stepped inside, and after a moment's hesitation Shea followed. Behind them the doors closed with a soft clunk, and the locks fell into place. Shea fought down a moment of panic; then a smokeless lamp brightened their surroundings as Rocan lifted it to guide them farther in.

"Stay close to me," the man said, but Shea found the advice unnecessary.

The ground floor of the building—or at least the considerable part of it that Rocan was leading him through—consisted of a maze of hallways and closed doors with no lights visible through the cracks. Gloom shrouded their path forward and back, and the air was filled with the smell of dust. Their footsteps echoed in the stillness—a steady tapping that measured their progress as they passed from one section of the building to another. Only once did they find a door ajar, and there appeared to be nothing within. It was impossible, from anything he was seeing, for Shea to identify the use to which this warehouse was being put.

Rocan glanced back at him and saw the look on his face. "Don't be fooled. All this is just to discourage the curious and the suspicious, should any manage to gain entrance. What matters lies ahead and higher up. Be patient. You'll see."

Shea nodded, but he was not convinced. Increasingly, he was coming to consider his decision to leave Varfleet with Rocan as foolhardy. It would not take much at this point to send him back the way he had come.

They reached a steel door in an alcove off to one side that the boy would have passed without notice, wrapped in shadows as it was. But Rocan steered him over, and through a series of rapid finger movements on the indented face of a blank keypad, he released the locks. The door opened onto a set of narrow stairs, leading up. Holding his smokeless lamp before him, Rocan ascended, with Shea at his heels. They climbed to the top of that set of stairs and then to the top of a second. The steps ended at yet another of the by-now-familiar steel doors, this one every bit as formidable-looking as the last two.

Once more, Rocan manipulated the indentations of a blank keypad until the locks released and the door swung open. But this time, instead of using the lamplight to show them what lay ahead, he engaged a huge metal switch affixed to the wall beside the door, and bands of light blazed to life from every direction.

The boy looked around in wonder. They were in a cavernous room—a chamber much larger than anything he had ever been in before. A quick perusal suggested it must occupy the entirety of the third floor, stretching far enough from end to end and side to side that the most distant points were indistinct and slightly hazy, despite the bright lights.

"Solar-powered by light sheaths stretched across the roof of the building," said Rocan. "Another new form of energy in this ever-expanding world of diapson-crystal-powered machines."

Crates and boxes of all sizes and shapes were grouped about the room. Settled in the spaces between were a series of machines the like of which the boy had never seen, their casings of smooth and polished metal, suggestive of powers that the boy could only guess at. Radian draws ran in thick tentacles across the floor from place to place, connecting to the machines and to the heavier cables tied against the walls that stretched upward through the ceiling and presumably to the light sheaths above.

For the first time since he had met Rocan and Seelah, Shea Ohmsford was impressed.

"All this," Rocan said, his hand sweeping the room and taking in all the machines and stores, "is what the credits I win are used for. It's taken three years of hard work while enduring hardships I could very easily have lived without. But I believed in Tindall's dream, and now it's come to pass."

He paused. "Because, finally, *that's* done!"

He pointed. At the center of the room, surrounded by all the rest of the equipment and supplies, was the strangest machine the boy had ever seen. It was a jumble of boxy compartments fused together, a maze of flexible cables and connectors running everywhere around and through it. Series of panels with dials and lights were embedded in the construct (although these were dark at present), and atop it all was a huge funnel formed of polished metal with its mouth facing toward the ceiling and its narrow end embedded in the largest of the compartments. Heavy supports braced the funnel to secure it in place, and the entire machine sat on a broad pallet of crossties and heavy wooden floorboards.

Shea took a few steps forward, conscious of Rocan following. "What *is* that thing?" he asked finally.

"The future," Rocan answered in a voice that reflected both pride and awe. His face was wreathed in a smile so broad that the boy was instinctively suspicious.

"The future," he repeated softly. "My future. Your future. The future of everyone in the Four Lands and beyond." He came closer and placed a hand on the boy's narrow shoulder. "This," he said, his voice dropping almost to a whisper, "is how we change everything."

TWENTY-THREE

---◆---

"OVER THERE!" SAID THE soldier, who had appeared with the news earlier that morning, after they had walked to the west perimeter of their camp.

The small group of four walked over to the spot indicated, and Arraxin Dresch knelt. The body lay sprawled on ground still dark with blood. The Federation commander remained where he was for a few moments, then rose and nodded.

The group walked on a short distance. "There," the soldier said again.

Dresch moved over to examine this spot, too. Another body.

The morning was all bright sunshine and sweet forest scents. Birdsong rose from within the trees. In the distance, the steady rush of the Mermidon River was clearly audible. Everything was peaceful. Everything fresh and promising. Nothing to suggest the events of last night.

"Here and here." Two more bodies lay on bloodied patches of earth, two more victims cut down as they stood watch, unaware of what was happening. They had been taken from behind while they were looking forward, their staggered lines preventing those in the front rank from realizing the fates of those behind.

They kept counting. Dresch grew sick to his stomach.

"The last three are over here," the soldier guiding him said finally. "The entire watch."

They walked to where the last of the bodies lay. Thirteen in all. Thirteen sentries dead. It shouldn't have been possible. How could all of them have been killed without any warning being given to the larger camp? Dresch shook his head. An enemy should not have been able to get behind them without at least one sounding an alarm.

He knelt by the last of the fallen and tried to envision the dead man's final moments. He closed his eyes and imagined what it must have been like. It didn't help in any tangible way, but it gave him a moment to empathize with these men who had been under his command. It fueled his rage, and anger was necessary where the deaths of any of his men were concerned. It wasn't enough simply to record them and pass on to other matters. It required more. It *demanded* more.

Admittedly, he didn't know these men. The command was too large, and his time was spent in planning and strategizing and issuing orders, so he did not have the personal contact with the soldiers that his junior officers had. He regretted this. But regret was a part of life as a soldier. You accepted it and then you put it aside and forgot it.

He stood again and looked around. There was nothing to see, of course. Not by now. He was just doing it out of habit.

He beckoned, and the soldier who had led him to the carnage came over. "Any sign of who did this?" Dresch asked quietly. "Any footprints or weapons or anything?"

The soldier shook his head. "They must have been ghosts."

Or ghostlike, Dresch thought.

"I want the entire area searched—upstream and down. Carefully. Report anything you find. Anything at all. No exceptions, no matter how insignificant or meaningless they might seem."

The man saluted and stepped away, turning back for the camp.

Almost immediately Murian Croix was at his shoulder, leaning close. "This is the work of our friends across the river," he said quietly.

Dresch nodded. "Seems so."

"The Skaar," Edeus Pressalin hissed, coming up to join them. "Why?"

Dresch looked over at him. "They're throwing what they have done in our collective faces and challenging us to do something about it."

There was a hushed silence. "They think we won't do anything?" Pressalin snapped in disbelief. "That we'll just sit on our hands?"

The first commander shrugged. "I'm not sure what they think. Maybe they are taunting us because they feel the Federation hierarchy will take a more cautious approach if there is any question at all about who's responsible. There's no physical evidence that the Skaar did this, after all. There are no witnesses. If Ketter Vause orders an attack, he does so with the clear knowledge that he might be making a mistake. If he sits tight . . ."

He trailed off. "What?" Pressalin demanded.

"He loses credibility with his enemies and allies alike." Croix finished Dresch's sentence, arms crossed, face intense. "Word will get around that he let an army of one thousand intimidate the Federation. How will that sit with the Coalition Council? How will it play with the Southland population once word gets out? And it will get out."

Arraxin Dresch was staring off into the distance, considering. "I've sent a small command to see if these assassins perhaps left a sign, but I doubt they will find much. They were too clever to make that sort of mistake. If they managed to get behind the sentry line without anyone hearing or seeing something, they could manage to avoid leaving tracks."

"What then?" Edeus Pressalin was impatient and angry. "What will you do? We can't sit around and do nothing."

"Agreed. If we just sit tight, the Skaar will simply look for another way to get our attention." He turned to Croix. "Send a message by arrow shrike to the Prime Minister. Give him the details of what has happened, including our suspicions about the origins of the attack. Ask for orders on how to proceed."

"Yes, Commander."

Dresch turned to Pressalin. "I want the defenses along the shoreline expanded and strengthened. I want scouts in place all up and down the Mermidon for five miles in either direction. I want call signals established during the day and watch fires by night. We are to expect an attack at any time, but sit tight nevertheless until we hear back from Arishaig. Go."

His subcommanders were off at once to carry out his orders. But Dresch lingered, troubled by what he could not understand. Why did any of what the Skaar had done matter in the overall scheme of things? What did it accomplish? It had to have been carried out with Ajin d'Amphere's permission—and very likely on her orders. She was too seasoned a veteran and experienced a leader, her age notwithstanding, to have been given this command by someone else. But smart, too. She would have a reason for killing those men beyond offering a challenge or engaging in a taunt. She would know, too, that an engagement with the Federation would be disastrous. There were simply too many Federation soldiers and too few Skaar. So why did she think it necessary to offer him a reason to come after her?

He hesitated a moment longer, then turned back for the center of the camp. He needed to do what he could to find out. His gaze drifted skyward. It was a fine day for flying.

An hour later, he was airborne over Callahorn, following the Mermidon River east toward Varfleet. He was alone save for a pilot, crew, and personal guards. They were flying in a well-equipped and heavily armored clipper that was armed with flash rips fore and aft. He did not expect they would encounter problems if they circled in from behind and flew once over the Skaar defensive lines along the river. He just wanted a look at how those defenses were formed and how large this army might actually be. It would not surprise him to discover it was much larger than was first claimed—that others were now being brought forward to add support to those already in place. While the reports had remained unchanged over the last five days, that did not mean they would stay the same.

Take no chances with this one, he told himself, thinking of the Skaar princess, Ajin d'Amphere, watching their camp from across the river.

Once they were ten miles downriver, he ordered the pilot to turn the clipper left and cross the Mermidon. The pilot did so at once, the sleek vessel slipping swiftly and silently across a narrows in the river. Everyone on board was on standing orders to watch for signs of Skaar occupation on the far banks, but no one spoke as they finished their crossing and headed out over the forests fronting the Dragon's Teeth. The mountains rose in front of them, huge and majestic peaks sharpened as if meant to chew up and spit out those puny humans in their airships who dared to come too close.

Dresch had no intention of taking such chances. He ordered the pilot to bring the ship left again, and they flew west now, back the way they had come, but away from the river to follow the line of the peaks as they continued west toward the Streleheim. He told the pilot to fly low above the trees, seeking to blend in as much as possible and to limit the chance of being seen by anyone not directly underneath. The clipper made no sound as it flew—a silent shadow passing just above the forest and well back from the Mermidon.

The point at which they needed to turn and fly directly over the enemy had been charted, so that they would risk as little as possible. If the Skaar were looking to avoid a direct engagement or any act of aggression that would be seen as an act of war, they would let the Federation airship pass overhead unharmed. Any move to bring it down would precipitate an immediate response. Retaliation would be swift and massive, and the Skaar would be annihilated.

Not that it would do Dresch any good if he were dead, but sometimes you had to take chances, even when you were the commander.

He had considered sending Croix or Pressalin or even bringing one or the other along, but in the end he had decided it might be better if he did this alone. Not only did it leave both of his seconds safely back should something happen to him, but it also allowed him to have his own look, to give close and careful study to what he was observing, and to consider it without interference or advice. If he was still uncertain at the end of the day, he could send one of the other two for another look and a second opinion.

When they were still just east of the Skaar defenses, Arraxin Dresch ordered their airship turned south toward the Mermidon, following a route that would carry them to the east edge of the Skaar lines. From there, they would turn west and fly over the length of the invader's defenses, providing an opportunity to see how many soldiers were in place and perhaps what sorts of weapons they intended to bring to bear. He would emerge at the far end of the Skaar lines, where he would continue on for a short distance before returning home.

All assuming no attack was launched that would bring the clipper down.

Or annihilate it.

He moved to the near side of the airship and stood at the railing where he could look directly down at the Skaar. In minutes the river came into view, a churning grayish rapids swollen by recent rains and high against its banks. As the airship swung west, he saw the first of the enemy soldiers scattered along the near riverbank, hunkered down behind earthen fortifications with a fair number of flash rips that, from the look of them, had obviously been stolen from the Federation. The line was staggered to provide cover against flanking assaults, and the high ground was manned with huge crossbows. These, he realized, might be powerful enough to send a bolt through the hull of his airship. But he did not call out for any change in their course. He still believed they would let him be.

And so they did. His vessel sailed on unscathed down the defensive lines to the far end before wheeling south to cross the Mermidon according to plan. He had seen what there was to see and it confirmed the reports. He could not be certain of the Skaar numbers, but at a guess he did not believe it to be more than a thousand. There was no movement on the lines and no indication of hostile intentions. Whatever they were planning, it did not include an immediate assault.

He returned to the pilot box and directed the pilot to take him back to the Federation encampment. There was nothing for him to do now but wait for a response from Arishaig and Ketter Vause.

Ajin d'Amphere watched the airship pass overhead, noting the insignia emblazoned on the hull and observing the figures peering down over the railing. *Well, well, Vause's first commander wants a look for himself,* she thought with no small measure of satisfaction. She remained where she was, nestled in among her Skaar soldiers, until the airship was out of sight. No one on the ground had done anything to threaten its passage. They were under strict orders not to give the Federation cause for retaliation. She wanted the Federation advance force convinced of their superiority and their control of the situation. She wanted First Commander Dresch (his name supplied by the dependable Kol'Dre) and his subcommanders complacent and confident.

Wheels within wheels, but in the end those that turned the gears of fate would be hers.

She remained where she was, visiting with her soldiers, joking and trading stories, being one of them for an hour until at last Kol'Dre came to find her. He had been hunting for her until she leapt up to greet him, and his impatience by that time was pronounced.

"You might have made it easier on me," he grumbled. "I had no idea where you were or what you were doing. Not a good idea for the commander of an army."

She smiled. "I was watching our friends do a flyover, taking in the size and shape of our army and our defenses. I wanted to be sure of what they were doing, and hiding among our soldiers seemed the best idea. No sour faces now, Kol. We have them where we want them. Do you have news?"

She guided him out of the trenches and back into the trees where they could talk in private. "Good news," he advised, his anger forgotten. "As you thought they might, they dispatched an arrow shrike to Arishaig with a message. Our archers brought it down."

He reached into his pocket and produced a folded sheet of paper and handed it to her. "Have a look at what our first commander has to report to Prime Minister Vause."

She took the paper, unfolded it, and read it through quickly. "About what we thought. He sets out the facts and then makes his conclusions. Correct conclusions, as it turns out—save for the one that matters. Too bad for him."

Kol'Dre peered at the message. "And he doesn't actually *say* what he wants Vause to do. He leaves it up to his superior. Smart. If something goes wrong, he will have evidence of his blamelessness. The tone of his report suggests he would like to attack us, but he wants Vause to give the order."

Ajin sat, and her Penetrator joined her. Side by side, they peered off into the trees, listening to the sounds of the forest.

"Vause would never order an attack without more evidence. He will prevaricate—perhaps consult the Coalition Council, but bide his time." Ajin's voice was low and thoughtful, her young face lifted toward the treetops. "He won't have the chance to do anything, of course, but were we to let him have his message, that is what he would do. He might agree with Commander Dresch's analysis, but he doesn't know for sure that he's right, and suspicions alone are not cause enough to start a war with an enemy who has already sued for peace."

"How will he see things when this is done?" Kol'Dre asked. "We have our plan; we have our chance. But if all goes well for us, what does he do then? What if he doesn't do what we think he will? Do we stay the course?"

She glanced over. "This was essentially your plan. You made the call to implement it; I simply approved. What reason do you have to doubt it now?"

He shrugged. "None. The plan will work. After we finish with Dresch, a message will be dispatched to Arborlon to inform the Elven king we are being threatened and there is reason to believe the advance force sent to intercept us at the Mermidon might attack us. Let our messenger advise the king that we are holding our position and doing nothing to give the Federation cause to attack us. But they are mobilizing and we fear the worst. Will the Elves stand with us if we are attacked?"

She stared at him. "Bold words, but I see what you intend. What if he rejects the request and tells us we are on our own?"

His smile was brittle. "Then we are no worse off than before, are we?"

"No." She thought about it. "We might gain sympathy and a change of heart if we are seen as having been deliberately attacked."

"More to the point, we might gain respect if we defend ourselves successfully. A man who stands his ground and wins is better than one who runs away and cowers in hiding." He paused. "Besides, he is infatuated with you. He desires you, and he will pursue any alliance that will bring you to his bed. Correct?"

"At the very least—even though doubts will nag at him when he takes time enough to think it through."

"If he allows himself to be rational rather than emotional. Where you are concerned, I'm not sure he can manage it."

She laughed. "I did not encourage him all *that* much! Just enough to stir what is left of his youth. But an old man, even a king, holds no interest for me."

"Not even your favorite Penetrator wields such power where you are concerned," he said wryly. "To his regret."

She rose. "There are good reasons we cannot be more than we are, and you are well aware of them. Let it go for now, and perhaps one day things will change."

She could see from his expression that he did not believe her, even if he could not help hoping it was so. But Kol'Dre was not for her. He never had been, and he never would be. Rank, station in life, profession, and tradition all worked against him becoming anything more than a friend.

As they walked back to the encampment, she found herself thinking suddenly of Dar Leah. He wasn't even a Skaar, and any logical assessment would define him as an enemy. Yet thoughts of him came unbidden and did so frequently. She could not manage to make herself forget him, even where any rational assessment of the prospects for a relationship said she must. If a partnering with Kol'Dre was unlikely, one with Dar Leah was beyond imagining.

But her heart wanted her to be wrong—wanted what was not possible to be possible. Throwing up barriers of logic and common sense did not change anything. In her young life, it never had. If she wanted something badly enough, she always managed to find a way to get it. Why not here? She was indisputably attracted to him, and if he gave himself half a chance he would feel the same toward her. She could not stop believing they could find a way to be something other than enemies. Her feelings, on which she always kept a tight wrap and which she'd come to trust, told her this was so.

He is someone I could be partnered with. Never with Kol'Dre, but possibly with Darcon Leah. I feel it down inside me where truths hide and wait to be discovered. I do not mistake them.

She sensed Kol'Dre looking at her, and she realized her face had gone hot and flushed.

"Everything is arranged?" she asked abruptly, trying to distract herself.

He nodded. "We have our soldiers in place. We have our airships and weapons ready. When the time comes, we can act."

"We're risking everything," she said quietly, stopping suddenly and pulling him about to face her, hands gripping his arms to hold him fast. "If this fails, we will be finished. Even if we survive, my father will abandon us, and my efforts to win his support will have been for nothing."

"We won't fail."

"You cannot know that . . ."

"Listen to me, Ajin. We will not fail. Not you and I. Not our brave Skaar. We will not fail. And when we succeed . . ."

He left the sentence unfinished. His sudden smile said it all.

She smiled back. "When we succeed," she echoed.

TWENTY-FOUR

◆

IT WAS NEARING SUNSET, two days later, and Arraxin Dresch was standing on a hilltop well back from the water's edge, watching as the Mermidon churned against its banks in heavy swells, fed anew by rains that were falling farther west. He glanced skyward and could see a dark line of clouds moving in. It would reach their encampment soon and make the ensuing night an uncomfortable one for those caught out in it. Overhead, the sky was still bright blue and clear, although the light was beginning to dim as the sun gradually sank behind the storm front to his left, and the coming night made a stealthy advance from his right.

He was alone at the moment, save for his personal guards—two soldiers who had served in this capacity for nearly ten years now. It was a career choice as much as an honor. The men had been assigned not only because they had showed courage and strength in battle but also because they had applied to enter into his personal service at the end of their fifteen-year tour of duty.

Anstase and Rijer. He genuinely liked these men—and respected them, too. They served at his pleasure, but they were independent-minded and kept their eyes and ears open for indications of dissatisfaction within the army. They did not gossip, but they felt no compunction about reporting things that needed it. Their relationship with their fellow soldiers was strong, and their commitment to the betterment of the Federation army thorough. He had told them recently that he would make them high-ranking officers and give them a portion of the autonomy he himself enjoyed. It was easy enough to find men willing to fight and die for the Federation; it was not so easy to find men smart enough to know how to avoid both.

Footsteps coming up behind him caught his attention. He turned.

"Commander," Edeus Pressalin called out, approaching at a quick trot, a determined look on his rugged face. An aide and a bowman accompanied him, but as they neared the first commander, Pressalin gestured for both to fall back. Whatever had brought him in such a hurry, he wanted to be alone with his superior to reveal it.

"Fresh news?" Dresch queried as the other came to a stop before him.

Without a word in response, his subcommander handed him a tiny rolled piece of paper. Dresch took it from him, unfolded it, and gave the contents a quick read:

Arraxin Dresch,

First Commander of the Federation Army
 Enough of this nonsense with the Skaar. Engage and destroy.
 Leave no survivors. An example is needed.
 Deploy soldiers at first light. Attack at dawn.

      Ketter Vause, Prime Minister

At the bottom of the page, the official seal of the Prime Minister had been imprinted.

"An arrow shrike carried it. It landed on one of the roosts we use for our birds while in the field." Pressalin was breathing hard. He must have run the whole way. "This one just arrived a few minutes ago. I read the message, saw what it meant, and came directly here."

Arraxin Dresch nodded, reading the message again. "This was one of our birds?"

"It must have been. According to the trainer who watched it land, it flew in from the south." Pressalin gave him a look. "You're worried it might not be genuine? That it might be a Skaar trick?"

"It had crossed my mind."

"It bears Vause's seal. How could they get their hands on that?"

Dresch shook his head. "I don't want to take anything for granted where the Skaar are concerned."

"But what reason would they have for inviting an attack on their fortifications? What would be the point? We outnumber them five to one and they are cut off from their homeland and any reinforcements. It doesn't make any sense."

Doesn't it? Arraxin Dresch wondered. That princess was bold in a way few he had encountered had even thought of being. Still, his subordinate had a point. Whatever else might or might not be true, there was no denying that the strength of the Federation advance force was far superior to that of the Skaar.

And there was no denying the authenticity of the message. The seal was genuine and the handwriting was Vause's—even if the decision seemed a departure from what he expected of the normally cautious-to-a-fault Prime Minister. But there was also the matter of the duty he owed to those who commanded him. If he was given an order, he was expected to obey it. Vause had put him in his present situation exactly because he had a history of doing what he was told without arguing or complaining. And now seemed a bad time to change that.

Besides, if he was to be completely honest with himself, he wanted the Skaar dead and buried, too. He wanted them gone from his life and from his country. The longer they stayed around, the more uncomfortable he felt. Smash them now, as ordered, and the discomfort and threat would both go away.

"Find Murian," he ordered. "Order a mobilization of the transports and warships for two hours before dawn. We will board just before sunrise and set out for the Skaar fortifications. We'll come at them on the flanks and roll them up from either end. Flash rips and cannons from the air, then soldiers on the ground to finish the job. Leave one company here to ward against a river crossing—although I cannot imagine anyone navigating the Mermidon in its present condition. Now go."

He watched as Pressalin and his companions hurried away, Edeus already giving orders and gesturing for quick action. Arraxin Dresch shook his head. Quick action wasn't needed now. It might not even be needed later. Quick thinking, maybe, if matters took a dramatic turn. The Federation commander yawned. He needed to get some sleep, but that wasn't likely to happen anytime soon. He never slept more than a couple of hours a night when he was in the field. But he might be home sooner than he expected if their strike on the morrow did the damage he expected, and he could catch up on his sleep then. Still, it was never a good idea to anticipate success. Fate had a way of fooling you when you did—and never in a pleasant way.

He stood for a few moments longer, watching Pressalin and then looking off toward the far bank of the river once more. Watch fires weren't even lit yet. The gloom of night was approaching. A mistiness rising off the warm earth and a steady drop in temperature partnered to form a heavy brume that was steadily thickening. He couldn't see any sign of movement among the Skaar ranks. He was struck by a disconcerting suspicion that his enemy had simply disappeared.

He signaled to Rijer and Anstase. "Let's go have a look at our airships and make sure they are ready for what's to come."

Without waiting for a reply, he departed the hilltop and moved toward the airfield farther inland. As always, movement helped ease his momentary concerns. His worries faded along with the last few rays of sunlight, and night settled in.

At exactly two hours before dawn, the night still black beneath a heavy layer of storm clouds and the air chill and smelling of rain, both companies that made up the Federation advance force began to mobilize. The men and women who filled their ranks woke quietly, dressed in darkness, armed themselves, and moved into previously designated positions on either side of the airfield, back where their huge transport and sleek black warships awaited boarding. They did so swiftly and efficiently, well trained for such contingencies, so all knew in advance what to expect and how to behave.

One-third of those assembled were dispatched to staff the defensive lines along the south bank of the Mermidon, there to settle in and keep watch for any sort of counterstrike by the Skaar, either before or during the Federation attack. The orders had been given, and the entire advance force was already anticipating an end to the Skaar threat.

Across the river, everything was quiet. Watch fires burned, but otherwise there was no sign of activity. The arrival of the anticipated rainstorm had blocked the light of moon and stars, and now the first raindrops were beginning to fall.

Standing with Subcommanders Croix and Pressalin, First Commander Dresch glanced at the sky and momentarily considered holding off until the storm had passed, even if it meant attacking in daylight. But at the end of his deliberation, he brushed aside his concerns. A little rain would hardly interfere with the maneuvering of his warships or the use of his flash rips, and the storm might even pass by entirely in the next two hours.

But things did not work out that way. The storm struck with an hour still left before sunrise and his soldiers not yet aboard their transports. And the rain was heavy—a deluge that drenched everyone to the skin. Winds howled and the waters of the Mermidon churned wildly, and the storm did not pass on as hoped, but hung around for another hour.

It was still pouring when the soldiers were given orders to board, and the slow, steady process of bringing nearly four thousand men aboard transports and warships commenced. Croix and Pressalin took command of one company each, boarding separate transports to be with their men, leaving Arraxin Dresch standing alone with Anstase and Rijer. The first commander would wait until the other airships were launched and then follow in his own much smaller craft, observing the attack from this side of the river. For the remainder of the fleet, it would be a swift crossing to meet the Skaar enemy. The warships would swing around to the ends of the defensive line and roll it up with weapons from the air. Transports would then fly farther inland to selected landing sites to unload their foot soldiers so they could pin the hapless Skaar between themselves and the river. In the end, the entire enemy force would be annihilated. It was the plan Dresch had determined had the best chance of success.

Except he was wrong.

The Skaar were one step ahead of him.

The transports, slow and ponderous, were to lift off first so that they could get under way and reach the river just as the warships came up to ward them on either side. But as the first of the transports—the one that Subcommander Edeus Pressalin had chosen to board—rose into the clouded, rain-filled sky and reached an altitude of just under a thousand feet, its diapson-crystal-powered engines began to fail. They did so without warning and not all at once, so that the airship lurched ahead for a few minutes longer, shuddering as it tried to stay aloft. But by then, the vessel was lost from view to those still on the ground, hidden by low-hanging clouds and engulfed by the rainstorm's deluge. One by one, its engines ceased functioning, but the vessel continued forward under the faltering power of a sole remaining engine until that one, too, failed entirely and the airship plummeted into the murky waters of the Mermidon. It struck with stunning force, and hundreds were killed by the impact alone. Others made it into the river and were quickly caught up in the pull of the rapids and drowned. Of those who stayed afloat, a few lost their sense of direction, swam to the wrong bank, and died on its shores. Edeus Pressalin was among them. Skaar soldiers who cared nothing for his rank or his value to them hauled him from the water, spread-eagled him on the rain-soaked earth, and cut him to pieces.

Those few who made it back to the south shore—no more than two hundred of the nearly fifteen hundred who had filled the ship's hold—found the Federation encampment in chaos. The remainder of the Federation airships had either tumbled from the sky or exploded shortly after their thrusters were engaged. No one knew the actual cause, although educated guesses were that either the diapson crystals in use had overheated due to a blockage of their parse tube exhausts or the replacement crystals stored in the holds of the airships had ruptured. In either case, the consequences were the same. Every remaining vessel either caught fire amid incendiary explosions that engulfed and destroyed them while they were still on the ground, or lost power when their engines failed on liftoff and crashed.

First Commander Arraxin Dresch watched in horror and disbelief as the first of the transports lost power and fell away into the river, and as the remainder of his fleet turned to tinder and ash when they began to explode. He was in a daze when his guards dragged him to safety. The four thousand men and women aboard those transports and warships were killed in minutes. Only a handful escaped. The carnage was indescribable. Some of those caught in the conflagration that engulfed the warships fought their way free of their doomed vessels while on fire, burning as they sought a safety that couldn't be found. Some fell out of the sky, thrown from the transports, helpless to save themselves. But most died while still aboard, unable to get clear.

Arraxin Dresch watched and tried to process what he was seeing and could not. Any semblance of command disappeared. All around him, his soldiers were dying by the hundreds and his airships were falling to pieces. Of Pressalin and Croix, he knew nothing. Their fates were already decided, but he was unaware of this.

At the river's edge, a new battle was beginning, but the Federation first commander could not know that it was between those Federation soldiers manning the defensive line and the unfortunate survivors of the first transport who had made it clear of their fallen airship and swum for safety. The latter were mistakenly seen as members of a Skaar attack and summarily slaughtered by their fellows. In the darkness, the smoke and ash and the rain and mist, it was impossible to tell who anyone was. Federation soldiers were killing one another because no one knew who was friend or foe. By the time anyone realized the mistake, most of those around them were already dead.

Screams filled the night. Howls of despair and cries for help rose from everywhere, and amid the chaos the terrifying explosions continued while the blanketing hiss of the heavy rain fell. Confusion was rampant, and order broke down at every turn. Survivors had no clear idea of what had happened and were seeing enemies everywhere they looked—even when they looked into the faces of their fellows.

And then the Skaar attacked.

• • •

Kol'Dre led the assault from the left flank of the Federation encampment while Ajin led the attack from the right. The Skaar had come across the Mermidon in separate units of two hundred soldiers each at dusk the day before, one choosing a point of crossing more than ten miles downstream, and the other crossing ten miles upstream from their enemy, doing so in small numbers so there would be no chance of discovery. When night arrived, both units had moved into place so they were well behind Federation scouts watching the river and its banks, in place for what they already knew was going to happen.

It had been Kol's plan to send First Commander Dresch the false message. He had stolen a seal and a handwritten note off the Prime Minister's desk during his visit a week earlier, and he could forge a false response accurately. Stealing one of the Federation's arrow shrikes from their pens, which were left unguarded in the false belief that no one would attempt the theft of a bird, was simple enough when you could render yourself invisible.

Ajin had approved his plan. She knew from experience that if there was to be a Federation attack, it would either come at dawn or, if the approaching storm settled in, be postponed until the weather improved. The Skaar only needed to be in place and ready to thwart it. It was a gamble to send soldiers across the river and set them in place the night before, but a gamble worth taking. It was a stroke of luck that the first commander had chosen to ignore what should have been common sense and engaged while the storm was still in progress. The concealment offered by the clouds and rain had worked in favor of the Skaar, giving them exactly the cover they had sought.

During the night, a handful of scouts led by Kol'Dre had crept into the camp, invisible to the eyes of the few Federation soldiers who were keeping watch or loitering about the airships. Boarding the warships unseen, they had blocked the parse tubes so they would overheat, and replaced all but a few of the sound diapson crystals in the transports with ones that were cracked. It had only required that the engines be engaged and the thrusters for lifting off be fired for the crystals either to explode as they overheated or simply to fail mere minutes after liftoff.

After the airships were destroyed, chaos enveloped the Federation encampment, and the chain of command that all armies relied on crumbled completely.

The orders Ajin d'Amphere gave were clear. The Skaar would emerge from hiding once the explosions were complete, swoop down on the disoriented and frightened soldiers, and begin the slaughter. The orders given to the separate units of the advance force were simple. Everyone found in the camp was to be killed. Not a single Federation soldier—man or woman, injured or healthy—was to be spared. The destruction was to be complete—an object lesson to the Federation that they had underestimated the power and experience of the Skaar, and that in spite of superior numbers they could not save themselves. Their false confidence in the strength of their army had undone them, and they would be undone again if the Skaar chose to come after them.

"What do you anticipate this will achieve?" Kol'Dre had asked her as they split up to lead their separate units. "Besides the obvious, of course. You're hoping for something more, aren't you?"

He was correct, as usual. Insightful, her Penetrator. She had smiled and nodded. "I want my father to acknowledge my ability to lead," she admitted. "I want him to see how invaluable I am. I want whatever doubts Sten'Or has created with his treacherous reports to be proved false. I want to persuade him to place me in command of the larger army he will most certainly be bringing with him, and allow me to finish what I started." She paused. "I want to keep him from finding a reason to dismiss me as his legitimate child and heir. Most of all, I want to reduce the influence of *the pretender* who has taken my mother's place in his bed."

"Which you think will happen if you succeed?"

"*The pretender* has sought to put an end to my mother from the beginning, so undermining her is necessary. A victory here, resulting in a new home for the Skaar people, would negate her influence considerably." She paused, seized his shoulders, and looked him in the eye. "What other reasonable choice do I have?"

Kol'Dre knew better than to attempt an answer to that question. Once Ajin had made up her mind about something this extreme, it was best to just stay out of her way. Besides, she might well be right in her assessment of the king's response. Cor d'Amphere was a hard man, but he valued success and loyalty. If his daughter could give him that, he might forgive her for losing Paranor and its treasures. He might accept everything that had happened since their arrival as the natural course of things and look to the promise of what was to be gained if he let his daughter follow through.

They parted company then, each going to a separate command to prepare for the events that would follow with the coming dawn.

And now those events had come to pass, and Ajin d'Amphere led her soldiers into battle from the right perimeter of the Federation encampment, blades drawn and ready. Those Federation soldiers still alive—dazed and disoriented and in many cases already injured—put up little resistance. They died by the dozens, most cut down before they even knew what was happening. The rain continued to fall in sheets, and the ground was soon soaked with comingled water and blood. The Skaar worked their way through the survivors with mechanical precision, maintaining lines that swept up everyone in their path. When the lines met, they split apart again, and one half of each unit was sent down to the river to attack the defenders entrenched at its edge. Coming up on the Federation soldiers from behind, they found them still waiting for orders, and—unable to see their attackers until they were upon them—these unfortunates were dispatched as swiftly and thoroughly as their fellows.

Soon the Federation camp was growing steadily quieter and the presence of those soldiers still living was diminishing. The sounds of death and dying faded, and only the pounding of the rain and the crackle of the flames engulfing the Federation airships remained.

Ajin was standing at the center of the carnage, watching as the last few of the enemy soldiers were sent to their deaths, when one of her junior officers appeared.

"Princess," he said, dropping to one knee.

"Ke'Rija," she acknowledged, giving him her hand to kiss.

She saw the warmth in his eyes as his gaze lifted to meet hers, saw the flush in his rain-streaked face. She never forgot a soldier's name, and such a small thing carried a great reward.

"We have a prisoner," Ke'Rija said, rising as she gestured. "His guards fought hard to protect him from us, but failed. We think he might be the army's leader."

"The first commander?"

"He won't say, but we think so."

"Show me," she said.

They walked through the killing ground to the back of the encampment, where a small cluster of soldiers was gathered about a man who had been forced to his knees in the mud. His head was hanging down, his hair fallen forward over his face, and his hands tied behind his back.

She took it all in and then turned to Ke'Rija. "Find Kol'Dre. Ask him to attend me."

Ke'Rija hurried away. Ajin stood looking at the prisoner. He was beaten and humiliated, unable even to look at her. She did not know if this was Arraxin Dresch. She needed Kol to confirm it; he had accumulated knowledge of such things from his time in the Four Lands previous to her arrival. She glanced toward the river while she waited, noting a sudden absence of sound. The killing was over. The battle was finished. She considered what she had done, but did not regret it.

Minutes passed, and then Kol'Dre appeared. He was soaked to the skin and covered in blood, but his gaze was steady. She pointed at the prisoner, and the Penetrator bent to lift the other's chin, studied his face a moment, and then stepped back.

"First Commander Dresch," he said to the man. "You seem dispirited."

The prisoner said nothing. He was clearly waiting to be executed, expecting it, perhaps even welcoming it. Ajin debated. Should she let him live? If she did, he would return to Arishaig and report on what had happened here, a witness to the carnage. And a firsthand report would carry weight with those who heard it. It would serve as a testament to what the Skaar could do to a superior force.

But it would also provide Dresch with an opportunity to set the record straight. He would tell of the false message he had received. He would reveal how a trap had been set to destroy the entire advance force by luring it into an ill-advised attack. Or if he chose to keep all of that to himself to avoid the attendant shame it would heap on him, he would likely be executed for acting precipitously. Or executed simply to provide an example of what could happen to those who failed so badly.

Nothing good would happen to him if he lived. And the benefit to her would be negligible. She looked down on his broken body with a twinge of pity. Better to end it here.

She nodded to Ke'Rija, gesturing toward his sword. He gave her a questioning look, then saw the determination in her eyes and drew his blade. Stepping to one side of Dresch, he lifted his weapon overhead and in a single swift stroke brought it down again.

Arraxin Dresch's head toppled away, and his body slumped forward.

"Finish up," she ordered Kol. "Gather up the bodies and burn them. Strip the airships of anything useful. Bring our aquaswifts over to carry back our soldiers. Tonight we celebrate the beginning of the end of the Federation."

TWENTY-FIVE

◆

SHEA OHMSFORD STARED AT the gambler who called himself Rocan Arneas and who now claimed to be involved in an enterprise that would change the world and wondered if the man was perhaps delusional. His strengths seemed to revolve around gaming and an ability to relieve almost anyone willing to play with him of their credits. And he was in possession of some sort of machine that might conceivably do almost anything, given its strange configuration. Nothing the boy had seen or heard so far had done much to convince him that this whole business wasn't simply a lot of hot air and unreasonable expectations.

Not for the first time, he thought it might be time to fold up his tent, pocket the credits the man had already paid him, and slip away into the night.

"I see doubt in your eyes, young Shea Ohmsford," the other said suddenly, as if reading his thoughts. "You think I am a braggart or a fool, a man somehow self-deceived into believing the impossible. You think you have heard nothing but words and have seen no proof of anything. Am I right?"

The boy shuffled his feet, measuring the distance to the doors through which they had entered earlier and judging how far it was from there to the street outside. He shrugged. "If you were me, what would you think?"

Rocan did not laugh. Instead, he gestured toward a bench to one side of the strange machine. "Sit with me a few minutes before you finish passing judgment. Let me try to convince you I am more than my words would suggest."

He moved over to the bench, leaving a clear path to the doorway leading out of the cavernous chamber. He sat and looked back at Shea, who was still standing where he had been left. The boy hesitated, then joined him on the bench.

Rocan studied him a moment. "Do you know why I brought you to Arishaig with me? I mean, why I *really* brought you?"

Shea shook his head. "Probably not."

"For all the reasons I told you before, of course. Those weren't lies I spoke; they were promises. But while they were honest, they weren't the entire truth. Tell me, does your name mean anything at all to you?"

Another shake of his head, but Shea was wondering by now where this was leading.

"And you don't know how you got it? No one ever told you?"

"I'm an orphan. No one ever told me anything. I never knew my parents. I was on the streets before I was five years old. I had some people who helped me, a friend or two to protect me. I learned how to look after myself otherwise. I don't know anything about my name."

Rocan sat back, drawing one leg up on the bench and placing it between them in a gesture that suggested both a distancing and a reflection.

"Your name is a famous one, my young friend. You are named after one of the most important young men ever to walk the Four Lands. You must have heard of the Wars of the Races? Of the Warlock Lord and his Skull Bearers?"

"Some. Not much. That was a long time ago."

Rocan's eyes assumed a faraway look. "A very long time ago. But I know the history well. It is a tribute to my people's culture that we consider it important to preserve our history through storytelling, and we keep those stories close as the generations pass. I am of Rover blood—all the way back to the time when my ancestors survived by their wits and their quick hands, and later by their skill as builders of airships. They mostly inhabited the Westland then, and many still do now. They still build the best airships in all the Four Lands—claims by the Federation notwithstanding.

"When the first Shea Ohmsford walked the Four Lands, he came out of a tiny village called Shady Vale, located just below the Rainbow Lake. And he walked in the company of one of *my* more famous ancestors, a man named Panamon Creel. Together, they stood against the terrible threat of the Warlock Lord and his Skull Bearers—a threat that would have destroyed everything of value in all these lands and would likely have put an end to the world we live in now."

"So the Warlock Lord was real?" Shea was still doubtful. "And all that stuff about the War of the Races really happened?"

His companion nodded. "All of it. But here's what you need to know. I don't believe in chance, and I don't believe in luck, but I do believe in fate. It was no accident that Panamon Creel and Shea Ohmsford ended up as companions on that fateful journey to the Skull Kingdom all those years ago. Fate caused them to meet, and made them friends—friends who would do whatever it took to help each other. It kept them together long enough for each to save the life of the other, and the lives of many more besides."

He paused, then reached out and tapped Shea on the shoulder. "It was fate that brought you to me, as well, don't you see? It was fate that placed you in that gambling room, drew my attention, and made me decide to take a chance that you were as ready and able as you appeared. Fate persuaded me you were the one to extricate me from a somewhat dangerous situation, and fate that convinced me to bring you here. I believe that. You and I are meant to be partners and comrades in a grand adventure!"

By now he was so wound up, so enthusiastic about fate and its complicity in his life, that Shea was left speechless. Homeless for so long, used to being dependent on nothing and no one, Shea was not much of a believer in fate. So while this wild-eyed gambler might be certain it played an important role in his life, Shea was much less sure. His experience had taught him that if you wanted things to improve, you had to do it on your own.

Rocan was staring at him with a look that bordered on amusement. "I know what you are thinking. You think I've lost my mind. You think I am a dreamer or a fool or worse. But if you stick with me, my young lad, you will find out that what I have just told you is correct. Now, then. Are you ready to hear about my grand scheme, my plans for changing our world and our people? Or are you just going to walk out the door?"

For a moment, Shea knew he was going to make the second choice. And then a bit of movement caught his eye, and when he looked over, there was Seelah, easing along through the shadows on the far side of the room. In the excitement and trauma of the fight to escape their attackers, he had forgotten her. But seeing her again, catching the light dancing in her strange eyes and the smile that curved her lips, he was reminded again of how entranced he was with her. He was not foolish enough to think that it could ever come to anything, but he was also unable to resist his infatuation.

And he didn't want to give up his chance to spend time with her just yet. He didn't think Rocan presented any danger, in spite of his wild ideas. What could it hurt to stick around for just another day or so? It would be time spent in the company of Seelah—a pleasure he very much desired.

Suddenly she was there next to him, her golden eyes fixed on him, her slender body leaning close. He stayed where he was as her face neared his, all but hypnotized by those eyes. A rumbling sound filled the air as she pressed close.

Was she *purring*?

Then she placed her face next to his cheek and licked him with her rough tongue in long, slow, languid laps.

"Enough, Seelah," Rocan snapped. "He is aware of your affection for him, if not for the cause. Back away."

The Fae did so reluctantly, her gaze drifting away. In less than five seconds, she had disappeared once more.

Shea brushed at his cheek in spite of himself. "Where does she go when she does that?"

Rocan shrugged. "Not very far. She stays close unless I tell her otherwise. She's watching you right now. You just can't see her."

The boy looked around carefully. His companion was right; he couldn't see her. "Like a moor cat," he ventured.

"Which is not surprising, since she has moor cat blood." He held up his hands quickly. "Don't ask. At least not now. Are we partners or not? You still haven't said."

"All right. For the moment, at least, we're partners. But if you can't convince me that whatever it is you intend is worth the time and effort, the partnership is over."

In the shadows across the room, something moved, catching his attention.

"She's exploring," Rocan offered. "She does it all the time. The cat in her, I suppose. Anyway, let me continue with what I started. I still owe you an explanation about what we are going to attempt. I will keep nothing from you, nor use any deceptions to convince you of falsehoods. Just hear me out."

Shea Ohmsford nodded and gave Rocan his full attention. He had already decided it was the least he could do.

Sitting alone in Drisker Arc's darkened cottage while Tavo Kaynin slept in the next room, Clizia Porse reached an epiphany. She had returned to the house with Tavo after the confrontation in the forest imp's underground lair, enraged at losing Tarsha to this creature and his companions, but confident about getting the girl back. It was only a matter of discovering where she had gone and what she intended to do next.

Tavo had wanted to set off in pursuit at once, but Clizia knew better. The Elf and the Blade both had the use of magic, and while Tarsha was weakened and disoriented for the moment, she would not remain that way for long. Together, the three might be a match for her—although having Tavo stand with her in a confrontation appealed to her; he had powerful magic at his command. But he was also borderline insane. His ability to do much more than strike out blindly was likely to overwhelm whatever common sense remained to him. She might have been better off getting rid of him, but she still could not shake the feeling that somehow he would prove useful. He could still be a pawn in this game; only his place on the board and his purpose remained to be determined.

On arriving back at the cottage, she had made him eat and drink a portion of bread and ale and then sent him off to bed. He had been more than willing to obey after unknowingly ingesting the potion she had mixed in—a drug that left him weak and disoriented. Because his behavior was so unpredictable, the trick was to keep him under control until she could figure out what to do with him. But at the moment she needed to think things through.

Starting with the odd demise of the forest imp.

That one still troubled her. An ancient creature with centuries of life behind him and no reason to give his life for a young mortal girl, yet he had done so. Why had he made such a choice? Why had he deliberately chosen to sacrifice himself? That would be impossible for most, but he had managed it effortlessly. What had persuaded him that this was a good idea? Why not just give the girl up and be done with it?

She would likely never know the answers to these questions, and she didn't like mysteries.

So she shifted her thinking to the three who had escaped her, the ones she intended to track down. They would band together, but where would they go with Drisker locked away inside Paranor? She frowned, the wrinkles on her aged face deepening. A highlander, an Elf, and a young girl from the deep Westland. They had nothing in common but the Druid and the girl's brother. Would they risk coming back for Tavo after having just escaped Clizia? She didn't think so. Not without help and a plan for besting her in a fight.

Would they go to Leah? To Arborlon?

It was easy enough to find out, of course. She had marked the girl, and unless Tarsha had discovered it and found a way to remove it, she could be located easily enough.

Suddenly she had a suspicion she knew exactly where they would go. *Paranor.* Or where Paranor had once stood. Drisker might even have called them there. Somehow he might have found a way to contact them—or maybe just the girl—to tell them what had happened. Which meant that he would know Clizia no longer had the upper hand, because now Tarsha Kaynin was free.

And if he had managed by now to recover the Black Elfstone . . .

Which was exactly what he had done! Of course he had. Why else would he continue to ignore her?

Yet he wasn't back in the Four Lands, and if he had the power of the Elfstone at his command, he would have returned at once. So maybe he didn't have it, but only knew that she didn't . . .

She shook her head in frustration. The entire business was a confused mess, and she needed to do something to clear it up before she could be sure of anything.

She rose and walked outside and stood on the steps leading out to the roadway, staring into the darkness. If Drisker *had* found the Black Elfstone, why was he still inside the Keep? Why hadn't he used the Stone's magic to return Paranor to the Four Lands and free himself? She needed to answer both questions before she did anything further. How could she do that?

But then, she realized suddenly, she knew.

A smile crossed her sour features, shedding years from her face as it broadened. The scrye orb. If she wanted to get a peek at how things stood, she could use the orb to summon Drisker. Find out where he was. Listen to what he might say. His situation would reveal itself, and then she would know what to do next.

She went into the cottage and took out the orb from where she had hidden it. Then she stopped by Tavo's bedroom and peered through the doorway to ensure he was still asleep. He was, his breathing deep and even, so she pulled his door closed and went back down the hall.

Once outside again, she sat in the wicker chair and willed the orb to do her bidding. Instantly it brightened. She commanded the magic to connect to its twin, readying herself for the confrontation that would follow.

A few seconds passed. A minute. Two minutes. She grew uneasy.

Then, all at once, Drisker was magnified in the magic's glow, facing her from within its bright wrapping. "Clizia," he said in what seemed a pleased tone. "I thought you had abandoned me."

"I made you an offer. It was yours to accept or decline. Have you come to a decision?"

She took quick note of his surroundings. The gray tones and haze, the dimness of the light surrounding him, and the stone and mortar walls looming in the background, told her all she needed to know. He was still trapped inside Paranor.

"I have," he acknowledged. "I'm afraid I have to decline."

"You do know what will happen to the girl, don't you?"

He shook his head. "Not anymore. Nor, I think, do you. Things have changed a bit, haven't they?"

A cold certainty swept through her. She tried not to show anything in her expression. He knew she'd lost Tarsha, which meant he knew she no longer had a bargaining chip with which to persuade him to return.

She gave a small shrug. "I admit she's run off. I'll find her and bring her back quickly enough." She paused. "I think we both know she won't be meeting with you, however. You're still trapped in Paranor. Do you really like it in there so much?"

Drisker shook his head. "I was puzzled for a time, but now I've figured out the solution. I won't be here much longer." He leaned forward to be close when he spoke next, his voice lowered. "But there's time for me to free myself now, isn't there? Tarsha has friends to help her, and you won't be finding her all that easily. Your hold over me is gone, Clizia. If I were you, I would find the deepest hole in all the Four Lands in which to hide. I would be covering up and praying hard I don't find you. Because I will be looking very hard."

"You don't scare me, Drisker!" she snapped.

He leaned back, and just before the scrye orb went dark, he said, "I'm coming for you."

"You have to understand," Rocan Arneas began, still seated beside Shea, "I've spent a good many years of my life just knocking about, trying to stay out of trouble and mostly finding it, anyway. I didn't have much direction in my life—which wasn't the fault of my parents, who tried to steer me right. But they had five other children, and I was young, headstrong, and eager to experience everything I could."

Oh, brother, Shea thought. *Now he's going to tell me the story of his life.*

But this time it appeared Rocan couldn't read his thoughts; he continued on. "I was making my money in gambling halls by then. I was good at games of chance; I had a knack for knowing what to do and when to do it. I'd left home while still young and gone east to the Southland cities. No one knew me there. No one knew of my reputation. The gamers in the big cities were easy pickings. They took one look at me and saw an easy mark. They thought they knew how to play, but they were amateurs next to me. I took them for everything I could wherever I went. And just before I could build a damaging reputation, I picked up my stakes and moved on. I lived frugally—sort of, if you don't count the women and the drink—saving everything else for when I would need it. I didn't know when that would be, but I believed I would find it one day."

He paused. "And then I met Seelah. You've already heard a little of the story. I found her locked away in a cage in an outlying village in the upper Borderlands, east of Varfleet. I was traveling through, saw the cage, and asked what was in it. The villagers didn't know. All they knew was that they'd never seen anything like it, so that meant it was bad and probably dangerous—especially since it reminded them of moor cats. But when I looked into that cage, I saw something beautiful. I don't know how they ever got her in there in the first place, but she couldn't get out. I found out later it was the iron that bound her. Iron saps the strength from some of the Fae, and Seelah couldn't break free."

"So you let her out," Shea said, interested now that the story was about Seelah. "And you've been together ever since."

"We weren't together at first. After I let her out, she raced off into the forest. It was the dead of night, so there was no one around to see it. I went back to bed, and woke the next morning to find the village in an uproar. I pretended to be just as surprised as everyone else, stayed around long enough to enjoy a bit of lunch, and left. I never saw a sign of Seelah after that. Eventually, I just chalked it up to another strange episode in my life."

Shea started to ask a question, but Rocan quickly held up his hand in a cautionary gesture. "Bear with me," he said. "I haven't finished."

Seelah was suddenly beside him once more, appearing out of nowhere to nuzzle his hand; he stroked her silky hair in response. Her golden eyes found Shea, and her purring was so loud it seemed to cause the air to vibrate. In that moment, she seemed more cat than woman.

Rocan shook his head and smiled. "Several months passed, and I was working the smaller cities below Leah when I got myself in trouble. Overstayed my welcome without intending to, and a bunch of dissatisfied players who had lost a king's ransom to me earlier came searching. They caught me unaware and hauled me off to the woods, where they were going to hang me. They had the rope and everything.

"Unfortunately for them, they made a mistake by choosing to finish me off deep in the woods. If they'd hung me in my rooms or dragged me out onto the village green, I'd be dead. But Seelah had been following me around all those weeks—watching me, studying me maybe. She shot out of the trees like the mad, wild thing she sometimes is, and those men broke and ran so fast they must have set new land speed records. She slapped a few of the slower ones around, but let them all go in the end.

"Then she chewed through my ropes—quicker for her that way rather than using those dainty fingers—and off we went. I didn't know what she wanted from me at first, but she made it known soon enough. She wanted a companion. Well, she wanted *me* for a companion, at any rate. So that was how we ended up traveling together. Right up until now."

There were a whole bunch of questions Shea wanted to ask about Rocan and Seelah's relationship, but none of them seemed quite appropriate—or any of his business. It was enough that they were partners and now he was being asked to join them. Was this good or bad? He couldn't tell yet.

"But none of this explains what we are doing here now, or how that machine is going to change the world," he pointed out instead.

"Prologue," the other said, smiling. "I like my stories complete. But here's the answer to your question. I stumbled on Tindall during my travels. I found him here in Arishaig, after some acquaintances had told me there was an old man working with diapson crystals in new and unusual ways. Mostly the Federation employs the crystals in weapons and vehicles—airships and flash rips and the like. War equipment that serves only a single purpose. Tindall thought that was insane. He thought the power of the crystals could serve other uses. Peaceful uses. He thought this fixation on war was leading us down a dangerous path that could well cause another Great War."

Shea shook his head. "I didn't think anyone had that kind of power anymore. I was told the Great Wars were the result of massive explosions—ones that destroyed entire cities."

"And poisoned the air and water and food and practically everything else. Sickness was deliberately introduced into whole populations to wipe them out. And no, we aren't yet at that point, but we could get there. Tindall believes we aren't that far away from seeing it happen. The Federation is a militant power with ambitious plans for dominating the other Races and occupying all of the Four Lands and perhaps beyond—and their leaders reflect that ambition. So something has to be done to blunt its direction. Tindall decided awhile back to see if he couldn't find a way."

"So he's a scientist?" the boy interrupted. "Like in the old days, only with diapson crystals?"

"A fair description. He has developed some amazing inventions. He invented a device that allows people to talk to each other from miles off through hand-sized units. Voice messaging, he calls it. But the Federation knows about it and wants to use it for military purposes—not for public communications. It's still in the improvement stages at the moment, but it won't be long before it's ready."

"So why did he tell them about it in the first place?"

"He thought it would be a good idea at the time. He thought they would listen to him when he suggested public communications. He thought wrong. When he realized what they intended, he refused to give them any plans. That's probably why he's locked up just now—he didn't do what they wanted."

"But they don't know about this?" Shea pointed toward the machine. "How did he keep *that* a secret?"

"He doesn't know where it is."

Shea stared at him. "How can that be? He invented it, didn't he? Whatever it is?"

Rocan stood. "Long story. Come with me."

He walked over to the strange machine with Shea following. Together they stood next to it, gazing up at all the odd components. The machine was huge—at least as big as a small house, if somewhat more strangely shaped. There was the funnel with its mouth pointed skyward, a cluster of wheels and gears, parse tubes of varying sizes, light sheaths that were furled but connected to the tubes by radian draws, catch basins closed and sealed, and cables, wires, and connector tubes going everywhere.

"This is Annabelle," Rocan said softly, placing one hand on the side of the machine as if to pet it.

Shea glanced over at him. "You named it?"

"Seemed the right thing to do, given what she is."

The boy frowned. "And are you going to *tell* me what she is?"

Rocan turned to him and placed both hands on his shoulders. "Annabelle can control the weather."

Shea gave an audible sigh, now quite certain that Rocan Arneas was crazy.

TWENTY-SIX

◆

Tavo Kaynin woke while it was still dark, confused and logy, his thinking clouded and his head pounding. He was not feeling well, and he wondered if something he had eaten had sickened him. But he had no memory of having eaten or, if he had, what he had eaten, so there was nothing to be done about it. His thoughts turned instantly to Tarsha and her escape. He was riddled with anger and frustration at the thought that he might have to track her down all over again. The old woman had tried to help, but her help had been insufficient, and now he was wondering if there was any reason to stay with her any longer.

He sat up slowly and waited for his head to clear enough that he could attempt to leave his bed. He remembered the old woman bringing him back to the cottage after Tarsha had fled, and that creature that had helped her had killed itself. He remembered the old woman giving him medicine to help him sleep. He seemed to recall her saying she would help him find his sister, but that might have been his imagination. After all, his magic was much stronger than hers. She was so ancient she could barely move around.

No, it was best if he thanked her, bid her a quick goodbye, and went on his way.

He wondered suddenly about Fluken. It had been awhile since his companion had spoken to him. Awhile, in fact, since he had even appeared. Tavo wondered suddenly if Fluken was gone—if he had tired of waiting and simply decided to go off on his own.

But Fluken would never do that. Fluken would always be there for him, no matter what.

Nevertheless, he grew nervous thinking about life without his only friend. So finally he dragged himself from his bed and stumbled over to the door. It was closed, but not all the way, so he peeked out to see what might be waiting for him. There was no one there, and the cottage was as dark as the night. He paused for a few moments longer, just to be sure it was safe, then crept from the room. Down the hall he slipped, quiet as a mouse, afraid of what might be lurking in the shadows. He had no reason to be afraid, of course. He was a match for anything, his magic capable of snuffing out a threat as quickly as breath could a candle. He was invincible, and that was why Tarsha was doomed.

When he reached the front room, he could see the old woman through the window, sitting in her high-back wicker chair on the porch, staring into the night. At first he thought to turn around and slip out the other way, but he was afraid if he did that Fluken might not see him go. Besides, he wasn't afraid of this old woman, was he? This . . . her name was . . .

For a moment he couldn't remember. Then it came to him. Clizia. Clizia Porse. Yes, that was it. And no, he wasn't afraid of her. Or anyone, for that matter. Why should he be?

He walked out onto the porch and stood looking at her. She turned her head to look back at him, and there was a coldness reflected in her eyes.

"You thought about running off, but you shouldn't do that," she said. "I would have known the moment you tried and stopped you."

He stared at her in surprise, startled that she could somehow know what he was doing. "I'm not afraid of you!" he snapped.

She rose to face him, taking her time. "Nor should you be," she replied. Her voice was suddenly warm and reassuring. "I'm not your enemy. I'm your friend. I'm the one who is going to find Tarsha for you. And her friends, as well—all of whom are plotting against you."

Tavo nodded slowly. "They are, aren't they? Plotting with her. She wants to hurt me. She is afraid of me!"

The old woman smiled, her sharp eyes holding his fast, trapping him like a fly in a spider's web. "We have to do something about them. We have to take them away from her. Then she will belong to you again."

"I know. They have to be taken away." He understood without entirely knowing why. "How do we do that?"

She stepped close. "We'll go where they are and we'll kill them, Tavo. All of them. One at a time. You and I. I will be there to aid you, but the most important of them is the one you must kill first. Will you be able to do so? Will you be strong enough to kill someone who is just as dangerous as either you or I? Will you be afraid of someone like that?"

He shook his head. "I'm not afraid of anyone! My magic protects me."

She reached out, took hold of his wrist, and made him kneel beside her. She stroked his cheek gently. He was reminded of another woman's touch in that moment, but he could not think whom the woman was. "I will help you," she whispered. "I will give you something even stronger than your wishsong. I will give you a weapon nothing can stop. Would you like me to do that?"

"What weapon?"

"I will show you when there is daylight. And then you will practice with it. You will learn to use it. It will become a part of you. With this weapon and your wishsong magic, you will be invincible. No one will be able to stand against you. But you must listen to my instructions. You must let me teach you."

He nodded, his gaze gone blank and unseeing. He was seeing now with his ears, listening to the pleasant hum of her voice. He was feeling her presence—strong, reassuring, and protective. There was no doubt in his mind that she wanted to help him—that she *would* help him. He only needed to listen to her. He only needed to pay attention.

"Tell me you will do as I say," she whispered once more, closer now—so close he could feel her breath on his face. "Tell me you are my friend and my companion, and that you will never disobey me."

He repeated the words, not even caring what they meant, only caring that he do as she said. When he finished, she handed him a cup of tea. "Drink this, and go back to bed. Rest until the sun rises."

He did as she asked, draining the tea in a few quick gulps before handing her the empty cup. "Who are the ones who took Tarsha?" he asked her. "Who is it I must kill? Then will I be allowed to kill Tarsha, too?"

"We will see about Tarsha," said Clizia Porse. "But you most certainly must kill the others. A highlander, an Elf, and one more. A Druid. He will be the hardest one of all. Then you may decide what to do about your sister."

"A Druid," he murmured. "Then Tarsha." He was growing very sleepy, and thinking was suddenly very hard. He looked blankly at her. "What is this weapon you will give me? What does it look like? I want to see it."

He was insistent now, wanting a look. He needed to see if it was right for him. He needed to be certain. "Show me now!" he demanded.

She seemed to think on it for a moment—or maybe it was longer—before reaching into her robes and withdrawing a wicked-looking long knife as black as night. "This," she told him, "is called the Stiehl. See the smooth line of the blade, the way the finish glistens? See the runes carved into the handle? There is only one of these in the entire world. It can cut through anything. No armor no matter how thick, no wall of stone or weapon of any kind can withstand it."

Tavo reached for it, but she jerked it away. "Ah, ah, Tavo Kaynin. First you must learn how to hold it properly. You must learn what it can do by testing it. For that, we need light. Morning will be soon enough for you to begin your lessons. We mustn't rush. There is time for what is needed. Now go back to sleep."

Tavo hesitated, wanting suddenly to find Fluken, to see him and know that he was still there, but Fluken failed to appear. Clizia was watching him, measuring him in the darkness, waiting on him to do as she had ordered.

He nodded finally and rose to his feet. There was no reason to delay longer. He was so tired. He needed badly to go to his bed. He went back inside the house and down the hall to his room.

In minutes, he was sound asleep.

The Coalition Council was in session and an argument over the allotment of expenditures for soldiers and equipment in various locations was in progress when an aide appeared next to Ketter Vause. He looked up, reminding himself that her name was Belladrin. She was young and relatively new to the position, but smart and efficient, so he knew that his standing admonition not to disturb him unless it was an emergency had not been forgotten. The troubled look in her eyes confirmed that something was seriously wrong.

She bent close, her voice a whisper. "Can you step outside, Prime Minister? It's extremely urgent."

Vause knew immediately what this was about. He had heard nothing from Arraxin Dresch and his advance force—which had departed Arishaig a week ago for the Mermidon and the Skaar—since their leaving. More than once, his patience almost beyond bearing, he had contemplated dispatching scouts to bring back information on what was happening, haunted by a growing suspicion that things were not proceeding as they should. He had confidence in his first commander, but these Skaar invaders were an enemy not to be underestimated.

Especially that cold-blooded princess and her clever envoy.

He left his place at the head of the room and followed Belladrin into the hallway.

"What's happened," he demanded, but she shook her head and motioned for him to follow, glancing right and left at the guards standing at the various doorways.

This must be important, Vause realized, and his suspicions must be correct. They went down the hall to the first vacant conference room and stepped inside.

Belladrin closed the door and locked it.

"A message, Prime Minister," she advised, handing him a small sheet of paper that had been rolled into a tight cylinder—the kind used for communications via arrow shrikes. "It just arrived and I brought it directly to you."

"Do we know . . . ?"

"Who sent it?" She shook her head.

He took the message from her and unrolled it.

To Prime Minister Ketter Vause:

Perhaps by now you are aware of the fate of your advance force.

I can only hope that their treacherous and unwarranted attack against the Skaar was not your idea.

Be that as it may, please know that any further attacks will be met with a similar response.

We had hoped to find a peaceful welcome to these Four Lands. We are disappointed in the Federation's failure to provide us with one.

Do not think for one minute that we will be driven off.

Consider making a new start.

We await a response that indicates you are willing to discuss how we might arrive at a peaceful resolution to our mutual problem.

With respect,
Ajin d'Amphere

Ketter Vause felt the world drop away. *The fate of his advance force?* What was she talking about? What had happened that he did not know about? He gave Belladrin a quick glance. "Have we heard anything from Commander Dresch and his advance force?"

She shook her head. "Nothing, Prime Minister."

Vause looked away. "Leave me. Wait outside. No one is to enter."

She did as he commanded, closing the door behind her. Vause remained where he was for a moment, then moved over to a small side window that opened out into the heart of the city. For the first time in forever, he felt vulnerable. He felt as if he were on a cliff edge, teetering toward the precipice, in danger of falling into the abyss. Dresch and the advance force were gone. He didn't need to consider the possibility further. He was sure of it. Five thousand soldiers, gone. He didn't have to be told this—he had only to read the message to know it was so. Nothing he had ever encountered before—in or out of office—had rocked him quite as hard as this. He had not in his wildest speculations imagined the Skaar were capable of standing up to the Federation. Not even after he had learned of the fates of the Troll tribes had he thought they were any serious threat.

Now he wondered.

It was not a good feeling.

"Belladrin!" he shouted.

She was through the door instantly, her young face turning pale as she caught sight of his. "Yes, Prime Minister?"

"I want scouts dispatched to the Mermidon immediately. Use Sprints. I want them there and back as quickly as possible, and I want a full report when they return."

He made a motion of dismissal and she went back out the door at once, leaving him alone.

Ketter Vause was suddenly furious. The audacity of this Skaar princess was galling. Did she think he would not act to crush her and her upstart bunch of invaders? Did she think he would stand for this nonsense? A discussion to find a resolution to their mutual problem? Was she insane?

But then he caught himself, ever the politician. Was it possible that Dresch had acted as she said, that he had chosen an unauthorized sneak attack in an effort to put an end to the Skaar threat? Could he have decided to attack without permission from Vause and the Federation's Coalition Council? Could it be that no provocation had been given and the Skaar had simply responded out of necessity?

But in those circumstances, how had a force of less than a thousand managed to destroy one so much larger? How had his soldiers failed in their attempt to catch the Skaar off guard? Was First Commander Dresch so much worse in battle than anyone could have anticipated?

Vause moved over to a bench by the window and sat, looking out into the city once more. He should not act in haste, he thought, even though the temptation to do something at once was very strong. He must think this through carefully before making any response. If the Skaar had dispatched an army of five thousand so easily, they were far more dangerous than he had given them credit for. It would be a mistake to underestimate them. The question of what to do about the destruction of his advance force needed thought. The facts of what had happened were not yet clear, and any reaction from the Federation must wait.

His scouts would be back within three days and would confirm if what he suspected was true. Perhaps they would be able to unravel some of the uncertainty surrounding what had happened.

And in the meantime, he would say nothing to anyone; he would simply bide his time.

As much as he wished he didn't have to.

"High King," Ajin said to Gerrendren Elessedil when he moved to receive her in the palace reception room allotted for their meeting.

She bowed in deference, and he quickly took her hands and brought her upright once more. "You are a princess of the Skaar," he told her with a smile. "You need not bow to me."

She had flown all day and the night following to reach Arborlon with Jen'Na as her guard and a crew of four to man the airship. And all the while she had rehearsed the words she needed to persuade him to her cause. Once Ketter Vause had decided her message was false and that it was the Skaar who had attacked the Federation and had done so without provocation—and he would do that, eventually— she would be facing an army dozens of times the size of hers. So she needed the Elves to provide at least the appearance of an ally until her full plans came to fruition.

So she faced her prospective ally now, returning his smile with one of her own. "You are very kind to receive me on such short notice. I apologize for the abruptness of my arrival, but events have taken an unfortunate turn, and I . . ." Her voice faltered, a trick she had mastered early on. "I have to do something. I fear for my life and the lives of my soldiers."

A tear trickled down her cheek, and the king had an arm around her shoulder at once, steering her toward a nearby couch. Gently, he eased her into place and sat next to her, taking her hands in his once more. "There, now. Would you like something to drink?"

She shook her head, appearing to collect herself. "I had such high hopes for the future of our peoples, those of Skaarsland and of the Four Lands. It is a crushing disappointment to find I have misjudged so badly. But you, at least, give me hope. You show me kindness."

"Of course I do. How could I do otherwise?" Gerrendren Elessedil's voice was sympathetic as he squeezed her hands reassuringly. She thought momentarily how easily she could crush his, should she choose to do so. "You must tell me what has happened. You must take your time and tell me everything. I am certain something can be done."

Ajin tried hard to look as if she was gathering herself to speak before doing so, bringing a stricken look to her face as she began to relate what had befallen the Skaar. Two nights earlier, while the Skaar were sleeping, she said, the Federation army that was positioned on the south banks of the Mermidon attempted to cross the river in force. Fortunately, sentries spotted movement on the far bank almost immediately and sounded the alarm. It was apparent at once what was happening. This was a full-on assault. Under orders to defend the advance force against any adversarial movements, the Skaar crews manning the flash rip cannons appropriated earlier began firing at both transports and airships. Some excellent marksmanship and confusion within the Federation ranks allowed the cannons to bring down three of the five attackers in the first few minutes. The other two collided and tumbled earthward. The Skaar repelled the rafts trying to cross the river and sent soldiers of their own to fight against Federation forces still gathering on the south bank.

The battle raged for several hours, but the end result was a victory for the Skaar. Most of the Federation soldiers died in the struggle, and a fair number of Skaar, as well. There was no provocation for what happened, and no one left who could explain it afterward. The Southlanders they had taken prisoner knew nothing of the reason for the assault, and the rest had fled. Ajin sought to learn more through messages sent to Ketter Vause, but there had been no response.

Recognizing the danger to the Skaar, she had flown directly to Arborlon and the Elves to report what had happened and seek help for her beleaguered soldiers.

"We have done nothing any reasonable person wouldn't have done. The attack was unprovoked, and no attempt at negotiation was made. We had only the warning of our sentries to rely on, and we were fortunate it was enough."

She paused, and the look she gave him was a mix of hope and desperation. "I ask you, King of the Elves, to help us. You know I only want to find a home for my people. You know I have sought to make alliances with all of the Races—Southlanders included. If they come for us now with their mighty army, we will be destroyed. Will the Elves stand with us to stop this from happening?"

The king nodded slowly. "We will do what we can, Princess Ajin. I cannot act on my own, but must go before the High Council to plead your cause. Yet I will be happy to do this. I think they can be persuaded to help, though I cannot promise what the form or extent of that help will be."

She leaned into him, her hands tightening about his. "Surely you will not leave us on our own? You will prevent the Federation from putting a complete end to us, will you not? Or will the Elves leave us as sheep to be devoured by wolves?"

He chuckled. "Oh, I don't think it will come to that."

His casual treatment of the danger to the Skaar and to herself infuriated her, but she did not let it show. Time enough for that later. For now, she needed the Elves to make at least a show of coming to her aid if she expected the Federation to hold off until her father's army arrived. And arrive it would; Sten'Or's treachery had made certain of that. Still, she knew a few things that her scheming commander did not, and there would come a reckoning.

But the presence of the Elves at her elbow when Ketter Vause and the Federation came calling was essential to her plans. And the High King's refusal to promise Elven support outright was troubling.

She assumed she had charmed him sufficiently that he would do so without hesitation. But now he was suggesting it was up to the High Council to decide, not to him. What sort of king was he, anyway?

She gave him a knowing nod. "You must do what you feel is best, Gerrendren," she said. "And I must be content to rely on your persuasive powers. I must be brave in the face of imminent destruction. I must rally my tired and wounded soldiers and stand fast against the forces that are sent against us."

She released his hands and rose. "I will wait to hear further from you, hoping the decision I receive is a favorable one." When she had taken a few steps, she turned back to him and bowed. "Please pray for me and my soldiers."

Then she departed, worrying as she did so she might well have wasted a lot of good time on courting this old fool. She had worked hard to give him the impression that he could bed her if he allied with the Skaar, and he had seemed intent on doing both. Now she had to wonder. It might be that the Skaar would have to stand against the might of the Federation without aid.

She did not much care for the prospect.

TWENTY-SEVEN

---◆---

AS TIME PASSED AND nothing changed, Drisker Arc came to realize that he was not going to survive his imprisonment in lost Paranor. It was a harsh realization, but whatever else the Druid might be, he was first and foremost a practical man. It was not all that difficult for him to come to terms with the reality—that if he didn't escape, he would die. Death was always close at hand for members of the Druid order, and his exile had not changed his condition in any significant respect. He was still reviled in some quarters, and attempts to kill him were not infrequent. It was only good fortune and training that had allowed him to survive the assassins of the Orsis Guild.

But his current situation was a bit more problematic.

What troubled him most was his inability to understand why he could not invoke the power of the Black Elfstone. Others had done so before him—others who were members of the Druid order. Walker Boh had even done so before he was actually a Druid, but simply a man trying to find a way to stop the Shadowen. So what was the matter with Drisker? What sort of blockage kept the magic from responding when he tried to summon it? How was he so different from those others who came before him? How had they managed to discover the secret that continued to elude him?

He had read the books of the Druid Histories—everything that

pertained to or mentioned Cogline—until he could practically re-
cite the pertinent passages from memory. He had read everything
he could find on the use of the Black Elfstone over the past three
thousand years of recorded history, searching for the clue that would
unlock his understanding of how it worked. He had spent hours before the west gates attempting to open them, attempting to summon
the magic of the Stone in every way he could imagine. He had gone
to Paranor's highest towers, to her lowest depths, to her farthest and
darkest corners in an effort to cause something to happen.

But nothing had helped.

In the meantime, he was beginning to sense his mortality draining
away. He still ate when he was hungry and drank when he was thirsty,
but his strength was steadily fading. Because time had no meaning in
disappeared Paranor—neither night nor day evident—he had trouble
telling exactly how much he had changed. But it was enough for him
to be certain that it was happening. It was gradual, it was incremen-
tal, but it was still a fact of his existence. He was disappearing a little
bit at a time, growing less clear, less substantial, less . . . *here.* And he
couldn't do anything to stop it.

He continued to speak regularly with the ghost of Cogline, but
their conversations were increasingly irritating. The failed Druid
was of no further help, and once Drisker got away from pursuing the
topic of the Black Elfstone's use, everything else seemed irrelevant.

"You could tell me more than you have," Drisker said on this particular day, during this particular conversation. They stood together
in the cold room staring down at the still, unresponsive surface of the
scrye waters. "You have secrets you are deliberately withholding. You
need to tell me what they are."

Cogline shook his head, his wispy hair flaring with the movement
like tendrils of mist. "I have no such need, Drisker Arc. You *think*
you need me to tell you more. You are fixated on it, and it has kept
you from doing what you must. Nothing will change if I do what you
ask. Which I cannot—as I have repeatedly told you. It is forbidden to
me to speak of such things. Forbidden by the certainty that the pun-
ishment for breaking that taboo would be more than I could bear. I

would be banished back to the underworld, and I have no intention of allowing that to happen."

He smiled. "Besides, I don't think things will work if I just tell you the answer. I think they only work if you come to whatever realization is needed on your own—as Walker Boh did. He never revealed how he had made the leap, but he found a way, didn't he? So now it is your turn, and asking me to give you the answer is a waste of time."

Drisker nodded absently. He had expected this. It was essentially the same answer Cogline had given him every time before. He supposed he understood. Use of magic was peculiar to every individual who sought to wield it. Others could not bestow its secrets; those had to be discovered. Cogline had never been a magic user, in any case. Science was what interested him. It was his reason for leaving the order; it was his passion for the remainder of his life both before and after his death. He was always going on about the diapson crystal technology that the Federation so heavily relied on—a new science that had facilitated practically all of the advancements their people had made.

Drisker shook his head in irritation. "The answer to the problem— I can practically reach out and touch it, but it's just beyond where I can make it out. I hate how it leaves me feeling so helpless not to be able to see it clearly. Or even to catch a momentary glimpse of it!"

"Yes, well." Cogline shrugged. "These things take time. Why don't you turn your attention to something else for a while? You made contact with this girl—this Tarsha Kaynin—awhile ago. Have you gone back to her to see if her situation has improved?"

Drisker had told Cogline everything about Tarsha, of course. He had no one else to talk to and a burning need to discuss her captivity with someone—even the enigmatic ghost—in case even a hint of something he could do to help her might surface. Nothing had, beyond his discovery that he could project himself outside the Keep, but the subject was still relatively new and everything else they had talked about had a stale, pointless feel to it.

Besides, Cogline was right: He needed to see if Tarsha had gotten free—even if there was a risk to both of them if he did so. It was easy enough for him to track her down as a shade, though difficult for him to explain why that was. But he knew from his last experience that every time he did this, it accelerated his diminishment. Whether it was the stress of his efforts or simply the act of disconnecting from Paranor, he couldn't say. But he could feel it. Each act caused him to disappear further. And if Clizia Porse detected his presence, she would shut him down once and for all, using her magic to prevent even his ghost from reaching out. But it had been long enough now that he felt he had no other choice but to seek Tarsha out once more.

The decision made, he closed his eyes and brought an image of his young student to mind. For this type of search, all that was required was that he picture her face, imagine him with her, then reach out and bring her close. It would all take place in his mind and hers, but it would seem to each as if they were really face-to-face and speaking.

Her image filled his thoughts, and he held it fast.

Tarsha.

Instantly he was with her.

Tarsha had traveled east with Dar Leah and Brecon Elessedil, leaving Emberen behind. She would have stayed if she had thought there was anything she could do, but by the time she had fled Flinc's underground home, made her way through the forest, and encountered Brecon, she was an emotional and physical wreck. Days of being drugged by Clizia and her subsequent battle with Tavo and imprisonment in Drisker's cabin had worn her down to nothing. She might have been saved from all that, but it would take awhile before she was back to herself.

Leaving was necessary, if only to ensure her safety, but it was also incredibly hard.

Her brother, after all, was back there, still in Clizia's clutches.

Nor could she pretend she did not know what had happened to Flinc. Clizia and her brother had discovered his home, and the forest imp had chosen to stay behind to face them in order to save her. For that alone, Clizia would have killed him—and Tavo would have helped, because he saw anyone who gave aid to Tarsha as an enemy. She had heard the sounds of fighting, and then the terrible silence.

No, Flinc was gone, and it was her fault. She should never have left him. She should have stayed to protect him.

But Dar and Brecon would not listen to her protestations or pleas, telling her they were in terrible danger, filling her in as they hurried to Brecon's airship on how they had found her and what had been required to rescue her.

"It was a diversion by Dar that made it possible," the Elven prince told her, cradling her in his arms as the Blade took the helm. "He risked everything to save you."

She nodded wordlessly. She had begun shaking after they boarded, and now could not seem to stop. Not willing to leave her alone, Brecon had chosen to wrap her in a blanket and hold her against him to share his warmth.

"He stood up to Clizia by himself and fought her off," Brecon continued. "He gave the forest imp and myself time to enter from the back of the cottage and sneak you out. The plan would have worked if not for Flinc's foolish decision to carry you away on his own when I went to Dar's aid. He brought it on himself."

She shook her head. "He was trying to protect me! He didn't understand the cost of such a decision. He lost his way."

"He lost his mind," Dar muttered, mostly to himself, but she heard him, anyway.

"I shouldn't have abandoned him." She kept her voice soft and steady, not wishing to argue the matter. "I should have found a way to help him."

"Staying would have cost you your life!" Dar insisted fiercely, and she let the subject drop.

They flew on through the day and into the night, their pace steady and unbroken save for a single stop to eat and briefly rest. Conversations were short and revolved mostly around what they were going to do once they arrived at the former site of Paranor. How were they going to help? But Tarsha felt strongly that this was where she needed to be in order to speak to Drisker Arc again. *He will find a way to reach out to us,* she repeated over and over in answer to the doubts and misgivings of the other two. *When he does, we will help him find his way out of his imprisonment.*

It was an odd insistence. After all, how could she know what it would take to free the Druid? But his appearance in her bedroom three nights before had instilled a certainty in her that was unshakable. She believed she could help him return to the Four Lands. She felt she was meant to do this. It was her destiny to work with him and try to become like him—not a Druid exactly, for she could never be that, but at least a magic user of some skill. It was a bold task she was setting herself, with so little reason to believe there was any hope of seeing it come to fruition, but she had never been one to back away from a challenge—even one as seemingly hopeless as this. And she felt in her heart that she was doing the right thing.

Of course, the alternative was to go back and face Clizia and try to save her brother. And that was not something she could do just now.

By midnight, they were still well shy of their destination, but exhausted. So they landed in a clearing in the deep woods, hoping to stay hidden from anyone who might be watching. They unpacked their bedrolls, ate a cold dinner, and went to sleep under the stars in the shadow of their transport.

While Tarsha slept—an unsettled, restless sleep—Drisker came to her. He appeared just as a voice at first, calling out to her in an urgent summons. She responded in her mind and then, on coming awake, found him waiting only a few yards away. A faded, shopworn image frayed around the edges—a pale imitation of the man she had once known.

He knelt before her. *Are you well?*

She nodded quickly. "Well enough. And you? You look so pale, Drisker. Tell me what is happening. Wait! Let me wake the others first."

He did not object, so she woke Dar and Brecon. Dar looked relieved to see Drisker, his lean face calm and his gaze steady. Brecon just stared in what appeared to be disbelief.

Tarsha, Drisker said when all were gathered. *My time in this limbo existence grows short. I am draining away. There is no pain, no sense of loss beyond my fading, but I feel it coming on. I must get free.*

"What can we do?" she asked at once. "How can we help you?"

He shook his head. *I don't know that you can. I cannot yet help myself, so I'm not certain what helping me might require. I am searching for an answer. Once I have it, it would be good to have you close by.*

"We are not far from you," Tarsha told him. "Less than a day's flight from where Paranor once was."

Good. Once you arrive, stay there for another few days to give me time to consider further. Although just now I feel defeated.

"We will stay as long as we need to," Tarsha answered firmly, missing the look that passed between the other two. "You must find a way out of there, Drisker! We will help you if we can."

Then she paused, her face twisting with the pain of what she was feeling. "You mustn't give up. You can't!"

The wraithlike figure turned its head momentarily, then said, *Is Clizia dead?*

Dar shook his head. "We left her behind when we rescued Tarsha." He quickly explained what had happened the day before, ending with how they'd found Tarsha and spirited her away. "But Clizia and Tarsha's brother are probably still there, in your cottage."

Drisker shook his head. *She will be tracking you. She has the scrye orb, and she may be able to use it to find you. Stay hidden as best you can, but if I haven't secured my freedom soon, you will have to leave. Don't underestimate her. She is a match for all three of you, talismans and magic notwithstanding.*

"I think she might have hurt Flinc," Tarsha said, and told him of how the forest imp had tried to save her.

Flinc is resourceful but foolish. He should have known better. But he is fascinated with you. He took you once before, you know, and I had to come and release you. I suppose he wanted you for himself this time, too. He brought this on himself, Tarsha. You must let it go. And perhaps, you will have to let me go, as well.

The girl stepped forward, determination reflected on her young features. "Don't ask that of me. You find a way out of there! And don't try to force us to leave, because we won't!"

I don't suppose you will. A smile and a nod. *Very well. Watch for me.* And then he vanished.

Back inside the Keep, Drisker found himself staring at nothing for a moment as he recovered from sending his astral projection to Tarsha, taking deep breaths to steady himself as he looked around the room. Cogline was still staring at him, taking the measure of what he had witnessed.

"You are satisfied?" the old man asked.

"She's safe for the moment," Drisker told him. "But only for the moment."

The other nodded, and a smile momentarily brightened his ghostly features. "Then you must go to her."

He backed away in a swift, floating movement and melted into the wall.

Drisker barely registered his disappearance, his thoughts already shifting back to the matter of mastering the magic of the Black Elfstone. He considered the short list of what he knew.

He couldn't summon it.

He should be able to.

Walker Boh had done so centuries ago.

Others before and after him had done so, as well.

His frustration surfaced anew. "What am I missing?" he whispered to himself.

Cogline's voice spoke from within the blank wall. "The obvious."

Drisker hesitated, then walked away. He did not need further advice from Cogline, not when it was completely unhelpful. What he needed was sound reasoning and a place to start. He pondered the matter as he walked the cavernous halls of Paranor, heading for the High Druid's offices where the Druid Histories were stored, but his thoughts wandered. *The obvious.* Maybe the old man was telling the truth. Maybe what he was missing *was* obvious—if he could just figure out why it wasn't obvious to him.

He went down another flight of stairs, then along the lower hallway to where the Histories were stored. The books sat out on a reading table within the vault that housed them. Some were opened to the pages he had been reading earlier and some were closed, stacked on top of one another and set aside. The room was gloom-filled and shadowy, the light diffuse and pale. Everything Drisker could see was indistinct and emptied of color.

The Druid took one of the reading chairs and sat back in contemplation. It was a way to clear his mind, and never had his mind needed to be sharper than it did now. He looked down at his body, examining the way it had faded. He had not become transparent yet—or even translucent—but he expected that would come with time. For the moment, he was still reasonably opaque; the main difference lay in the lack of any color. His body was graying, dimming—a change that had increased steadily since he had found himself trapped.

There was definitely a diminishment of substance.

He looked away quickly. Enough. He had to think. He needed answers—and quickly.

He went back to the book that chronicled the events leading up to Walker Boh becoming the sole member of the order well back before the Druids returned to the Four Lands and began to grow strong again. In those days, there had been no Druids at all. There had only been Walker, living with Cogline, summoned by Allanon to serve as the first of a new Druid order. Walker had not wanted to do so. He had resisted. But in the end, he had found himself trapped in a Paranor that Allanon had sent into limbo, forced to become the very thing he had sworn he would never be in order to escape his prison.

Just as it appeared Drisker must do now.

So they had that in common. Like Walker, he was not a Druid—at least not any longer. And like Walker, he had been given the task of returning Paranor to the Four Lands in order to escape it. But where Walker had been able to make that happen, Drisker could not. Why? What was the difference between them? What had Walker known that he did not?

He stopped short and shifted his perspective. Maybe he was asking the wrong question. Maybe it wasn't what Walker had known that had freed him to use the magic, but what he had discovered. There was a secret hidden somewhere in all this, a bit of knowledge that his predecessor had managed to uncover while he had not. Walker Boh and Drisker Arc, so much alike in so many ways. The answer had to lie somewhere in the similarity of their situations; somewhere in their mutually shared need to bring back the Druid's Keep from its limbo existence.

Use of magic, use of magic, use of magic . . .

He repeated the words, whispering them. Again, he stopped himself. What did the use of magic require in order to command it?

A price.

A cost to the user. Always and always. That cost was not always clear at the time the magic was summoned and used, but it was always revealed at some point. It would have been so for Walker Boh in his time. And it would be so now for Drisker.

But what determined the nature of the cost? Sometimes, it was flesh and blood. Sometimes, it was a life given in sacrifice. Sometimes it was harsh, and sometimes barely noticeable. It varied wildly with each use. History had taught the Druids as much. So what was the cost here? It would be substantial for such powerful magic. Did it require his life? What would it take? What would be enough to satisfy the payment demanded?

And abruptly, he knew the answer. He had known it all along, he thought in despair; he had simply refused to accept it. There would be no bargaining. There would be no easing of the weight the price would carry. He would simply have to bear it. It was in the nature of who he was and who he always would be.

He lowered his head into his hands. *Don't cry,* he told himself.

But he was already weeping.

TWENTY-EIGHT

---◆---

THE NIGHT WAS DEEP, and time seemed to have stopped. The city of Arishaig rose about them in a dizzying array of impenetrable black shapes and mysterious purposes. Here and there, lamps glowed yellow and dim in an evening mist that spread all through the city before climbing the walls and disappearing across hilly grasslands in a liquid flow. Overhead, a tapestry of stars peeked out from the vast firmament of a clouded sky.

But Shea Ohmsford was not looking at the stars or contemplating their mysteries. He was barely aware of his surroundings. Instead, his attention was completely focused on the massive walled structure situated just ahead of where he stood with Rocan Arneas, in the heavy shadows of a building's overhang.

Assidian Deep.

It was the name given to the complex of Federation prisons that had been built close to the outer walls that warded Arishaig on the south perimeter of the city, hunkering down atop a vast underground river that flowed beneath its formidable bulk for miles in either direction—a river born in the Anar and dispersed in miles of tributaries that snaked their way across vast regions of the Southland. That a prison was built across one of those tributaries, even given the narrowness of the river's channel, seemed at first glance a fool's choice. But those who had constructed Assidian Deep had been privy to the reasons for this choice and told not to reveal them—although, as with all such things, the truth had leaked out, anyway. The river was a delivery system, a means of disposal for all those who met their end within the prison's walls—they were tossed down chutes to be carried away by the river's swift flow and made to disappear.

For this underground river was so deep and so furious, it was said, it would never give up its bodies.

Shea Ohmsford knew the stories. Everyone living in the Southland knew them. Everyone knew someone who had gone into Assidian Deep and not come out again. The stories came back to the boy now as he stared at the forbidding structure and felt a raw, overwhelming terror fill him.

"I'm supposed to go in there?" he whispered, because his voice failed him and a whisper was all he could manage.

"*We're* supposed to go in there," Rocan corrected calmly, "if we want to get Tindall back."

Massive walls fronted them—barriers to everything Rocan had insisted must happen, a warning to stay clear. Shea felt an unspoken certainty vibrate in his bones—a conviction that, if he took one more step, it would be the beginning of the end of his life. It was the same as if he were standing in front of a flash rip, its charge loaded in the parse tube chamber, its barrel pointed at his heart, and a finger on the trigger readied to pull. Stepping back, giving way and turning around, would save his life. Anything else, and he would be gone from the world of men and from any chance of a future as quick as a flash of lightning in a rainstorm.

"I told you there would be uses for a boy like you," Arneas said, turning to look at him. "This is one of them. You can do what I cannot. I would rather we began your service to me in some other way, but fate deals us the hand she chooses. You know this. We must free Tindall from these walls. We must have him back, or all our plans come to nothing."

All *our* plans. All *your* plans, the boy thought. *My* plans were for something far different.

And his mind drifted back momentarily to four nights earlier.

. . .

"I know it sounds strange to hear that such a machine might exist," said Rocan Arneas, "but it does. Tindall invented it. He developed and explored the science that allowed for it. And once he knew the science well enough, he had the pieces built to assemble Annabelle. I financed his work with my winnings over a three-year period. It was very expensive, but I was convinced it was something worth doing. So I gave him what help I could."

"And you built a weather machine?" Shea was incredulous. "How can anyone change the weather? Nature makes the weather, not Men. Besides, what's the point of changing the weather, anyway?"

Rocan was nodding along as he spoke. "You voice the same questions I did. But Tindall saw what you and I didn't. So much of what impacts our lives is weather-driven. Too hot, too cold, too wet, too dry. Floods, fires, hail, snow, and cold; periods of endless drought and winter. Winds can destroy our homes and threaten our safety. We don't have enough food when we need it. All sorts of aberrations over which we have no control can dominate everything we do. Think about it. One nation has abundant rain while another swelters in endless heat. Floods destroy the crops in one nation while another has perfect weather for growing and harvesting. The number of combinations is endless."

Shea shook his head. "But a *machine*? How can a machine change something as powerful as weather?"

"Science can change anything, once you understand how the system works. Sure, nature determines the weather, but Tindall saw that a machine could replicate this. Climate conditions are not set in stone; they are variable and can be altered for short periods of time—sometimes even permanently."

But Shea was having none of it. This was so bizarre, so far removed from anything he had even thought was possible, that he could not bring himself to accept it.

"You say all this like it could really be done, but no one has ever done it, have they? What's to say that this one man—this Tindall—

will be the first? How do you know you haven't thrown all your credits down a rathole for the last three years?" He gestured at the strange machine. "Do you even know how to make this thing work?"

"No," the other admitted at once. "I don't. But Tindall does. He built it; he understands it. And you're missing the point. We aren't guessing. Everything I've just told you isn't a theory. This machine has been tested—several times now. Tindall has used it to alter the weather, and I was there to see it happen. Annabelle works. She can do exactly what she is supposed to."

The boy stared. "You saw this machine change the weather?"

"Three times. Once changing clear skies to a thunderstorm; once changing the temperature from boiling to freezing; and once from wind to calm. Do you see how incredibly useful this will be for the Races? Can you imagine what it could accomplish?"

Rocan paused. "Understand this, Shea. I am committed to this course, because I think it will impact the way the world works in ways we can't even begin to imagine yet. Weather is geographically segmented, changing in different places in different ways. And regional change allows for those in a certain location to benefit. Think of all the ways the people of those regions could improve the condition of their lives. Think of all the ways using a machine like Annabelle can provide needed help. The results are more far-reaching than you can imagine! When people are content, dissatisfaction diminishes, aggression lessens, and peaceful coexistence becomes more realistic. I want that. I want to help make that happen."

"You really believe all this," Shea said quietly, studying the gambler. "You think this can happen?"

"I know it can. I've knocked around for most of my life with no particular purpose in mind. But now, finally, I have a chance to accomplish something important. I don't want to look back and realize my life has meant nothing. I could keep gambling and gathering in my winnings and salting them away, but that isn't much of a legacy. But this . . . this incredible chance that Tindall is offering . . . this is something I knew right from the first that I needed to grab hold of. And now that I have, I'm not letting go." He paused, flushed with the passion of his words. "And I'm offering the same chance to you."

Shea frowned and shook his head. "And why would you do that? What would be the point of bringing me into this business? You said you wanted me to fetch and carry. You said you wanted me to get in and out of places you couldn't. And I can do all that; it is what I signed on for. But I can't do anything to help with this weather machine of yours, even if I believed everything you just told me. Which I don't."

"I think you do believe." Rocan put a hand on his shoulder. "You're just reluctant to let yourself do so. I was like that at first, too. I didn't believe. I couldn't see the point in such a machine. Besides, if it could do what Tindall said, the Federation would take it away from him the moment they found out about it. They wouldn't let some half-baked scientist share that sort of discovery with other nations. They would want it for themselves. That's why Annabelle is here, in my warehouse, where even Tindall doesn't know how to find it without my help. You see? He believes in me as much as I believe in him. I financed this whole project; I made it possible for him to build his dream and test it."

Shea started to say something more, then stopped himself. Rocan was right. He did half believe, because the idea of such a machine was so incredible that he *wanted* to believe. But it was so far removed from anything he had ever encountered or thought to imagine that he was struggling.

"I don't know," he admitted. "Believing in this is hard."

"Like believing in Seelah was? A mix of human and moor cat? A shape-shifter? And then you saw her. And you saw what she could do."

"I guess . . ."

Rocan edged closer. "I need you, Shea Ohmsford—namesake of the boy who once needed my ancestor Panamon Creel. We need each other. We can make this machine a part of everyone's life in the Four Lands, and I can help you escape your circumstances by providing you with a purpose in your life and the credits to do anything you want."

He squeezed the boy's shoulders tightly. "But I need you now—at this moment, it happens—for exactly the reasons I first told you. I need someone who can get in and out of places I can't. The unfortunate fact remains that, without Tindall, the machine is useless. Only he can operate Annabelle. Only he understands enough to keep her running or fix her if she breaks down. But now that Commander Zakonis has him locked away in Assidian Deep, I'm afraid the old man won't survive. Zakonis cares nothing for Tindall; what he wants is to get his hands on me. And he's using Tindall as bait. He knows I'll come for him."

Rocan smiled. "So I need you to go instead."

Months ago, Rocan then explained, he had been told by Tindall that the individual pieces of his weather machine were ready to be assembled and tested. At that time, everything was stored in a building just outside the city walls in a less desirable part of the extended city. Arishaig had grown since its destruction and rebirth, and much of it had sprawled out onto the plains beyond the protective walls of the central city. But there was privacy, too, in such marginalized places, and Tindall was free to work without interruption.

Now, though, since the individual components and housings for the machine had all been constructed, they needed to be taken to a more secure location—one that would allow for final assembly and testing without the danger of attracting attention. Rocan arranged for such a place, and under cover of night Annabelle's separate parts were airlifted into the city and lowered through hatches in the roof of the warehouse that was to be their new home. It took two weeks and a dozen flights, each one risking a discovery that would put an end to the entire project. But Rocan Arneas was nothing if not resourceful, and he imported members of his Rover family from the Westland to undertake the task of transport—men who, once paid and paid well, would then return to their homes and say nothing of what they had seen.

When the repositioning of Annabelle's individual parts was finished, Tindall undertook the assembly, checking to make certain all would work as expected. Upon completion of that task, the testing of the machine began. Rocan was there for each experiment, still hopeful—but doubtful, as well.

After the very first test, all his doubts were gone.

"It was after midnight and there were clouds masking the stars on a moonless night. The weather was forecast to be nothing but sun for weeks to come. It had been the same for weeks before, and the prospect of drought was starting to become a concern." Rocan shook his head in wonder. "But Tindall wasn't worried. There would be no drought, he insisted. Annabelle would make sure of that.

"So on that night, the old man had me roll back the roof hatches so he could test Annabelle. She had been absorbing sunlight for days, storing sufficient power to allow her diapson crystals to release the energy necessary to change the weather. I stood there and watched him, excited for what might happen and worried for what might not. I was not yet wholly convinced. I was not the believer Tindall was. So even to see the machine come to life—to hear its sounds grow louder and watch its lights brighten—was astounding. A deep whining rose from the machine, and I was afraid it might bring unwanted attention. But Tindall assured me the city's other sounds would mask it.

"Most of Arishaig was sleeping, anyway, and we were in this district of the homeless and lost, far from the mansions of the well-off and respectable—and far from the districts where nightlife flourished. The results would happen quickly, Tindall assured me; no one was likely to notice anything. Or if they did, it would only be to note the unusual change in the weather."

Shea listened intently, caught up in the story now, wanting to hear it all. Seelah had returned from wherever she had gone and was curled up on the bench with her head in her companion's lap, golden eyes fixed on Shea in that disconcerting way she had. All around them, the warehouse was silent, and Annabelle was inert and inactive, no more than metal parts and radian draws and light sheaths—no more than a promise. But in the story Rocan was telling, she came fully alive.

"She began to vibrate with a deep rumbling. Tindall was working levers and turning wheels and adjusting gauges. It was exhilarating to watch, even though I had no idea what he was doing. He continued with his preparations for long minutes, taking readings and waiting for his creation to ready herself.

"Then all at once he threw this huge lever that released a blaze of particle-filled light out of the machine's funnel through the open roof and into the night sky. There is no other way I can describe it—a pillar of light with dark bits of matter caught within its grasp. It was a burst of brightness that became a pillar and twisted upward through the dark—like a tornado or a waterspout, but one formed of light. It rose and held position for I don't know how long, because I lost all track of time, and then it shattered like glass into millions of glowing pieces that swept through the ragged layer of clouds and disappeared. It was over and done with in less than a minute."

Rocan shook his head. "Tindall turned off Annabelle and closed the roof again. Nothing had happened, and I thought he had failed completely. I was embarrassed for him and angry with myself. Three years of hard-won earnings, lost. Three years of work, wasted. Mostly, I was heartbroken, despondent—knowing that my dream of changing things was gone. I could not even bring myself to speak.

"Then Tindall told me to listen. I did as he asked and heard the sound of thunder rumbling across the skies. I saw a flash of lightning through the warehouse windows. Suddenly a downpour opened up, the rain pounding down, drops striking the walls and windows with such ferocity that I could scarcely hear myself shouting. Tindall shouted along with me, and we danced around the room like madmen as the rain fell. The proof I was looking for—hoping so hard for—was right in front of me."

He grinned at Shea, his eyes alight with passion. "It can be done, my young friend. It has been done before, and it can be done again. We can change the weather. And by doing so, we can change the world."

Thus Shea had come to believe in Tindall's machine and been persuaded help Rocan Arneas in his efforts to free the old man from the prisons of Assidian Deep. And now here he stood, right outside the jaws of the beast, at the doors of the prison, ready to carry out his part in what even Rocan admitted was a risky plan. He found himself wishing—not for the first time—that Seelah could be there with him. But Rocan had explained that she could not enter a place like Assidian Deep because its walls were constructed of so much iron that she would not be able to function. Iron was anathema to a creature like herself, and to willingly enter a place like Assidian Deep was not only impossible for a Faerie creature, but also life threatening. Otherwise Rocan would have considered sending her in to rescue Tindall instead of Shea.

So now the responsibility for this endeavor belonged solely to him. Shea was willing to try to make the plan work, but down inside, where you took a true and unburnished look at such things, he found himself doubtful of success. Still, everything Rocan had told him of the effort that had gone into the construction of Annabelle and the stunning successes of the testing she had undergone, coupled with the other's certainty that only Tindall could operate the machine, was enough to persuade him he should at least try.

He glanced over at Rocan. Would this subterfuge work? Would any of what Rocan Arneas had planned for this rescue have any chance of success?

"Time to go," the other said, and not quite dragging a still-reluctant Shea behind him, he started for the prison gates.

At that same moment, Ketter Vause was standing at the floor-length windows of his office, looking out over the brightly lit buildings of the city. He had been doing so for some time, thinking through the dilemma of the Skaar invaders and the destruction of his advance force. It was confirmed now; his scout had returned. The man stood not ten feet away, waiting for Vause to bid him to either stay or go, but Vause was ignoring him.

The scout had returned well after sunset. Faithful Belladrin, still on duty—though Vause was sure not willingly at this hour—had brought him to the Prime Minister immediately upon his arrival.

"Prime Minister." The scout had bowed deeply, his uneasiness palatable. "I did as you ordered and flew to the Mermidon to make contact with the advance force. There was no one there. The camp was destroyed—everything burned, blackened, smashed to pieces. There were clear signs of explosions. All of the warships and transports had obviously been destroyed, along with their crews. There were bodies—or parts of them—everywhere."

Vause had felt his heart constrict, his fears confirmed. "Our soldiers?" he asked, wanting to be certain. "All of them dead?"

The scout nodded. "There was no one alive in that camp."

Still Vause could not believe it. "Surely someone escaped! Did you conduct a search?"

"I found no one alive anywhere, Prime Minister."

All dead. Everyone who had gone with Dresch to the Mermidon was dead. He had known it from the moment he had read that message from the Skaar princess, and yet he had not wanted to believe it. He felt fresh rage building inside him, red hot and hungry for redress.

"Was there any evidence of how this happened?" he had pressed the other man.

The scout shook his head. "But everyone who was dead, everything that was destroyed? I found it all on our side of the river—or in the river itself. Bodies had washed up here and there—our soldiers, not theirs. The battle appears to have been fought entirely on our ground, not theirs. If we attacked them, wouldn't some of the fighting have occurred on their side of the river?"

Vause had turned away then without a word and walked to the window of his office, where he continued to stare out into the night. The more he examined things, the more certain he had become that Ajin d'Amphere's claim that the Skaar had only been defending themselves was patently false. This was a deliberate act of aggression intended to demonstrate the Skaar military superiority. By now, it was clear and undeniable that these Skaar were invaders and, in spite of the protestations of that princess, that they intended to take what they wanted by force.

"You may go," he said to the scout, addressing him finally, with a quick glance over his shoulder. "You have done well. But you are not to speak a word of this to anyone. Not a word!"

He waited until he heard the door close, scuffing the floor with the toe of his slipper, looking at nothing as he thought through it all. It galled him no end that there were no survivors. An eyewitness might have provided a better explanation for how such attacks were carried out. That at least might have given some insight into why such wholesale destruction was possible. But even more infuriating was the sense that he was being toyed with. He could not escape the feeling that there was something more to all this than was apparent, that he and the Federation were somehow pawns in a larger game.

Yet his course of action now was clear. He must report the loss of Commander Dresch and his advance force to the Coalition Council. The response would be predictable—outrage followed by insistence on action followed by endless debate that would disintegrate swiftly into dithering. Whatever they chose to do, they would not want to make a mistake. They would not want to expose themselves to public censure for acting too swiftly or inappropriately. They were politicians, no matter their individual titles, and they all thought pretty much the same way—condemnation was to be shifted onto someone else and blame was to be avoided at all costs.

Ketter Vause was something similar, but not entirely. He was a politician and shared an inclination to proceed with caution. But he was also a soldier. He had come up through the ranks of the Federation army, attaining the rank of commander before he was drafted to become Minister of Defense and eventually Prime Minister, when his predecessor became ill and died. His mindset as a military man was to act, not to debate. When you were threatened, you responded. When you were attacked, you fought back. If you were mistaken or if there was collateral damage, you accepted blame and argued necessity. But you acted. You did not sit on your hands.

Now he would be asked to wait while the council debated the matter. This could take days, even weeks. The council would be troubled by the lack of witnesses. They would be disturbed by an absence of convincing evidence. How could they be expected to know exactly what had happened? How could they make a decision on the matter when everything surrounding the incident was so vague? What if these Skaar, these people from another land who protested their innocence, were telling the truth about what happened?

But Vause knew the truth. He was as certain of it as he was certain the Skaar were not finished with whatever had brought them to the Four Lands in the first place. And a small part of him had begun to wonder if war with these invaders might not prove too much for the Federation army.

He turned from the window and walked into the center of the room. He was sickened by the idea of a delay. He was incensed by the thought of the Coalition Council debating endlessly. He was furious with all of it—and he was not going to wait around any longer.

"Belladrin!" he called to his young aide.

She came at once. He knew she would still be there. She always was, never leaving his offices until he had left himself. She had been a find—a young woman of great capability and intelligence. Eager to serve him, anxious to advance her station, not making any pretenses otherwise but still smart enough to remain respectful of her duty to him.

"Prime Minister," she said. "What can I do?"

"Summon Commander Bashonen. Wake him, if you have to. Tell him he is to muster the Fifth Army and its fleet of airships and have them ready to set out by tomorrow afternoon. In the meantime, I will be informing the Coalition Council of my decision."

She stared at him. "They will claim you are overstepping your authority."

"By the time any of them has gotten up the courage to do so, I will be gone with Commander Bashonen and his soldiers to the Mermidon. I need to see this enemy for myself."

"You will destroy it?"

The gleam in her eyes did not escape his notice. "Utterly. Would you like to see it happen?"

She nodded eagerly. "I would. Are you taking me?"

"If you wish. You could be my aide on the flagship. Interested?"

"I would be honored. I will be ready when you are."

She turned and left the room, a bit of extra spring to her step. He liked her eagerness to participate in this endeavor. He thought having her learn more about how things worked would serve them both well in the future.

He took a final look out the window. In three days' time, the Skaar would be no more. That was his promise to himself.

TWENTY-NINE

◆

Two nights later, a snowstorm rode in on the back of an early winter wind, blowing down out of the northwest and across the Streleheim. It reached the former site of Paranor a little before midnight—a clear indicator of an early winter and a truncated autumn. Tarsha was seated around a small campfire with Dar Leah and Brecon Elessedil, wrapped in travel cloaks and blankets to ward off a deepening chill, when the first flakes began to fall.

All three glanced up at the same time, watching as the fat white crystals began to flutter down, spiraling earthward like tiny creatures.

"Snow," Brecon said in wonder. "Awfully early."

"Awfully inconvenient," Dar replied with a tinge of disgust in his voice. "We've nowhere to take shelter if it worsens."

They were settled back in the trees, away from the open space where Paranor had once been, talking about Drisker Arc's appearance in ghost form six days earlier, trying not to show their impatience with having to wait around to see if the Druid would find a way to negate the spell that had dispatched Paranor into limbo and bring it back into the Four Lands so he could free himself from its imprisoning magic.

"We're well enough protected by the trees," Tarsha ventured after a moment. "We can move camp farther back under the conifers if need be."

No one said anything for a minute, caught up in the dance of the snowflakes as their fall steadily increased and the ground began to take on a whiter cast. Finally Dar rose, kicked out the fire, and led them back under a massive old fir with broad limbs that offered better shelter. They built a new fire, gathered more wood for the remainder of the night, and then resumed their places.

"Happy now?" Brecon teased the highlander.

Dar shook his head. "I'll be happy once we have Drisker back again. Every moment we spend sitting out in the open like this is another opportunity for Clizia and Tarsha's brother to find us. They won't be confused about where we are for long."

"Even with the mark removed from Tarsha?"

Dar had found it four days earlier. He was familiar enough with how this form of magic worked—and how often, over the years, it had been applied by various Druids—to be aware he should look for it. Once Brecon had used the Elfstones to find it embedded in Tarsha, Dar had used a root extract the Druids had discovered years ago to negate its power. Drisker had been the one to teach him about it, and what Drisker had taught him, Darcon Leah always made sure he remembered.

"She will use other means to track us, Brec," he assured the other. "She won't give up until she finds us."

Brecon sighed and rose. "In that case, I think I'll take a look around, just to make sure your worries are pointless."

Off he went into the trees, disappearing into darkness and snowfall. Dar glanced up and away again. Tarsha thought he should be more concerned about the Elf going off on his own in this weather, but he seemed unconcerned.

She took a moment to consider Brecon Elessedil. She was more than a little curious about him, although not quite understanding why. Not that she'd had much of a chance to be attracted to anyone, given the way her life had unfolded. But she remembered still the moment during her flight from Flinc's underground lair when she had run straight into Brecon's arms. All sorts of emotions had rushed through her then—relief, joy, and a strange sense of homecoming coupled with a deep feeling of contentment and security. Something about Brecon had triggered all this—and while she knew it was mostly the circumstances, she had come to believe it was something more, as well.

Traveling with him to Paranor had given her a chance to test those feelings out, and to her surprise they had lingered. In fact, if she was being honest, they had strengthened. She had given herself a chance to step away from those emotions, to allow them to diminish, but each time she looked at him or spoke to him or just walked next to him, they were renewed. She liked Brecon Elessedil; she liked him a lot. Enough so that she didn't feel compelled to examine the attraction too closely yet. She just wanted it to continue.

Which, under the circumstances, was ridiculous. They were running for their lives, under constant threat of being discovered and likely killed, and facing the very real possibility that the Druids would be completely wiped out if Drisker did not get free, leaving the entirety of the Four Lands under siege from the Skaar invaders.

"Are you warm enough?" Darcon Leah asked suddenly, his question scattering her thoughts.

She nodded. "Yes, thanks."

She wanted to say more, but she couldn't think of anything. The Blade was a formidable figure, radiating a dangerous power and possessing a willingness to use it. She still marveled that he had chosen to stand alone against Clizia Porse. If not for him, she would still be Clizia's prisoner.

Which made her wonder anew about her brother. Tavo was likely still with the old woman, held in her thrall and doing her bidding. Clizia would use him if she could find a way, and it would not be in her interests to seek a cure for him. He was simply a tool she would employ before casting him aside, as she did everyone.

"You look troubled," Dar Leah was saying. "Are you worried for your brother?"

"I don't see how I will ever get him back again," she admitted. "Clizia has him, and she won't ever let him go."

"Maybe we won't give her a choice," the Blade replied, pulling his cloak tighter about his slender form. "If Drisker gets free, he will deal with Clizia, and we will get Tavo back. Don't give up hope."

She smiled. "I'm not. And it isn't just Tavo I'm worried about. It's Drisker, too."

"Not to mention the three of us."

They were silent a moment, and then she came to a decision, speaking of something she had been mulling over for days. "Can I tell you about something that happened to me while I was traveling to Backing Fell?" she asked.

The Blade smiled, a reassurance. "Of course."

She gathered herself. "I met this old woman. I was staying at an inn, sitting in the tavern by a window, when she appeared. She was old—and yet she wasn't. I was never sure about her age, and I'm still not. She stood there and pointed at me, and I knew she was asking if she could come inside and join me. She asked for a glass of ale and drank it, but afterward it was still there, untouched. In fact, the innkeeper told me later he never saw her at all, that he thought I was playing games with him. As far as he was concerned, she was never there."

"But she was?"

"I spoke with her. She was as real as you are and sitting just as close. She told me about something she called the rule of three. Do you know about it?"

"I've never heard of it."

Tarsha nodded. "Neither had I. This woman said she was a seer. She told me her name was Parlindru. The rule of three was her rule—a kind of schematic for how the world worked. She said she wanted to share something of my future with me, and that she would use the rule of three to reveal it. She took my hands in hers and held them for a time. I don't know how long; I couldn't be sure afterward. But long enough for me to feel something—a kind of intrusion, like someone reaching inside me. I saw the color of her eyes change, over and over."

Dar Leah had shifted his position and was leaning closer. Tarsha hesitated, momentarily unsure of herself, but then continued.

"Then she released my hands and told me three things that would happen to me. She said I would love three times and all three would be true, but only one would endure. She said I would die three times, but that each death would see me born anew. Finally, she said, I would have a chance to make a difference in the lives of others three times, but that one of those times I would change the world."

She went quiet then, staring at him, waiting for a response. "Did you believe her?" he asked.

"Not at first. But later, yes. I can't explain why. I don't usually believe in such things. Seeing the future seems more like a parlor trick; it shouldn't be possible. But I think maybe she really could."

He frowned, his dark features tightening. "There are seers. We had one or two among the Druids of Paranor while I was there. I never spent much time with them—nor did anyone else. No one really wants to know their future."

"I didn't, either. And I didn't ask her to tell me all this. I was just trying to be nice by giving her that glass of ale. But she claimed she had come to find me specifically, and I think—looking back on it— she had. Too much of it felt real. Then and now."

The Blade shook his head. "Sometimes things feel real when they aren't. It might all just be nonsense you've persuaded yourself is something more. But that's for you to decide, not me. Why are you telling me this, anyway?"

She shrugged. "I don't know. Mostly because I wanted to tell someone. I would have told Drisker if he had been here when I returned. But since he wasn't . . ." She shrugged. "I decided to see what you thought."

"Lucky me." He smiled—but neither the smile nor the words were intended to mock her. "I like it that you value my opinion enough to ask it, and I wish I had something insightful or inspiring to say in response. But I'm afraid I don't."

The wind gusted, and a smattering of snowflakes blew into her face. She wiped away their dampness and smiled back. "I didn't think you would. I just needed to get it out of my system."

"Maybe you will still have a chance to tell Drisker," Dar said.

She looked off into the distance toward where the Keep had once been. "Maybe."

Moments later, Brecon returned, trudging out of the darkness, a ghostly figure in a thin covering of white. He must have seen something in their faces because he slowed as he looked from one to the other and back again.

"What did I miss?"

"Nothing," Darcon Leah said.

"Nothing," Tarsha echoed.

The Elven prince settled himself next to them and related what he had seen and heard in his search, which was precisely nothing. No sign of life, no indication that anything or anyone was out there in the darkness. The sky was masked with clouds. Snow was falling steadily and beginning to accumulate. Winter appeared to be on the verge of staking its claim to a new season.

But Brecon Elessedil was mistaken.

In the darkness eyes watched them, unseen.

That same evening, some miles farther south and on the far side of the Dragon's Teeth, Ajin d'Amphere sat staring across the Mermidon River into the darkness, talking quietly. Kol'Dre sat close, listening, a silent presence providing company she was happy to have. They were situated on a rise where they could look out across the river and into the countryside beyond. It had been six days since the Skaar had wiped out the Federation advance force under the command of Arraxin Dresch and she had sent Ketter Vause, Prime Minister of the Federation, a message advising him of what she had done to his soldiers and warning of what would happen if he tried to do anything like that again. She had lied about who was at fault, shifting the blame to the Federation force she had destroyed and claiming, falsely, that the Skaar had been attacked, suggesting that Vause meet with her to achieve a peaceful solution. It was a suggestion she was certain he would ignore, choosing instead to come at her with what he assumed were enough men and airships that her much smaller Skaar force would simply be overwhelmed.

Old news to Kol, but a necessary lead-in to something that wasn't.

"Things have not worked out the way I had thought they would," she began, the words a bitter taste in her mouth.

"Well, it's true the Elves haven't come to your support as you thought they would," he said, after she was quiet for a moment.

True enough, she thought. Gerrendren Elessedil and his Elves had failed to appear, apparently still undecided about whether to stand with her. She had been so sure the Elven king would be moved by her impassioned pleas for assistance, given his obvious feelings for her. And the look on Ketter Vause's face when he registered *that* alliance would have been priceless. But it appeared she had misjudged badly, and she was disappointed and resentful.

"You think perhaps that I expected too much," she said. "Because if the Federation chooses to respond by striking back at us now, it is unlikely we possess sufficient strength to fight them off. But you misunderstand. Gerrendren Elessedil was never the one I was counting on to save us. My father was."

Kol stared. "Your father? But I thought you didn't . . ."

"Want him to intervene? Want him to steal my victory by dismissing me and claiming credit? I didn't. But when Sten'Or brought me the message from my father and I realized what my traitorous general had done, I saw an opportunity."

She paused. "I have a confession to make, Kol. I lied to you. It was a lie of omission, but a lie nevertheless. And I suspect you will be very angry with me for doing so."

Kol'Dre shook his head at once. "I would never be angry with you, Ajin. You know that."

"We are about to find out. You were there when Sten'Or brought my father's message. You should remember the glee he exhibited at the news that my father was coming. It was clear enough that he had orchestrated it, probably by revealing my failure to take and hold Paranor after losing all my soldiers while seizing it. He thought that I would be sent packing. But while I could not undo his actions, I thought I could change their impact. I messaged my father right afterward—without telling you what I was doing—admitting I had overreached and asking forgiveness. I reminded him of my value over the years. I told him that everything I had done had been for him, and that my intentions this time were no different. I did not try to dissuade him from coming; instead, I urged him to come. If he did, I said, I had a gift for him. If he arrived at a particular time and place with the rest of our army, I would present him with an opportunity to crush the Federation for good. Or, if not to crush them, then at least to force them into negotiating an agreement that would allow us to stay and give us time to plan further. But he must come when and where I asked him to."

She paused. "I never told you this. I never told anyone. It was to be my personal redemption when the plan unfolded. Everything I have done since learning of my father's arrival has been directed toward bringing Vause and the Federation army to bay. The deliberate ambush of those Federation sentries. The subsequent slaughter of his entire advance force. A message that practically dared him to come after me, a challenge to his vaunted Federation invincibility. And I am certain it worked; he's probably on his way at this very moment. Everything is falling into place, just as I had hoped."

She shook her head wearily. "Except for the one thing I needed the most. My father hasn't done his part."

"When was he supposed to arrive?"

"The night of the new moon. Yesterday."

"He told you this? He promised he was coming?"

"He didn't have to. He is my father. I know him well enough to be certain that Sten'Or's summons, coupled with my own admission of guilt and my offering, would bring him—if for no better reason than to sort matters out. No, something has gone wrong."

"Ajin, Ajin." Kol whispered her name in soft reproach. "You have taken on too much. You have risked us all."

"I have risked as much on every campaign we have ever undertaken, Kol'Dre!" She was angry that he should question her. "I have built my reputation on taking such risks. Every victory I have achieved required risks. To sit back and simply let events unfold with no attempt at intervention is anathema to me. I would rather die ten times over than fail to take a necessary risk and be forced to crawl in abject defeat because of the poison a weasel like Sten'Or feeds my father! Risks are a part of life, when life is war. Now is not the time to draw back and forsake what got me where I am."

She kept her voice quiet, but the power and certainty in her words were unmistakable—just as she intended. Yet there was a poignancy reflected, too. She had gambled everything on this chance at victory and redemption combined, and it seemed she had failed. Never had she felt so alone, and she did not care to lose the support of her best ally at this juncture. So however things might turn out, she needed to be honest with Kol. She still believed she had done what was necessary and right, and she believed he would see this as she did.

But Kol'Dre said nothing. He simply looked away. Ajin waited for a response—any response. When there was none, she closed her eyes, feeling a bitter despair bloom in the pit of her stomach.

Scattered flakes of snow began falling around her in the darkness. *Well, there you are,* she thought. *A touch of my homeland come for a visit. But why do you come now? What does your appearance portend?*

"You did what you felt you had to," Kol said softly. "You did what you believed was right."

She felt a pinch of gratitude, quickly replaced by renewed anger. She was not going to leave it at this. She was not going to be the sacrifice Sten'Or intended her to be. Not while she still had breath in her body and the ability to act.

Suddenly she was on her feet. "I'm going to have a talk with Sten'Or and find out exactly what he knows. I'm going to put him on his knees and hear him beg me to spare his life!"

She started off without waiting for Kol's response, certain he would follow her, just as he always had—protective and committed. And in seconds he was there, matching her stride for stride. "Better watch yourself," he cautioned.

But she was beyond listening to such advice, incensed at what Sten'Or had done to her or—if she was honest about it—what she had done to herself. Her own safety no longer mattered. She was about to lose everything she had worked so hard for. She was about to become a footnote in Skaar history, an afterthought. She was about to be killed along with her entire army and reduced to inconsequentiality.

If this were to be her fate, she would know exactly why first.

She found Sten'Or's tent, dismissed his personal guards with a look that sent them off without a word, swept through the tent flaps, and dragged him from his blankets, half awake and thrashing madly.

A foot on his neck and a sword point in his face calmed him sufficiently that he went still and looked up at her with undisguised malevolence.

"Your father will not appreciate how you treat his generals," he hissed at her. "Especially given that you are already in such deep trouble."

"Which does not much concern me, given how you have betrayed me!" she snapped in reply. "What did you tell my father in your message?"

He laughed, and it took everything she had not to jam the sword down his throat. "The irony of this moment is sweet. You are so blind to how the world works, so caught up in your unshakable belief in yourself. Did you even stop to ask yourself this—what if you are mistaken? What if I didn't send him a message?"

She pressed down with her boot. "He wouldn't be coming if you hadn't sent him a message! He would have no reason to come."

She pressed down harder. "Gently, Princess." His voice was strained, rife with pain. "I sent no message."

"You lie!"

"No, I speak the truth. Look in my eyes and you will see. I sent your father no message. Not a single word. I have had no communication with him since we left Skaarsland."

She experienced a tremor of uncertainty. He seemed so sure of himself. She could detect nothing in his eyes or his voice to suggest he was lying. Usually, she could tell at once.

He glared up at her, and she eased up the pressure on his neck. "Remove your boot," he snapped. "I have given you my word. I sent no message to your father. I had no reason to."

She hesitated, undecided. Something . . . was still wrong . . .

But it was Kol who saw it first. "No, of course you had no reason. Because the message you sent wasn't to the king—it was to his queen!"

Sten'Or shifted his gaze swiftly to the Penetrator, and Ajin saw the truth in his sudden change of expression.

Down came the boot once more. "You messaged *her*? You conspired against me with *her*? Of course you did, you coward! A clandestine liaison with that *pretender* to undermine my authority and my competence—so like you, General!"

He was choking now, gasping. His big hands were scrabbling at her leg in a panic. "Your . . . boot! I can't . . . breathe!"

"I should kill you right now and be rid of you." She growled the words in a tight rage. "But I want you alive to tell him yourself what you have done. And tell him you will, or you will die screaming for mercy!"

She eased off. "You and *the pretender*. How fitting. Two snakes cursed with the same poisonous character. Conspirators intent on destroying my family. My mother and me—and perhaps, one day soon, my father, as well? Have you royal ambitions, General? Do you see yourself as a queen's consort? Or perhaps even as a king? What fun my father will have with you when he arrives."

Sten'Or rubbed his throat. "You father has made up his mind about you, Princess. You won't change it. He won't believe you. His wife makes his decisions for him now."

She moved her foot up to his chest and pinned him fast to the ground. She exchanged a quick glance with Kol'Dre, who nodded. "I sent him a new message, General," she said to the man on the ground. "I acknowledged my mistakes and asked him to come see for himself how matters stood. By now, I think he might be having second thoughts about me."

"He will be having no new thoughts about you," Sten'Or said. "The queen has convinced him that she is better suited to the task of keeping you in line. To be sure he doesn't falter, she intercepts all messages and destroys the ones she thinks he doesn't need to see. She has been doing so for months."

"She would never dare do that!" Ajin hissed in fury.

Her treacherous commander sneered. "Clearly you haven't been paying attention to how things have shifted in court for the past year or so. He's allowed her greater access to his affairs than ever he did to any councilor. And so she steers him in the directions she thinks best. He has become more puppet than king, girl."

Ajin nearly killed him then, even though she suspected that this time he spoke the truth. It would explain so much about his abandonment of her when she called for help. But Kol'Dre reached her before she could act and pulled her away. "Let him be," he whispered. "Your father might not be as stupid as he thinks. And Sten'Or will die, anyway, when the Federation comes."

She glared at him for a long moment, then turned and walked away.

A short time later, Kol caught up with her. She was waiting for him pretty much where they had been sitting earlier, looking out over the river. Without a word, he sat down beside her. Together, they watched the flow of the Mermidon's swift waters as starlight reflected off its choppy surface. To the south, on the far bank and beyond, all was dark and quiet. There were no signs of life. The skies, clouded and snow-filled north of the Dragon's Teeth, were clear and untroubled here.

"What did you do with him?" she asked finally.

"Trussed him up and put him under guard, with orders that no one was to be allowed to see him."

"Better than he deserves," she muttered.

"You should go to your tent, Ajin," he said. "You've been awake for too long. You need sleep."

"I can't sleep. Not now, knowing what I do. Knowing why my father hasn't come as I asked. Knowing he is *the pretender's* puppet, and we are doomed."

"Rest then."

"I keep thinking the same thing over and over again. I've schemed and manipulated and tried so hard to make things right, and it's all come to nothing. I wanted my father to come with his armies and save our brave soldiers—even if he also steals away all the credit for what I have achieved. But I don't think he will. I think Sten'Or is right—*the pretender* has taken control of him."

Her father—strong of mind and body, confident of his ability in all things—had become a puppet of that creature. It was more than she could endure—more than any daughter should have to.

"Perhaps the Federation has decided not to retaliate," her companion suggested. "Perhaps the loss of his army was sufficient to persuade Vause we would be too much for him to handle."

She shook her head slowly, long hair shimmering. "He will take whatever small amount of time he needs to think it through, but in the end, he will arrive at the only obvious conclusion about what really happened. Then he will come for us with a force that even we cannot stand against, and he will crush us like bugs beneath his boots."

"You cannot be sure."

"I can, Kol'Dre. So stop trying to comfort me."

"You make it sound like I am asking for you to make the sun rise in the west."

She looked at him and smiled. Loyal Kol'Dre, her partner in so many conquests of foreign lands. So clearly in love with her, so determined to find a way to make her his. He was beneath her station, not of royal blood, and she had done nothing ever to suggest that such an arrangement would happen, and yet he persisted. If she didn't find it so endearing—and he so very useful—she would have shucked him off ages ago. But here he was. She might have other friends among those many men who curried her favor, but none so genuine as Kol'Dre.

"It would be interesting to see what a westerly sunrise would look like," she said after a minute. She looked at him. "I am constantly amazed by your positive outlook, Kol'Dre. You really are quite extraordinary."

He shrugged. "If you don't believe in the impossible, you don't stand a chance of seeing it happen. Can we go in now? It's getting cold."

"Skaarsland is colder," she said quietly.

"Freezing out here won't help our people back there."

She nodded. "Just a few minutes longer, Kol. Then we'll go in."

She did not look at him again, and they sat in silence, watching the darkness deepen as storm clouds began to fill the sky over the river.

THIRTY

◆

IN ARISHAIG, ROCAN ARNEAS and Shea Ohmsford had slipped from hiding and were standing at the gates leading into Assidian Deep. A watch called down to them for identification, and Rocan replied with a single word. The watch disappeared from view, and within seconds the gates began to swing open on their hinges with deep growls of protest.

"So far, so good," the boy's companion whispered.

Shea wasn't inclined to agree. Having the gates opened to receive them did not make him feel any better—even if they were gaining the admittance they sought. What he kept thinking was that getting in might turn out to be a whole lot easier than getting out.

"Keep your head down and your face out of sight," Rocan added, and started through the opening.

Shea followed, head lowered, eyes on his companion's boots as they entered the prisons. He was all the way inside before he risked a quick glance around and instantly regretted it. They were in a tiny courtyard, surrounded by massive stone walls that soared skyward and seemed to lean inward. There were no doors leading out save the ones they had come through; the rest only led deeper into the complex. Shadows and gloom shrouded everything, and the windows he could glimpse were as dark as the surrounding night. The looming walls were capped with barbed wire and iron spikes. At each corner of the Deep's front wall were watchtowers, but there were no guards in sight. There was no one to be seen anywhere, for that matter. There was no sign of life at all.

The massive scale of the structure pressed down on Shea like a great weight, which seemed to grow heavier with each step he took. He realized he was shivering and was sorry he had ever agreed to come. He felt trapped and helpless and impossibly vulnerable. He wanted to flee, but already he could hear the gates closing behind him. He breathed deeply to steady himself—to stop the shaking—but the air was foul and dead, and he choked on it.

Nothing could live in a place like this for long, he thought. Nothing could survive.

He had just managed to stop shaking when the door of the huge building just in front of him—a structure not quite as high as the walls, but every bit as intimidating—began to open. A black-cloaked figure appeared, hooded and faceless. A wraith, it seemed, come out of the darkness to gather them in. But Rocan kept walking toward it, anyway, and Shea followed him, trying not to look as frightened as he felt.

When they reached the shadow-wrapped form, a hand emerged and a piece of paper appeared. Rocan took it silently and nodded. Then the black-cloaked figure turned back toward the door leading into the building, and the Rover and the boy followed.

As with the gates, once they were past the entrance, the door closed solidly behind them.

They were standing in an entryway with a scattering of wooden chairs and tables pushed up against the walls, and in the open spaces between, several closed doors were visible. The cloaked form pointed to one before disappearing through another, leaving Rocan and Shea alone. The boy looked around doubtfully. He had no idea what they were supposed to do next.

Rocan, however, did. He moved quickly to the door the cloaked figure had indicated and opened it. There was a solitary torch burning in a stanchion just inside, and on the floor a pair of smokeless lamps. Rocan picked up the lamps, handed one to Shea, and kept the other for himself. Then he unfolded the paper he had been given and motioned the boy closer.

"This is where we are," he whispered, pointing to a black dot. A maze of connected lines angled away from one another as they meandered across the entire width of the paper. Beside each line was a number.

Shea stared at the paper and then at Rocan. "What am I looking at?"

"A map!" Rocan snapped, as if it were as plain as the nose on the boy's face. "This is the waste system that runs through the prisons. It has vents to prevent the gases from collecting, and it's flushed out regularly so you can breathe in there." He pointed again to the black dot. "This is us." Then he traced the connected lines with his finger across the paper to an X. "This is Tindall."

"A waste system?" The boy shook his head vehemently. "I'm not crawling through any waste system!"

"Well, if you won't, we might as well turn around and go home. This is the only way to get Tindall out. He's in a cell nineteen floors up. All you need to do is follow the map, crawl through a duct on each floor until you come to a ladder, then climb for as many floors as the number on the map tells you to. Do this until you reach him."

Rocan paused. "It won't be as bad as you think. The ducts were washed out this morning, so there will only be a few bad spots to get past. Just hold your nose."

"Easy for you to say!" Shea was furious. "You're not the one doing the crawling . . ."

"Because I can't!" Suddenly Rocan was right in his face. "You're going in because we have no other option. I won't fit, and Seelah can't expose herself to all this iron. That leaves you."

His tone was harsh and certain, and there was an unmistakable edge to it. If Shea tried to back out now, he would likely find himself inside these walls for good.

He gritted his teeth. "When this is finished, we'll be setting up some ground rules about what I will and won't do from now on!" he snapped.

Rocan cocked an eyebrow. "We'll discuss it later. Here." He produced some rubber gloves. "Wear these. It will at least keep your hands clean."

Wordlessly, Shea slipped the gloves on his hands. When he was finished, Rocan handed him the map. "Don't lose it—and pay close attention to the numbers. If you mess up, you'll get lost for sure, and likely end up living here for the rest of your life."

"You're so thoughtful," Shea sneered.

His companion took him by the shoulders and held him fast. "Shea, I need you to do this. Tindall is an old man. He will not survive for long if we abandon him, and there's too much at stake as it is. Trust me when I tell you that the risk you are taking is worth it. *Annabelle* is worth any risk, and only Tindall can make her work! Here."

He released his grip on Shea's shoulders and reached into the front of his tunic, pulling out a package of something cold and pliable and wrapped in a piece of leather, handing it to the boy. "When you get to the nineteenth floor, find Tindall's cell, dab a small bit of this on the lock, then spit on it. The substance will ignite and burn away the lock. Then do the same with all four bars on his cell window. Just be sure to use the substance sparingly."

Shea shook his head. "What happens once I've done all that?"

"You wait."

"*What?*"

"You hang a bit of cloth outside the cell window after you've burned away the bars to let me know you've finished, and then you wait. Help will come, to get you and Tindall the rest of the way out."

"What sort of help?"

Rocan shook his head. "Just trust me. Help will come."

"What if someone sees me in there while I'm waiting on this help you promised?"

"No one will see you." He gave the boy a firm pat on his back. "Bribery still works, lad, and credits still provide information. And silence. No one will bother you."

"Well, if bribery still works, why didn't you just find a way to walk in and walk out with Tindall? Why am I going through all this?"

Rocan shook his head. "If it looks like the watch helped us, my source would likely be compromised. I promised that wouldn't happen. Walking in and walking out again would be a dead giveaway."

"And you're sure this will work?" Shea could hear the doubt in his own voice, and it reflected the myriad suspicions he harbored about this whole plan. "Seems like I'm the one taking all the risks."

Rocan straightened. "If something happens, Shea Ohmsford—if something goes wrong—I will come for you. You have my word. No matter how long it takes or what I have to do, I will come for you."

The way he said it—the gravity of his words, the insistence in his voice—convinced the boy that he meant it, and he felt a measure of reassurance.

He took a deep breath and exhaled sharply. "All right, I'll do it," he agreed reluctantly.

"Good lad! I knew you would. Now let's get on with it." Rocan paused. "Ah, one thing I forgot to mention." He actually looked sheepish. "At night they put scrubbers inside—mechanical cleaners designed to remove anything larger than a bug. It's a precaution against clogging the ducts, but also against anyone trying to escape."

"Wait! You mean there's something in there that might kill me if it finds me?"

Rocan made soothing gestures with his hands. "We have to enter the Deep at night. That was the deal I made with the guard I bribed. There are too many guards around in the daytime; one would be bound to notice something. I've been assured the scrubbers have all been shut down tonight, however. You'll be safe enough."

Safe enough? The boy shook his head. "But you're warning me about them, anyway?"

"Just so you know. Just in case. Also, there are guards besides the one I've bribed scattered throughout the building. While there are definitely fewer of them at night, some will still be . . ."

"I think this is a mistake," Shea interrupted angrily. "I've heard no one ever gets out of this prison unless they are carried out. Add in the guards, and these scrubbers, and what chance do I have?"

"Stop worrying. Yes, there are guards, but not at every turn. They ward the doors and the cells, working in shifts, but they can't be everywhere at once. And the scrubbers have been disabled. Shea, the reputation of the Deep relies on the myth that no one has ever escaped—that everyone who has ever tried has been caught or killed. But this isn't so."

He stared. "You're making this up. Who ever escaped that you know?"

Rocan smiled. "I did."

"How could you have escaped?"

"I'll tell you sometime. Just trust me for now—it can be done. Going in through the waste ducts is viable. If a scrubber appears—which it won't—use some of the compound I gave you to disable it. If you are quiet and careful enough, no guards will know you are there. I paid a pretty penny for these plans and the assistance of the guard I bribed, and your own quick thinking will be enough to see you through."

"What if I decide not to do this?" the boy demanded suddenly. "What if I decide it is monumentally stupid and I am almost certainly going to die?"

Rocan shrugged. "Then we leave here now, I take you back to where I found you, and we will likely never see each other again." He paused. "But that would be a real shame."

Shea was quiet for a long time. The way the other spoke of taking him back, the unspoken implication of this dismissal, was chilling. He had already decided that this was an instance when taking a risk was necessary. He had never given any real consideration to how large the risk would be before it became unacceptable. Was it so large now that he was unwilling to embrace it—so large he was ready to walk away?

"Are you going to do this or not?" Rocan asked finally.

Shea Ohmsford thought back momentarily to his old life in Varfleet. Although it was by now far too late, he wished he had stayed where he was.

He gave a reluctant nod.

Clizia Porse had set out for Paranor three days after losing Tarsha, taking Tavo Kaynin with her, thinking that he still might serve a purpose. If nothing else, he would prove a useful sacrifice in her efforts to rid herself of Drisker and the two who accompanied Tarsha Kaynin. The girl, on the other hand, had more potential—if she was handled in the right way. For now, she thought of Clizia as an enemy, but that could change.

Whereas Tavo Kaynin was hopeless.

Not so long ago, she had harbored great hopes for him. His attraction to the Stiehl was obvious, and he was certainly capable of killing. Then she had spent a frustrating two days trying to teach him how to wield the fabled blade—and had failed miserably. Though he had been given the deadliest weapon in all the Four Lands, Tavo Kaynin saw it only as a knife—a blade that could cut and slice and skewer. He failed to understand its nuances. Because a weapon of this sort—a weapon of such sophisticated magic—was so much more. No prison could hold its owner; no barrier could keep him out. No armored juggernaut or implement of war could defeat him so long as he understood how to wield it in the right way.

But Tarsha's brother did not understand. He didn't even care to try.

Worse still, it quickly became apparent that he could not control his madness sufficiently to be trusted. She had explained to him over and over the value of sparing his sister and killing the others; with endless patience, she had explained that they were the real threat. They were the ones who had stolen Tarsha away and disabled him. Once they were out of the way, there was nothing and no one that could protect his sister. But he kept insisting he must kill her first— that she had betrayed and abandoned him and he was determined to see to it that she joined the others . . . Stark raving mad, he was. Just look at the course he had embraced, the path he traveled with his imaginary friend Fluken—this creature who always agreed with him, who always stood by him, and whom Tavo believed to be utterly real, even though there was no evidence of his existence whatsoever.

So yes, Tavo was expendable, and turning him loose on the Elf and the Blade was a good way to put an end to all three of them. If she handled it right, Tavo would kill Drisker first, then engage the other two in a struggle that would kill them all while she disabled

Tarsha Kaynin. Then she could take the girl back to Drisker's cottage and begin the process of bending her mind to serve her new mistress.

With this in mind, she had set out from Emberen on the third morning in a small two-man craft she had stolen from the airfield manager's own collection while he napped—a condition she had helped to foster. Finding the girl and her companions was now her first order of business, and while it should have been a simple chore, there was one significant complication. She had marked Tarsha, of course, as a prevention against losing her. But suddenly the marker was no longer in evidence. She had to assume it had been discovered and negated by one of the three. She could no longer rely on it.

Even without the mark, though, Clizia was pretty sure she knew where the girl had gone.

Flying east, she and Tavo traveled that day and much of that night, stopping only briefly to sleep, and—toward the evening of the second day—reached a clearing in the forest surrounding lost Paranor's former site and landed. A quick scouting mission confirmed that Tarsha and her companions were indeed present and waiting. That done, she faced her unpredictable companion and talked slowly and carefully about what she intended to do, what his part was to be, and how he was to behave as they neared their destination. Tavo was to carry their camping gear, which they needed so they could be comfortably settled while they waited for Drisker's reemergence from Paranor— still assuming, of course, that he remained inside. She had no idea how long that would take, but she was sure it would happen soon. He had undoubtedly retrieved the Black Elfstone since he was threatening to come after her, so it only remained for him to make use of it. Whatever else he had planned, his first order of business was to bring himself back into the Four Lands where he could protect his beloved student and endeavor to dispose of Clizia.

Others had sought to do the same over the years, she recalled with a smile, and all had failed. Drisker would fail, too.

With camp established far enough away from where Tarsha and her protectors waited, and a cloaking spell in place to hide them from discovery, she hunkered down to wait. But Tavo was not good at waiting. He was restless and bored and eager to make an end of his sister. He spent time talking to his imaginary companion when he thought she wasn't paying attention, his words hushed and furtive, his body hunched over and protective. She was afraid she was losing control over him—despite the medications she slipped into his food and drink, and her constant attempts at reassuring him he would get what he wanted.

Two further days had passed by now, and still nothing had happened. Even she was growing impatient. It was close to midnight, and she was sitting up and keeping watch. Easy enough for her to do since she slept so little these days and liked the quiet and calm of being alone. Tavo was sleeping nearby—sleeping more these days, it seemed to her, as if he was drifting farther away from the real world by the moment. He talked in his sleep—nonsense words and vague mutterings, his body twitching, his eyes fluttering as if he might be half awake.

She kept thinking of ways she could speed things up, but everything she could do other than wait always came back to using the scrye orb, and she didn't want to give anything away by doing so. Drisker Arc was nothing if not observant, and if he thought she was close to Tarsha, he would know it was a trap.

Snow had begun to fall. She watched it for a time, then reached into her pack and produced a pair of heat stones—magic that could warm the body for hours if tucked into clothing. She slipped one into her dress first and then went to Tavo.

She was tucking his in place when he suddenly woke. "What are you doing?" he demanded at once.

The tone of his voice was troubling, but she held up the heat stone regardless. "It's snowing and getting cold. This will keep you warm. Put it inside your tunic."

The boy stared at her suspiciously for a moment, then did as she asked. He nodded once it was in place. "You shouldn't do things like that," he muttered.

"Next time I won't."

Tavo lay back, looking up at the sky. "Never mind."

She was returning to her watch when suddenly he said, "What are those?"

She followed his gaze skyward. Dark shapes were passing silently overhead like giant birds on migration, only much more slowly. They were vague shadows amid the curtain of falling snow, traveling just under the clouds as they passed in silence through the skies in a southward direction.

She watched in fascination as they came and went. There were dozens of them—some huge creatures, some smaller. They were so dark she imagined Tavo might have missed them entirely had they not been moving through the snowfall.

"Warships," she murmured to herself. But to Tavo, she said, "A freighter convoy. Go back to sleep."

When he returned to his bedding and lay quiet, she glanced skyward again as the last of the airships disappeared. A smile played across her thin lips.

Well, well, well.

THIRTY-ONE

---◆---

IN THE BOWELS OF Assidian Deep, Shea Ohmsford was making his way through the tangled system of ducts that made up the prison waste system and trying not to gag. Indeed, the system had been flushed recently, as Rocan had promised; the floors and walls were still damp. But the smell of waste still lingered, embedded in the metal from constant use over the years. The vents helped to clear the air, but not enough. In Shea's opinion, no amount of venting would have been sufficient.

Still, there was nothing for it now but to continue on. And so he did.

He had entered the maze immediately after ending his argument with Rocan Arneas, removing the grate to the duct opening and slipping inside. He wasn't sure by now how long he had been in there, crawling through the ducts and climbing the narrow metal ladders between floors. It was just as dark as the night he had left behind, and he had no idea what time it was. Without the smokeless lamp, he would have been completely lost. All he could think about at this point was reaching the nineteenth floor, getting Tindall free of his cell, steeling himself for the journey back, and getting out of there once and for all.

Now that his journey was under way, it seemed endless. Climbing up between floors, crawling through stench-filled metal tunnels and the occasional piles of unspeakable filth, was almost more than the boy could bear. He kept telling himself to remember what was at stake, to ignore anything but putting one elbow and knee in front of the other. It was a tiny space, even for him.

Several times there were loud bangs and shouts that echoed down the ductwork, and each time he paused and took a deep breath to remain steady. Whatever was happening was likely a good distance off and had nothing to do with him, but still he slowed automatically. If he were discovered, Rocan had promised to come for him. But it seemed just as likely that his companion would choose to abandon him. After all, what would it cost him to toss aside a homeless street kid, no matter what promise he had given?

The darkness pressed close, partly mitigated by the weak circle of light provided by his lamp. The smells threatened to overpower him. The ragged sound of his breathing was a constant reminder of how quickly his life could be snuffed out. His knees and elbows and back were all aching. Every time he glanced at the map to make sure he was doing what he should, he despaired over how far he still had to go.

Once, as he climbed the ladder from the thirteenth floor to the fifteenth, he found himself wondering what all this was going to achieve. Oh, sure, he knew it would free Tindall. And he understood Annabelle's value. But how was anything permanent supposed to come to pass? What exactly were Tindall and Rocan planning on doing with Annabelle to change the destiny of the Four Lands? They couldn't expect to travel the countryside using her to change the weather everywhere they went. That would take years—not to mention that Annabelle was far too big to move easily. In fact, even if they could figure out how to move the big machine, wouldn't they be fugitives from the Federation prisons? Wouldn't they be hunted at every turn? How could they do what they needed to if they were constantly fleeing pursuers? The prospect of such a life left the boy cold, and he told himself again that once he had finished freeing Tindall, he was going home.

When he reached the eighteenth floor, he found himself facing a metal grate identical to, but much larger than, the one he had come through earlier. It was securely fastened in place and barred any possibility of passage down the length of the horizontal ductwork ahead. He peered through the slots into the corridor beyond, using his lamp, but there was nothing to see. He listened for voices or other sounds of occupation and heard nothing. Scooting backward, he looked for another means of passage, but the ladder ended on his floor and the duct only ran one way. He looked at his map to see if there might be an explanation for this barricade, but there was none.

For a moment, a spike of panic hammered thought him. Had he miscounted a floor or taken a wrong turn? Would he, as Rocan had said, be lost in here forever? But no, he had gone slowly and consciously through this labyrinth, counting each level carefully and triple-checking the map at each junction. This had to be the right path. All that was different was this grate. He forced himself to relax, trying to decide what to do.

Then he remembered the substance Rocan had given him to burn his way through Tindall's cell door.

He wriggled onto his side so he could reach the leather-wrapped package and take it out. Then he crawled forward again until he was back at the grate. A quick study revealed that it had been fastened to the walls, ceiling, and floor with metal clamps. If the substance worked as he had been told, it should be easy enough to burn those clamps away from their fastenings.

He decided to test it first. Opening the wrapping, he scooped out a little of the substance and placed it against the closest fastening. When it was in place, he leaned forward and spat on it—twice, because he missed the first time. On the second try, the substance flared with white brilliance and the metal dissolved instantly.

Powerful stuff, he told himself. Best not to let any of it get on him. Or to stick his fingers in his mouth.

Emboldened, he began to work on the remainder of the fastenings and was done with all but one when he heard something moving in the darkness on the other side of the grate.

He paused what he was doing and listened carefully. A slow scraping broke the silence, a stealthy creeping.

Something was back there, and its movements were growing louder.

And closer.

Kol'Dre stood with his Skaar princess on a rise that gave them a broad view of the Mermidon River and everything that lay south for twenty miles. They had watched the sunrise as it colored the skies earlier—first crimson, then orange and pink, and finally deep blue. The colors had been spectacular, even for a sunrise in the Four Lands, and the cold of the day and the thin layer of snow that the deep night had brought to announce winter's coming failed to diminish their beauty. Now they kept watch. For both of them, the end might be coming—today or tomorrow or, with luck, perhaps a bit longer. Every day was an exercise in patience as they waited along with their soldiers for the arrival of a Federation force that would crush them. Sooner or later, Ketter Vause would lose patience. And when he did, he would give the order.

Ajin had been hopeful the Elves might yet lend assistance, but so far they had failed to do so. Kol'Dre knew from years of working alongside her how persuasive she could be. She had given everything she had to winning over Gerrendren Elessedil—including the possibility of a visit to her bed. Not that she would have allowed it, but she would have made certain he believed it might happen, and that should have cemented his thinking.

But for some reason, it had not.

So now they were faced with the unpleasant prospect of having to fight the Federation on their own. Especially now that it seemed clear that her father was not coming.

The minutes passed slowly, time dragging her leaden feet as they waited and watched. On the lower banks of the river, small movements were apparent within the trenches and shelters where the Skaar soldiers were hidden, waiting for orders. Runners moved back and forth between concealments, cloaked in their invisibility, their presence a series of ripples on the air apparent only to the trained eye.

Kol'Dre watched and considered. If the attack came, Ajin would have to decide whether to stand and fight or flee. She would be reluctant to do the former and unlikely to choose the latter. There were no good choices in a situation as untenable as theirs.

He gave her a quick glance, and she met his gaze. "Thank you for being with me, Kol. Now and all the other times you could have abandoned me. I speak in haste and with ill-advised words sometimes, as you, most of all, well know. And for that, I am sorry."

He nodded slowly and looked away again, taking in her words, her look, her demeanor. She meant what she said, he believed. She was not simply trying to mend things between them.

"Kol," she said suddenly, pointing southward.

In the far distance, black dots were appearing, filling the skies as they multiplied. Swiftly, they emerged from the horizon's bright haze to take the forms of airships, spanning a broad swath of blue space in the morning sky.

"They're coming for us," she said.

Already, a runner from the Skaar defensive line was charging up the hill to make certain she knew. He was running hard and fast, zigzagging through brush and rocks, lithe and agile in his leaps and bounds. Ajin and Kol watched him come, saying nothing as he drew closer, their eyes shifting between the runner and the airships, each growing larger as the seconds passed. Ajin would have to make a decision now—one that would determine all their fates.

He glanced at her one last time. "What do we do?"

"What we have always done, Kol. We stand our ground. We do not yield and we do not flee. We do not show fear. We are the Skaar. We die if we must, but we die facing what comes for us."

"What of our airships? They might prove useful if we are attacked, offer some protection for our soldiers."

"No. The ships remain where they are, behind our lines and concealed. When it becomes apparent there will be an attack and no quarter given, we will withdraw into the forests and make for our aquaswifts. Those soldiers who can reach them will fly home to kindred and king and tell our story. It will be a testament to our courage and our steadfastness. And perhaps my father will forgive me for failing him."

Kol was indignant. "You did not fail him, Ajin! He failed you."

"He apparently does not see it that way."

"How he sees it, and how it really is, are two very different things."

"Not in his eyes."

Kol thought to say more on the matter, but chose not to. "So you will not attempt to escape? Not even where it looks hopeless?"

She looked over once more. "What sort of princess—what sort of commander—would I be if I fled in front of my soldiers? No, I will not be remembered that way. I do not hold my life so precious. Fate will decide what becomes of me, but fate will not name me a coward. You may go, my friend. In fact, you should."

He looked away. "Where you go, I go. You should know that by now."

She studied him for long moments, and out of the corner of his eye he saw her nod. "Yes, I should."

The runner reached them, stumbling at the end as he drew up short before her. "Princess, there are airships approaching from the south. As many as fifty or sixty. Some are clearly identifiable as warships and transports. What are your orders?"

Kol waited for her answer. She wasn't even looking at him. She was looking south at the approaching enemy and then down at the Skaar defenses. "Divide the command into three units and move them back from the riverfront into the trees to make their stand. Separate the three by at least two hundred yards each. There is to be no response to any attack until I give the order. If the battle goes against us, the units are to disband and our soldiers are to find their way back to the airships and fly home. Send fifty of our soldiers to me to create a defensive response if one is needed. This will give the others in the command time enough to slip away. Tell them I . . ."

But the runner was no longer listening to her. He was no longer even looking at her. He was staring upward at the sky behind them, his mouth hanging open in shock, his eyes wide.

Kol'Dre wheeled about at the same time Ajin turned, and together they looked into a sky filled with a second fleet of warships, their dark shapes hovering above the trees like birds of prey.

"The Elves!" Kol exclaimed in joyful recognition. "They've come!"

But Ajin shook her head at once. "No, Kol. Not Elves. Those are Skaar vessels." The expression on her face spoke volumes, a mix of joy and regret. "It seems my father has arrived after all."

THIRTY-TWO

DRISKER ARC WALKED THE deserted halls of lost Paranor, a faded presence in this tomb of faded dreams, alone for the moment since Cogline had gone elsewhere, thinking about what lay ahead. He knew now what was expected of him, understood what he must do in order to return Paranor to the Four Lands and free himself of his imprisonment. He knew the sacrifice he must make, but not yet the toll it would take on him to make it. His experience as Ard Rhys of the Fourth Druid Order gave him many insights, but not this one. Nothing, he had come to accept, would prepare him for what lay ahead.

The Druid Histories had not fully explained what the cost would be, and he imagined it was better not to know. It had happened only once before that a Druid had been required to use the Black Elfstone to bring back Paranor after it had been dispatched into limbo. But the circumstances had not been the same. Walker Boh had not been deliberately imprisoned. Instead, he had entered willingly, though without knowing what doing so would cost him, and then once within had been forced to make the same choice Drisker was now required to make hundreds of years later.

Drisker slowed, then stopped at the west-facing doors leading from the building's interior to the walls beyond and freedom. That he had been brought to this was incomprehensible. If only he had been a little more careful, a bit more wary, Clizia Porse would not have been able to place him in this situation. But his desperate need to prevent disaster and his overconfidence in his ability to do so had propelled him to his doom, making him return from exile in a futile effort to change the fate of an order that had brought about its own demise. For it was undeniable that the failure of the Druids to govern themselves was the direct cause of their downfall. It hadn't happened in a day or a month or even a year. It had happened over a considerable time, but they were all complicit in the result.

And he included himself in this assessment, accepting for the first time his failure to lead the order with a stronger, surer hand. He, too, must share responsibility for the lapses of judgment and reason he visited on the other members of his order. And having acknowledged such, he must pay the price.

He reached into his cloak and withdrew the Black Elfstone. It was surprisingly light in his hand, and its polished surface—matte black and nonreflective—shone with an odd glimmer. It knew. It was waking in response to his decision. It was awaiting his call.

As if sensing what was about to happen, Cogline appeared beside him—a pale and ghostly creature, a wraith of a Druid long gone from this world and not yet passed into the next. The old eyes looked into his and saw the truth, and he nodded his understanding.

"You've found what is needed," he said. "Your eyes have been opened."

Drisker nodded. "I studied enough of the Druid Histories and thought enough on Walker Boh to understand. Although it did not come to me easily. I resisted it."

"Walker, too, struggled."

"I imagine he did. He faced a similar dilemma. To bring back Paranor, a sacrifice of self is required—letting go of personal considerations and giving in to what fate demands. His fate will now be mine. He did not want it, either, but he did what was required. I must do the same."

"So you would return to the Four Lands? You would go again into the world of the living?"

Drisker shrugged. "I can do nothing else if I want to see things set right. I will use the Black Elfstone. I know now that I can. I have accepted what needs to happen, and what I must become once more. Walker Boh did not face a return to something he once was; he faced becoming something he never was. I, on the other hand, face becoming something I once was and had told myself I would never be again."

"Ard Rhys."

Drisker nodded. "I wonder if I am up to it? I wonder if I have the strength?"

"You understand the price?"

He did. If he were to bring back Paranor, he must restore it to what it was before. He must eventually return the life that was stolen by the Skaar. It must become again a home for Druids, a gathering place for those who would protect and preserve the Four Lands and their people. And at least one Druid was necessary to set those wheels in motion. Drisker must become Ard Rhys of a new Druid order—a Fifth Druid Order—creating at least the possibility of carrying on what his predecessors had begun. What Galaphile had first envisioned thousands of years ago, in the wake of the destruction of the Old World. His life would no longer be his own, but one of service to the larger order, his wants and needs subsumed by his duties, his intention to live a private life a dream he would never realize.

He looked down at the Black Elfstone where it rested in the palm of his hand. The gem shone brighter, he thought, more radiant even though it was still opaque. He could feel its warmth on his face and clothing. It was alive with hope, and it wanted him to acknowledge it. It wanted him to embrace his calling, to cast aside his doubts and fears, to believe in himself as he had never believed before.

"Will you do this now?" Cogline pressed, stepping closer.

"When my mind is ready and my thoughts clear. When there is no longer any hint of doubt."

"You ask too much of yourself. Your confidence in yourself will carry you through. I can sense it."

Drisker was examining himself. He was all but transparent by now, almost a ghost, ready to join those long dead. Only a small part of him felt real anymore, and that part was fragile and weak. He had let himself decay to the point where he was not sure he could survive the demands of the magic. Such magic was not easily accessed and less easily withstood. It would try to break him with its power; it would test him in the most severe ways.

Yet he had no choice. Movement in any other direction would indicate the extent of his weakness, and he could not bear that.

"Stand back from me, Cogline," he said. "I must be alone to do this properly."

Cogline stepped away without a word, and Drisker moved forward until he stood directly before the doors that would open out toward the west. Somewhere outside Paranor's walls, he would find Tarsha, Dar Leah, and Brecon Elessedil waiting for him. Somewhere out there, Clizia Porse and Tarsha's brother would be waiting, too. And somewhere farther along the road, his future waited.

He closed his hand tightly around the Black Elfstone and stretched forth his arm. In his mind, he spoke the words he believed were needed for a summoning of the magic.

I am ready now. I am willing. I understand what is needed. I embrace who I am and what I must do. I shall not run or hide or shy from what that means. I will dedicate my life to the Druid order from henceforth until my time is over.

He felt the Black Elfstone warm further.

Come to me. Become part of me. Do to me what you must to accept the truth of what I have pledged.

The warmth increased. An inky darkness rose from the talisman to mingle with the hazy air of the Keep, enfolding him in a cocoon that caused his surroundings to disappear.

He was alone.

Time stopped.

He could hear his heart beating and the inhaling and exhaling of his breath, but he could feel something else, too. A gathering of the darkness that cloaked him was under way. Without realizing he was doing so—and without knowing or understanding why—he allowed his fingers to unfold and his fist to fall open so that the Black Elfstone was revealed.

Instantly, the darkness that surrounded him exploded, and he could sense it spreading through the Keep, mingling and mixing with the brume that lingered in the wake of the Guardian's passing. It went everywhere—down hallways and through passages, into rooms and nooks and tiny dark spaces, from floor to ceiling and wall to wall. Its presence was unmistakable, and even with his senses curbed and muted he could tell it was becoming . . . what?

Something different, something more.

Then, with the ferocity and power of an attacking moor cat, it came roaring back to him, a whirlwind of sound and fury. He shrank from it, but there was no escape. It wrapped him with suffocating intent, then entered him. It burrowed through him—a hot and fierce intrusion that burned him from the inside out. He heard himself scream—as much from its intense pressure as from the pain. He was possessed by it, his defenses insufficient and quickly overwhelmed.

A change was taking place within him. Another presence had entered his body—an intruder that did not belong. He fought back, struggled to expunge it, but he was a child fighting to hold back a giant. This pain, this occupation, far exceeded what he had felt when the mix of darkness and mist had entered him earlier. It was searing and raw; it was unbearable. Yet he did not burn away as he thought he surely must. Somehow, he withstood its fury and held himself together.

And then it was gone, as suddenly as it had come.

In its place? A different kind of pain, a new source of agony. Memories and images began to appear. Words spoken and visions revealed. All of it was recognizable—a recitation of stories and truths long since told or revealed. He knew their source instantly. They were from the Druid Histories, from times mostly forgotten. They were the writings of Druids dead and gone. A voice was speaking to him, whispering all through him, and what it was saying left him stunned. It was not so much the telling as the manner of the telling. The emotion he felt conveyed far more than the words and images. It brought tears to his eyes—revelations of sacrifice and loss, of failure and despair, of intentions gone wrong and efforts fallen short. All the suffering caused by the Druids in their efforts to help—some of it willfully and some accidentally; some visited on the people of the Four Lands and some on themselves; some expended with memorable success and some wasted futilely.

Suddenly he knew who was speaking, who had entered his body to possess him and would remain until the revelations were complete.

It was Walker Boh.

It was his predecessor from centuries back—the reluctant Druid who had once been visited in the same way he was being visited now. Walker Boh, who had not wanted to be a Druid, either, but who had been brought to his fate in the same way Drisker had. Need and duty; the knowledge of what failure would mean; an understanding that sacrifice was what the magic demanded—those were the ropes that had bound him.

And that were now binding Drisker.

Look at what you have done. Look at the destruction you have wrought. Look closely at what you are.

The words were spoken in a calm, cold voice that demanded a response, yet gave no sense of comfort. Drisker looked and saw how his weakness had caused so much damage. If not for his abandonment of Paranor, spurning his duty to serve as Ard Rhys—if not for his collapse of faith and willingness to walk away, for his acceptance of exile and withdrawal to a life of solitude and self-indulgence—the Fourth Druid Order might yet exist. It was his decision to leave that had set everything in motion. He had allowed an inferior to occupy the position and wield the power with which he had been entrusted. It was his lack of perseverance and courage that had opened the doors to the Skaar and invited the destruction of everything that his predecessors had built.

Abruptly, they were there to bear witness—a line of faces and dark robes, come to confront him. Galaphile, Bremen, Allanon, Grianne, Aphenglow. They and so many others appeared out of the ether. And then Walker Boh materialized, the first and foremost of his accusers, revealing his weaknesses and forcing him to admit the truth. Drisker stood before them all, broken and ashamed. He saw what he was, what he had known secretly and tried to deny. He felt the burden of the guilt he must bear. These men and women who had preceded him had given so much so that the work of the Druids could survive. Much sacrifice had been required of them, yet they had not walked away from their responsibility as he had.

Each had a story to tell, and each told it. The words burned through Drisker like live coals. The images they conjured caused him to shrink further inside himself. He thought more than once that he might break down completely. He thought more than once he was going to descend into a despair from which he would never recover. But even so he weathered it. He would not fall apart.

And then, with shocking suddenness, all disappeared. The ghosts of Druids past faded away. Their words and images ceased, and all the pain and sorrow with them—vanished in the blink of an eye, leaving him alone once more in his black cocoon. The abruptness of it made him catch what little remained of his breath. And the silence that followed left him strangely bereft and vulnerable.

He had only a moment to dwell on it before a swirling of dark magic caught him up and carried him away, plunging him downward into a vast emptiness. He fought against it, but his strength was insufficient. He was being drowned, the magic of the Black Elfstone submerging him in its vast darkness.

Walker Boh's voice followed him down, filled with anger and recrimination. The words Drisker heard were unintelligible, yet he knew by their tone what they were saying. He had been Ard Rhys and given it up. Now he was asking to be saved from a fate he had brought upon himself. To be saved, he must become that which he had cast aside, yet why should he be granted this privilege? What was he willing to expend to secure it? He must embrace his destiny as Ard Rhys unconditionally and forever. He must submit himself to its needs. He must bow to it. His immediate reflexive response was to resist, and he fought it as he would a physical threat.

But he was helpless before such power. He was brought to his knees and made to bow. He was made to beg. The condition of his life would be forever changed if he went down this path he was seeking, and his acceptance of the inevitability of it must be total. Look what the others had given up: everything! In the end, even their lives. Was he willing to abide by this demand? Was he committed in a way he never had been before? Did he understand that there was no middle ground here, only that same patch of ground on which every Ard Rhys before him had stood, every Druid who had fought alone and in pain and in despair to protect what those before them had achieved?

Drisker quailed before the barrage of expectations. His resolution crumbled. He spiraled farther down into the darkness, and at some point he understood that he was never coming back if he did not embrace what was being demanded of him.

He would do this, he knew. But not while on his knees, and not when under such terrible duress.

He fought back anew, rising and straightening beneath the attack. He began to swim against the darkness, to claw his way through the oily depths to which he had been dragged. He was hammered back, but he would not give in. He fought on relentlessly. He knew what was needed and he had made his commitment, so there was nothing for it but to rise to it. To rise to the surface of his life, to the place where he belonged—back in the Four Lands, back among the Races, back with those few who had stood by him.

He surged through the pain and the dark magic and the gloom, feeling them beginning to give way, to acknowledge his determination and commitment to the future they wanted him to forge.

I'm coming back to you—Tarsha, Darcon Leah, Brecon Elessedil. I am ready to become what Walker Boh once became. Beware, Clizia!

Against the tide he swam, and as the tide lessened and the current died, the black began to fade and daylight flickered in the distance. The balance between life and death, success and failure, shifted in his favor. Casting away everything holding him back—fear, doubt, the past and its failures—he broke the surface of the magic that had fought to stop him.

Reborn. Remade. Arrived.

He took the first breath of his new life.

He was aware right away that something was different. It took him a moment to identify what it was. The light within the Keep was no longer hazy and dim. It was brighter and clearer and more intense than he remembered. Nor was the light beyond the walls an empty gray nothingness. Through the high windows of the hallways, he could see clouds massed and shadows trailing across the sky. He could see the branches and trunks of trees.

He could hear birdsong.

He could smell the forest.

He looked down at himself. His transparency was gone, and he was a solid presence once more, whole and complete. In spite of his resolve, he broke down in tears. The joy he felt was indescribable. He was home again. He had brought Paranor out of limbo and back into the Four Lands, and himself with it.

Cogline appeared next to him. *You are now Ard Rhys once more, Drisker Arc.*

His voice was not the same as before; it had changed, become more ethereal, more indistinct. More ghostlike. Drisker looked at him. "You can see this?"

It's written all over you. Were you to look into a mirror, you would see it, too.

"I can feel it." He paused. "It was grueling, old man. I was tested in ways I cannot describe. Mostly by the ghost of Walker Boh, but there were others, as well—men and women who were once Ard Rhys and now are gone. They stood before me and they made me see myself. They made me recognize my failures and weaknesses. They hammered at me with words and images like they were working a piece of iron. I was remade, reshaped . . ." He trailed off. "It turned me into what I had sworn I would not be again. It infused me with belief and power beyond what I have ever known. I do not know what it will mean for the future, but for now I am something more than what I was."

You are what they once were, Drisker Arc. You are all of them. You become them when you take up their mantle. They infuse you with their knowledge, and they make you over. I saw it happen with Walker. I saw him become another Allanon and more. He had not Allanon's presence or physical strength, but he had his determination and his conviction. I see all that in you, too.

Drisker moved over to a bench and sat. He was suddenly shaking, the ordeal he had endured washing over him, stealing his strength away. "I was made to see it. To see what is required of me."

He buried his face in his hands, but Cogline let him be, standing silently to one side. A long time passed as they remained where they were, neither speaking nor even looking at each other. Drisker had his eyes closed and did not try to open them. He was reliving what he had gone through, what he had experienced—reminded of what he had agreed to, of what he now must do. It was humbling and a bit terrifying to know the depth of the commitment he had made.

But he embraced it and did not try to shy away.

Will you go out now? Cogline asked him finally. *You are free to do so.*

Drisker raised his head and looked at him. "In a minute."

They wait for you, those who have stood vigil. I have already seen them, although they could not see me. I have looked at their faces and seen the wonder in their eyes. Paranor appeared before them out of nowhere, brought them to their feet and left them stunned. Now they wait for you to emerge. You must go.

He was right, of course. He could leave now, and he should. Drisker rose and started for the doors.

Ard Rhys! Cogline called out sharply, and Drisker turned. *I must leave you now. You will not see me again. We are back in the world of the living, where the dead and the living are not meant to mingle. We are no longer ghosts together in a ghost world. Can you not tell from my voice? I am in spirit form, while you are once again flesh and blood. Our time is over. But know that I will still be within the walls of the Keep, still watching over things. Now and then, I expect I will see you. I wish you well.*

"And I wish you the same," Drisker said. "Thank you for giving me the chance to find myself. Had you not repeatedly provoked and challenged me, I might have given up. I owe you, old man, and I do not know how to pay you back for that."

Cogline was sliding back toward the wall, fading as he went. *Be what you have sworn you would. Protect the Druid order. Protect its legacy. Do not let Paranor be violated again. That will be payment enough.*

A moment later he was gone, fading away to nothing.

Drisker stared after him, surprised by the sense of loss he was feeling. A page in his life had been turned—everything now changed, everything new.

He went out through the building's doorways and into the courtyard that led to the Keep's walls. And transformed, he returned to the real world.